P9-CFO-128

PRAISE FOR

# THE PLAGUE OF DOVES

"Writing in prose that combines the magical sleight of hand of Gabriel García Márquez with the earthy American rhythms of Faulkner, Ms. Erdrich traces the connections between these characters and their many friends and relatives with sympathy, humor, and the unsentimental ardor of a writer who sees that the tragedy and comedy in her people's lives are ineluctably comingled."

—Michiko Kakutani, *New York Times*

"Wholly felt and exquisitely rendered tales of memory and magic. . . . By novel's end, and in classic Erdrich fashion, every luminous fragment has been assembled into an intricate tapestry that deeply satisfies the mind, the heart, and the spirit."

—*O, The Oprah Magazine*

"You could read Louise Erdrich's latest book for its wisdom. . . . Erdrich writes from a philosophical, cultural, and historical perspective that is rich and deeply rewarding. Or you could read *The Plague of Doves* for its poetry. . . . In the end, you'll read this book for its stories. . . . The stories told by her characters offer pleasures of language, of humor, of sheer narrative momentum that shine even in the darkest moments of the book."

—*Boston Globe*

"Erdrich moves seamlessly from grief to sexual ecstasy, from comedy . . . to tragedy, and from richly layered observations of nature and human nature to magical realism. She is less storyteller than medium. One has the sense that voices and events pour into her and reemerge with crackling intensity, as keening music trembling between sorrow and joy."

—*Los Angeles Times*

"Masterfully told. . . . One can only marvel, while reading her twelfth novel, at Erdrich's amazing ability to do what so few of us can—shape words into phrases and sentences of incomparable beauty that, then, pour forth a mesmerizing story."

—*USA Today*

"Erdrich's characters have rich inner lives, expressed in language that's often achingly poetic. . . . The question of who really murdered that farm family adds suspense to the plot, but deeper, more satisfying discoveries arrive with the slow unspooling of the community's bloodlines, with their rich and complex romantic entanglements."    —*New York Times Book Review*

"To read Louise Erdrich's thunderous new novel is to leap headlong into the fiery imagination of a master storyteller. By turns chilling, funny, astonishing, wild, wrenching, and mournful. . . . A rich, colorful mosaic of tales that twist and turn for decades."
    —*Miami Herald*

"The great web that connects Erdrich's vivid characters is so subtly drawn and so surprising in its configuration, the novel, like every good story, yields new insights and surprises with each immersion."
    —*Chicago Tribune*

"Louise Erdrich, a fearless and inventive writer, has created a unique species of American magical realism, interweaving mysticism with storytelling that unfolds and operates on multiple levels, at once mythic and down-to-earth. . . . Beautiful, funny, moving, and unexpected, *The Plague of Doves*, her most complex, ambitious, and interesting work, expertly moves forward and backward in time."
    —*Elle*

"Erdrich's latest novel . . . is so natural you forget there's a writer behind it. . . . Instantly gripping."    —*Marie Claire*

"Fine and engaging. . . . A marvelous novel. . . . There is a symphonic achievement in Erdrich's capacity to bring so many disparate stories to life, and to have their thematic echoes overlap in such compelling harmony."    —Claire Messud, *New York Review of Books*

# THE PLAGUE OF

# DOVES

*Also by Louise Erdrich*

# THE PLAGUE OF

# DOVES

❧

## LOUISE ERDRICH

HARPER ● PERENNIAL

NEW YORK ● LONDON ● TORONTO ● SYDNEY ● NEW DELHI ● AUCKLAND

HARPER ● PERENNIAL

FIRST HARPER PERENNIAL EDITION PUBLISHED 2009.

*Designed by Fritz Metsch*

Library of Congress Cataloging-in-Publication Data
is available upon request.

ISBN 978-0-06-051513-3

10  11  12  13   WBC/RRD   10  9  8  7  6  5  4  3  2

# THE PLAGUE OF

# DOVES

# SOLO

The gun jammed on the last shot and the baby stood holding the crib rail, eyes wild, bawling. The man sat down in an upholstered chair and began taking his gun apart to see why it wouldn't fire. The baby's crying set him on edge. He put down the gun and looked around for a hammer, but saw the gramophone. He walked over to it. There was already a record on the spindle, so he cranked the mechanism and set down the needle. He sat back down in the chair and picked up his work as the music flowed into the room. The baby quieted. An unearthly violin solo in the middle of the record made the man stop, the pieces of the gun in his hands. He got up when the music was finished and cranked the gramophone and put the recording back on. This happened three times. The baby fell asleep. The man repaired the gun so the bullet slid nicely into its chamber. He tried it several times, then rose and stood over the crib. The violin reached a crescendo of strange sweetness. He raised the gun. The odor of raw blood was all around him in the closed room.

# *Evelina*

# The Plague of Doves

☙❧

IN THE YEAR 1896, my great-uncle, one of the first Catholic priests of aboriginal blood, put the call out to his parishioners that they should gather at Saint Joseph's wearing scapulars and holding missals. From that place they would proceed to walk the fields in a long, sweeping row, and with each step loudly pray away the doves. His human flock had taken up the plow and farmed among German and Norwegian settlers. Those people, unlike the French who mingled with my ancestors, took little interest in the women native to the land and did not intermarry. In fact, the Norwegians disregarded everybody but themselves and were quite clannish. But the doves ate their crops the same.

When the birds descended, both Indians and whites set up great bonfires and tried driving them into nets. The doves ate the wheat seedlings and the rye and started on the corn. They ate the sprouts of new flowers and the buds of apples and the tough leaves of oak trees and even last year's chaff. The doves were plump, and delicious smoked, but one could wring the necks of hundreds or thousands and effect no visible diminishment of their number. The pole-and-mud houses of the mixed-bloods and the bark huts of the blanket Indians were crushed by the weight of the birds. They were roasted, burnt, baked up in pies, stewed, salted down in barrels, or clubbed dead with sticks and left to rot. But the dead only fed the living and each morning when the people woke it was to the scraping and beating of wings, the murmurous susurration, the awful cooing babble, and the sight, to those who still possessed intact windows, of the curious and gentle faces of those creatures.

My great-uncle had hastily constructed crisscrossed racks of sticks to protect the glass in what, with grand intent, was called the rectory. In a corner of that one-room cabin, his younger brother, whom he had saved from a life of excessive freedom, slept on a pallet of fir boughs and a mattress stuffed with grass. This was the softest bed he'd ever lain in and the boy did not want to leave it, but my great-uncle thrust choirboy vestments at him and told him to polish up the candelabra that he would bear in the procession.

This boy was to become my mother's father, my Mooshum. Seraph Milk was his given name, and since he lived to be over one hundred, I was present and about eleven years old during the time he told and retold the story of the most momentous day of his life, which began with this attempt to vanquish the plague of doves. He sat on a hard chair, between our first television and the small alcove of bookshelves set into the wall of our government-owned house on the Bureau of Indian Affairs reservation tract. Mooshum would tell us he could hear the scratching of the doves' feet as they climbed all over the screens of sticks that his brother had made. He dreaded the trip to the outhouse, where many of the birds had gotten mired in the filth beneath the hole and set up a screeching clamor of despair that drew their kind to throw themselves against the hut in rescue attempts. Yet he did not dare relieve himself anywhere else. So through flurries of wings, shuffling so as not to step on their feet or backs, he made his way to the outhouse and completed his necessary actions with his eyes shut. Leaving, he tied the door closed so that no other doves would be trapped.

The outhouse drama, always the first in the momentous day, was filled with the sort of detail that my brother and I found interesting. The outhouse, well-known to us although we now had plumbing, and the horror of the birds' death by excrement, as well as other features of the story's beginning, gripped our attention. Mooshum was our favorite indoor entertainment, next to the television. But our father had removed the television's knobs and hidden them. Although we made constant efforts, we never found the knobs and came to believe that he carried them upon his person at all times. So we listened to our Mooshum instead. While he talked, we sat on kitchen chairs and twisted our hair. Our mother had given him a red coffee can for spitting snoose. He wore soft, worn, green Sears work clothes, a pair of battered brown lace-up boots, and a twill cap, even in the house. His eyes shone from slits cut deep into his face. The upper half of his left ear was missing, giving him a lopsided look. He was hunched and dried out, with random wisps of white hair down his ears and neck. From time to time, as he spoke, we glimpsed the murky scraggle of his teeth. Still, such was his conviction in the telling of this story that it wasn't hard at all to imagine him at twelve.

His big brother put on his vestments, the best he had, hand-me-downs from a Minneapolis parish. As real incense was impossible to obtain, he prepared the censer by stuffing it with dry sage rolled up in balls. There was an iron hand pump and a sink in the cabin, and Mooshum's brother, or half brother, Father Severine Milk, wet a comb and slicked back his hair and then his little brother's hair. The church was a large cabin just across the yard, and wagons had been pulling up for the last hour or so. Now the people were in the church and the yard was full of the parked wagons, each with a dog or two tied in the box to keep the birds and their droppings off the piled hay where people would sit. The constant movement of the birds made some of the horses skittish. Many wore blinders and were further calmed by the bouquets of chamomile tied in their harnesses. As our Mooshum walked across the yard, he saw that the roof of the church was covered with birds who constantly, in play it seemed, flew up and knocked a bird off the holy cross that marked the cabin as a church, then took its place, only to be knocked off the crosspiece in turn. Great-uncle was a gaunt and timid man of more than six feet whose fretful voice carried over the confusion of sounds as he tried to organize his parishioners. The two brothers stood in the center of the line, and with the faithful congregants spread out on either side they made their way slowly down the hill toward the first of the fields they hoped to clear.

The sun was dull that day, thickly clouded over, and the air was oppressively still so that pungent clouds of sage smoke hung all around the metal basket on its chain as it swung to each direction. The people advanced quickly. However, in the first field the doves were packed so thickly on the ground that there was a sudden agitation among the women, who could not move forward without sweeping birds into their skirts. The birds in panic tangled themselves in the cloth. The line halted suddenly as, to our Mooshum's eyes, the women erupted in a raging dance, each twirling in her own way, stamping, beating, and flapping her skirts. So vehement was their dance that the birds all around them popped into flight, frightening other birds, so that in moments the entire field and the woods around it were a storm of birds that roared and blasted down upon the people, who nonetheless stood firm with splayed missals on their heads. The women forsook modesty, knotted their skirts up around their thighs, held out their rosaries or scapulars, and moved forward. They began to chant the Hail Mary into the wind of beating wings. Mooshum, who had rarely been allowed the sight of a woman's lower limbs, took advantage of his brother's struggle in keeping the censer lighted, and dropped behind. In delight, watching the women's naked, round, brown legs thrash forward, he lowered his candelabra, which held no candles but which his brother had given him to carry in order to protect his face. Instantly he was struck on the forehead by a bird hurtled from the sky with such force that it seemed to have been flung directly by God's hand, to smite and blind him before he carried his sin of appreciation any farther.

At this point in the story, Mooshum became so agitated that he often acted out the smiting and to our pleasure threw himself upon the floor. He mimed his collapse, then opened his eyes and lifted his head and stared into space, clearly seeing even now the vision of the Holy Spirit, which appeared to him not in the form of a white bird among the brown doves, but in the earthly body of a girl.

Our family has maintained something of an historical reputation for deathless romantic encounters. Even my father, a sedate-looking science teacher, was swept through the Second World War by one promising glance from my mother. And her sister, Aunt Geraldine, struck by a smile from a young man on a passenger train, raised her hand from the ditch she stood in picking berries, and was unable to see his hand wave in return. But something made her keep picking berries until nightfall and camp there overnight, and wait quietly for another whole day on her camp stool until he came walking back to her from the stop sixty miles ahead. My uncle Whitey dated the Haskell Indian Princess, who cut her braids off and gave them to him on the night she died of tuberculosis. In her memory he remained a bachelor until his fifties, when he married a small-town stripper. My mother's cousin Agathe, or "Happy," left the convent for a priest and was never heard from again. My brother, Joseph, joined a commune in an act of rash heat. My father's second cousin John kidnapped his own wife and used the ransom to keep his mistress in Fargo. Despondent over a woman, my father's uncle, Octave Harp, managed to drown himself in two feet of water. And so on. As with my father, these tales of extravagant encounter contrasted with the modesty of the subsequent marriages and occupations of my relatives. We are a tribe of office workers, bank tellers, book readers, and bureaucrats. The wildest of us (Whitey) is a short-order cook, and the most heroic of us (my father) teaches. Yet this current of drama holds together the generations, I think, and my brother and I listened to Mooshum not only from suspense but for instructions on how to behave when our moment of recognition, or perhaps our romantic trial, should arrive.

## The Million Names

IN TRUTH, I thought mine probably had occurred early, for even as I sat there listening to Mooshum my fingers obsessively wrote the name of my beloved up and down my arm or in my hand or on my knee. If I wrote his name a million times on my body, I believed he would kiss me. I knew he loved me, and he was safe in the knowledge that I loved him, but we attended a Roman Catholic grade school in the mid-1960s and boys and girls known to be in love hardly talked to one another and never touched. We played softball and kickball together, and acted and spoke through other children eager to deliver messages. I had copied a series of these secondhand love statements into my tiny leopard-print diary with the golden lock. The key was hidden in the hollow knob of my bedstead. Also I had written the name of my beloved, in blood from a scratched mosquito bite, along the inner wall of my closet. His name held for me the sacred resonance of those Old Testament words written in fire by an invisible hand. Mene, mene, teckel, upharsin. I could not say his name aloud. I could only write it on my skin with my fingers without cease until my mother feared I'd gotten lice and coated my hair with mayonnaise, covered my head with a shower cap, and told me to sit in the bathtub, adding water as hot as I could stand.

The bathroom, the tub, the apparatus of plumbing, were all new. Because my father and mother worked for the school and in the tribal offices, we were hooked up to the agency water system. I locked the bathroom door, controlled the hot water with my toe, and decided to advance my name-writing total by several thousand since I had nothing else to do. As I wrote, I found places on myself that changed and warmed in response to the repetition of those letters, and without an idea in the world what I was doing, I gave myself successive alphabetical orgasms so shocking in their intensity and delicacy that the mayonnaise must surely have melted off my head. I then stopped writing on myself. I believed that I had reached the million mark, and didn't dare try the same thing again.

Around that time, we passed Ash Wednesday, and I was reminded that I was made of dust only and would return to dust as soon as life was done with me. This body written everywhere with the holy name Corwin Peace (I can say it now) was only a temporary surface, fleeting as ice, soon to crumble like a leaf. As always, we entered the Lenten season cautioned by our impermanence and aware that our hunger for sweets or salted pretzels or whatever we'd given up was only a phantom craving. The hunger of the spirit, alone, was real. It was my good fortune not to understand that writing my boyfriend's name upon myself had been an impure act, so I felt that I had nothing worse to atone for than my collaboration with my brother's discovery that pliers from the toolbox worked as well as knobs on the television. As soon as my parents were gone, we could watch the Three Stooges—ours and Mooshum's favorite and a show my parents thought abominable. And so it was Palm Sunday before my father happened to come home from an errand and rest his hand on the hot surface of the television and then fix us with the foxlike suspicion that his students surely dreaded. He got the truth of the matter out of us quickly. The pliers were also hidden, and Mooshum's story resumed.

## Apparition

THE GIRL WHO became my grandmother had fallen behind the other women in the field, because she was too shy to knot up her skirts. Her name was Junesse. The trick, she found, was to walk very slowly so that the birds had time to move politely aside instead of startling upward. Junesse wore a long white communion dress made of layers of filmy muslin. She had insisted on wearing this dress, and the aunt who cared for her had become exhausted by her stubbornness and allowed it, but had promised to beat her if she returned with a rip or a stain. Besides modesty, this threat had deterred Junesse from joining in that wild dance with a skirt full of birds. But now, attempting to revive the felled candelabra bearer, she perhaps forced their fate in the world by kneeling in a patch of bird slime and then sealed it by using her sash to blot away the wash of blood from Mooshum's forehead, and from his ear, which he told us had been pecked halfway off by the doves as he lay unconscious. But then he woke.

And there she was! Mooshum paused in his story. His hands opened and the hundreds of wrinkles in his face folded into a mask of unsurpassable happiness. There was a picture of her from later in that era, and she was lovely. A white ribbon was tied in her black hair. Her white dress had a flowered bodice embroidered with white petals and white leaves. She had the pale, opaque skin and slanting black eyes of the Metis or Michif women in whose honor the bishop of that diocese had written a warning to his priests, advising them to pray hard in the presence of half-breed women, and to remember that although their forms were inordinately fair their hearts were savage and permeable. The devil came and went in them at will. Of course, Junesse Malaterre was innocent, but she was also sharp of mind. Her last name, which comes down to us from some French voyageur, describes the cleft furrows of godless rock, the barren valleys, striped outcrops, and mazelike configurations of rose, gray, tan, and purple stone that characterize the badlands of North Dakota. To this place, Mooshum and Junesse eventually made their way.

"We seen into each udder's dept" was how my Mooshum put it in his gentle old reservation accent. There would be a moment of silence among us three as the scene played out. Mooshum saw what he described. I can't imagine what my brother saw—after the commune, he seemed for a long while immune to romance. He would become a science teacher like our father, and after a minor car accident he would settle into a dull happiness of routine with his insurance claims adjuster. I saw two beings—the boy shaken, frowning; the girl in white kneeling over him with the sash of her dress gracefully clutched in her hand, then pressing the cloth to the wound on his head, stanching the flow of blood. Most important, I imagined their dark, mutual gaze. The Holy Spirit hovered between them. Her sash reddened. His blood defied gravity and flowed up her arm. Then her mouth opened. Did they kiss? I couldn't ask Mooshum. Perhaps she smiled. She hadn't had time to write his name even once upon her body, though, and besides she didn't know his name. They saw into each other's beings, therefore names were irrelevant. They ran away together, Mooshum said, before each had thought to ask what the other was called. And then they both decided not to have names for a while—all that mattered was they had escaped, slipped their knots, cut the harnesses that relatives had already tightened.

Junesse fled her aunt's sure beating and the endless drudgery of caring for six younger cousins, who were all to die the next winter of a choking cough. Mooshum fled the sanctified future that his half brother had picked out for him. The two children in white clothes melted into the wall of birds. Their robes were soon to become as dark as the soil, and so they blended into the earth as they made their way along the edges of fields, through open country, to where the farmable land stopped and the ground split open and the beautifully abraded knobs and canyons of the badlands began. Although it took them several years to physically consummate their feelings (Mooshum hinted at this, but never came right out and said it), they were in love. And they were survivors. As a matter of course they knew how to make a fire from scratch, and for the first few days they were able to live on the roasted meat of doves. It was too early for there to be much else to gather in the way of food, but they stole birds' eggs and scratched up weeds. They snared rabbits and begged what they could from isolated homesteads.

## *The Burning Glare*

ON THE MONDAY that we braided our blessed palms in school, braces were put on my teeth. Unlike now, when every other child undergoes some sort of orthodonture, braces were rare. I have to say it is really extraordinary that my parents, in such modest circumstances, decided to correct my teeth at all. Our off-reservation dentist in the town of Pluto was old-fashioned and believed that to protect the enamel of my front teeth from the wires, he should cap them in gold. So the next day I appeared in school with two long, resplendent front teeth and a mouth full of hardware. It hadn't occurred to me that I'd be teased, but then somebody whispered, "Easter Bunny!" By noon recess boys swirled around me, poking, trying to get me to smile. Suddenly, as a great wind had blown everyone else off the bare gravel yard, there was Corwin Peace. He shoved me and laughed right into my face. Then the other boys swept him away. I walked off to stand in the only sheltered spot on the playground, an alcove in the brick on the southern side facing the littered hulks of cars behind a gas station. I stood in a silent bubble, rubbing my collarbone where his hands had pushed, wondering. What had happened? Our love was in danger, maybe finished. Because of golden teeth. Even then it seemed impossible to bear such a radical change in feeling. Because of family history, though, I rallied myself to the challenge. Included in the romantic tales were episodes of reversals. I had injustice on my side and, besides, when my braces came off, I would be beautiful. Of this I was assured. So as we were entering the classroom in our usual parallel lines, me in the girls' line, he in the boys', I maneuvered right across from Corwin, punched him in the arm, hard, and said, "Love me or leave me." Then I marched away. My knees were weak, my heart pounded. My act had been wild and unprecedented. Soon everyone heard about it, and my bold soap-opera statement brought fame even among the eighth grade girls, one of whom, Beryl Hoop, offered to beat Corwin up for me. Power was mine, and it was Holy Week. The statues were shrouded in purple, except for our church's exceptionally graphic stations of the cross.

Nowadays, if you see them in churches, they are carved in tasteful woods or otherwise abstracted. But our church's stations were molded of plaster and painted with bloody relish. Eyes rolled to the whites. Mouths contorted. Limbs flailed. It was all there. The side aisles of the church were wide, and there was plenty of room for schoolchildren to kneel on the aggregate stone floor and contemplate the hard truths of torture. The most sensitive of the girls, and one boy, destined not for the priesthood but for a spectacular burnout in community theater, wept openly and luxuriantly. The others of us, soaked in guilt or secretly admiring the gore, tried to sit back unobtrusively on our bottoms and spare our kneecaps. At some point, we were allowed into the pews, where, during the three holiest hours of the afternoon on Good Friday, with Christ slowly dying underneath his purple cape, we were supposed to maintain silence. During that time, I had decided to begin erasing Corwin's name from my body by writing it backwards a million times, ecaepniwroc. I began my task in the palm of my hand, then moved to my knee. I'd only managed a hundred when I was thrilled to realize that Corwin was trying desperately to catch my eye, a thing that had never happened before. As I've mentioned, our love affair was carried out by intermediaries. That fist in the arm was the first time I'd ever touched him, and that now famous line the first words I'd ever spoken to him. But my fierce punch seemed to have hot-wired deep emotions. That he should be so impetuous, so desperate, as to seek me directly! I was overcome with a wash of shyness and terror. My breath tugged. I wanted to acknowledge Corwin but I couldn't now. I stayed frozen until we were dismissed.

Easter Sunday. I am dressed in blue nylon dotted swiss. The seams prickle and the neck itches but the overall effect, I think, is glorious. Not for me a Kleenex bobby-pinned into a bow on top my head. I own a hat with fake lilies of the valley on it and a stretchy band that digs into my chin. But at the last moment, I beg to wear my mother's lace mantilla instead, the one like Jackie Kennedy's, and the headgear of only the most fashionable older girls. I am splendid, but I am nevertheless completely unprepared for what happens when I return from taking Holy Communion. I am kneeling at the end of the pew. We are instructed to always remain very quiet and to allow Christ's presence to diffuse in us. I do my best. But then I see Corwin in the line for Communion on my side of the church, which means that returning to his seat farther back he will pass only inches from me. I can keep my head demurely down, or I can look. The choice dizzies me. And I do look. He rounds the first pew. I hold my gaze steady. And he sees that I am looking at him—dark water-tracked hair, narrow brown eyes—and he does not look away from me. With the host of the resurrection in his mouth, my first love gives to me a burning glare of anguished passion that suddenly ignites the million invisible names.

## Mustache Maude

FOR ONE WHOLE summer, my grandparents lived off a bag of contraband pinto beans. They killed the rattlesnakes that came down to the streambed to hunt, roasted them, used salt from a little mineral wash to season the meat. They managed to find some berry bushes and to snare a few gophers and rabbits. But the taste of freedom was eclipsed now by their longing for a hot dinner. Though desolate, the badlands were far from empty, and were peopled in Mooshum's time by unpurposed miscreants and outlaws as well as honest ranchers. One day, they heard an inhuman shrieking from some bushes deep in a draw where they'd set snares. Upon cautiously investigating, they found that they had snared a pig by one hind leg. While they were debating how to kill it, there appeared on a rise the silhouette of an immense person wearing a wide fedora and seated on a horse. They could have run, but as the rider approached them they were too amazed to move, or didn't want to, for the light now caught the features of a giant woman dressed in the clothing of a man. Her eyes were small and shrewd, her nose and cheeks pudgy, her lip a narrow curl of flesh. One long braid hung down beside an immense and motherly breast. She wore twill trousers, boots, chaps, leather gauntlets, and a cowhide belt with silver conchos. Her wide-brimmed hat was banded with the skin of a snake. Her brown bloodstock horse stopped short, polite and obedient. The woman spat a stream of tobacco juice at a quiet lizard, laughed when it jumped and skittered, then ordered the two to stand still while she roped her hog. She proceeded to do so, then with swift and expert motions she tied him to the pommel of her saddle and released his hind leg.

"Climb on," she ordered them, gesturing to the horse, and when the children did she grasped the halter and started walking. The roped pig trotted along behind. By the time they reached the ranch, which was miles off, the two had fallen asleep on the back of the companionable horse. The woman had a ranch hand take them each down, still sleeping, and lay them in a bedroom in her house, which was large, ramshackle, partly sod and partly framed. There were two little beds in the room, plus a trundle where she herself sometimes slept, snoring like an engine, when she was angry with her husband, the notorious Ott Black. In this place, my Mooshum and his bride-to-be would live for six years, until the ranch was broken up and Mooshum was nearly lynched.

In Erling Nicolai Rolfsrud's compendium of memorable women and men from North Dakota, "Mustache" Maude Black, for that was the name of my grandparents' benefactress, is described as not unwomanly, though she dressed mannishly, smoked, drank, was a crack shot and a hard-assed camp boss. These things, my Mooshum said, were all true, as was the mention of both her kind ways and her habit of casual rustling. The last was a kind of sport to her, said Mooshum; she never meant any harm by it at all. She rustled pigs sometimes. The one in the bush had not belonged to her. Mustache Maude sometimes had a mustache, then sometimes not, when she plucked it out. She kept a neat henhouse and a tidy kitchen. She grew very fond of Mooshum and Junesse, taught them to rope, ride, shoot, and make a tasty chicken and dumpling stew. Divining their love, she banished Mooshum to the men's bunkhouse, where he quickly learned all the ways that he could make children in the future with Junesse. He practiced in his mind, and could hardly wait. But Maude forbade their marriage until both were seventeen years old. When that day came, she threw a wedding supper that was talked about for years, featuring several delectably roasted animals that seemed the same size and type as many lost to the dinner guests. It caused a stir, but there were only bones left when the wedding was over and Maude had kept the liquor flowing, so most of the surrounding ranchers shrugged it off. But what was not shrugged off, and what was in fact resented and what fostered an undercurrent of suspicion, was the fact that Maude had thrown a big and elaborate shindig for a couple of Indians. Or half-breeds. It didn't matter which. This was western North Dakota at the turn of the last century. Even years later, when an entire family was murdered outside Pluto, four Indians including a boy called Holy Track were blamed and caught by a mob.

In Mooshum's story, there was another foul murder, of a woman on a farm just to the west; the neighbors disregarded the sudden absence of that woman's husband and thought about the nearest available Indian. There I was, said Mooshum. One night, the yard of pounded dirt between the bunkhouse and Maude's kitchen and sleeping quarters filled with men hoisting torches of flaring pitch. Their howls rousted Maude from her bed and she didn't like that. As a precaution, having heard they would come to get him, Maude had sent Mooshum down to her kitchen cellar with a blanket, to sleep the night. So he knew what happened only through the memory of his blessed wife, for he heard nothing and dreamed his way through the danger.

"Send him out to us," they bawled, "or we will take him ourselves."

Maude stood in the doorway in her nightgown, her holster belted on, two cocked pistols in either hand. She never liked to be woken from a sleep.

"I'll shoot the first two of youse that climbs down off his horse," she said, then gestured to the sleepy man beside her, "and Ott Black will plug the next!"

The men were very drunk and could hardly control their horses. One fell off and Ott shot him in the leg. He started screaming worse than the snared pig.

"Which one of you boys is next?" Maude roared.

"Send out the goddamn Indian!" But the yell had less conviction, and was punctuated by the shot man's hoarse shrieks.

"What Indian?"

"That boy!"

"He ain't no Indian," said Maude. "He's a Jew from the land of Galilee! One of the Lost Tribe of Israel!"

Ott Black nearly choked at his wife's wit.

"She's got a case of books, you damn fool idiots!" He took a bead on each of them in turn. The men laughed nervously, and called for the boy again.

"I was just having fun with you," said Maude. "Fact is, he's Ott Black's trueborn son."

This threw the men back in their saddles. Ott blinked, then caught on and bellowed, "You men never knowed a woman till you knowed Maude Black!"

The men fell back into the night and left their fallen would-be lyncher kicking and pleading to God for mercy in the dirt. Maybe Ott's bullet had hit a nerve or a bone, for the man seemed to be in an unusual amount of pain for just being struck by a bullet. He began to rave and foam at the mouth, so Maude got him drunk, tied him to his saddle, and set out for the doctor's as she didn't want him treated at her house. On the way, he died from loss of blood. Before dawn, Maude came back, gave my grandparents her two best horses, and told them to ride hard back the way they had come. That's how they ended up on their home reservation in time to receive their allotments, upon which they farmed using government-issue seed and plows, where they raised their five children, one of whom was Clemence, my mother, and where my parents let us go each summer to ride horses just after the wood ticks had settled down.

## Story

THE STORY COULD have been true, for, as I have said, there really was a Mustache Maude Black with a husband named Ott. Only sometimes Maude was the one to claim Mooshum as her son in the story and sometimes she went on to claim she'd had an affair with Chief Gall. And sometimes Ott Black plugged the man in the gut. But if there was embellishment, it only had to do with facts. Saint Joseph's Church was named for the carpenter who believed his wife, reared a son not his own, and is revered as the patron saint of our bold and passionate people, the Metis. Those doves were surely the passenger pigeons of legend and truth, whose numbers were such that nobody thought they could possibly ever be wiped from the earth.

Mooshum slowed down that spring and had trouble putting in the garden. As he got more enjoyment out of his chair, our parents relaxed their boycott. More often now, our father fixed the magic circles of plastic onto their metal posts and twiddled them until the picture cleared. We sometimes watched the Three Stooges all together. The black-haired one looked a lot like the woman who saved his life, said Mooshum, nodding and pointing at the set. I remember looking at his gnarled brown finger and imagining it as the hand of a strong young man gripping the plow or a boy holding the candelabra, which, by the way, my grandparents had lugged all the way down to the badlands, where it had come in handy for killing snakes and gophers. They had given their only possession to Maude as a gesture of their gratitude. She had thrust it back at them on the night they escaped.

That tall, six-branched, silver-plated candelabra with the finish worn down to tin in some spots now stood in a place of honor in the center of our dining room table. It held beeswax tapers, which had recently been lighted during Easter dinner. The day after Easter Monday, in the little alcove on the school playground, I kissed Corwin Peace. Our kiss was hard, passionate, strangely mature. Afterward, I walked home alone. I walked very slowly. Halfway there, I stopped and stared at a piece of the sidewalk I'd crossed a thousand times and knew intimately. There was a crack in it—deep, long, jagged, and dark. It was the day when the huge old cottonwood trees shed cotton. The air was filled with falling down and the ditch grass and gutters were plump with a snow of light. I had expected to feel joy but instead felt a confusion of sorrow, or maybe fear, for it seemed that my life was a hungry story and I its source, and with this kiss I had now begun to deliver myself into the words.

# A Little Nip

※

ON THE KITCHEN wall beside the black tin clock whose hands of poisoned radium glowed in the dark, three pictures hung. John F. Kennedy, Pope John XXIII, and Louis Riel. The first two were color photographs that my father and mother had acquired through school and church. The last was a newspaper photograph, yellowed and frail. My mother had clipped the picture out and placed it carefully into a dime-store frame. In the picture, Riel looked morose and disheveled, a little blurry. Yet he was the visionary hero of our people, and the near leader of what could have been our Michif nation. Mooshum and our mother venerated him, even though Mooshum's parents had once lived in neat comfort near Batoche, Saskatchewan, and their huge farm would have passed to their sons, if not for Riel. That farm was put to the torch before Mooshum gained the power of speech, because the Milk family had harbored the genius of Riel, supported his cause with money, taken in his wife and child, fed his lieutenants, fought beside him, and angered the priests who threatened excommunication to Riel's followers and ultimately betrayed them to their killers.

After the rout at Batoche, the family had fled south and crossed the border in darkness, not knowing exactly where they were. As soon as they found an agreeable setting, they tried to homestead again, but the heart was out of them. They lost a baby, settled into a despondent subsistence, and were crushed when they heard Riel was tried and hanged.

Riel went to his death wearing moccasins and holding in his hand a silver-worked crucifix. His last words to the attending cleric were *Courage, mon père*. Joseph Milk, our great-grandfather, had been particularly fond of the moody prophet of the new mixed-blood Catholicism, and he cursed the priests even though his son Severine had just been ordained.

Mooshum had a younger brother, a violin player named Shamengwa, who was neat and dignified as Mooshum was happily disordered and profane. Except for his folded-up arm, Shamengwa was stark elegance. The last of their generation, these two enjoyed each other's company in spite of their differences. They had grown up in that melancholy house and the history affected them in different ways. Shamengwa was driven to music and Mooshum to stories. Both escaped as soon as possible but history followed them, of course, and now as old men they took comfort in chewing it over. When Shamengwa visited, he sat straight up in a hard kitchen chair, and often played the old tunes, while Mooshum liked to lounge or slouch beating time on his knee. Outside in summer, Mooshum claimed an old bench car seat that he refused to let Mama haul away. Inside, the nubbly, sagging, overstuffed couch was his. Sometimes the two brothers sat at the kitchen table drinking hot sugared tea into which Mooshum "slipped a little something." But nothing made them happier than the chance to fling history into the face of a member of the hated cloth. And so, on days that the old retired priest, frail as dried flowers and all but forgotten up there on the hill, would laboriously totter down to pay the brothers a visit, or when he arrived in a kind of huge, makeshift baby carriage pushed by an obliging Franciscan sister, the brothers grew much excited. They took special pains to procure whiskey and badgered Mama or Aunt Geraldine for boulettes or the special high-risen and light galette they had learned to make from Junesse. Other foods sat heavy on their bowels, but all three of the old men claimed that the meat soup and bread unbound them wonderfully if soaked in sufficient grease. The old priest used a polished diamond willow stick to negotiate the rutted road, and would plant it hard between his feet as he lowered himself into the wine-dark billows of the couch. From there, nodding his eggshell-thin skull, he'd opinionate in whispery, gentle tones, which were maybe too agreeable to the brothers. Sometimes they fell silent in disappointment at the priest's lack of opposition, but the visits always ended in polite toast after toast. But then the good priest died and the brothers had no ecclesiastic to play off until a big, whey-faced, pompous, and painfully hearty priest was transferred from Montana. He was nicknamed Father Hop Along because of his cowboy origin, his real name, Cassidy, and an unfortunate tendency to pop a bit too daintily along on his pointed feet when using his aspergillum to sprinkle holy water upon worshippers at High Mass.

THE SUMMER AFTER my first kiss, the TV faltered and all sound was lost. We could raise only random buzzing noises and the picture spun so rapidly it made us queasy. But we lived outdoors anyway. Joseph and I were allowed to catch and ride the paint horses belonging to Aunt Geraldine whenever we wanted. Both were swift and loved to run. The black and white was fairly good-natured, but the other, a flighty brown and white pinto, had been struck in the face and bit viciously if you stepped into her blind spot. We rode them bareback with rope halters and tied them at the edge of the yard when we stopped long enough for food. One day, as we were sopping up bowls of soup across the table from Mooshum and Shamengwa, our horses tied under the trees in the backyard, it began to rain lightly down. Sheltered by thick leaves, the horses busily cropped the long grass all around them, so when Mama answered the door and ushered in Father Cassidy we did not attempt to escape, but decided to play gin rummy against the door until the sky brightened.

The two old men greeted the priest with huge delight.

"Tawnshi! Tawnshi ta sawntee, Père Cassidy! How good of you to visit us! How well you look, please sit down, sit down with us, have a bite to eat, a bowl of soup, a crust of bread."

"Perhaps a pour from the jar, too. Clemence?"

"I wouldn't mind," said Father Cassidy, shivering a bit, though with anticipation, for it wasn't cold. "A little nip would take the chill off me."

Joseph looked at me, raised his eyebrows and drew his mouth down in that way he had. It wasn't even the least bit cool outside. The air had stayed hot and the rain made steam rise off the grass, by which it was immediately obvious that here we had a thirsty priest. Mooshum crowed with pleasure and tipped Clemence's hand up when she poured stingily.

"Daughter, be more hospitable!"

Mama frowned, and sighed huffily, but left the bottle on the table.

"So, Father Cassidy, you have been here for several months now. What do you think of our ways?"

But the priest had his head tipped back to catch the last drip from the shot glass.

"Oh yai! I remember when priests used to take their whiskey with water, but this one takes the firewater straight. My brother, let us do the same!"

"That's a Montana boy for you," said Father Cassidy, trying to appear as though he'd not tossed his shot back too greedily. "We don't stand on ceremony and we don't water down our whiskey, but we do believe in going to Holy Mass. Now Clemence attends regularly and she drags along Edward, and the young are of course obliged to make Holy Confession every Friday and attend at least three Masses during the week. But you, now I haven't seen the two of you at church since I arrived here. So that means at the very least that your confessions are much overdue."

"Tawpway, Père Cassidy, you speak the truth. But old men have no chance to sin much," said Mooshum in a regretful voice. He looked at Shamengwa. "Brother, have you had a chance to sin this year yet?"

Shamengwa made a long face and sighed in reproach. "Frère, you would know it, as I would tell you immediately in order to make you jealous. Hiyn, no, I have been pure."

"I, too, completely pure," said Mooshum. His chin trembled.

"Are you sure," said Father Cassidy, eyeing the bottle. His hand clutched his empty water glass. He lifted the glass toward the bottle. "Great sins are not required. Have you not, perhaps, taken the name of the Lord in vain?"

"Mon Dieu! Never!" The brothers looked quite shocked and displeased at the notion, and hastily poured the priest a double shot and refreshed their own glasses.

Father Cassidy looked thoughtful, and perhaps a little downcast to find the two old brothers sinless. But then he sipped deeply and brightened. "There are so many ways of sinning not readily apparent! You may for instance share in the guilt of another's sin without actually committing it yourself, via the Sin of Silence. Has anyone you know sinned?"

The brothers shook their heads in blank surprise. The priest cast about, waving a plump hand for inspiration. "You may have sinned against the Holy Ghost by resisting known truth—the worth for instance of Holy Mass—thus hardening your soul to the penetrations of grace!"

Father Cassidy looked extremely pleased with himself, but the brothers seemed most offended that he should imagine their souls hardening and they put their hands protectively upon their pulsing hearts. The priest did not give up, however, and quickly rattled off a list of venial sins: "a stab of envy or pride or . . . , no? Bad temper or even a minor untruth, no? Or even, I hesitate to say . . ." The priest's soft hand wobbled a bit as he closed it around the glass, and he smiled in tender delight at its contents, swirling the golden liquid gently as he spoke. He was now a bit dreamy. "Impure thoughts," he whispered. "Very common."

At this, Mooshum gave his brother a look of wounded puzzlement, and raised his eye questingly to the ceiling. Shamengwa made the sign of the cross with his good arm, and then took a small sip of his drink.

"We *should* know what he is talking about," said Mooshum, touching his poor maimed ear, "but we must admit, we are completely ignorant of these . . ."

"Impure thoughts," said Joseph, from the doorway, frowning at the cards in his hand.

"Gin," I said.

"Aw."

"Impure thoughts," said Shamengwa. "Dear priest, could you explain to us—exactly what *are* these impure thoughts you mention? As you say, if they are common, we must have experienced them, and yet we haven't noticed somehow."

"Perhaps we sin unknowingly," said Mooshum, his eyes sincere as he gazed at the priest over his poised shot glass. He tried for dignity, but his chewed-up ear always made him look ridiculous. "Which would be something . . ."

"Tragic!" said Joseph. He tried to cover a snorting laugh with several quick card shuffles.

"Tragic . . . as we'd end up in the bad place without warning, were we to die!"

"Could these impure thoughts send us to hell?"

Paralyzed with alarm, both men sat bolt upright. The priest frowned cross-eyed into his empty glass and Mooshum neatly filled it.

"Concupiscence," said Father Cassidy, raising one finger beside the glass, which he held slightly out at the level of his clerical collar. With his other hand, he tugged at the collar itself, as though it was tightening. "From the Latin, *concupisserry*, I believe, meaning, ah, to dwell upon unclean emissions in one's past or to anticipate such as . . . any act of imaginary or ejaculatory fornication. Bluntly speaking!"

"Ah, fornication!" The brothers grew animated and tipped their glasses to each other, then to Father Cassidy, who inadvertently tipped his in automatic fellowship and then stared confusedly down, mumbling, "from the Latin . . ."

"From the Latin *forn*, as in *foreign*, for relations with foreigners," cried Joseph.

"Ho, ho!" exclaimed the brothers, toasting again as Joseph set his cards down and skimmed out the door.

I quickly followed, but Father Cassidy and Mama were out the door right behind us and Mama said, "Now you two stop right there, and apologize to Father." But Father Cassidy, perhaps to prove what a horse-savvy Montanan he was, strode up behind us with his great chin of dough bulging over his collar and said, "No need, no need, yours, eh? Nice little docile scrub ponies, awful conformation, of course, positively knock-kneed and they do need the currycomb something worse." A nasty light sparked in the long-necked pinto's eye. Father Cassidy stepped up to her face and put his hand out. Quick as a rattlesnake, she struck and crushed his fleshy bicep in her teeth. Father Cassidy screamed and began to skip in place. But the mare held on firmly, like a mother might grip a naughty boy. Father Cassidy tried to swat her nose with his open hand. Her eye rolled back, she gave some coughing grunts that sounded like sobs of laughter, and bit down harder before she finally released his arm. There was hot shock in Father Cassidy's eyes.

"Oh," said Mama, "I am so sorry, Father. Please come back in and let me ice that little nip."

"Little nip!" cried Father Cassidy. He clapped his hand over his upper arm as if to keep the meat of it in place and was edging backwards now, heading for his automobile, which was parked in the road before our house. "Good-bye, Clemence, much gratified, the drop did no harm. Aghhh. Who knew I'd need the anesthetic!"

"From the Latin *anesthed*, meaning numskull," said Joseph to me.

Father Cassidy got into the car. "Tell your father and his brother that they flirt with damnation by resisting Mass!"

"I'll tell them, Father, yes, don't you worry."

Mama stepped forward to wave politely to Father Cassidy, and by the time she'd turned around to come at us full steam we'd mounted up and sped away. So I believe on that day she walked into the house and poured her frustration out on her father and her uncle, even though she was normally gentle with the two old men, whom she loved as greatly as she loved us. They were chastened and quiet when we returned for supper. Shamengwa stayed on because she had not allowed him to "slink off," as she put it. The television blared out and the picture scrolled slowly along, edging up the screen and sticking halfway so that a woman's legs would be on top of her talking head. Then her head would rise and the legs would tremble for one moment beneath her, until her head disappeared and popped up below. The two old men leaned back and closed their eyes, unable to bear the disorienting sight. They fell asleep. They were snoring lightly in profound innocence.

❦

THAT WAS NOT the end of it. Mooshum and his brother attended Holy Mass and then lapsed intentionally in order to provoke a visit from Father Cassidy. His hopes had been raised by seeing the two old men, so close to eternity, in the pew before him, and he wished to secure their souls. This second visit was as ridiculous as the first. Mooshum promised to make an heroic attempt to sin, so he would have something to confess. Joseph watched all of this with a teenager's long suffering omniscience.

Life as a boy was hard on my brother. To be the son of a science teacher in a reservation school cast him under suspicion, while it was to my advantage. It is always good for a girl to have a visible father. Worse for Joseph, he loved science and actually was teaching himself the Latin names of things. To make up for this, he rode one or the other of Aunt Geraldine's pintos all over, way back into the bush, and got drunk on bootlegger wine whenever he could. We both had friends, as well as eight or nine Peace cousins first to third, about sixteen others that we could count, and Corwin. I had girlfriends and I did not mind going to school, but somehow the closeness of my family was enough for me outside the classroom. We were not social. Plus Joseph and our father were somewhat isolated by their fascinations— collecting stamps, of course, which was a way of traveling without leaving, but also stars and heavenly phenomena, grasses, trees, birds, reptiles and happenstance insects, which they collected methodically, pinned to white squares of cardboard, and labeled.

Joseph was particularly interested in a species of fat black salamander that he believed endemic to the region, and he'd persuaded Dad to help him follow the life cycle throughout the year by observation in the field. Thus, they would be off even in dead winter with shovel and pick to unearth a hibernating creature from the rock-hard mud of Aunt Geraldine's slough. Or in summer, as now, they created false playgrounds for the creatures and watched their every move, taking notes in precise printing. For some reason they had agreed to avoid cursive.

Maybe the fact that I grew up admiring Joseph made him softer-hearted toward me than most brothers. We also knew that there would be no other children. Mama said so, and when we fought she shut us up by saying, "Just imagine how you'd feel if *something happened*." Imagining the other dead helped us enjoy each other's company. I helped Joseph collect specimens in stolen canning jars, and memorized a few Latin names just to please him. It helped that I also liked the salamanders—or mud puppies, as they were commonly known. They were lumps of earth, dark with yellow spots, helpless when they left the water. During heavy rains, they swarmed with slow gravity out of wet cracks in the ground. There was something grand and awful about their mute numbers. Mooshum said that the nuns had believed they were emissaries from the unholy dead, sent up by the devil, and hell was full of them. We shuffled slowly through the grass, gently kicking the plump things over. We picked them up and stashed them on higher ground, covering them with wet leaves. They dropped in piles down low wet spots around the school buildings—ten or twenty could be found in the window wells. Joseph always woke me early when the drowning rains came, late in warm spring, and we got to school first so that we could fish the creatures out before the boys found and stomped them to death.

That summer, using picks and shovels, Joseph and my father had dug a deep pond in the backyard. The water table was high that year, and it immediately filled. They planted cattails and willow around the edges, then added frogs and salamanders. The pond was not for fish, those enemies of neotenic larvae, but they stocked it well with chorus and leopard frogs transported from Geraldine's slough, and then the salamanders, which we carried home in buckets. To Joseph's disappointment, the salamanders seemed to vanish into the earth. Even if he did find one, they were hard to observe actually doing anything. It took all day to see one open its mouth. Joseph grew impatient and swiped a dissection kit from Dad. The cardboard box contained a scalpel, tweezers, pins, glass slides, a vial of chloroform, and some cotton balls. There was a diagram of an opened frog with all of its organs labeled.

Joseph laid the instruments out carefully on the windowsill of the small room we had divided between us. He took a jar from under the bed. It contained a specimen of *Ambystoma tigrinum*, the eastern tiger salamander. Into the jar, he dropped a cotton ball dabbed with chloroform, then he stashed it under the bed. Our father didn't really like dissections.

•

That night, I moved a candle to shed more light where Joseph needed it. I watched as he sliced the belly of the salamander open and revealed the slippery muck of its insides—a tangled set of tubes filled with transparent slime.

"It was just about to release its spermatophore," said Joseph with awe, poking at a little white piece of mush. There was a footstep outside the door. I blew out the candle. Dad opened the door.

"No candles," he said. "Fire hazard. Hand it over."

I rolled the candle to his feet from under the bed and he said, "Evey, get out of there and go to bed!"

The next morning, I got up before Joseph and found that the salamander had revived and tried to crawl away, unraveling the piece of entrails that Joseph had pinned into the soft wood of the dresser. The trail of its insides stretched to the windowsill, where it had managed to die with its nose pressed against the screen. That day, at the funeral, Joseph buried the dissection kit beside the salamander. He sighed a lot as we covered the plump little graying body, but he did not speak and neither did I. It was months before he dug up the dissection kit, and a year might have passed before he used it on something else.

✄

BOTH MOOSHUM AND Shamengwa insisted that if Louis Riel had allowed his redoubtable war chief Gabriel Dumont to make all of the decisions preceding and at Batoche, not only would he have won for the mixed-bloods and Indians a more powerful place in the world, but this victory would have inspired Indians below the border to unite at a crucial moment in history. Things would have been different all around. The two brothers also liked to speculate about the form that Metis Catholicism would have taken and whether they might have had their own priests. Mooshum insisted it would be better if the schismatic priests were allowed to marry, and Shamengwa was of the opinion that even Metis priests should keep their chastity. Both agreed that Louis Riel's revelation, which he experienced upon learning of his excommunication and that of his followers, was probably sound.

After much meditation, Riel the mystic had announced that hell did not last forever, nor was it even very hot.

"And I believe this," Mooshum insisted, "not only because Riel was comforted by angels, but because it stands to reason."

"Enlighten me."

Dad went to Mass to please Clemence and vanished at the first sight of Father Cassidy. He was a Catholic of no conviction whatsoever.

"If hell was hot enough to eat the flesh, there would be no flesh left to suffer," said Mooshum. "And if hell was meant to burn the soul, which is invisible, it would have to be imaginary fire, the flames of which you cannot feel."

"So either way, hell is seriously compromised."

"Either way." Mooshum nodded.

"I find that totally believable." Dad nodded. "It really makes a great deal of sense. Scientifically speaking, of course, nothing can burn forever without an unlimited fuel source. So you have to wonder."

Clemence, who said that she believed in hot fires that burned forever to the bone, shook her head in pity at the men. She considered it a weakness of character not to believe in hell, a convenient mental trick to excuse slack conduct. She had noticed the failure was most pronounced and useful in those who had no expectations of heaven. But although she wished intensely to rear her children in such a way that they would surely join the kingdom of God (her legacy), she was somehow foiled in her intentions, and by her own sympathies.

For instance, she could be persuaded to pour for Mooshum with a too liberal hand; and she took a shot herself now and then. Also, anyone could tell she did not think much of Father Cassidy. Her lack of enthusiasm in his presence, after that first visit, was obvious. She sometimes let slip a word or two behind his back. Joseph and I were certain we had heard her mutter, *Fat fool*, after one of his sermons on God's plan for creating babies in the wombs of women. Father Cassidy preached against interference with this plan, but in terms so obscure that I couldn't understand what he was talking about at all. When I asked Mama what it was Father Cassidy meant, she gave me a long stare and then said, "He means that God's plan was for me to get pregnant again and die. However, the doctor I spoke with did not agree with God's plan and so here I am, alive and kicking."

She saw the worry on my face and realized, I suppose, how her words sounded. "I'll explain when you're fourteen," she said in a voice meant to sound reassuring. I wasn't reassured at all and had to ask Joseph if he understood Father Cassidy.

"Sure," said Joseph, "he's talking about birth control. Aunt Geraldine's the one to ask if you need sex information. She'll draw it out on paper."

So the next time I went to catch a horse, I came back with knowledge. Thanks to Geraldine I also understood about impure thoughts, and I realized that the miraculous feelings that were part of God's plan for me, and which I had experienced in the bathtub with a headful of mayonnaise, were considered sins.

"Do I have to confess those?" I had been aghast at the prospect.

"I don't," said Geraldine.

The next time Father Cassidy appeared at the door, I greeted him with a pure conscience and took his light jacket and hat and put them on the chair beside the door. Then I retreated to a corner of the room. This time, once the priest was ushered inside to the table, Mama did not leave the bottle after she'd poured the shots. She took it with her to the other room. With the bottle gone, there came a dampness of feeling among the men.

"Ah, well," said Mooshum, "they drank no wine in the trenches at Batoche, and the priests were halfway starved, too. Father Cassidy, are you familiar with our history?"

"I'm a Montana boy," said the priest. "I know how they put down the rebellion."

"Rebellion!" Mooshum puffed out his cheeks. He didn't drink from his little glass yet.

"With a Gatling gun!" Shamengwa said. "Trucked from out east. A coward's invention, that."

Father Cassidy shrugged. Mooshum suddenly became very angry. His face went livid red, his mangled ear flared, his brows lowered. He grit his teeth, shivering with hatred.

"It was an issue of rights," he cried, slapping the table. "Getting their rights recognized when they had already proved the land—the Michifs and the whites. And old Poundmaker. They wanted the government to do something. That's all. And the government pissed about this way and that so old Riel says, 'We'll do it for you!' Ha! Ha! Howah! 'We'll do it for you!'" He raised his glass slightly and narrowed his eyes at Father Cassidy.

A look of happiness had taken hold of Shamengwa. He took a tiny sip of the liquor on his tongue, and beamed. "Why," he said, "this is sure smooth."

"My lease money come in last week," said Mooshum. "Clemence, she purchased me a special bottle. My, but she's stingy! If we had our rights, as Riel laid 'em out, Father Cassidy, you'd be working *for* us, not *at* us. And Clemence would pour a deeper glass, too."

"Well, I doubt that," said Shamengwa, "but there are so many other things." Shamengwa's joy had stirred him to sudden life. "I've thought about this, brother. If Riel had won, our parents would have stayed in Canada, whole people. Not broken. We would have been properly raised up. My arm would work."

"So many things," said Mooshum, faintly. "So many . . . But there is no question about one word, my brother."

"What is that word?"

"Respect."

"Respect is as respect does," Father Cassidy commented. "Have you respected Our Lord's wishes this week?"

"Did Our Lord make us?" Mooshum asked belligerently.

"Why, yes," said Father Cassidy.

"As we are, in our bodies," said Mooshum.

"Of course."

"Down to the details? Down to the male parts?"

"What are you getting at?" asked Father Cassidy.

"If Our Lord made our bodies down to the male parts, then He also made the male part's wishes. This week, I have respected these wishes, I will tell you that much."

Before Father Cassidy could open his mouth, Shamengwa jumped in. "Respect," said Shamengwa, "is a much larger subject than your male parts, my brother. You referred to political respect for our people. And in that you were correct, all too correct, for it is beyond a doubt. If Riel had carried through, we would have had respect."

"To our nation! To our people!" Mooshum drained his glass.

"Land," said Shamengwa, brooding.

"Women," said Mooshum, dizzy.

"Not even the great Riel could have helped you there."

"But our people would not have been hanged . . ."

"Ah, yes," said Father Cassidy, eyeing the bottom of his glass. "The hangings! A local historian—"

"Don't speak ill of her, Father. I am in love with her!"

"I wasn't . . ."

"Let us not speak of the hanging," said Shamengwa firmly. "Let us speak instead of requesting another glass of this stuff from Clemence. Oh niece, favorite niece!"

"Don't favorite me." Mama came back into the room and poured the men a round. She swept out with the bottle, again, so quickly that she didn't see me. I had sunk down behind the couch because I didn't feel like being stuck with weeding the beans right then. That she wasn't more hospitable with the priest confirmed her low opinion of him, but then I realized he'd also come to see her.

"Could we have a little word?" Father Cassidy tried to loop his voice around her swift ankles, to drag her out of the kitchen, but she had passed through the back door out into the garden.

❧

MOOSHUM WAS, INDEED, in love with Mrs. Neve Harp, an annoying aunt of ours, a Pluto lady who called herself the town historian. She often "popped in," as she called it. We were never free of that threat. She was what people called "fixy," always made-up and overdressed. She was rich and spoiled, but a little crazy, too—she sometimes gave a panicky laugh that went on too long and seemed out of her control. Mama said she felt sorry for her, but would not tell me why. Neve Harp seemed proud of having beaten down two husbands—one she had even put in prison. She was working on a third, bragging of stepchildren, but had already started using her maiden name in bylines to reduce confusion. As he was not allowed to visit Neve Harp often enough to suit his desires, Mooshum wrote letters to her. Some evenings, when the television worked, Joseph and I watched while Mooshum sat at the table composing letters in his flowing nun-taught script. He prodded our father for information.

"Is your sister fond of flowers? What is her favorite?"

"Stinging nettles."

"Would you say she favors a certain color?"

"Fish-belly white."

"What were her charming habits when she was young?"

"She could fart the national anthem."

"The whole thing?"

"Yes."

"Howah! Did she always have such pretty hair?"

"She dyes it."

"How did she come to have so many husbands?"

"Obscene talents."

"What does she think? What is her mind like?"

Our dad would just laugh wearily. "Mind?" he'd say. "Thoughts?"

"She's got her teeth, no? All of them?"

"Except the ones she left in her husbands."

"I wonder if she would be interested in memories of my horse-racing days here on the reservation. Those could be considered historical."

"You only quit two years ago."

"But they go way back . . ."

And so it would continue until Mooshum was satisfied with his letter. He folded the paper, setting each crease with his thumb, fit it into an envelope, and carefully tore a stamp from a sheet of commemoratives. He would keep the letter in his breast pocket until Mama went to the store, then he'd go along with her and put it directly into the hands of the post lady, Mrs. Bannock. He knew that his pursuit of Neve Harp was frowned upon, and he believed that Clemence would throw his letters in the garbage.

⋊⋉

I PROBABLY DID not fully realize or appreciate our family's relative comfort on the reservation. Although everyone in the family except my father was some degree of Chippewa mixed with some degree of French, and although Shamengwa's wife had been a traditional full-blood and Mooshum abandoned the church later to pursue pagan ways, the fact is, we lived in Bureau of Indian Affairs housing. In town, there was electricity and plumbing, as I've mentioned, even an intermittent television signal. Aunt Geraldine still lived in the old house, out on the land, and hauled her water. Her horses were the descendants of Mooshum's racers. We also had shelves of books, some of which were permanent, others changed every week. But because we lived in town we were visited more often by the priest. There was, in fact, one final visit from Father Cassidy, a drama that had far-reaching effects in our family. For one, our mother blamed the argument on liquor and banned Mooshum from drinking it as best she could. For another, the grip of the church on our family was weakened as Mooshum thrillingly broke away.

It was a low and drizzly summer day. Joseph and I had caught a number of salamanders after a rain and were busy restocking the back pond from a galvanized tin bucket, when Father Cassidy appeared in the yard and skipped his bulk along the grass to inspect our work. We looked up from beneath his vast belly, and were surprised to see him crossing himself double time.

"What's wrong?" asked Joseph.

"There are some who believe those creatures represent the devil," said the priest. "I, of course, do not hold with superstitions."

But perhaps there was something to it, as we later found.

By the time Joseph and I had finished releasing the salamanders and come back in the house, the conversation was in full swing and the bottle, too, was out because Mama was out. The three men nodded happily at us. They were drinking not from shot glasses, but from hard plastic coffee cups, Mama's favorite new set, harvest gold.

"We better stay here and watch over them," said Joseph to me, low, and I dipped out cold water for us to drink. We sat down on the couch. There was no doubt things were preceding swiftly. Father Cassidy had asked of Mooshum a particular question, one he never answered the same way twice. The question was this: What had happened to Mooshum's ear? The ear had not actually, he'd tell us later, been pecked away by doves.

Mooshum squinted, curled his lip out, and asked Father Cassidy if he'd ever heard of Liver-Eating Johnson.

Father Cassidy smiled indulgently and tried a weak joke: "He must have been from Montana!"

"Tawpway," said Mooshum.

"Paint the picture in words, mon frère!" said Shamengwa.

Mooshum made himself into a hulking beast and clawed at his chin to show the man's scraggly blood-soaked beard. He then related the horrifying story of Liver-Eating Johnson's hatred of the Indian and how in lawless days this evil trapper and coward jumped his prey and was said to cut the liver from his living victim and devour that organ right before their eyes. He liked to run them down, too, over great distances.

Father Cassidy gulped and laughed weakly. "That's enough!" But Mooshum drank from the coffee cup and barged ahead.

"Me, I was a young boy, not yet a man, alone on the prairie hunting for some scrap to eat. Turned out of my family, eh? Away across in the distances I see a someone running, a hairy and desperate man. But me, I have no fear of anything."

Shamengwa glanced at us, tapped his head, and winked.

"I kept to my own pace, as I was searching for something to eat. A rabbit, maybe, a grouse, even a rattlesnake would have set me up good. I myself was very hungry."

"Boys get hungry," said Shamengwa.

"I glance around in hopes that maybe this stranger has some food to spare. He's coming at me, still running. He's covered with ragged skins and he has a scrawly beard and that beard, eh? I suddenly see, when he gets close enough, how that beard is all crusted with old blood. And I know it's him."

"Liver Eater," said Shamengwa.

"I see that light in his eyes. He's very hungry, too! And I begin to spring, I'll tell you, I take off like a rabbit, quick. I've got speed, but I know Liver Eater's got endurance. He'll outrun me if we go all day, he'll exhaust me. And sure enough, the minute I slow my pace, he's on me. I speed up. It's cat and mouse, lynx and rabbit. Then he puts a burst on and he jumps me!"

Father Cassidy looked aghast, forgot to drink. Mooshum slowly touched what was left of his ear.

"Yes, he got that. His teeth were sharp. But he must have lost his hunting knife, for he did not stab me. I struggled out of his grip." Mooshum struggled out of his own arms, burst free of his own clutching hands. "I hopped out, running once again, just ahead of him, but as I charge along, blood from my ear flying in the wind, I get to thinking. Riel, if he'd won there would be some justice! This devil would not dare to chase an Indian. Hey, I think, I'm hungry too! Let's give Liver Eater some of his own medicine, anyway. I've got sharp teeth. So I stop, quick."

Mooshum jolted in his chair.

"The hairy white man flips over me, and as he does, I bite off one of his fingers."

"Which one?" said Shamengwa.

"I just got the pinkie," said Mooshum. "But now he's foaming mad, so I let him come at me again. This time, I strike like a weasel. Snap, a thumb comes off!"

"Did you eat it?" said Joseph.

"I had to swallow it down whole, no chewing. It tasted foul," said Mooshum. "I needed it for strength, my boy. We blasted out again. The next time I slowed he went for my liver—but only ripped a chunk out of my left cheek here." Mooshum pointed at the baggy seat of his pants. "I tore a bite from his hindquarters, too, and wrestled him down and got a piece of thigh, next. I kept after him. I was young. We must of ran for twenty, thirty miles! And over those miles I whittled him down."

"Howah!" cried Shamengwa.

"By the time he dropped from blood loss, he was down six fingers. I got one of his ears, the whole thing. I took a couple of his toes just to slow him down. Those, I spit right out. And I got his nose."

"Yuck," I said.

"It's my lucky piece," said Mooshum. "Want to see it, Father?"

"No, I do not!"

But Mooshum had already drawn his handkerchief from his pocket, and with an air of reverence he unwrapped it to show a blackened piece of leatherlike gunk.

"A bit of *Thamnophis radix*," said Joseph, peering at it over Mooshum's shoulder. "Why'd you keep it?"

"It's his love charm," Shamengwa said.

"That is . . . positively pagan!" Father Cassidy spluttered the words out and Mooshum's eye lighted.

"In what way, dear priest?" he asked with an air of curious innocence, pouring whiskey into the coffee cup that Father Cassidy gripped in his shuddering fingers.

"A nose!" cried Father Cassidy.

"And what piece of good Saint Joseph is lodged in our church's altar?" asked Mooshum. He spoke in a nunlike voice, gentle and reproving.

Father Cassidy's mouth shut hard. He frowned. "To *compare*, even to *compare* . . ."

"I was told," said Joseph readily, "as he is my name saint of course, I was told that our altar contains a bit of Saint Joseph's spinal material."

Father Cassidy drank the whole cup back.

"Sacrilege." He shook his head. Wagged his empty cup, which Mooshum promptly filled again.

"It saddens and outrages me," Father Cassidy said, sipping moodily off the brim. "Saddens and outrages me," he repeated in a fainter voice. Then he got all stirred up, as if some thought pierced the fog. It was the same thought he'd had already.

"To *compare* . . ." he blurted out, almost tearful.

"Compare, though, I must," said Mooshum. "When you stop to consider how the body of Christ, the blood of Christ, is eaten at every Mass."

Father Cassidy's tears vanished in a wash of rage. He blew up at this—his cheeks puffed out and he swayed monumentally to his feet.

"That is the *transubstantiation*, which is to say you speak of the most sacred aspect of our Mother the Church as represented in the Holy Mass."

Father Cassidy was building up more and more gas, and soon a froth of fresh bubbles dotted the corners of his mouth. Mooshum leaned forward, questioning.

"Then do you mean to tell me that the body and the blood is just, eh, in your head, like? The bread stands in for the real thing? Then I could see your point. Otherwise, the Eucharist is a cannibal meal."

Father Cassidy's lips turned purple and he tried to roar, though it came out a gurgle. "Heresy! What you describe. Heresy. The bread *does indeed* become the body. The wine *does indeed* become the blood. Yet it does not compare in any way to the eating of another human." Father Cassidy wagged a finger. "I fear you've gone too far now! I fear you have stepped over the edge with this talk! I fear you will be required to make a very special, and grave, confession for us to allow you back into the church."

"Then back to the blanket I go!" Mooshum was incensed with delight. "The old ways are good enough for me. I've seen enough of your church. For a long time I have had my suspicions. Why is it you priests want to listen to dirty secrets, anyway?"

"All right, be a pagan, burn in hell!" Father Cassidy restrained a belch and put out his cup for another shot. The bottle was nearly empty now.

"We don't believe in the everlasting kind of hell, remember that?" Shamengwa said primly.

"We put our faith in a merciful hell," said Mooshum.

"Then there's nothing for me to do!"

Father Cassidy threw his hands up and staggered to the door, fumbled his way out, made it down the steps. Joseph and I sat on the couch still sipping cold water. Shamengwa and Mooshum stared musingly at the door. Shamengwa had just stirred himself to pick up his fiddle when there was a terrific sound from outside, a resounding thud, like a dropped beef. I was closest to the door and got out first. Father Cassidy was laid out on the grass like a massive corpse. He looked quite dead, but when I bent over him I saw that his breath still moved the froth bubbles at his lips.

"Oh no!" Joseph cried out, kneeling at the other end of Father Cassidy. He peeled something from the sole of Father Cassidy's black cleric's shoe, and cradled it in his two hands. He walked away with the flattened salamander, glaring back once at the felled priest.

Mooshum gaped at us, holding on to the wood railing. He and Shamengwa did not trust their feet to negotiate the front steps and were picking their way down sideways, as if descending a steep hill.

"He slipped on a salamander," I said.

"Does he live yet?"

"He's breathing."

"Payhtik, mon frère," he said as Shamengwa stepped carefully down the road to his own house. Shamengwa waved his good arm without turning back. Mooshum went out to his car seat on the back lawn, lay down across it, and fell asleep. I stayed with Father Cassidy, who snored in the grass for a little while. I helped him to his feet when he came to, and then to his car, which he drove wanderingly up the hill.

Things would be harder, now, for Father Cassidy. As I went back inside to stash the empty bottle and wash out Mama's cups I knew that word would spread—the priest drunk, tripped up by the devil in the form of a mud puppy, cursing an old man to hell, all of these things would be recounted by Mooshum and Shamengwa when talking to their cronies. And Mooshum really did follow through with what had seemed like a drunken threat. He cast his lot in with the traditionals not long afterward and started attending ceremonies, which took place out on the farther reaches of the reservation and to which our dad drove him secretly. For Clemence was furious with Mooshum's defection. When I asked my grandfather why he'd decided to change so drastically, so late in his years, Mooshum told me.

"There is a moment in a man's life when he knows exactly who he is. Old Hop Along did not mean to, but he helped me to that moment."

"You were drunk, though, Mooshum."

"Awee, tawpway, my girl, you speak the truth. But my drunkenness had cleared my mind. Seraph Milk had a full-blood mother who died of sorrow with no help from the priest. I saw that I was the son of that good woman, silent though she was. Also, I was getting nowhere with the Catholic ladies. I thought that I might find a few good-looking ones out in the bush."

"That's not much of a reason."

"You are wrong there, it is the best reason."

And Mooshum winked at me as if he knew that I went to church because I hoped to see Corwin.

# Sister Godzilla

❧

MY LOVE FOR Corwin Peace turned to outraged betrayal when he told the other boys that he had kissed me. I was wretchedly angry with love now, determined to revenge myself on Corwin no matter how much my heart broke to do it. But I soon found that my heart didn't break at all, and I enjoyed tormenting Corwin. That whole summer, I struck him out whenever he dared join a game, and I looked forward to the moment when he slung his bat behind him in despair, sometimes cracking the shins of his teammates, turning their jeers to cries of pain. I shot at him with a BB gun. Years later, he claimed that my BB had migrated through his body and came out his kidney, causing him agony. My brother and I rode our ponies everywhere and took turns giving everybody rides except Corwin, around whom I barrel-raced one day in a circle, slowly obscuring him with dust as he stood and watched, hands out, helpless.

Yet, no matter how I tried to humiliate him, Corwin stayed in love with me. We grew side by side. I don't know what happened to him underneath his clothes, but that summer my breasts turned to sore buds, and I almost cried when I found hair where it didn't belong. Stoically, I endured my body's new secrets. Summer went and the air cooled. I got a new dress, saggy in the bust. We were in the sixth grade, at last, and it was the first day of school. Mama got us up and shoved us onto the dirt road that led up the hill. We dawdled until we heard the other children on the playground, then we ran. Two lines formed as always. We went in, already knowing our classroom. The door banged shut and we were alone with our teacher.

The habits of Franciscan nuns still shrouded all but their faces, and so each of the new nun's features were emphasized, read forty times over in astonishment. Outlined in a stiff white frame of starched linen, Sister's eyes, nose, and mouth leapt out, a mask from a dream, a great raw-boned jackal's muzzle.

"Oh, Christ," said Corwin, just loud enough for me to hear.

I had decided to ignore him for the first month, at least, but the nun's extreme ugliness was irresistible.

"Godzilla," I whispered, turning to him, raising my eyebrows.

The teacher's name was really Sister Mary Anita. People who knew her from before she was a nun said she was a Buckendorf. She was young, in her twenties or thirties, and so swift of movement for all her hulking size that, walking from the back of the room to the front, she surprised her students, made us picture athlete's legs and muscles concealed in the flow of black wool. When she swept the air in a gesture meant to include all of us in her opening remarks, her hands fixed our gazes. They were the opposite of her face. Her hands were beautiful, white as milk glass, the fingers straight and tapered. They were the hands in the hallway print, of Mary underneath the cross. They were the hands of the apostles, cast in plastic and lit at night on the tops of television sets. Praying hands.

Ballplayer's hands. She surprised us further by walking onto the gravel field at recess, the neck piece cutting hard into the flesh beneath her heavy jaw. When, with a matter-of-fact grace, she pulled from the sleeve of her gown a mitt of dark mustard-colored leather and raised it, a thrown softball dropped in. Her skill was obvious. Good players rarely seemed to stretch or change their expressions. They simply tipped their hands toward the ball like magnets, and there it was. As a pitcher, Mary Anita was a swirl of wool, graceful as the windblown cape of Zorro, an emotional figure that stirred something up in me. By the time I got up to bat, I was so thoroughly involved in the feeling that, as I pounded home plate, a rubber dish mat, beat the air twice in practice swings, and choked up on the handle, I decided that I would have no choice but to slam a home run.

I did not. In fact I whiffed worse than Corwin, in three strikes never ticking the ball or fouling. Disgusted with myself, I sat on the edge of the bike rack and watched as Sister gave a few balls away and pitched easy hits to the rest of the team. It was as if, from the beginning, the two of us had sensed what was to come. Or then again perhaps Mary Anita's information simply came from my former teachers, living in the redbrick convent across the road from school. Hard to handle. A smart-off. Watch out when you turn your back. They were right. After recess, my pride burned, I sat at my desk and drew a dinosaur encased in a nun's robe, the mouth open in a roar. The teeth, long and jagged, grayish white, absorbed me—I wanted to get the shadows right, the dark depth of the gullet behind them. I worked so hard on the picture that I didn't notice as the room hushed around me. I felt the presence, though, the tension of regard that dropped over me as Mary Anita stood watching. As a mark of my arrogance, I kept drawing.

I shaded in the last tooth and leaned back to frown at my work. The page was plucked into the air before I could pretend to cover it. There was silence. My heart sped with excitement.

"You will remain after school," the nun pronounced.

The last half hour passed. The others filed past me, smirking and whispering. And then the desk in front of me filled suddenly. There was the paper, the carefully rendered dinosaur caught in mid-roar. I stared at it furiously, my thoughts a blur of anticipation. I was not afraid.

"Look at me," said Mary Anita.

It was at that moment, I think, that it happened. I couldn't lift my head. My throat filled. I traced the initials carved into the desktop, my initials.

"Look at me," Mary Anita said to me again. My gaze was drawn upward, upward on a string, until I met the eyes of my teacher. Her eyes were the deep blue of Mary's cloak, electrically sad. Their stillness shook me.

"I'm sorry," I said.

When those two unprecedented words dropped from my lips, I knew that something terrible had occurred. The blood rushed to my head so fast that my ears ached, yet the tips of my fingers fell asleep. My eyelids prickled and my nose wept, but at the same time my mouth went dry. My body was a thing of extremes, contradicting itself.

"When I was young," said Sister Mary Anita, "young as you are, I felt a great deal of pain when I was teased about my looks. I've long since accepted my . . . deformity. A prognathic jaw runs in our family. But I must admit, the occasional insult, or a drawing such as yours, still hurts."

I began to mumble, then stopped, my throat raw. Sister Mary Anita waited, then handed me her own handkerchief. I buried my face in the cloth. She'd used it to mop her brow when beads of sweat crept down beneath the starched white square that cut into her forehead. There was no perfume whatsoever, of course, but something cleaner. Maybe lavender. Or marigold. Some pungent leaf.

"I'm sorry." I was intoxicated by the handkerchief. I wiped my nose. I asked to keep the square of white material, but Sister Mary Anita shook her head and retrieved the crumpled ball.

"Can I go now?"

"Of course not," said Mary Anita.

I was confounded. The magical two words, an apology, had dropped from my lips. Yet more was expected. What?

"I want you to understand something," said the nun. "I've told you how I feel. And I expect that you will never hurt me again."

Again the nun waited, and waited, until our eyes met. My mouth fell wide. My eyes spilled over again. I knew that the strange feelings that had come upon me and transfixed me were the same feelings that Mary Anita felt. I had never felt another person's feelings, never in my life.

"I won't do anything to hurt you," I babbled in a fit of startled agony. "I'll kill myself first."

"I'm sure that will not be necessary," said Sister Mary Anita.

I tried to rescue my pride, then, by turning away very quickly. Without permission, I ran out the schoolroom door, down the steps and on, into the road, where at last the magnetic force of the encounter weakened and I suddenly could breathe. Even that was different, though. As I walked I realized that my body still fought itself. My lungs filled with air like two bags, but every time they did so, a place underneath them squeezed so painfully the truth suddenly came clear.

"I love *her* now," I blurted out. I stopped on a crack in the earth, stepping on it, then stamped down hard, sickened. "Oh God, I am *in love*."

><

CORWIN TRIED EVERYTHING to win me back. He almost spoiled his reputation by eating tree bark. Then he put two crayons up his nose, pretend tusks. The pink got stuck and Sister Mary Anita sent him to visit the Indian Health Service clinic. He only rescued his image by getting his stomach pumped in the emergency room. I now despised him, but that only seemed to fuel his adoration.

Walking into the school yard the second week of September, on a bright cool morning, Corwin ran up to me and skidded to a halt like he was stealing base.

"Godzilla," he cried. "Yeah, not too shabby!"

He picked himself up and wheeled off, the laces of his tennis shoes flapping. I looked after him and felt the buzz inside my head begin again. I wanted to stuff that name back into my mouth, or at least into Corwin's mouth.

"I hope you trip and murder yourself," I screamed.

But Corwin did not trip. For all of his recklessness, he managed to stay upright, and as I stood rooted in the center of the walk I saw him whiz from clump to clump of children, laughing and gesturing, filling the air with small and derisive sounds. Sister Mary Anita swept out the door, a wooden-handled brass bell in her hand. When she shook it up and down, the children who played together in twos and threes swung toward her and narrowed or widened their eyes and turned eagerly to one another. Some began to laugh. It seemed to me that all of them did, in fact, and that the sound, jerked from their lips, was large, uncanny, totally and horribly delicious. It rose in my own throat, its taste was vinegar.

"Godzilla, Godzilla," they called underneath their breath. "Sister Godzilla."

Before them on the steps, Sister Mary Anita continued to smile into their faces. She did not hear them . . . yet. But I knew she would. Over the bell, her eyes were brilliantly dark and alive. Her horrid jagged teeth showed in a smile. I ran to her. Thrusting my hand into my lunch bag, I grabbed the cookies that my mother had made from recipes she clipped from oatmeal boxes and molasses jars.

"Here!" I shoved a sweet, lumpy cookie into the nun's hand. It fell apart, distracting her as my classmates pushed past.

☀

MY FELLOW STUDENTS seemed to forget the name off and on all week. Some days they would seem to have passed on to new disasters—other teachers occupied them, or some small event occurred within the classroom. But then Corwin Peace would lope and careen among them at recess; he'd pump his arms and pretend to roar behind Sister Mary Anita's back as she stepped up to the plate. As she swung and connected with the ball and gathered herself to run, her veil lifting, the muscles in her shoulders like the curved hump of a raptor's wings, Corwin would move along behind her, rolling his legs the way Godzilla did in the King Kong movie. In her excitement, dashing base to base, her feet long and limber in black-laced nun's boots, Mary Anita did not notice. But I looked on, helpless, the taste of a penny caught in my throat.

☀

"SNAKES LIVE IN holes. Snakes are reptiles. These are Science Facts."

I read to the class, out loud, from my Discovery science book.

"Snakes are not wet. Some snakes lay eggs. Some have live young."

"Very good," said Sister. "Can you name other reptiles?"

My tongue fused to the back of my throat.

"Yes," I croaked.

She waited, patient eyes on me.

"There's *Chrysemys picta*," I said, "the painted turtle. And the Plains garter snake, *Thamnophis radix*, and also *T. sirtilis*, the red-sided garter snake. They live right here, in the sloughs, all around here."

Sister nodded in a kind of thoughtful surprise, but then seemed to remember that my father was a science teacher and smiled her kind and frightful smile. "Well, that's very good.

"Anyone else?" Sister asked. "Reptiles from other parts of the world?"

Corwin Peace raised his hand. Sister recognized him.

"How about Godzilla?"

Gasps. Small noises of excitement. Mouths opened and hung open. Admiration for Corwin's nerve rippled through the rows of children like a wind across a field. Sister Mary Anita's great jaw opened, opened, then snapped shut. Her shoulders shook. No one knew what to do at first, then she laughed. It was a high-pitched, almost birdlike sound, a thin laugh like the highest keys played on the piano. The other students' mouths opened, they all hesitated, then they laughed with her, even Corwin. Eyes darting from one of us to the next, to me, Corwin laughed.

But I was near to puking with anxious rage. When Sister Mary Anita turned to new work, I crooked my fist beside me like a piston, then I leaned across Corwin's desk.

"I'm going to give you one right in the bread box," I said.

Corwin looked pleased, and so with one precise jab—which I had learned from my uncle Whitey, who fought in the Golden Gloves—I knocked the wind out of him and left him gasping. I turned to the front, my face clear and heart calm, as Sister began her instruction.

✄

FURIOUS SUNLIGHT. BLACK cloth. I sat on the iron trapeze, the bar pushing a sore line into the backs of my legs. As I swung, I watched Sister Mary Anita. The wind was harsh and she wore a pair of wonderful gloves, black, the fingers cut out of them so that her hand could better grip the bat. The ball arced toward her sinuously, dropped, her bat caught it with a clean sound. Off the ball soared, across the playground boundaries, over into the yard of the priest's residence. Mary Anita's habit swirled open behind her. The cold bit her cheeks red. She swung to third and glanced, panting, over her shoulder and then sped home. She touched down lightly and bounded off.

My arms felt heavy, weak. I dropped from the trapeze and went to lean against the brick wall of the school building. My heart thumped in my ears. I saw what I would do when I grew up. Declare my vocation, enter the convent. Sister Mary Anita and I would live over in the nuns' house together, side by side. We would eat, work, eat, cook. Sometimes we'd have to pray. To relax, Sister Mary Anita would hit pop flies and I would catch them.

Someday, one day, the two of us would be walking, our hands in our sleeves, our long habits flowing behind.

"Dear Sister," I would say, "remember that old nickname you had the year you taught the sixth grade?"

"Why no," Sister Mary Anita would say, smiling at me. "Why, no."

And I would know that I had protected her.

≽⊀

IT GOT WORSE. I wrote letters, tore them up. My hand shook when Sister passed me in the aisle and my eyes closed. I breathed in. Soap. A harsh soap. Faint carbolic acid. Marigolds, for sure. That's what she smelled like. Dizzying. My fists clenched. I pressed my knuckles to my eyes and loudly excused myself. I went to the girls' bathroom and stood in a stall. My life was terrible. The thing is, I didn't want to be a nun.

"There must be another way!" I whispered, desperate. The white-washed tin shuddered when I slammed my hand on the cubicle wall. I decided that I would have to persuade Mary Anita to forsake her vows, to come and live with me and my family in our BIA house. Someone was standing outside. I opened the door a bit and stared into the great, craggy face.

"Are you feeling all right? Do you need to go home?" Sister Mary Anita was concerned.

Fire shot through my limbs. The girls' bathroom, its light mute and brilliant, a place of secrets, of frosted glass, paralyzed me. I gathered myself. Here was my chance, as if God had given it.

"Please," I whispered to her. "Let's run away together!"

50

Sister paused. "Are you having troubles at home?" she asked.

"No."

Sister's milk-white hand came through the doorway and covered my forehead. My anxious thoughts throbbed against her lean, cool palm. Staring into the eyes of the one I loved, I gripped the small metal knob on the inside of the door, pushed, and then I felt myself falling forward, slowly turning like a leaf in wind, upheld and buoyant in the peaceful roar. It was as though I'd never reach Sister's arms, but when I did, I came back with a jolt.

"You *are* ill," said Sister. "Come to the office and we'll call your mother."

※

AS I HAD known it would, perhaps from that moment in the girls' bathroom, the day came. The day of reckoning.

Outside, in the morning school yard, after Mass and before first bell, everyone crowded around Corwin Peace. In his arms, he held a windup tin Godzilla, a big toy, almost knee-high, a green and gold replica painted with a fierce eye to detail. The scales were perfect overlapping crescents and the eyes were large and manic, pitch-black, oddly human. Corwin had pinned a sort of cloak upon the thing, a black scarf. My arms thrust through the packed shoulders, but the bell rang and Corwin stowed the thing under his coat. His eyes picked me from the rest.

"I had to send for this!" he cried. The punch hadn't turned him against me; it had made him crazy with love. He turned and vanished through the heavy wine-red doors of the school. I stared at the ground and thought of leaving home. I could do it. I'd hitch a boxcar. The world went stark, the colors harsh. The small brown pebbles of the school yard leapt off the play-sealed earth. I took a step. The stones seemed to crack and whistle under my feet.

"Last bell!" called Sister Mary Anita. "You'll be late!"

※

MORNING PRAYER. THE PLEDGE. Corwin drew out the suspense of his audience, enjoying the glances and whispers. The toy was in his desk. Every so often, he lifted the lid, then looked around to see how many of us watched him duck inside to make adjustments. By the time Sister started the daily reading lesson, there was such tension in the room that even Corwin could bear it no longer.

Our classroom was large, with a high ceiling, floored with slats of polished wood. Round lights hung on thick chains and the great, rectangular windows let through enormous sheaves of radiance. Our class had occupied this room for the past two years. I had spent every day in the room. I knew its creaks, the muted clunk of desks rocking out of floor bolts, the mad thumping in its radiators like a thousand imprisoned elves, and so I heard and registered the click. Then the dry grind of Corwin's windup key. Sister Mary Anita did not. She turned to the chalkboard, her book open on the desk, and began to write instructions for us to copy.

She was absorbed, calling out the instructions as she wrote. Her arm swept up and down, it seemed to me, in a kind of furious joy. She was inventing some kind of lesson, some new way of doing things, not a word of which was taken in. All eyes were on the third row, where Corwin Peace sat. All eyes were on his hand as he wound the toy up to its limit and bent over and set it on the floor. Then the eyes were on the toy itself as Corwin lifted his hand away, and the thing moved forward on its own.

The scarf it wore, the veil, did not hamper the beast. The legs thrashed forward, making earnest progress. The tiny claw hands beat like pistons and the hollow tin tail whipped from side to side as it moved down the center of the aisle, toward the front of the room, toward Sister Mary Anita, who stood, back turned, still absorbed in her work at the board.

I had got myself placed in row one, to be closer to the one I loved, and so I saw the creature close up just before it headed into the polished space of floor at the front of the room. Its powerful jaws thrust from the black neck piece. The great teeth were frozen, exhibited in a terrible smile. The painted eyes had an eager and purposeful look.

Its movement faltered as it neared Mary Anita. The whole class caught its breath, but the thing inched along, made slow and fascinating progress, directly toward the hem of Mary Anita's garment. She did not seem to notice. She continued to write, to talk, circling numbers and emphasizing certain words with careful underlines. And as she did so, as the moment neared, my brain finally rang all of its alarm bells. I vaulted from my desk. Two steps brought me across that gleaming space of wood at the front of the room. But just as I bent down to scoop the toy to my chest, a neat black boot slashed down inches from my nose. Sister Mary Anita had whirled, the chalk fixed in her hand. Daintily, casually, she lifted her habit and kicked the toy dinosaur into the air. The thing ascended, pedaling its clawed feet, the cape blown back like a sprung umbrella. The trajectory was straight and true. It knocked headfirst into the ceiling and came back down, in pieces. The class ducked beneath the rain of scattered tin. Only Sister Mary Anita and I stood poised, unmoved, absorbed in the moment between us.

There was no place for me to look but at my teacher. But when I lifted my eyes, this time, Sister Mary Anita was not looking at me. She had turned her face away, her rough cheek blotched as if it bore a slap, her gaze hooded and set low. Sister walked to the window, back turned against me, against the class, and as the laughter started, uncomfortable and groaning at first, then shriller, fuller, becoming its own animal, I felt an unrecoverable tenderness boil up and rise around my ears. Inwardly, I begged Mary Anita to turn and stop the noise. But Sister did not. She let it wash across us both without mercy. I lost sight of her unspeakable profile as she looked out into the yard. Bathed in brilliant light, her face went blank as a sheet of paper, as the sky, featureless as all things which enter heaven.

# Holy Track

❧❦

ALTHOUGH SHE TREATED me with neutral interest from then on and did not punish me, I was grieved by Sister Mary Anita's disregard. I wrote letters, tore them up, and at last, as there was no other course of action, I collected facts, and I studied Sister Mary Anita. In a fit of longing, I retrieved papers she had written on and thrown away. Her sloping hand was absolutely uniform. You could put her capital letters one on the other, hold the pages up to the light, and see no variation in the size or ornamentation. Yet her handwriting wasn't strictly Palmer script, but very much her own invention.

One startling day I learned that she was allergic to chocolate and broke out in hives. The red welts across her face gave her a warrior's intensity. She never scratched, but they must have tormented her. Even so, sometimes she could not resist chocolate and was known to take a piece of candy or cake at a wedding, saying, "Darn the consequences!" even though for a nun "darn" was considered a swear.

Unlike the other nuns who taught at the school, and came from a mother house in Kentucky, Sister Mary Anita had grown up near the reservation, on a farm between Hoopdance and Pluto. She told this to us in the middle of our history class. None of the other children thought that unusual, but I perceived it as some sign. At home, I spoke of her constantly, and one day my mother gave me a long look.

"Sister Mary Anita this, Sister Mary Anita that. You sure talk about Sister Mary Anita a lot. What's her full name anyway?"

I turned aside but muttered, "Sister Mary Anita Buckendorf." I stole a look back at my mother, but she raised her eyebrows and glanced at my father. He gave no sign that he found the name of significance, but continued to paste stamps into his stamp album. He had inherited these polished leather albums and was adding slowly to some arcane arrangement which had originally been assembled by Uncle Octave, the one who had died tragically, for love. When attending to his albums, my father's absorption was so complete that he was unreachable. Mooshum was sitting at the table playing rummy with Joseph. He caught the name though, and said, "Buckendorf!" He tried to keep on playing, but Joseph jogged his arm to make him quit. My mother went outside to hang the wet laundry on the line, in spite of the storm brewing. I'd caught the same note in Mooshum's voice as my brother had, and checked again on my father, who was examining through a magnifying glass some stamp he held up with a tweezers. Our father drew a rapt breath and smiled as though the frail scrap of paper held a mystic secret. I moved to the end of the table and asked, "What about the name?"

"What name?" Mooshum knew that he had us hooked.

"You know, my teacher, Sister Mary Anita Buckendorf."

"Oh yai! The Buckendorfs!" His mouth twisted as he said it.

"She's a nun!"

Mooshum packed his jaw and nodded at his spittoon. Joseph made a retching noise but went outside carrying the snoose can—a red Sanborn coffee can with the man in a yellow robe walking across it sipping coffee. We always emptied the can onto the roots of Mama's struggling blue Colorado spruce—eventually, it surrendered to the killing juice, turned black, and dried up.

"You know why she's a nun, after all, my girl," said Mooshum, while Joseph was outside. "Not too many people have the privilege of seeing right before their eyes there is no justice here on eart." He said "eart," he hardly ever used a *th*.

Mooshum put his hands down before him and pushed the air

twice. He pushed the air like he was stuffing it into a box. "She saw it. No justice."

"Yeah?"

Joseph came back in and we waited, but Mooshum suddenly turned his back on us and rummaged in his shirt pocket. We could not see what he was doing. He turned back to us and spat into the empty coffee can with such a loud ping that my father glanced up, but his eyes didn't even focus on us before the stamps reclaimed his attention. Mooshum shifted the wad a little and kept squinting at us. Measuring us. We sat still and stared at him, trying to contain ourselves. The television had succumbed to some disturbance in the atmosphere and no delicate adjustment of its long wire antennae had cleared the snow from the picture. We were very bored, but there was more—perhaps I could add to my facts about Sister Mary Anita. It seemed that Mooshum had knowledge of something new about her, or her family at least, and I suspected that it might be something that no one else would tell me.

Mooshum straightened with a creaky groan and rocked himself forward. He found his balance, launched himself. We followed as he walked out the screen door, down the wooden steps, onto the tortured lawn. He lowered himself into the peeling yellow kitchen chair that he brought out in spring and took back inside after frost. It was late September, but the day was very warm. He liked to sit outside on the dead grass of the yard and inspect people as they walked the road to the agency offices. We grabbed a pair of camp stools and sat watching him think. His mouth fell slack and then his face seized up; he scratched his jaw and glared at us. Mooshum's strange reluctance to tell this story was compelling. The less he wanted to tell, the more we wanted to hear. He turned away from us again, bent his head and with a furtive squint reached into his shirt. He took a snort of something that we couldn't see. Whirling quickly, he focused on our mother. She put a wooden clothespin between her teeth and picked up two others. Then she bent down, grabbed a pillowcase, and snapped it once, briskly, before she pinned it with the two pins she had in one hand. The pin in her teeth always was an extra, or she used it for securing her underwear beneath thin top sheets, she was that modest.

Mooshum spat, ringing the can again, and waited to see if our mother would turn around. She didn't, so he began to talk to us in a low voice, returning to that time when he had been young, though not as young as when the doves filled the sky. They were gone when this next thing happened, he said, and Joseph asked if the prayers had worked to drive them off. Mooshum said that everything had dwindled away by then, even the buffalo, which he'd been told were once limitless. Killed off, he said, shrugging and spitting at the same time, a gesture we tried to imitate later, with stolen snuff. Mooshum told us that we should not tell our mother or father the things he was about to tell us. This of course squeezed our breathing tight, and we huddled closer.

## The Boots

MOOSHUM SPAT THOUGHTFULLY and repacked his lip. He repeated the name Holy Track several times, his voice trailing. Then he suddenly roused, as the old do, and told us in a rain of words how, when he and Junesse rode Mustache Maude's good horses back onto the reservation, they were accused of stealing those horses. For a time, they had had trouble fending off the newly appointed tribal police, who coveted good blood stock. They kept the horses only through the intervention of Father Severine. Scolded by the priest, the authorities quit. The young mare Junesse rode had long legs, a great keg of a barrel, and a fighting heart, and so raced very well. Mooshum made enough on bets to buy a cow and to outfit the farm with a windmill. He traded the stud services of his horse for help building a cabin of hewn oak. But having fallen in with the sort who raced horses—not a good sort, said Mooshum—he began, for the first time, to drink whiskey.

"I could always take or leave it," he paused, crumpling his face with an odd wince, and added, low, that sometimes the whiskey would not just take or leave him. The whiskey had its own mind. Or spirit, he said. A cunning spirit. Sometimes it fooled him. Sometimes it set him free.

A boy and his mother, who was a cousin to Junesse, lived on the edge of Mooshum's land, and it was pitiful. The mother's lungs had rotted. Mooshum spread his hands across his own chest. She was so weak that she could hardly stir out of her bed to care for the boy. He was thirteen years old and getting rangy, but he was an innocent boy. Until his mother weakened, he walked her to church every day. She remained after, sunk in prayer, while her son memorized the Latin Mass and learned exactly how to help Father Severine change bread and wine into the body and blood of the Son of God. Sometimes Junesse came with her and the three walked back together, Junesse and the boy holding the sick woman between them. From time to time she stopped and coughed blood carefully into the dust of the road, bending way over so that it would not stain her dress.

This went on all autumn until the weather got too cold. Through the winter, the mother wasted. By the time the snow was entirely gone and the bitter new leaves had darkened, she was nearly dead. Junesse sent Mooshum by the house every day to see if her cousin had survived the night. One spring morning, he brought along the hammer and fine nails she had requested. The boy was there as well as an aunt who worked in Canada at a sanatorium for tubercular patients. That place did not as a rule take Indians, but because of the aunt's piety the nuns had agreed to make an exception and had prepared a bed.

The boy's mother had a small cross in each hand, prizes given to her son for memorizing the long prayers. She nodded at her boy's crude, thick-soled boots and gestured that he should remove them and give them to Mooshum. She then told Mooshum to fix a cross to each sole. He nailed carefully through the inside of the boot, and covered the tops of the nails with pieces of her blanket that she'd cut away for this purpose. When Mooshum was finished, she staggered toward her sister, who helped her into the bed of a small cart, hitched to a tough old pony.

"Wear them," she whispered to her son. "The sickness will not follow you. Evil will not cross your tracks. You will live."

The boy put his feet in the boots and stood miserably beside Mooshum as his aunt led the horse and cart off down the grass trail, then turned onto the broader road leading north. Mooshum brought the boy to an old man called Asiginak, who was named for a great chief, Blackbird, and lived alone farther back in the bush. The old man was the boy's great-uncle.

At first the boots must have cut, said Mooshum. But by the time he saw the boy again, he had bound his feet in strips of leather and had gradually gotten used to their weight. People came to believe that his mother was right about the boots, for her son did not begin to cough. After some time, because he left tracks printed with a cross, the people began to call him Holy Track.

## The Clothesline

MOOSHUM LOOKED UP, brightened his eyes, and nodded. Mama had finished pinning up everything in the basket. Dad's blue teacher's shirts, all of our denim pants, white bedsheets, and the brown dress I hated flapped there, lightly soaking in the sun. Through the box elder leaves, we could see clouds massing to the west, building radiant pink towers against a blue-gray backdrop of distant rain. Mama watched us. She had a talent for looking at a person with no expression—you filled in whatever you felt guiltiest about. Mooshum stopped talking. She set down the empty basket under the wire lines and stepped across the dry grass. Dust puffed up behind her firm steps.

"They don't need to hear it," she said.

"Hear what?" asked Mooshum.

"You know."

"Ah, that, tawpway, my girl!"

Mama would usually have made sure that Mooshum left off, or given us each some task to ensure that her directions were followed, but she seemed distracted that day and simply walked up the back steps. The moment she passed into the house, we leaned close to Mooshum.

## The Basket Makers

BIG STANDS OF willow grew around their cabin, so Asiginak taught Holy Track the art of making baskets. That spring, they cut willow and bundled it away in a cool place, then split the ash to make the framework of the baskets—some with carved handles, tikinaganan for babies, wide and flat baskets, even heart-shaped baskets for the farm women. Every day, they wove pliable willow into ash frameworks until their fingers were tough as sticks. When they had thirty or forty, as many as they could carry, they went out selling.

People readily bought baskets from Holy Track. The boy's big childish teeth were white and crooked; his smile was shy and his eyelashes were so long they shadowed his cheeks. Asiginak had tried to give him a whiteman's haircut and it got clipped so short in places that the hair stood out like brushy quills.

One day in early summer, when the little strawberries ripen along the edges of the field and the ducklings whisk across the sloughs, the two set off walking to the towns and farms off the reservation. They sold a basket or two everyplace they went. Only ten baskets were left when they met Mooshum and Cuthbert Peace coming down the road.

"Us two rowdies," said Mooshum, winking at us, "were unhappily sober. We fell in with Asiginak and Holy Track hoping that we could persuade the old man to spare enough of his basket money to get his old friends drunk."

"Gewehn!" Mooshum swiped his hand in the air, remembering. "Go home!" the old man told us.

"Ah, no, brother, I replied, let us carry these things for you!"

Mooshum put his hands out as if to help carry the baskets, but told us how Holy Track held tight to his baskets and tramped steadily beside his uncle.

Mooshum's friend Cuthbert was dark as a bear, round, and his nose was like his nickname, Opin, a potato. Something had gone wrong with it after a fight and it had kept growing out of control on one side. It took up most of his face now and was an odd, lumpy shape. He spat tobacco and tugged at Holy Track's arm.

"Leave him alone," said Asiginak. "Your nose will sprout."

Cuthbert took offense, dropped his hands away, and kicked his feet like a dog scratching dirt on its shit. Holy Track was still studying catechism with Father Severine, but he couldn't help laugh at Cuthbert. The rascal pranced down the road, then stopped, jiggled his dodooshag and preened like a pretty girl. Mooshum showed us, doing a little dance in his chair. Then he sat back, laughing, and mimicked Cuthbert: "You'd be surprised what this nose gets me, and this belly, but it's down here the women love the best!"

Asiginak tried to shut up the two other men, saying, "This boy is going to be a priest. He can't hear things like that."

Mooshum said that he and Opin walked in silence behind the two basket makers, still hoping, until Asiginak turned and warned them, "Don't step in his tracks."

Mooshum shook his head slowly back and forth, shifting his wad of chew, frowning as he did. "The old man meant that we were not worthy to step in the boy's tracks. Evil had us in those days."

## The Lochren Farm

THEY WALKED DOWN the wagon path into a farmyard bounded by a scraggle of cottonwood. The farm was set near the town of Pluto, but the entrance was obscured by a low rise and the brushy tangle of a slough. When they got to the farm, Mooshum said he wished they had not followed the boy's tracks. He said he knew there was something wrong from the beginning, with the smeared door to the house wide open and no smoke from the chimney. When they got close, the cows in the barn set up a sudden groaning to be milked. The desperation in their resonant bawls stopped the men in the trampled yard.

Asiginak set down his baskets. One of the cows screamed like a woman in pain, and everything went abruptly quiet. After a moment the frogs started up again, trilling and sawing in the slough.

"Let's not go any closer," said Asiginak. "The devil has this place."

And then they heard the baby crying. It was a scratchy cry, a thin, exhausted wail from inside the house.

Asiginak picked up his baskets and turned to leave.

"That's a baby," said Cuthbert, and he grabbed Mooshum's shirt and stood rooted, staring, his stained jaw working.

The baby continued to cry as if it knew they were out there, but they did not move and soon the little sound died away. The wind struck up in the leggy young cottonwoods. Bits of fluff whirled high above them. There was the clatter of stiff, new leaves. As Asiginak started to walk away, the cows started up even louder. Maybe the baby did, too, but now they couldn't hear it over the vast moans from the barn.

"I feel the devil," Asiginak cried. "Look there!"

But Cuthbert had gone through the door marked with blood. He vanished into the house. When he came out, he was carrying the baby and his eyes were bugging out—that's how Mooshum put it, his eyes were bugging out. Cuthbert staggered to the barn with the baby. It wore a tiny white dress and a reeking diaper. The others followed. On the way there, they saw two boys curled on their sides, in the weeds, like they were sleeping, and then a man, his fingers clutched in the green black grass, his head up and still staring at the boys when he died crawling. His back was blasted out.

"Don't look in that direction," Asiginak told Holy Track.

The men cracked the barn doors wide and entered the mad wall of sound.

There were ten cows, one dead. Mooshum helped Holy Track put down the baskets somewhere in the dark, and blinked until he could see the nearest cow. He began on that one, then found another. Soon there was just the hiss of milk and a few last cows. The milked ones sounded like they were weeping, softly, in relief. Cuthbert cradled the baby in one arm and squeezed a teat to its lips—the bud of its mouth was hardly big enough, but he squirted the milk in deftly. At last the baby relaxed and its head lolled back. A smile played around its chapped scarlet lips. Mooshum turned the cows out to pasture and the men fled outside, rubbing their eyes, dazzled.

"I'll carry this baby back," said Cuthbert, peering anxiously into its face.

"Back where?" said Asiginak.

"To the sheriff."

"The white sheriff?"

Asiginak saw that his nephew was gaping at the yard. He gently pushed the boy's face so that Holy Track was facing not the sleeping forms but the watery blue line of the horizon.

Asiginak turned back to Cuthbert. "You're not drunk, so why do you say this? We are no-goods, we are Indians, even me. If you tell the white sheriff, we will die."

"They will hang us for sure," said Mooshum. He picked up Holy Track's baskets.

"It's all right," said Holy Track. "I know what to do. I will tell the priest."

The other men looked at him.

"Do not tell the priest," said Mooshum.

Cuthbert held the baby tight. "We cannot put this little one back. If we go, we take it with us."

"We cannot," said Asiginak.

"I will not go in that house again," said Cuthbert.

"You know how to write," said Asiginak to the boy. "You will write this down: *One lives yet on Lochren.* Tonight, I will place your message in the sheriff's box where he receives his papers. They will come for the baby in the morning."

Cuthbert nodded slowly and gave the baby to Asiginak, who went back into the house. When he came out, he was looking at the ground. He noticed the tracks.

"We must brush your tracks out wherever we find them," he said, in a serious, distracted voice. "Take your shoes off."

The men walked around the yard brushing out marks of the cross in the loose dirt. When they were satisfied, they left, melting down along the edge of the cow pasture, off into the woods, then down paths that raveled out for miles.

## A Little Medicine

MOOSHUM QUIT. WE thought he'd had enough of talking, and as this was such a strange and awful thing that he was telling us, we just sat there. I twisted my hair around and around my finger and Joseph frowned at the rock-hard ground.

The door creaked open, and Mama leaned out to look at the sky. The blazing balls of clouds were getting sucked back into the dark, though the rain seemed far away yet. The wind had started up in the box elder grove and the laundry flapped on the line. She bent her head like she was shouldering a yoke, and let the door slam behind her. She strode over to the line to feel whether the clothing was dry enough. Something was definitely bothering her that day, but we did not find out until later what that was. Maybe if she hadn't been so absorbed in her irritation she would have stopped Mooshum from telling us the whole story, or from sipping at the brown medicine bottle under his green zippered Sears work jacket. He drew the bottle out, swirled its contents round and round, and popped a small slug back into his throat. We caught a whiff of bitter, wild leaves. His eyes watered as he replaced the bottle.

Mama took down a couple of flat sheets, leaving some of her own nylon underwear on the line. I'd never seen her underwear right out there on the line. The pale blue and tissuey pink panties puffed with air and stayed true to her rounded shape. She walked past and said to Mooshum, "Geraldine's coming and I know what she's going to tell me already." She went up the steps and shouted back down to Mooshum. "And I don't like it."

Mooshum popped his eyes out comically as the door slammed, and made an *oooh, she's mad* ducking gesture.

"What happened to the baby?" Joseph asked.

"A man named Hoag came and got that baby," said Mooshum. I thought the story was over and got up to follow Mama—she was going to want me to help her fold the clothing, or roll it for ironing. She was so perturbed already that I didn't want to test her patience. But then Mooshum took another toot from his medicine bottle and said, "They came for Asiginak at night."

"They?" I turned back.

"They who?" said Joseph.

"The town men," said Mooshum. "That's why I'm telling this to you. Wildstrand, the Buckendorfs . . ."

"The Buckendorfs?" I said.

"Oh yai! They're the ones! They came for Asiginak at night, but he heard them first and bolted. Me, I had come to warn them and I dragged the boy out just in time."

## Confessional

THE LITTLE CABIN had a tiny window out back covered with a flap of hide. Holy Track and Mooshum were out that window in an iced second—blown by terror into the woods. They landed like leaves, sprang into the trees, and crept into a tangle of chokecherry and willow. Then they floundered into a slough and sank down among the reeds. There were dogs with the men, but they were cow dogs, not trained hounds, and they barked at everything. They smelled an animal or maybe Asiginak and started off in another direction. The men's torches played over the surface of the water. There was more trampling, shuffling, the dogs' mad barking, and they were gone. The noise got smaller and smaller. The two pulled themselves through the muck until they were on solid ground. There was no choice now but to run to Father Severine. Though he was unreliable and didn't like Mooshum anymore, he very much loved Holy Track.

As the two made their way down the trail that led around the hills, along pastures, the birds started up singing in the alder and wild raspberry. Mooshum asked the little birds for help, and Holy Track said Hail Marys. As they walked along, they talked about the priest's habits—how he took forever to fraction the Host and drawled his prayers out so it was nearly impossible to keep one's eyes open and not pitch forward on the floor. How soft the floor looked while listening to Severine's sermons and how dreadful it was when a louse or flea began to bite, or when a piss was necessary. They agreed that the most agonizing itches always developed while serving Mass. They revealed that both of their butt ends knew a sharp corner attached to the kneeler that afforded a merciful, secret scratch.

On the swelling side of a hill, along a small stream that ran slough to slough, they heard horses and rolled into the torn system of a tipped-up cottonwood tree. They hid in the cage of black roots and froze as the white men passed. Asiginak had not been caught.

"They might give up on us," said Holy Track.

The air was still fresh with night dew when Holy Track and Mooshum pulled open the door to the church and slipped inside. There was the odor of rotting burlap and field dust from all of the potato bags placed down as rugs. One tiny lamp flickered before the carved wooden cabinet where the priest kept the Hosts. It was covered with a towel embroidered in red letters.

"I don't like the taste of that bread!" Mooshum made a face. "You cannot call it bread! Not even a cracker. You could eat a thousand and not live."

"You're supposed to get everlasting life from it," said Joseph.

"That did not work for Holy Track," said Mooshum.

The boy knelt for a moment before the cabinet. Then he pushed aside the towel, opened the gilded door in its side, and ate all the wafers. He closed the door, and blew out the flame of the lamp. He told Mooshum that he hadn't eaten for days—ever since Asiginak had come home raving with fear saying there was drunk talk and now the white sheriff and maybe some farmers, also, knew that Indians had been in the presence of the murdered family. Holy Track's hands reached forward and he drank the rancid fat from the bowl of the lamp. His stomach immediately cramped up. He broke out in a sweat, ran outside, and leaned his head against the back wall of the church. He forced himself to keep down the spirit bread by breathing hard and concentrating on the presence inside of him. Father Severine had explained his soul to him. Now, he told Mooshum, it made sense that the bread he had eaten would feed this soul, this spirit, and increase its strength. He thought he would need this strength.

At last, when the boy felt better, Mooshum helped him creep back inside. There was an aperture of enclosed space in the church where the priest heard confessions. A sack curtain hung down the front. Holy Track ducked in and crouched on the dirt floor with his knees drawn up to his chin.

Mooshum left him there and sipped like an animal at the stale font of holy water. Then he fell asleep underneath a pew until morning sun filtered through the rough curtains. He peered into the brown light of the church. The door opened and a narrow band of white light struck across the floor. Father Severine approached the confessional with long, delicate, strides, and looked inside.

"My son!" he breathed. A dark cleft of anxiety formed between the priest's eyebrows. "Are the others here too?"

"No," said Holy Track.

Relieved, the priest let out his breath. The boy had formed himself into a ball on the floor. The priest's face worked back and forth between expressions of pity and disgust, and at last settled on peevish disappointment.

"I suppose you are here to confess." His voice was shaky and shrill. His breath was agitated. "You have done a monstrous thing!" He seemed to gather himself and stepped backwards.

"I will feed you, only that," he said, and left. But when Father Severine returned, he had such food. There were tears in his weak eyes as he watched his favorite eat the tinned crackers and the dried peaches, cold fried venison, a jar of honey, and bread soft as flower petals. Mooshum kept quiet although his stomach yawned.

Holy Track ate with gravity, devotion, and lust. He spoke with his cheeks bulging.

"They were all dead but the baby."

By the time he swallowed, there were men outside. The priest got up. His eyes were swimming.

"Nothing, we did nothing . . . we never," said the boy, but his tongue was weighed down with honey and his mouth too dry to swallow the food.

"They led you to it," said Father Severine, his eyes spilling over, the tears running down the furrows beside his beaky nose, splashing down inside his collar. "Stay hidden, I will talk."

## *The Sisters*

THE DOOR SLAMMED with a deliberate whack. Mooshum spat. Joseph started. I jumped up. Mama had Geraldine with her now and as they passed I heard my aunt say, "Who told you?" Then they were halfway down the yard, past the tangled brushy trees and the hanging clothes, which Mama didn't bother to touch for dryness this time. They were lost in a conversation. Mama's shoulders were hunched and her head was turned just a bit toward Geraldine. They looked a lot like each other from behind—their permanented black hair bobbed prettily just over their collars. Mama wore a green blouse and Geraldine's was yellow. Their dark skirts were long and full, belted tight with elastic cinch belts. Their feet were dainty in Keds shoes and anklets. Mama painted her canvas shoes with white polish to keep them spotless. Their clothing was always secondhand but they still looked dashing. People thought they went to Fargo to shop when their clothes really came from the mission.

They walked to the end of the yard where the old outhouse stood, now cluttered inside with hoes and shovels. There, they folded their arms and faced each other, mouths moving, skirts whipping in the hot rain-smelling breeze. Mooshum began to talk again, knowing that Mama's attention was absorbed. It wasn't like he was talking to us, though, or even using his usual storytelling voice. He wasn't drawing us in, or gesturing. This was different. Now it was like he was stuck in some way, on some track, like he couldn't stop the story from forcing its way out. This was the one time he told the story whole.

## *The Party*

OUTSIDE THE CHURCH, the men's voices were a tumble. First the priest's choked pleas, then a rolling barrel full of words. Mooshum made no sense of it, but dreamily shoved in the food Holy Track pushed over. He caught the back and forth of the talk. The words jammed together until the men and the horses made one sound, a heavy confusion of breath and stomping blood. Then a brief quiet in which the wind came up whining in the eaves. Suddenly Holy Track leapt up, stuffing bits of the boiled meat into his pockets, and rolled underneath the darkest bench with Mooshum.

The white men knocked Father Severine aside and banged into the church. They strode down the church aisle in their heavy boots and each genuflected. Some crossed themselves. Then they looked behind the altar and into the confessional.

"He run again," said a bright, clear voice.

"We got one anyhow, let's hang the one we got," sang a man from outside. It was a lovely, melodious voice with a German buzz.

As the men outside dragged Asiginak past Father Severine, the priest went rigid. He opened and shut his mouth like he was choking, and tried jerkily to bless the old man. Asiginak slapped his hands away.

"Don't be useless," he cried. "Get them off me!"

From under the bench, Holy Track heard his uncle cry out. Asiginak gave a wail of penetrating fear and shouted in Ojibwe, "I don't want to die alone!"

Father Severine swayed and propped himself against a tree in the yard. Suddenly everyone stopped. They sensed that someone had come to stand in the doorway of the church. They all turned as one.

"Uncle, I will go with you," said the boy.

Mooshum crawled from under the pew and jumped up to pull Holy Track inside. He struggled to bar the door against the men, but the Buckendorfs surged in and caught them both fast in their big hay-pitching arms. The men hoisted Mooshum and the boy out into the light. One held the boy by the nape of his neck. When he saw the horror and the shame on Asiginak's face, Mooshum knew that Holy Track regretted showing himself. But he stood his ground and made the sign of the cross over and over until the white men pinned his hands behind his back. They tied his wrists together and threw the boy along with Mooshum and Asiginak into the bed of their wagon. Father Severine cried something out in Latin and bolted to life. He clawed at the sides of the wagon and tottered awkwardly beside them. He blurted crazily useless threats and conflicted blessings as they rattled down the hill. Soon, his croaking died away. Asiginak hunched over at first, staring at his feet, and would not speak. At last, in a voice filled with anguish, he said to Holy Track. "I never knew you were hiding in there. My words were not for you to hear."

Holy Track glared, angry at his uncle for a moment, then he shrugged and pretended that he didn't care.

Wild plum trees were blooming in the scrub. Willow had leafed out narrow and green, and the sloughs glittered in the early light. The question of a tree and a place arose among the chimookamanag. However, they were diverted by two others who appeared dragging Cuthbert behind a horse. They pulled him slowly, so they could hang him, too. Cuthbert looked like a big caterpillar coated with gray dust. They cut him out of his ropes and hoisted him into the wagon. He lay still, blinking up at the others.

"Ah," said Cuthbert after a little while, from his bloody face, "they have rubbed off the worst of my nose. It is a pity to die now that I am handsome."

"You're still ugly, my brother," said Asiginak.

"Then I won't be such a loss to the women," said Cuthbert. "It is a comfort."

The wagon jostled them along in a friendly way. As they crossed the boundary into the fields and roads off the reservation, a farmer or two stood in his field, stilled and planted, and watched the slow procession of men, horses, dogs, wagon, and trussed Indians, pass by.

## The Baby

MOOSHUM LOOKED OVER at his daughters, who had begun arguing away at the end of the yard. He swigged precisely at his medicine. Suddenly, Mama and Geraldine quit talking and frowned up at the sky. They walked over to the clothesline, but before they had even plucked off one clothespin, they resumed arguing. Instead of taking in the rest of the wash, the two looked over at us to make sure that we weren't listening. When they saw us watching, they swished their skirts and strode swiftly around to the front of the house. We turned back to Mooshum. He told us other things he knew. How the little brother of a woman named Electa Hoag—well, he wasn't little, exactly, at seventeen—had run away in the night just after the murder, taking two of her newly baked loaves, his shoes, a woolen jacket, and an extra pair of overalls. Her husband Oric's cap was also missing from the hook by the door. Oric had gone off so quickly, summoned by Colonel Benton Lungsford and the sheriff, that he'd forgotten to wonder where he'd put the cap. Electa might have said something about Tobek running off when the men came back from the farm, not long after. She might have said something, but she was too surprised by the baby Oric held up there on the horse. She was too distracted by it, and then absorbed when he leaned over the saddle and transferred it into her arms. Instead of screaming, the baby just gave her a calm and trusting look, a direct look, like it was all grown up now but still caught in the tiny body. Oh, it screamed later, she told Mooshum, it turned into a baby again. That was once the men had rustled up some food for themselves and gone and she was alone cleaning it and trying to feed it. After she knew about the murders, Electa decided that she would tell Oric that he must have taken the cap with him and lost it, laid it down in shock somewhere on the farm. Knowing what had happened, she decided that she would not let on that Tobek was missing, run off, not for a while, not for as long as she could.

"If she had told . . ." said Mooshum. "If only she had told . . . and then there was Johann Vogeli. My old friend Vogeli. He was coming back from the barn when he saw his father, Frederic, smoke a cigarette in the middle of the day."

"What's so strange about that?" I asked.
"I don't know," said Mooshum.

## Vogeli

FREDERIC VOGELI WAS standing in the yard talking everyday German to the Buckendorfs. Johann's late mother had spoken a more complex German. Her voice was fading in his mind, or getting used up, like everything else about her. She had written letters back to her family in Heidelberg and made copies, written love letters to Frederic and notes to Johann himself, and she had kept a detail-filled diary of their little adventures and all that happened in their daily lives—except the beatings Frederic gave her once she got sick: those she hadn't written down. All the same, Frederic never liked all that writing and he ripped out a page of her diary or used the fine paper of a letter whenever he rolled himself a cigarette. Johann hated to see it.

He came around the corner of the house now, and there they were. The Buckendorfs were also smoking. His father had rolled cigarettes for them. The slender tube of paper and tobacco hung off the younger Buckendorf's boulder jaw. As they stood there, talking, Johann watched the men breathe the burning paper into their lungs. His mother's exact words vanished into their chests and emerged as form-less smoke.

Johann walked into the house and hid his mother's diary in a new place. He had grown about a foot in the months since she'd died and put on muscle. He wasn't used to how strong he was now. When he walked out again, Frederic grabbed him by the collar and said, "Catch the horses," then shoved him toward the pasture. He came back with a horse called Nadel and his father made him saddle Girlie, too. As they mounted their horses, his father said, "Now you will see some-thing." And they rode off after the Buckendorfs.

"So that was old Johann," I said. "That's the one you called the Deutscher."

"Ya vole," said Mooshum. "The Deutscher. Later on, he told me what happened when he and his dad caught up with the others, and when the sheriff and the old colonel tried to stand in their way."

## Death Song

COLONEL BENTON LUNGSFORD and the sheriff, whose name was Quintus Fells, caught up with the party of men as they were search-ing out a place that would do for hanging. Oric Hoag had fallen back and approached from a distance. The men were standing at the side of a well, peering down the hole, discussing the problem and testing the rope that held the bucket. The colonel and the sheriff maneuvered their horses in front of the wagon and they blocked the party of men from moving forward.

"Well, friends," said Sheriff Fells in his easy way, "I see you've done some of our work for us."

"We're going to finish it, too," said Frederic Vogeli.

Eugene Wildstrand, a neighbor of the slaughtered family, and William Hotchkiss, a locksmith and grain dealer, stepped their horses close to the sheriff. Some of the men were on foot. Two or three had even ridden in the wagon. Emil Buckendorf was driving the wagon. His pale-eyed brothers sat on the wagon seat with him, their hands in their laps. They looked like oversize boys in a pew.

"Step down," said Sheriff Fells. "I'm commandeering this wagon and it is my duty to drive the suspects to jail."

"Commandeer," said Emil Buckendorf. He snorted through his beard. One of his brothers laughed, and the other, with the big jaw, just stared at his knees.

William Hotchkiss craned forward over his saddle. He was carrying an old repeating rifle. Sheriff Fells had his shotgun out, and Colonel Lungsford had his hand on the revolver he had carried in the Spanish-American War, and kept oiled and clean on a special shelf ever since. The men and horses were so close that they grazed one another as the horses nervously tried to avoid a misplaced step.

"That's a boy you caught," said Colonel Lungford to them all. "No more than."

"That's a killer," said Vogeli.

"Don't you have no conscience?" Wildstrand, holding his horse tight up, spat and coldly addressed the sheriff and the colonel. His eyes stood out black as tacks on white paper. "Didn't you or didn't you step in that house?"

William Hotchkiss urged his horse up suddenly behind Colonel Lungsford and he poked his gun against the other man's back. Colonel Lungsford turned and spoke to Hotchkiss, pushing the barrel of the rifle away from his kidneys.

"Put that thing down, you idiot," he said.

Vogeli herded Hotchkiss away from Sheriff Fells.

"Sorry, boys," said Wildstrand. "We got to do what must be done."

He leaned across the space between them and shot Fells's horse between the eyes. The sheriff threw up his hands as he went down with the horse. There was the bullwhip crack of bone. The report made everybody jump. The men all looked at one another, and in the wagon Asiginak started toward the sheriff. He was thrown back by one of the Buckendorfs.

"We are done for," said Cuthbert. He began to gag on the blood soaking down his throat from his nose.

Emil Buckendorf slapped the reins and the wagon rolled smoothly ahead.

"We still ain't figured out a place to hang these Indians," said William Hotchkiss. "Maybe we could use Oric's beef windlass."

"I ain't in this!" cried Oric, who'd just caught up. He jumped off his horse to help Quintus Fells. The sheriff was breathing fast and saying, "Whoa, whoa, whoa . . ." He was still under the dead horse. His eyes rolled up to the whites and he passed out. Lungsford said "damn" and a few other words and got off his horse to help Oric free the sheriff, letting the wagon go by.

Jabez Woods, Henric Gostlin, Enery Mantle, and all the others stood quietly alongside the road watching the men who had guns and horses. Now they began to walk alongside the wagon, down the two-track grass road.

"Maybe over that swell," said Mantle. "Those trees this side of it are scrawny."

"All the good trees is back of us, over the reservation line," said a Buckendorf.

"We just need one tree branch," said Wildstrand. He looked into the wagon and his face was white around the eyes, like all the blood was gone underneath the field tan.

"We found those people already dead," cried Cuthbert, stirring Holy Track from a drowsy stupor. Mooshum was listening to everything. "We found them, but we did not kill them. We milked their cows for them and we fed the baby. I, Cuthbert, fed the baby! We are not your bad kind of Indians! Those are south of here!"

"Don't talk bad of the Bwaanag," said Asiginak. "They adopted me."

Cuthbert ignored him and badgered the white men. "Us, we are just like you!"

"Just like us!" Hotchkiss leaned over and slammed the butt of his rifle against Cuthbert's head. "Not hardly."

"You are right," said Asiginak in Ojibwe. "You are a madness on this earth."

Cuthbert's head was all blood now. His eyes were hidden in his bloody hair, his neck awash with blood, his dirty shirt was blood all up and down. He spoke Ojibwe from inside the bloody mask and said to Holy Track, "Don't worry. There is another boy among them. Pretty soon one of them will notice and remember the sheriff's words. They'll let you go. When you speak of my death to others, tell them of my courage. I am going to sing my death song."

"I hope you can remember it before you shit your pants," said Asiginak.

"Aiii! I am trying to think how it goes."

Both men began to hum very softly.

"To tell you the truth," said Cuthbert, after a little while, "I was never given a death song. I was not considered worth it."

"Make one up," said Asiginak. "I will help you."

They began to tap their knees and mumble a whine of melody beneath their breaths again. They did not address a single word to Mooshum. He gazed out over the fields, which were newly plowed and planted, the furrows straight and just sprouting a faint green fuzz. The sky was the sweetest color of blue. The horizon was dusty with a hint of green, just like the egg of a robin, and the clouds were delicate, no more than tiny white breast feathers way up high.

They came to a tree that looked all right, but the white men thought the limbs were too slanted and thin. They came to another tree and the men argued underneath it and measured with their arms and hands. Apparently, that tree wasn't good, either.

"They are giving us time to practice our song, anyway," said

Cuthbert. He wiped his face. It looked as though his nose-lump had been shorn away smoothly.

"Now that I look at you closely," said Asiginak, "I think you would have been handsome, my friend."

"Thank you," Cuthbert said.

"That tree over there will do," said Emil Buckendorf.

Mooshum heard someone begin to sob and he thought at first it was himself—it sounded just like himself—but then he realized that it was Johann Vogeli. The boy was riding next to him, his hands clutching the mane of his horse. His tears rushed down and wet the leather of the saddle. Frederic Vogeli rode up beside his son and swung his arm back, then smashed his knuckles and forearm across his son's face. Johann nearly fell off the back of his horse, but he caught himself. As he gained his balance, he changed, grew broader, bigger, and something in him could be seen to light. This thing took fire, and blew him right up. It propelled him off his horse: he lunged into an embrace with his father, who flew sideways out of his saddle and was still underneath his son when the two men landed and skidded— Frederic's back the sled. Johann sat on his father's chest and began to hit his face with the side of his fist like he was pounding on a table. He pounded with all his arm's strength, like he would strike through the wood, or the flesh. His other hand had closed around his father's throat. The wagon lurched on and the other men traveled with it, leaving the two rolling and kicking, then standing, then swinging and punching. Down again, then up, their battle looked more comical as they receded into the distance. Finally they were two black toy figures popping up and down against an endless horizon and beneath a boundless sky.

"The boy's heart was good, anyway," said Cuthbert.

"I hope he doesn't kill his father, yet," said Asiginak. "He could carry that hard."

Cuthbert agreed.

"So you talked to Cuthbert, too," said Joseph, his voice strained. "And Holy Track? Asiginak? They lived to be old men, right?"

"No," said Mooshum.

"Oh," said Joseph.

## The Clatter of Wings

THE OAK TREE had a generous spread. It had probably grown there quietly for a hundred years.

"I can show you that tree to this day, on the edge of Wolde's land," said Mooshum. "There's tobacco put down there. Prayer flags in its branches."

The men rode up to it and got down and walked around the base, peering up into the branches and pointing at one particular limb that ran straight on both sides of the tree and then bent upward, as if in a gesture of praise. They decided that it was the tree they had been looking for and drew the wagon up beneath it. Five or six ropes were neatly coiled underneath the straw on the wagon bed. Enery Mantle and the Buckendorfs took the ropes out and argued over which ones to use. Then they tried and repaired the knots, clumsily, several times, still arguing, and threw the ropes over the limb. They tested the slip of the rope and discussed who would hit the horses, and when.

"They don't know how to snare a rabbit," said Cuthbert, "or drop a man. This will not go easy."

Holy Track was sick and wild. Asiginak did not answer. Mooshum was staring into space and pretending to be already dead.

"The Michif will do all right," said Cuthbert, meaning Mooshum. "He knows how to jig."

Asiginak roused himself from deep thought and touched his nephew's shoulder.

"I regard you as my son," he said to Holy Track. "We will walk to the spirit world together. I would not have liked to walk that road alone. Howah! You made my old heart proud when you showed yourself in that church door!"

"Thank you, my uncle," said the boy, his voice soft and formal. "I regard you as my father, too."

"We will see them soon," said Cuthbert. "All our relatives." He touched the boy's arm, and smiled. His smile was awful in the dried blood. "Aniin ezhinikaazoyan?"

"Charles."

Cuthbert shook his head. "Not the priest's name. Not even our nickname for you, Holy Track. How do the spirits know you?"

Holy Track told him.

"Everlasting Sky. Good, you were named well. Give that name to the Person who will be waiting for you on the other side. Then you will go to the Anishinaabeg spirit world. Your mama and deydey will be waiting for you there, my boy. Don't be afraid."

"Don't fight the rope," said Asiginak. His voice shook.

Wildstrand made the four stand up and he refastened the ropes that tied their hands behind them. Emil Buckendorf arranged them on the wagon bed and lowered the loops of rope over their heads and then tightened the loops to fit more snugly.

Henric Gostlin stepped up to the wagon.

"He says he doesn't want the boy to hang," said Emil Buckendorf.

One of his brothers said, "Yah, just leave him."

Eugene Wildstrand's face darkened with a sudden rush of blood. "Were you there," he said, looking at Gostlin and the others, one after another. "Were you there, at the place? You were there. You seen it."

He held their gazes and his face burned strangely in the light.

"The girl," he continued. "The wife. The two boys. My old friend, too. All of them."

Emil stared at his brothers until they nodded and looked down at their feet. Henric Gostlin walked away, back down the path, slapping his hat on his thigh. The other men standing next to the horses started as Asiginak and Cuthbert suddenly burst out singing. They began high—Cuthbert's voice a wild falsetto that cut the air. Asiginak joined him and Holy Track felt almost good, hearing the strength and power of their voices. And the words in the old language.

*These white men are nothing*
*What they do cannot harm me*
*I will see the face of mystery*

They sang the song twice before the Buckendorfs shook themselves and prepared the wagon. Emil steadied the two horses and counted down to whip them at the same time. The boy tried to open his mouth to join in his uncle's song, but could only hum to himself the tuneless lullaby that his mother had always used to sing him to sleep. The Buckendorfs threw their arms back, cut the horses at the same time, then again, harder. The wagon lurched, stopped, then bucked forward. The men stumbled but did not stop singing. Finally, the horses bolted away. They halted after twenty feet. The men tried to keep singing even as they strangled. The boy was too light for death to give him an easy time of it. He slowly choked as he kicked air and spun. He heard it when Cuthbert, then his uncle, stopped singing and gurgling. Behind his shut eyes, he was seized by black fear, until he heard his mother say, *Open your eyes*, and he stared into the dusty blue. Then it was better. The little wisps of clouds, way up high, had resolved into wings and they swept across the sky now, faster and faster.

# Bitter Tea

❧

MOOSHUM FINISHED TALKING as the storm moved over us—the clouds low and black-bellied. In the yard, the sheets were thrashing wild, the overalls and Mooshum's work shirts were ballooning out. Even my mother's pastel underthings were flying straight back, wisps, and her bras corkscrewed around the wooden pins and line. She must have gone somewhere with Geraldine, leaving the baskets to tumble over empty.

I bolted forward as the first big drops splashed on my shoulders and began unpinning the clothes. The clothing flew from my hands, twisted off in the sharp wind. A circle-skirt wound me in its embrace. I was still caught in the story, and it took all of my concentration to struggle across the yard with my thoughts and that clothing into the quiet of the house.

My mother followed me into the kitchen, drenched. She had walked back from our uncle's place in the rain, but it hadn't put out her fire. Anyway, it was the kind of rain that passes quickly and leaves the air hot and clear right afterward, so she wasn't inside for long, talking to Mooshum, before I saw her outside with the basket again, pinning up the same clothes that I'd just taken down. This time she was carefully hiding her underwear. Mooshum had gone out with Mama and he stood, hunched a bit, beside her, holding the clothespin bag. I thought that maybe she was giving him hell for telling us what had happened, about the hanged boy, but when she came back in the door holding Mooshum's arm in hers, having left the basket outside again underneath the clothes, she only said, "I can't persuade her, she has to see him, she cares for him. And she even knows about that woman doctor he was loving on the sly. *You* know who, you know damn well."

I pretended like I was doing something else and not listening, but she was not in the least fooled. I wanted desperately to ask about the doctor.

"Oh, good. Evelina. I need you to peel potatoes."

"Can we put our hair up tonight, like Geraldine's?"

Mama gave me a sharp look, and I glanced away. I pulled up the ring on the square kitchen trapdoor rimmed with pounded tin and set into the linoleum. I gingerly let myself down the ladder into the cellar. She handed me a colander.

"I'll shut you down there if you mention Geraldine right now," she said.

I scrambled back up with the potatoes. While I was down there, though, I heard her say something about the judge to Mooshum, so I guessed this had to do with why she was so upset with Geraldine, only I got it wrong, entirely. I thought that Geraldine (surprisingly, for her!) had done something outside the law and would have to go before the judge, in court, pay some fine or go to jail. That's what I thought.

❊

THE NEXT DAY, Uncle Whitey and Shamengwa came over to the house. Uncle Whitey was teaching me how to hold my own in life and I was punching at his hands.

"You're quick," he said, "but not quick enough."

I tried to duck my head before he touched my ear, but never could.

"Think like a snake," he said. "Don't think, react."

But he could tell that I was a thinker and would never have lightning reflexes. Nor would Joseph.

"Boy, you're hopeless," said Uncle Whitey. He was a big, square man with an Indian Elvis face and a springy pompadour that he slicked back with hair oil out of a bright purple bottle. Sometimes he lived with us, sleeping on the couch.

"What's going on with Aunt Geraldine?" I asked him.

"I could get killed for saying," said Whitey. "It's classified."

"Let's get some gloves," said Joseph, "you come out back behind the sheds and they can talk all they want about Aunt Geraldine. Gossip is beneath us as men."

"I'm with you," said Whitey, and showed that inside his shirt he had a pint of Four Roses.

That left me with Shamengwa and Mooshum, and after I sat drinking water with them for a while I asked, because I knew they would not get mad at me, what Geraldine had done to make my mother so angry.

"Done?" said Mooshum, trying for once to look as if he didn't know. "She's not done nothing."

"Yet," said Shamengwa, his face still.

Shamengwa had brought his fiddle over, but he was only plucking and tuning it, frowning. He complained about the poor quality of the strings.

I asked what happened to the men who had lynched our people.

"You talked of that!" Shamengwa hissed through his teeth.

With a wary look at his brother, Mooshum turned to me. "The Buckendorfs got rich, fat, and never died out," he said. "They prospered and took over things. Half the county. But they never should of. And Wildstrand. Nobody hauled him up on a murder charge. Sheriff Fells turned into a cripple and old Lungsford, out of disgust, he went back to the civilized world he called Minnesota. He moved to Breckenridge, where in 1928 they went and hung the sheriff. He could not escape it. I think he died out east."

"And you," I said, "how did you live? Can you live after being hung?"

"They were never going to hang him *to death*," said Shamengwa.

"Why not?"

But Mooshum began to argue with his brother, saying things that made no sense to me. *I saw the same thing as Holy Track, the doves are still up there.* Their annoyance with each other grew, so I went away and turned all that I had heard over in my mind. Later on, someone drove up to the house, and I went out to see who it was. When I saw her, I ducked back in the door.

Aunt Harp had came over from Pluto to interview the two brothers for the local historical society's newsletter. My mother usually arranged to be out whenever Aunt Harp visited. But if she couldn't get away, Mama endured Neve because our father was still fond of his sister, even though she had kept their inheritance to herself with my other grandfather's blessing. Old Murdo never forgave my father for not becoming a banker. My father thought about getting a lawyer and making his sister divide what was left, but he never did. He insisted that he just wanted a few old stamp albums that had belonged to Uncle Octave.

Still, it wasn't that greed we held against Aunt Neve. She irritated and exhausted everyone around her with continual naïve questions that she would ask, and without waiting, answer herself.

"What did the Indians use for firewood?" she asked that afternoon. It became one of her more famous questions. "I can't believe I asked that!" She dissolved in self-appreciation.

Shamengwa wearily humored her, but Mooshum was delighted to have her near to work his charms on. He flirted with her outrageously, asking if she'd like to sit on his lap.

"You ever sit on a horse, in a saddle? Then you know there's a horn you got to grab on to. I got one too . . ."

Mooshum's brother turned his face away in distaste and I said, "What horn, Mooshum? Where is it?"

Mama came out the door and stood watching her father with a very quiet look on her face. I shut up. She was wearing a blue checked apron trimmed with yellow rickrack and had her arms folded over her breasts. Mooshum noticed her, straightened up, cleared his throat, and asked Mrs. Neve Harp if she had ever received his notes. She said yes, and that she'd come because she wanted material for her newsletter.

Mooshum said eagerly that he would answer her questions. Shamengwa folded his hands. But when Neve Harp said that she was going back to the beginning of things and wanted to talk about how the town of Pluto came to be and why it was inside the original reservation boundaries, even though hardly any Indians lived in Pluto, well, both of the old men's faces became like Mama's—quiet, with an elaborate reserve, and something else that has stuck in my heart ever since. I saw that the loss of their land was lodged inside of them forever. This loss would enter me, too. Over time, I came to know that the sorrow was a thing that each of them covered up according to their character—my old uncle through his passionate discipline, my mother through strict kindness and cleanly order. As for my grandfather, he used the patient art of ridicule.

"What you are asking," said Mooshum that afternoon, opening his hands and his mouth into a muddy, gaping grin, "is how was it stolen? How has this great thievery become acceptable? How do we live right here beside you, knowing what we lost and how you took it?"

Neve Harp thought she might like some tea.

"I'll make it," I said, and went inside the house. I filled the kettle with water and lit the front burner. Over the sink, there was a little window, and I stood there waiting for the water to boil. I was just able to see over the sill. I watched Aunt Neve waggle her tiny fingers at the two old men and squeeze smiles out of her face. Mama came in the door and stood beside me. She hardly ever touched me, so when she put her hand on my back I might have shaken it off, in surprise, and then regretted I had done so. I think I moved a step closer to her so that my shoulder lightly touched her arm. We stood there together, and for maybe the first time ever I understood that we were thinking roughly the same thing about what we were seeing.

"It's not her fault," said Mama, not talking to me. She was reminding herself to think charitable thoughts, so that she could stand having Mrs. Neve Harp in her yard.

"I think it is her fault," I said.

"Oh? Maybe you're thinking about the money," said Mama. "I know you know about that. We don't need it."

"There were no Harps at the lynching," I said without thinking. "But there was a Wildstrand. She married one."

It surprised me that Mama didn't question the fact that I knew what she had warned Mooshum not to tell us. She just took a little breath.

"Well," she said, "and Buckendorfs. That was a long time ago. And look how Mary Anita has come back to help the young children of the parish." Her voice took on that overcareful pious quality that always made me step away from her. I stepped away.

"Oh, her," I pretended, and we were quiet for a little while. Just before the tea boiled, Mama shook herself.

"Evelina, you know that your grandma, Junesse, was not all Chippewa."

"Yes," I said.

"Her father left her and of course she was raised by her aunt. Her father's name was Eugene Wildstrand."

I just kept looking out the window, as if I hadn't heard what she said. But inside I thought I now understood the reason that they hadn't hanged Mooshum *to death*, as his brother put it. Behind me, I heard her take the kettle off the stove. The handle rattled a bit as she set it down. She scooped the tea leaves out of a tin with her fingers, then dropped them in the teapot and tapped the lid back onto the tea can. I heard the pour of steaming water as she filled the brown teapot and then she came back to stand beside me. This time, when she put her hand on my back, I did not shrug it off. We waited, together, for the tea to brew the way the two old brothers liked it, dark and bitter. Neve Harp could add a pound of sugar and she'd never get it sweet enough.

"Oh, anyway," said Mama, "I might as well tell you everything. You'll hear it anyway. Your aunt Geraldine and Judge Coutts are having . . ." But she couldn't say it. She just gave a great, cracking sigh and put her hand on her chest.

"A baby?" I said.

Mama looked at me in surprise, then realized I didn't really know what I was saying.

"Your aunt can't have babies," she said, in a somber way.

"Oh?" I said. "Then what? What are they having?"

But Mama regretted her moment, I could tell, and sent me outside with the teacups.

## Lines

THE STORY MOOSHUM told us had its repercussions—the first being that I could not look at anyone in quite the same way anymore. I became obsessed with lineage. As I came to the end of my small leopard-print diary (its key useless as my brother had broken the clasp), I wrote down as much of Mooshum's story as I could remember, and then the relatives of everyone I knew—parents, grandparents, way on back in time. I traced the blood history of the murders through my classmates and friends until I could draw out elaborate spider webs of lines and intersecting circles. I drew in pencil. There were a few people, one of them being Corwin Peace, whose chart was so complicated that I erased parts of it until I wore right through the paper. Still, I could not erase the questions underneath, and Mooshum was no help. He bore interrogation with a vexed wince and silence. I persisted, kept on asking for details, but he answered in evasions, to get rid of me. He never spoke with the direct fluidity of that first telling. His medicine bottle, confiscated by our mother, had held whiskey. No one knew from what source. She'd never get him to stop. I still loved Mooshum, of course, but with this tale something in my regard of him was disturbed, as if I'd stepped into a clear stream and silt had billowed up around my feet.

*Judge Antone*
*Bazil Coutts*

# *The Way Things Are*

❦

THE MOMENT I passed Geraldine Milk in the narrow hallway of the tribal offices, I decided I had to marry her. As we swerved slightly sideways, nodding briefly, her breasts in a modest white blouse passed just under my line of sight. I was intensely aware of them and forced myself to keep my eyes level with hers, but still, I caught the delicate scent of her soap mixed with a harsh thread of female sweat. The hair at the back of my neck prickled, I stopped dead, swiveling like a puppet on strings, to watch her as she passed on down the hallway. Geraldine's walk was elastic, womanly. But there was no come-hither in it. There was a leave-me-alone quality, in fact. Geraldine was thought aloof because she'd never married—her first boyfriend, Roman, the one off the passenger train, had been killed in a car wreck and she had not become attached since. I had my own pains in that department. We had that in common.

Of course, Geraldine knows all. She is a tribal enrollment specialist and has everyone's secrets alphabetically filed. I must, in fact, call upon her expertise for many questions of blood that come my way. A few days later, I visited her office. I nodded as I entered the room and Geraldine glanced away.

"I'm Antone Coutts," I said.

"Yes," she answered.

Her eyes, black and upslanted in a pale, cool face, rested on me with an odd intensity, but no warmth. There was no sign of friendliness, although she made a gesture. Raised her eyebrows a fraction. That day, she was wearing a rose pink dress belted at the waist with a black tie. She wore sheer stockings and low black heels. She had on a gardenia perfume that left behind the suggestion of moist vegetation. A woman who smelled tropical, here in North Dakota. I watched her leave the office and Margaret Lesperance, who'd seen me rebuffed, said in a sympathetic tone, "Her old uncle is probably waiting outside for her." At the time, I thought Margaret said it just to cover the awkward moment. It seemed obvious that Geraldine wanted nothing to do with me. But later on I found that her uncle really had been waiting for her, and of course, she intended to get to know me all along. Yes, she had tried to avoid me, but the reason was not, as I imagined, the way she viewed my past or thought about my family. She was cool because that was her way. She was a woman of reserve.

It took a long time before Geraldine would even talk to me, longer still before she'd sit down and drink a cup of coffee in my presence. At a conference in Bismarck she finally had dinner with me—I'd maneuvered into the hotel smorgasboard line right behind her and when she walked over to a table I stuck tight. We talked of general and familiar subjects, getting acquainted, but all the while I longed to say, "I'm going to marry you, Geraldine Milk, and you are going to marry me."

Though impatient, I managed to keep my interest hidden. I heard the Milk girls had tempers, and I did not want to begin by sparking hers. After the conference, when we returned home, I boringly kept an appropriate distance, though sometimes I thought I'd die of all I didn't dare say in her presence. My love of her uncle's music helped—I often went to sit with him in the evenings. At other times I dropped by his house early in the mornings, made a pot of strong tea or took him out to breakfast. That was on the weekends. The first time Geraldine showed up at her uncle's house and found me there, I faked an elaborate surprise. She was not fooled.

"Are you here for a haircut, Judge? I brought my trimming shears." She drew a pair of scissors from her purse and snapped them in the air. I felt like telling her she could do anything she wanted to me. I am pretty sure she read this in my expression and took pity. She put the scissors down.

"Do you like to fish?" I asked her. Maybe it was an odd way to get to know a woman, but I was suffering.

"No," she said.

"Would you like to go fishing anyway?"

"All right."

So the next day we went out together in a cousin of mine's fishing boat, a little aluminum outboard with a 45-horsepower motor. She had on rolled-up jeans, a starched plaid shirt. Her hair was a curled graceful shape that brushed her shoulders. She wore a deep red lipstick and no other makeup, and I thought that if she let me lean toward her in the boat I would hold her face, graze her lips with the side of my thumb, look into her eyes, and slowly kiss her. I was picturing just what I'd do, when she said, "Watch out," sharply. We'd just missed a rock, which I knew was there, and she shook her head.

"You'll hang us up, Judge."

"I'm not a hanging judge."

"You know that story?"

"Sure."

I told her that the two older brothers of Cuthbert Peace, Henri and Lafayette, had long ago saved my grandfather's life. We reached what looked like a good spot, cast our lines out, reeled them in, cast out and reeled in without talking. The silence wasn't uncomfortable. We knew where we were from. After a while, we began talking in a general way of exactly that. We talked of history, mused a little on the future. Our reservation as it stands now is bordered by three towns—Hoopdance, Argus, and Pluto. That last—being closest, but on the western boundary and so off the most traveled roads—has ended up not benefiting from the slight stability and even occasional prosperity brought to the reservation by light manufacturing. Since the government offers tax incentives for businesses to locate here, we've begun to switch our economic base away from farming, even as the towns surrounding us empty out and die. It's a shame to see them go, but Geraldine and I agreed that we were not about to waste our sympathies. In the winter of our great starvation, when scores of our people were consumed by hunger, citizens of Argus sold their grain and raffled off a grand piano. More recently, when we traveled to Washington to fight a policy that would have terminated our relationship with the United States Government guaranteed by treaty, only one lawyer, from Pluto, stood up for us. That was my father. And in 1911, when a family was murdered savagely on a farm just to the west, a posse mob tore after a wandering bunch of our people. They chased down three men and a boy and hung them all, except Mooshum. The story Geraldine had just referred to. I told her that later on the vigilantes admitted that they probably were mistaken. She hadn't known that.

"But it happened in the heat of things, one of them said, I think Wildstrand. In the heat of things!"

Geraldine said, "What doesn't happen in the heat of things? Someone has seized the moment to act on their own biases. That's it. Or history. Sometimes it is history."

I caught a few small sunnies, and threw them back. Geraldine got a bite and her pole bent double.

"Bet you it's a turtle."

"Reel it in slow, let it swim to you. Coax it along."

Geraldine, of course, knew how to catch a turtle better than I did. We didn't have a net, so she was going to have to maneuver the creature alongside the boat. When she dragged it closer, I saw the bullet head and rounded humps and knew it was a giant snapper. I was surprised it hadn't bitten the line and dived. Big as a car tire, it floated just beneath the water. I carefully stowed my fishing pole and tried to figure just how I would pull the monster out of the lake. I would rather have cut the turtle free than drag it in, not because I had sympathy for it, but because snappers bite with tremendous force. When I suggested we let it go, Geraldine gave me an excited look and said, "No, Clemence will make French turtle soup!" So I resigned myself, flexed my fingers, and hoped I'd keep them.

"Now, now! Reach over and grab onto him!"

Geraldine's snapper swam alongside the boat and I leaned over, grabbed its shell, but failed to secure my grip. Twice I lost him, which exasperated Geraldine.

"Here, take this. I've caught lots of snappers before."

She set the fishing rod in my hand and pulled it in by the tail, right over the side. It was the biggest snapper I'd ever seen, with olive green slime growing in patterns on its back and that strange, unreconstructed dinosaur beak. The neck was massive, slack, and the nose came to a delicate, creepy point.

"They go back over a million years unchanged," I said. I planned to whack the turtle with the emergency oar if it attacked, but it lay there passively. Geraldine was staring hard at the shell, sitting stiffly with her hands folded in her lap. Her arrest became prolonged and her face went ash gray.

"Should I throw it back?" I asked. She didn't answer. I kept talking.

"The one my cousin kept as a pet tried to lay eggs after two years alone in the tank. I guess the female can conserve sperm for quite a long time, if the need arises."

I tried to stop myself, wondering how idiotic a man could be, but her silence rattled me.

"I know," she said at last. "My brother-in-law studies reptiles."

"Is something wrong?" I asked, after we'd both sat for much too long looking at that turtle in the bottom of the boat.

"Don't you see it?"

The turtle was becoming more responsive now. It opened its muddy eyes and poked its head out like a snake, then slowly stretched its jaws wide. The inside of its mouth was grotesque, ornately fleshy, and there was the low reek of turtle musk.

"We scared it," I said, feebly, holding the paddle out. The thing moved toward it and struck, crunching down hard on the wood. I cried out, but Geraldine ignored me.

"Can't you see? Take a good look," she said again.

Now that its jaws were solidly clamped down on the paddle, I was less distracted. But I still couldn't see until she traced the initials in air just over the turtle's back. G & R.

"Roman and I caught this turtle a long time ago, when it was small," she said. "He carved our initials in its shell. I was mad. I said he was going to kill it anyway, so we might at least have soup."

"So," I said stupidly after a few moments, "you've been fishing here before."

"So to speak."

I damned Roman for dying and the turtle for living on; I damned the turtle for biting her hook; I damned it for letting itself be pulled over the side. With this sign from the past, my courtship might be delayed another ten years. By now, I knew how the Milk romantic streak could turn fatalistic.

She took my pocketknife and cut the line. Although I felt at this point I could have eaten the turtle raw, we lifted it (still gripping the paddle) over the side. I steadied the boat. Geraldine held one end of the paddle and the turtle floated at the other end, eyeing us in a weirdly doglike way, until Geraldine commanded, "Let go now." It sank obediently and she sat frowning at the place it vanished. After some time, I started up the motor.

All is lost, I thought, definitely lost, more the luck. I wasn't surprised, though. Losing women is a trait inherited by Coutts men.

That night, as I put together my bachelor dinner (cans of this, cans of that), I tried to counsel myself in persistence. I thought of my grandfather's loves and hideous trials. He was part of the first, failed, town-site expedition, the youngest of a bunch of greedy fools, or venture capitalists, who nearly starved dead but eventually became some of the first people to profit financially from this part of the world. The lucky capture of a turtle had saved them way back then, a thought that cheered me now. I'd read his old journals. Some of his other books were piled deep in the other bedroom of my house, waiting for shelves. The living room walls were already stacked two volumes deep. Boxes of files and more books filled the basement. Although these books were valuable, I wasn't fanatical about the way I handled them. Yes, they were very old, but they were meant to be read by a living human and I did them that honor. As I held one of my other favorites open with one hand and read, I slowly spooned up hot beef stew and baked beans. Finally, I found the passage I was looking for. *The primary sign of a well-ordered mind is a man's ability to remain in one place and linger in his own company.* Lucius Annaeus Seneca, the Younger.

For dessert, as usual, fruit cocktail.

# Town Fever

THEN AS EVER it did not pay well to teach, and the youth of St. Anthony did not sufficiently appreciate the writings of Marcus Aurelius to make Joseph J. Coutts's vocation a labor of love. And besides, there was real love to think about. He felt that he should be traveling with more assurance in that golden realm as he was nearly twenty-six. But, tossing at night in the room he surely paid too much for in the home of Dorea Ann Swivel, widow, his prospects only gave him a galling headache. He had visited himself for a short time upon a woman named Louisa Bird—small, pretty, some four years older and unfortunately Presbyterian, but she certainly hadn't kissed him and was stolen away during a sleigh ride by a young St. Paul minister with a set of fabulous whiskers. That theft erased any hesitancy on Joseph's part, and now he could not get her out of his mind. So he burned, secretly enough, though sometimes as he walked through the chill early morning dark to light the stove in the former lumber mill office that served as a schoolhouse, he could almost feel the air scorch around him, and he wondered if the widow, for instance, understood the nature of his burden.

Shortly after Louisa flew to the arms of the minister, he realized that the widow did. One night, there was a rap on his door and Mrs. Swivel, who was large-hipped, plain, and shrewd, entered his cold little room. His bedstead did not seem sturdy enough to bear the weight of them both, and though the warmth and bread-dough fragrance of her body was sweet, he worried as he made his way toward bliss which one of them would pay for the bed if it collapsed. Their nights grew frequent and the bed more frail. He strapped the legs to the frame with strong rope and braced the base of the bed with river stones. She fed him better than her other boarders, which got their suspicions up. But real fear did not enter him until the first day of November, when she gave back half his rent and told him with a glint of tooth that she'd reduced it. So Joseph Coutts was ready to make a change in his life when he met up with Reginald Bull, who was looking for a man to join a town-site expedition heading for the plains.

Reginald was enough like his surname for that alone to stick. Bull was thick, wide-necked, powerful, but had the prettiest bashful brown eyes and a red bud of a mouth, which he was often teased for. As Bull laid it out, two land speculators, Odin Merrimack and Colonel LeVinne P. Poolcaugh, were getting up a party of men, which they would outfit at their own expense, and sending them out past the Dakota-Minnesota border to survey and establish claim by occupancy on several huge pieces of land that would most certainly become towns, perhaps cities, when the railroad reached that part of the world. The men would be paid in shares of land, said Bull, and there was already talk of millions in it; he'd heard that phrase. But they were not the only ones with town fever. Other outfits were making plans. They'd beat everyone by heading out in the dead of winter.

"I've seen men get richer out here," said Joseph, "but I never have seen a man poor to begin with obtain much wealth, not yet."

"It's a going proposition," Bull insisted. "And we're outfitted with the best. Two ox teams and a cook. Not only that, but we've got the cleverest guides in this country, Henri and Lafayette Peace. They'll get us through anything."

At this, Joseph was impressed. Henri Peace was known by reputation, though he'd never heard of Lafayette. There was also a German named Emil Buckendorf and three of his brothers, all excellent ox-team drivers.

"Give me one night," said Joseph. But when he thought of going back to his room and remembered the state of his bed legs, he changed his mind and agreed right there on the spot. That very afternoon, he visited his school district officer and put in his resignation; that night, he gave his landlady notice. He'd thought Dorea might be downcast to see him go, perhaps even angry, but when he explained his plan and told her of the interest he'd earn in the town-to-come, her face grew radiant, almost beautiful. The thought of so much money to be made just by camping out in a place made her so excited that she almost wanted to go herself. Alarmed, Joseph mentioned that they would be guided by *bois brûlé* or Metis French Indians, and her features shut tighter than a drumhead.

She left him alone that night and he was surprised at how much he missed her. Unable to sleep, he lighted a candle stub and paged through the *Meditations* until he found the one he needed, the one that told him no longer to wander at hazard or wait to read the books he was reserving for old age, but to throw away idle hopes (Louisa!) and come to his own aid, if he cared for himself and while it was in his power. He blew out his candle and put the book beneath his pillow. He had made the right decision, he was sure of it, and he tried not to think of Dorea Swivel's plush embrace. But the night was cold, his blanket thin, and it was impossible not to long for the heat she generated or to wish his head was pillowed on the soft muscles of her upper arm. There would be more of this deprivation, he told himself; he'd best get used to it. For the next year, he would be hunkering down for warmth with hairy men who soon would stink. What men call adventures usually consist of the stoical endurance of appalling daily misery. Joseph Coutts knew this, intellectually at least, already, and so that night he tried to discipline himself to put away all thoughts of Dorea's two great secrets—a mesmerizing facility with bad words, which she would whisper in his ear, and a series of wild, quick movements that nearly made him faint with pleasure. He would not think of these things. No, he would not.

## The Expedition

THE NEXT DAY, Bull came around with papers to sign and brought him over to Colonel Poolcaugh's establishment, where his outfit garments were being sewed and where, also, two Icelandic women were completing an enormous blanket of thickly quilted wool batting made expressly for the nine men to sleep together underneath. Emil Buckendorf was there, dark-haired, with fanglike teeth and eyes so pale that there seemed to be a light burning in his skull. He was a quiet, efficient young man; he was helping the women sew and doing a nice job of it, too. The two guides were very much unlike each other. Lafayette was fine-made and superbly handsome, with a thin mustache, slick braids, and sly black eyes. Henri was sturdy as Bull, though shorter and with an air of captivating assurance. There was also the cook, English Bill, a man whose brown muttonchops flew straight out from his face and would soon droop to cover his neck. Joseph had developed a suspicion of grand whiskers, but he liked English Bill's riveting energy as he dickered with and worried Colonel Poolcaugh. Bill was adamant about the necessity of provisioning the outfit well. He also insisted on bringing his dog, a stubby little brown and white short-haired terrier, and he made Joseph try on each garment. There were so many that Joseph was inclined to simply accept the pile, but when he put on the three woolen shirts and three woolen drawers, the three pair of stockings and moccasins over them, there were adjustments to be made. There was an overcoat of Kentucky jean to repair and his elkskin overshoes needed additional lacings as well. A grand-looking helmet made of lambskin came down over his shoulders with flaps to each side to draw over his nose and, last, there was a pair of fur mitts. When it was all on, Joseph was so hot he could hardly breathe, as it was a warm day for December. But, by the end of the month, when the party started out, the weather was already being called the worst and coldest in memory.

When he left Dorea Swivel, she gave him a picture of herself. He almost gave it back, thinking it unfair of him to accept it when he loved the heated bolster of her body but did not see a future with someone who didn't know how to read and could write little more than her name, though she was good at adding and subtracting. But something made him keep the small locket photograph of her, so plain and steadfast, her broad face symmetrical beneath a severe middle part in her hair. It was as though he had an intimation that he was embarking on a journey that would bring him to the edge of his sanity, and that he'd need the solid weight of her gaze to pull him back.

## *The Great Drive*

WITH FIVE YOKE of oxen and two sleds built for rough haul, the men started from St. Anthony. The only personal possessions Joseph brought were the locket and the book that contained the writings of Marcus Aurelius. One sled was loaded with corn and cob for the oxen and the other with provisions for the men, plus all of the tools that Bull, Emil Buckendorf, and Joseph Coutts would need to garden and live out a year. The other men were to be fetched back as soon as the prairie dried out in the spring, and at the same time those who stayed would be reprovisioned. Within two days, the road disappeared and Joseph, Henri, and Lafayette broke the trail with snowshoes before the oxen, who either foundered in the deep snow or cut their fetlocks on the burnt-over prairie where the wind had swept a vicious crust. By placing one step before another, they progressed about eight miles a day. At night, they raised their tent, built a good blaze, cut slough grass for bedding, piled it on the snow, then spread their buffalo coats and oilcloths over the grass and got into their huge communal bed fully clothed. The two guides took turns sleeping with their most important possession, a fiddle, which they kept in a velvet-lined case and kissed like a woman. Once they lowered the great woolen comforter over themselves, the men began to steam up under the batting, and they slept, though every time one rolled over so did the rest. The nights were lively that way, but not, at first, unbearable, thought Joseph. But this was only January and there wouldn't be a chance for any of them to bathe before spring. He had never been an overly fastidious person, but the food that English Bill prepared sat heavy on the gut and one night the men grew so flatulent they almost blew the quilt off. Halfway through the concert, Henri Peace began to laugh and cried out in the dark, praising the men for playing so loudly on their own French fiddles. Joseph started laughing too, but Emil Buckendorf took offense.

"Gawiin ojidaa, ma frère," said Henri, who spoke the French-Chippewa patois as well as either English or pure Chippewa, or Cree, "I am sorry to have insulted you. For you were playing the German bugle, were you not?"

Emil went silent and ground his teeth. Joseph could hear his molars and jaws working. But it was too cold to fight. No one wanted to get out from under the quilt.

When Joseph rose the next morning and looked out over the great white bowl of the universe, he saw the sun had two dogs at either side and was crowned by a burning crescent. It was a sight so immediate, so gorgeous, so grim, that tears started into his eyes as he stood transfixed.

"Oui, frère Joseph, weep now while you have the strength," Henri said, handing him a tin cup of boiling hot tea, "we shall be hit hard by afternoon." As with everything Henri said, this proved true.

They ran into heavy drifts on the unburned prairie and had to shovel all the way. Foot by foot, they made five miles. Henri and Lafayette found elk sign and went after the creatures, hoping to supplement English Bill's cured hog. No sooner were they gone than the blizzard swept down and the men set about making camp, hauling wood, trying to raise the tent. But the wind drove the snow in horizontal sheets, slapped out their fire, sucked the tent into its nothingness, confused and battered them until they stumbled uncertainly this way and that. Henri returned and shouted for them to make the bed where they stood and get in quick. As they spread the buffalo coats and oilcloths the snow drifted into the fur but the men got in, Lafayette on one end and English Bill on the other end, as he always was on account of sleeping with his terrier. For a long time the men shook so hard that Henri called something out to Lafayette in Chippewa that Joseph was to recognize, later, when he understood them better, as a reference to a sacred method of divination in which spirits entered a special tent and caused it to tremble. The shaking ceased gradually. The men relaxed against one another and Joseph, held fast between two Buckendorfs, drifted off wondering if he might not waken but too tired to really care.

A little before dawn, Joseph did wake to the sound of men singing. Edging his face from the bed, he realized that the blanket was covered entirely by a great and glowing white drift. Steam rose from the cracked snow at the edges. The wind had ceased and a steep cold now gripped them. Henri and Lafayette had built up the fire and were drying themselves before it. Henri was playing a jig of stirring joy. Lafayette was beating a hand drum and jumping up and down, singing a song loud and wailing wild as the blizzard. The Buckendorfs cursed and screamed as they emerged, damp, into the horrible cold, but the music, which Henri told Joseph was meant to pluck up their spirits, had an effect. Something in the song, which Joseph began to repeat with the guides, worked on him. As he turned himself to each direction before the fire, and sang, a startling awareness came over him. The violence of the storm, the snapping and growling of the fire, the flame reflected on the dark faces of the guides and on Bull's sweet features and in the strange white eyes of the Germans, struck him with indelible force. A sudden, fierce, black happiness boiled up in him. He laughed out loud and looked into Henri's eyes, glittering over the roan body of violin, and saw how narrowly they had escaped. If the drift hadn't covered them, they'd have iced up in this extremity of cold and frozen to death in their sleep, welded fast to one another by ice, a solid mass until spring allowed the weird human sandwich to loosen and rot.

Joseph didn't get much chance to reflect on that prospect; for the next four days they plunged along and even drove themselves through a black night and over the next day, their usual consecrated Sunday of rest, across a poker-table-flat belt of prairie twenty-five miles wide, for fear of the wind in that unsheltered expanse. The guides used the North Star for direction, and the party stopped in confusion when ice fogs swept over them every few hours. When the oxen stopped, the Buckendorfs dropped off the sledges as though shot, and fell asleep in the snow. Emil beat his brothers awake, and the men and oxen staggered on. At one point, drowsing as he walked, words came to Joseph. *Do not act as if you were going to live ten thousand years. Death hangs over you. While you live, while it is in your power.* . . . . Having been spared the night of the blizzard, Joseph determined that it would not be for nothing if he was also spared now. It was true that his original purpose on this expedition had been to become a rich man, but now in the measureless night he understood it was more than that. He'd seen the blizzard sweep out of nothing and descend in fury upon them and then return to the nothingness it came from, so like all men. There was something powerful in store for him. He must be ready for it. He fell completely asleep walking and when he woke, one of the oxen was down. The men were coaxing it with wild blows to rise. The poor beast's fetlocks had swollen big as teakettles and each step left a gush of blood in the snow. Joseph leapt toward the ox, hunched over the massive head, breathed his own breath into its foamy muzzle, and spoke in a calm clear voice until the animal groaned to its feet and labored on into the waste. It was the first one they killed for food.

This was a bad sign—to slaughter their oxen before they had even reached their destination. Henri looked a little grim. But that night as they roasted its withered heart and salted the charred flesh and ate, and as the little spotted terrier with the brown eyes worried a bone to one side of the fire, Lafayette played and the two guides sang again. Only this time it was a French chanson about a black-haired woman, and even the Buckendorfs, once they understood the refrain, roared it willingly and in good timbre until they turned in, still joking, as though drunk. The fresh meat and the French song did their work on the men and that night Joseph dreamed of Dorea for the first time. She'd put a new plank in his bedstead, she said as she drew him close. The other men also, from the looks of them at daylight, had been disturbed in their slumbers, for they began the next day hollow-eyed, downcast, subdued. Throughout the day Bull heaved cracking sighs and gazed too long at the horizon.

"Is she there?" said Henri at one point, gesturing at the line between the sky and the earth.

"Who? Where?" asked Bull.

"Ginimoshe! Is she there?"

But Bull could not be teased. He hadn't the stiff pride of Emil Buckendorf. He spoke in a kind of innocence.

"If she were. If she only were there!"

The guides nodded in approval at his devotion. The other men went quiet out of respect and envy. Bull had nearly dropped out at the last minute for reason of having fallen in love. It was not just any love, he'd told Joseph, it was unbearable, it was heaven. She had been introduced to him by the guides, and was the housekeeper and general assistant to a local doctor who advertised "Surgeries with or without chloroform, the latter on bargain terms!" Joseph had in fact thought the doctor's advertising card an excellent reason to become rich. He had also seen the girl Bull loved. She was a niece of the Peace brothers, daughter of their younger sister, a Metis Catholic whose family was very strict. Her skin was a dark cream. She was round and sweet as caramel, with brown-black hair and tiny cinnamon-colored freckles sprinkled across a sensible nose. Nice enough, a forthright look about her, but hard to see as the object of deathless passion. But then, thought Joseph, who was he to talk? He kept Dorea's locket in the heart pocket of his innermost shirt and fished it out in secret.

### Batner's Powders

THEY REACHED THE area they wanted to claim one month after they'd started off with just six oxen left and an alarming lack of flour. English Bill had insisted three barrels be provided and yet just one had been loaded. He cursed Poolcaugh up and down and spat till he was livid over the flour and then the quality of the beans, which he insisted were shriveled and had been switched on him. By now, though, having eaten one meal more scorched and strange than the next, the men had understood that English Bill's cooking was as big a challenge as the weather. Both were soon to get worse. The first blizzards had been nothing, and they were met at their destination by a four-day howler, which they survived only through the cleverness of their guides in choosing a camp, setting up their tent, and banking it with brush and snow so that it became quite snug by the end of the blow. With the flour nearly gone, they decided, after they emerged, to feed the oxen elm slash and keep the feed—rough corn and ground cob—to sustain themselves. They divided it up equally. Joseph filled his extra pair of socks with the stuff—hard as sand pebbles. There were still plenty of beans, but the men had now developed bowel trouble and ate their suppers with slow despair. By morning, beneath their suffocating quilt, they wanted to murder one another. In the beginning the men had coveted the warmest interior sleeping spots, but now they craved to sleep on either end, where at least they could gasp fresh air. They became so weak from the trots that Bull at last decided to break into the store of drug remedies he'd procured from his sweetheart's employer.

One night, consulting written instructions from the doctor, he prepared a solution of Batner's Powders for each of the men. Joseph took his ten drops like the others and crawled into bed. The effect upon them all was nothing short of magical. They slept like babes, dreamed lusciously, woke in the morning refreshed, pleasant, and actually did some surveying. Using a hand compass, a tape and chain, they completed the main lines, which would be filled in back in St. Paul. Joseph had dreamed a banquet so detailed that he thought for part of the morning he'd really eaten it. That night they boiled ox and hog meat with the last of the flour into a thick mush that Henri called booyeh. They ate as well as they could and eagerly accepted their treatment. Over the next weeks, the food dwindled. Lafayette killed a lynx and the guides replaced the broken strings of the fiddle with its entrails, but the rank meat sat hard in their scoured guts. At last they killed the final ox, and were glad the medicine helped also with hunger pains. Joseph noticed how loose his clothes were and how tightly his flesh now seemed strapped to his bones.

"We're nothing but gristle," he said one night to Lafayette, who grinned and took his laudanum. That night they all dreamed, fantastically, the same dream. Where they slept they saw lights twinkling on a great upraised wheel and giant cups, whirling in the dark, accompanied by an unearthly flow of music. Hundreds of people lived around them and walked, floated, emerged, and dove back into the shadows. There were towers and buildings and an array of lights that would rival the greatest cities in Europe. They all agreed, the next morning as they drank their tea and munched the hot corn- and cob-meal cakes they'd patted together for themselves with the last of the heated hog fat, that this was a great and wondrous sign. That day, too, Henri and Lafayette killed two buffalo calves and a cow. They hauled the carcasses to a brushy lean-to in the empty cattle enclosure, covered the meat with ice and snow, and stuck flags all around to keep away the wolves. That night they ate wonderfully, and all the next week there was clear weather. Believing that they now had food to last until the time when B. J. Bolt, the reprovisioner, was meant to appear, they worked with good cheer and roughed out a cabin of hewn log. They even set up a raised platform for their bed at one side and built a large fireplace. Soon, they meant to have a real door. Bull was using a ripsaw to work out a plank and casings for a door and even a window to let in a little light.

## The Emissary

THE MOST DEVOUT among the men were Henri and Lafayette Peace, who wore, it was revealed once the men had stripped down to only two shirts during a warm February day, a crucifix each next to their skin. They had an interesting way of doing things, thought Joseph. For instance, to get the buffalo, they'd slipped in amid the small herd that had ventured near, wearing wolfskins draped over their heads and shoulders. As there were always wolves scouting the herds, the bulls stepped near the men and smelled their caps, which must have made them think that the guides were dead wolves. The buffalo turned away and lowered their great muzzles into the snow to forage for grass. Once close to the animal they'd chosen, one of the two brothers rose slightly and killed it, a single shot at close range, then instantly sank down. Keeping their gun locks dry under the wolfskin, the guides kept still until the animals, who shifted uneasily at the noise but never panicked, went back to stirring through the snow.

Joseph was close enough to see that beneath the wolfskins both men made the papist sign of the cross, kissed their crucifixes, and in their stillness he could ascertain that they were giving thanks and praise to God. They loved their fiddle, and called her their sweetheart, their lover. But on Sundays she was the Virgin Mary to the *bois brûlés*; they played only sacred music. And no matter what the circumstances they always fished out their rosaries, first thing in the morning, and muttered as they moved their fingers along the beads.

English Bill had treated their religious practices with skepticism and even made a few jokes at their expense. He also thought it a good prank to hide the mirror Lafayette used every morning to conduct his scrupulous toilette. But one day a wolf surprised English Bill's terrier at the edge of camp, snatched it up, and bounded away in one fluid leap. Lafayette happened to be near and in a motion just as lyrical as the wolf's he prepared and raised his gun and in one blast brought the wolf down, although it had attained a good distance. The terrier jumped from the wolf's jaws unscratched, sniffed the carcass, and ran back to camp, behaving as though nothing had happened. After that, English Bill could not do enough for the two guides. And as it turned out it was a good thing Lafayette had saved the dog's life for, in turn, the bold little terrier was to save the men.

The weather stayed warm and then grew warmer, until the meat rotted and they were again reduced to beans. The meat had seemed to regulate the men's bowels. Meat or laudanum. Again, they began the drug regimen. Alarmingly thin by now, they tried all methods of snaring game, but even the Peace brothers had no luck and one night Bull declared the unspoken and said that they were all bound to die. He was leaving the next day, he said, making a last desperate effort for his life. He was walking back to St. Anthony. Back to his love.

"You'll not make it," Joseph said. He'd grown fond of Bull, and he was grateful to him for bringing along the laudanum, which was all that kept them from dying in the snow with their pants around their ankles, he was sure. "Don't go," he begged. "Don't let him," he entreated Henri. But the guides only nodded and looked away. They understood that the doctor's housekeeper was the only reason Bull was living yet. Like most men of large muscled stature, Bull had suffered the pangs of starvation more cruelly than the others. He had even gazed hungrily at English Bill's dog and so, that night, English Bill and the guides were the only of the men who did not try to dissuade Bull from making his attempt.

The ice broke and by morning the river was outside the door of the cabin. By noon that day, as Bull got ready to leave, the water had entered. The men gave him half of the cornmeal they had left, and he took a butcher knife. All of the men shook hands before he walked off, and nobody expected to see him again. The melt was grave—not only had they built too close to the river, they now realized, but the prairie between them and St. Anthony would be swimming. There would be no crossing. Bull would die in the mud. There would be no B.J. Bolt with a wagonload of food. Perhaps an Indian pony could get through, said Joseph, but the guides said no and Henri calmly sliced apart the extra pair of moccasins he'd brought and stewed them up. Joseph added the lacings and tops of his elkhide overboots. They had sent Bull off with more than his share of the laudanum and the dose they took that night, as it was the last, inflicted them with melancholy.

When they woke the next day the water had risen to just below their platform bed, and they resolved with their remaining strength to build a higher temporary shelter on a rise behind the cabin. As they were slowly attempting to build, Joseph had a sudden bolt of fear that he'd left the *Meditations* within reach of the water and he ran back to the cabin to retrieve the book. He had his gun with him because he was keeping that dry. As he entered the cabin, he saw a watery slur of movement. In the light from the open door an otter popped his head up and regarded him with the curious and trusting gaze of a young child. Slowly, not taking his eyes off the creature, Joseph aimed and shot. The otter died in a bloody swirl and Joseph found, when he fished it out, that his eyes had filled with tears. In a moment he was weeping helplessly over the gleaming and sinuous body of the creature.

The book was safe. He put it in his coat. Embarrassed at himself, he took the otter to a dry place and skinned and dressed it out. He'd got hold of himself by the time he brought the meat to English Bill, but he was unnerved by the great emotion he'd felt. For he'd had the instant horror that he had committed a murder. And that conviction still filled him. The creature was an emissary of some sort. He'd known as they held that human stare. Joseph himself was part of all that was sustained and destroyed by a mysterious power. He had killed its messenger. And the otter wasn't even edible. English Bill tried to roast the meat without parboiling it first, and the otter's taste of rotting fish gagged the men. Not so the terrier, who had a feast.

The dog was so full that the next day she didn't eat even one of thirty-six snow buntings that she found huddled in a pile, frozen dead and perfectly preserved. The Buckendorfs heaped the birds in their laps and with swift hands plucked them bare. Then the men put the birds on spits, roasted them, and ate, shivering with pleasure as they cracked and sucked the tiny bones. Joseph praised the dog, who flipped her ears up and seemed quite proud. Three times after that, the dog uncannily brought food. She dragged two great catfish, still gasping, off a piece of ice. She caught a squirrel and tried to pull a snapping turtle off a log by holding on to its tail. When Henri saw the turtle, he grinned and did not allow English Bill to touch it. He baited the turtle until it bit down on a stick, then sawed its head off. The head did not let go of the stick and the eyes continued to blink even after its body was chopped into a ravishing soup.

## The Millions

SO THE MEN were comparatively fit when Bull crawled back into the camp—a ghost, a skeletal thing, a flailed creature with great pools of eyes and a gaping mouth. His beard had grown all over his face and his chest had sunk. His knees and elbows were grotesquely swollen, his muscles shriveled onto the bone. He had lost his boots and socks and his feet had frozen black. Sick with pity, Joseph put his arms around the wasted man and lowered him onto a buffalo skin. He held Bull like a baby and let a bit of the soup trickle down his throat. As soon as the soup hit Bull's stomach, he straightened his legs out, kicked twice, and perished. Bull died looking up into the trees over them, just budding. Countless golden tassels winked in the sun, and the millions reflected in his baffled gaze.

## Lafayette Peace

THE BUDS SOON opened and the trees were wearing a denser film of green one week later, when B.J. Bolt arrived on foot, looking not much better than had Bull. Over a month before, B.J. Bolt had started with four men, three pack ponies, plus their own mounts, only to run into the melt. From then on, there was nothing but half-frozen mush and icy slough. After an argument over whether to continue, the other men deserted B.J. and left him just one horse, who ran right off. B.J. had eaten what he could of the food but then—remarkably, given that he could have made it back to St. Cloud—he strapped the rest of the food onto himself and headed west. There were times he waded chest-deep through ice water, holding the food over his head. Other times he cracked through fragile ice. Somehow, he continued. But he had to eat in order to walk. So by the time he arrived at the camp and unbuckled his pack, there was nothing left but a dozen hard biscuits. The men divided them and that night, as he slowly let each crumb dissolve on his tongue, Joseph thought of the otter and of his saved book, which he knew by heart. One phrase whirled in his head: *Wait for death with a cheerful mind.*

If only there was something afterward. Bull hadn't seemed to see anything in the branches and Marcus Aurelius had left that question up in the air.

"I envy your faith," Joseph said to Henri. The Buckendorfs slept in a heap. The night was clear and the flames of the outdoor fire snapped high. The two guides took turns playing soft music, and Joseph thought that if only they were not near death this would be a very pleasant night.

"Me," said Henri, putting down the fiddle and slowly stirring the fire with a stick, "I haven't much faith. The saints love my brother here."

Lafayette smiled, polishing his gun, and leaned over to breathe on the barrel. He had grown extremely beautiful and frail. Yet of them all he had remained most like himself in wit and action. His music had gained in depth. He alone seemed capable of effort.

"Do you believe we will die?" Joseph asked Lafayette, who continued to clean the gun with an absorption much like prayer. "Will you promise to bury me if I do?"

Lafayette suddenly leaned over, took the crucifix from around his neck, and with a tender gesture put it onto Joseph. The fire leapt in his extraordinary, sharp-bladed face. Three times he tapped Joseph on the chest and Joseph felt his heart leap, then Lafayette turned and walked off into the woods.

"Where is he going?" said Joseph, touching the cross at his throat. "What is he going to do?"

"We will have meat tomorrow," said Henri. That was all.

The Buckendorfs' eyes glowed with hunger like mystic stones and their yellow fangs had grown. There had been talk of eating Bull, and the guides had promised to kill anyone who tried. They were the ones who buried poor Bull and set a great pile of stones over his grave. They knelt with their rosaries and prayed to the Virgin Mary to rest his soul. Joseph had tried to help them, but had fallen down repeatedly. He was really asking Lafayette and Henri to do the same for him as for Bull. He was very tired now. Sitting beside Henri, he took the locket that held Dorea's picture from his inner pocket and he opened it to show the guide. Before this, he'd always looked at her picture when he was alone, ashamed, perhaps, of the fact that she was plain and older. Ashamed, perhaps, that someone might think she was his mother.

Henri placed the fiddle with great care into its velvet nest, and stroked it before he shut the lid. Then he took the locket from Joseph's hands, and looked into the face of Dorea for a very long time. At last he gave her back to Joseph.

"Such a pretty woman," he said. "Très jolie. You will be happy. She will give you many children and keep you warm at night."

This was the only untruth that Joseph heard Henri Peace to utter, for after that night in which Lafayette killed a crazed old female moose, and after the next week in which another outfit arrived with flour and they all stuffed themselves sick on pancakes and syrup then rolled in agony out in the woods, and after Joseph made his way back to St. Anthony more broke than he'd started out and with a deed for two hundred acres of worthless land in his pocket, he showed up at Dorea's doorstep only to be met by a man who introduced himself as her new husband, to whom he wordlessly gave the locket.

## *The Saint*

FOR A LONG time after the expedition, Joseph was sick, in a general way, and he gazed long at Lafayette's crucifix nailed onto his wall. He wondered where English Bill, his dog, the Buckendorfs, and Lafayette and Henri Peace were now. Except for B. J. Bolt, who looked in on him sometimes, the only one whose whereabouts he was sure of was Bull. So after he recovered, Joseph went to visit the doctor's housekeeper with the dark brown hair, sweet, coffee-milk skin, and freckled nose. She sat with him in the receiving parlor where the doctor's patients waited. From behind the shut door they could hear the clack of instruments and some muffled yelps. Joseph told the doctor's housekeeper all about Bull and how he had spoken of her looking at the horizon and how he had set off to walk across the dead swamp of the late winter prairie to be with her. She gazed at him with clear brown eyes and nodded when he had finished telling her about the turtle soup and how Bull had died looking up into the budding branches, with her name on his lips. The last part about the name was, he hoped, a pardonable embroidery. She did look sad, and a bit surprised. At last, she spoke.

"I was going to marry him, it's a fact. I loved him, I think, but the truth is I cannot recall what he looked like. Our affection came on sudden and he was gone so fast. He hadn't a picture of himself. But I do think I miss him and I am very sorry that he is dead."

She was so lucid in her puzzlement and her speech was so calm that Joseph nearly asked her to marry him right then and there. He held his tongue out of respect for Bull, and went back to the room B. J. Bolt had insisted he be given out behind Poolcaugh's establishment.

There, he pondered, as he had many times, the mystery of his survival and the meaning of the otter. He took down the crucifix and touched it to his forehead. *Alexander and Pompeium and Caius Caesar, after so completely destroying whole cities, and in battle cutting to pieces many ten thousands of cavalry and infantry, themselves too at last departed from life. Heraclitus, after so many speculations on the conflagration of the universe, was filled with water internally and died smeared all over with mud. And lice destroyed Democritas; and other lice killed Socrates. What means all this? Thou hast embarked, thou hast made the voyage, thou art come to shore; get out!*

He put the book down. He pressed the cross into his forehead as if to absorb its meaning. He thought of Bull's calm fiancée. Again the otter looked at him, an innocent saint. And Bull's fathomless eyes stared into the leaves.

"Well," he said out loud, "I'm cured of town fever."

He went out, bought a vested suit, and decided to become a lawyer.

# The Wolf

✴

HE WHO GOES to law holds a wolf by the ear, said Robert Burton. So there I was, here I am, the clichéd mixed-blood with a wolf by the ear. One of my advantages in holding on to the wolf is that I grew up dividing my time between my mother's family on the reservation, and the big house in Pluto. Thus, I know something about both sides of many cases I hear. My father built our house on land he had inherited from Joseph Coutts, whose own survey stones the railroad company tried to search out and steal when they came through, named, and platted out the town. That was some years after the town fever ordeal. Joseph Coutts was his own attorney, by then. In his first big case, he got back land for himself, therefore benefiting the Buckendorfs and any other of those original party members who cared to make a living near Pluto. Some did come back, drawn to where they'd lived the hardest, maybe, or where like Bull they had seen the truth of things flutter away in the pale leaves above them.

English Bill returned for a short time to open a saloon, but his terrier dog was thrown across the room in a poker dispute, shot right out of the air, and never did quite recover its vitality. Bill's liquor was as remarkably bad as his food. I don't know where he next tried his skill. As for the Buckendorfs, three of the four stayed on and were of course party to the lynching murder of the youngest Peace, whose older brothers had saved their lives.

After he got his land back, my grandfather was asked to move to Pluto and open a practice in what was thought of, after the mob had its way, as a town not quite fit to count itself part of the civilized new state of North Dakota. He did so, my father also went to law, and as they both married Chippewa women we became a family of lawyers who were also tribal members, an unusual combination at the time, but increasingly handy as tribal law and the complications of federal versus state jurisdiction were just beginning to become manifest.

As I look at the town now, dwindling without grace, I think how strange that lives were lost in its formation. It is the same with all desperate enterprises that involve boundaries we place upon the earth. By drawing a line and defending it, we seem to think we have mastered something. What? The earth swallows and absorbs even those who manage to form a country, a reservation. (Yet there is something to the love and knowledge of the land and its relationship to dreams—that's what the old people had. That's why as a tribe we exist to the present.) It is my job to maintain the sovereignty of tribal law on tribal land, but even as I do so, I think of my grandfather's phrase for the land disease, town fever, and how he nearly died of greed, its main symptom.

I have tried to keep some things about my Pluto self a secret here—my long defeat in love, for instance, by a woman who demolished my house, a few (mostly pardonable) youthful escapades, and a verbal mistake that resulted in my lengthy term of work digging graves in the town cemetery—a place for which I still have fond regard. But in one of my first law cases, I defended the perpetrator of a crime that had taken place in Pluto. This crime had also resulted in Corwin Peace. John Wildstrand was the perpetrator; he was also Corwin's father. He was tangled in with the rest of the family in complex ways as his grandfather had also fathered Mooshum's wife—but enough. Nothing that happens, *nothing*, is not connected here by blood.

I trace a number of interesting social configurations to the Wildstrand tendency to sexual excess, or "deathless romantic encounters,"

as Geraldine's niece, Evelina, puts it when listening to the histories
laid out by Seraph Milk. But of course the entire reservation is rife
with conflicting passions. We can't seem to keep our hands off one
another, it is true, and every attempt to foil our lusts through laws and
religious dictums seems bound instead to excite transgression.

At any rate, the entire story of the case, which became lurid in its
endless aftermath and was snapped up and salivated over by the Fargo
and even Minneapolis newspapers, began a chain of events that worked
its way through cultic religion full of inner dramas and hypocrisies,
and eventually ended up pretty well, considering that it may be said to
have started years ago when Corwin's uncle, Billy, decided to defend
his sister's honor with a jammed gun.

I represented John Wildstrand, Corwin's father, after the law
caught up with him on a Florida racetrack. That was years after the
crime. It was a disastrous criminal case—frustrating because Wildstrand was a jack-in-the-box. He continually popped out of his seat
during the proceedings and blurted out wildly incriminating blather—
he could not control himself. I debated whether to plead insanity, or
simply gag him, and ended up settling for what he seemed to wish
for—a conviction. He'd always wanted, I saw later, some sort of con-
tainment or certainty that would prevent self-harm. Of course, in the
interview process, he told me everything. He told me too much. He
told me things about himself that I could not forget.

Wildstrand's sinned-upon wife, Neve Harp, whom I still see now
and then when I visit my mother in the Pluto Retirement Home, hates
me for defending the man who so insulted their marriage. Neve is not
a resident there, she goes around collecting interviews for her historical newsletter. Neve glares at me, and looks away before I can catch
her eye, then she sneaks a look back. She cannot help herself either. It
is as if she wonders what I know about her, through him; she intuits
that I have an intimate level of information, and she both resents and
is curious about my knowledge of her former husband's life. In spite
of everything, I don't think Neve actually stopped loving John Wildstrand, and I understand that for many years she was the only person
who visited him in prison.

Burton's contemporary, Francis Bacon, believed it was only due to Justice that man can be a God to man and not a wolf. But what is the difference between the influence of instinct upon a wolf and history upon a man? In both cases, justice is prey to unknown dreams. And besides, there was a woman.

# Come In

✤

JOHN WILDSTRAND OPENED his front door wide and there was Billy Peace, his girlfriend Maggie's little brother. The boy stood frail and skinny in the snow with a sad look on his face and a big gun in his hand. As president of the National Bank of Pluto, John Wildstrand had trained his employees to stay relaxed in such a situation. Small-town banks were vulnerable, and John had actually been held up twice. One of the robbers had even been a jumpy drug addict. He did not flinch now.

His voice loud and calm, Wildstrand greeted Billy Peace as though he didn't see the gun. His wife, Neve, was reading in the living room.

"What can I do for you?" John Wildstrand continued.

"You may come with me, Mr. Wildstrand," said Billy, leading slightly to the left with the barrel of the gun. Beyond him, at the curb, a low-slung Buick idled. Wildstrand could see no one else in it. Billy was just seventeen years old and Wildstrand wondered if, and then wished that, Billy had joined the army as Maggie had said he was going to do. She was just a year or two older or younger than her brother. She would never tell. Her age was just one of the dangerous things about her. From the living room Neve called, "Who is it?" and Billy whispered, "Say kids selling Easter Seals."

"Kids selling Easter Seals," John Wildstrand called back.

"What? Tell them we don't want any," Neve yelled.

"Say you're going for a little walk," said Billy.

"I'm going for a little walk!"

"In this snow? You're crazy!" his wife cried.

"Put your coat on," said Billy. "So she doesn't see it's still hanging on the rack. Then come with me. Shut the door."

John Wildstrand went out into the snow and Billy pulled the door closed behind him. As Billy followed him down the walkway, presumably with the gun still out or slightly hidden, Wildstrand's confusion turned to a prayerful wish that he might find Maggie hidden in the car. That this was some odd prank. Some way of her seeing him. The windows of his house sprayed a soft, golden light all the way down the landscaped twist of pavers. There was a band of utter darkness where a stone wall and close-grown arborvitae cast a shadow onto the boulevard. The car sat beyond in the wintry shimmer of a street lamp.

"Get in," said Billy.

Wildstrand stumbled a bit in the icy snow and let himself into the passenger's side. The backseat was empty, he saw. Billy held the gun just inside the sleeve of a large topcoat, and kept it pointed at the windshield as he rounded the front of the car and ducked quickly into the driver's seat.

"I'm going to ease out of this light," he said.

Billy kept his gun out and his mild eyes trained on Wildstrand as he put the car in Drive and rolled forward into the darkness beyond the street lamp's glow.

"Time to talk." He put the car in Park.

Billy was a nervous-looking boy with deep brown eyes and a thin face. Toast-brown hair flopped over one eye and bent into his collar. There were little wisps of down on his chin. He was artistic. This sort of action, Wildstrand knew, did not come naturally to Billy Peace, though he was descended of the famous guide Lafayette Peace, who'd also fought with Riel. He might have gotten slightly drunk to force himself to drive to the Wildstrand residence with a gun and ring the bell. And what if Neve had answered? Would Billy have pretended to be selling candy bars for some high school trip? Would he have tried something else? Did he have an alternate plan? John Wildstrand stared at the gaunt little face of Billy. The boy really didn't seem likely to put a bullet in him. Wildstrand knew, also, that Billy's success in getting him into the car had depended on some implicit collaboration on his own part.

"So," Wildstrand repeated, using the patient voice he used with jumpy investors, "how can I help you?"

"I think ten thousand dollars should be just about right," said Billy.

"Ten thousand dollars."

Billy was silently expectant. Wildstrand shivered a little, then pulled his coat tight around him and felt like crying. He had cried a lot with Maggie. She had brought all of his tears up just beneath his skin. Sometimes they rushed out and sometimes they trickled in slow tracks down his cheeks, along his throat. She said there was no shame in it and cried along with him until their weeping slowed erotically and sent them careening through each other's bodies. Crying with her was a comfortable, dark act, like being painlessly absolved in church. There was an element of forgiveness in her weeping with him, he felt, and sometimes he became sentimental and sad about what his grandfather had done to a member of her family, long ago.

John Wildstrand heard himself make a sound, an *ah* of doubt. There was something about the actual monetary figure that struck him as wretched and sorrowful.

"It's just not enough," he said.

Billy looked perplexed.

"Look, if she keeps the baby, and you know I want her to keep the baby, she's going to need a house, a car. Maybe in Fargo, you know? And then there are clothes, and, what, swing sets, that sort of thing. I've never had a child, but they need certain equipment. Also, she needs a good doctor, hospital. That's not enough for everything. It's not a future."

"Okay," Billy said, after a while. "What do you suggest?"

"Besides," Wildstrand went on, still thinking out loud, "the thing is, in for a penny in for a pound. This amount will be missed just as much as a larger amount will be missed. My wife sees our accounts.

There needs to be an amount like, say, let me think. If it's just under a hundred thousand, the papers will say nearly a hundred thousand anyway. If it's a hundred thousand, they'll say that. So it might as well be over fifty thousand. But not seventy because they'll call that nearly a hundred."

Billy Peace was quiet. "That's just over fifty thousand," he said finally.

Wildstrand nodded. "See? But that's a doable thing. Only there must be a reason. A very good reason."

"Well maybe," said Billy, "you were going to start some kind of business?"

John Wildstrand looked at Billy in surprise. "Well, yes, that's good, a business. Only then we'll need to actually have the business, keep it going, make a paper trail and that will lead to more deception and the taxes . . . it all leads back to me. It gets too complicated. We need one catastrophic reason."

"A tornado," said Billy. "I mean in winter maybe not. A blizzard."

"And where does the money come in?"

"The money gets lost in the blizzard?"

Wildstrand looked disappointed and Billy shrugged weakly.

"A cash payment?"

They both cast about for a time, mulling this over. Then Billy said, "Question."

"Yes?"

"How come you don't get divorced from your wife and marry Maggie? A while ago, she said you loved her and now it sounds to me like you still love her. So maybe I didn't have to come here and threaten you with this." He wagged the gun. "I'm not getting why you don't leave your wife and go with Maggie, like run off together or something. You love her."

"I do love her."

"Then what's the problem?"

"Look at me, Billy." John Wildstrand put his hands out. "Do you think she'd stay with me just for me? Now be honest. Without the money. Without the job. Just me."

Billy Peace shrugged. "You're not so bad, man."

"Yes, I am," said Wildstrand. "I'm . . . a lot of years older than Maggie and I'm half-bald. If I had my hair, then maybe, or if I was either good-looking or athletic. But I'm a realist. I see what I am. The money helps. I'm not saying that's the only reason Maggie cares for me, not at all. Maggie is a pure soul, but the money helps. I'm not losing one of my biggest assets—if I divorced Neve now I wouldn't have a job. All gone. I took over from her father, who is, yes, old and in a nursing home. But perfectly lucid. Neve is a fifty-one percent shareholder. Besides, here's the thing. Neve has done nothing wrong. She has never, to my knowledge, betrayed me with another man, nor has she neglected me within her own powers. It is not her fault. Until I really *saw* Maggie, you understand, one year ago, I was reasonably happy. Neve and I had sex for twenty minutes once a week and went to Florida on winter vacations; we gave dinner parties and stayed two weeks out of every summer at the lake. In the summer we had sex twice a week and I cooked our meals."

Billy looked uncomfortable.

"Besides, we're a small bank and we could get bought out. That would change my situation. I'd like to be with Maggie. I plan to be with Maggie. If she'll have me."

Now Wildstrand leaned questioningly toward Billy.

"What does your presence here mean, actually? Did she send you?"

"No."

"What happened? She won't talk to me, you know."

"Well, she told me about her being pregnant. She was kind of upset and I thought you were ditching her. That's what I thought. You know there's always been just the two of us. Our mother froze in the woods when I was eleven. Maggie raised me in our grandparents' house. I would die for her."

"Of course," said John Wildstrand. "Of course you would. Let that be our bond, Billy. Both of us would die for her. But here's the thing. Only one of us . . . right now anyway, only one of us can provide for her."

"What should we do?"

"Something has come to me," said Wildstrand. "Now I'm going to propose an act that may startle you. It may seem bizarre, but give it a chance, Billy, because I think it will work. Hear me out? Say nothing until I've laid out a possible plan. Are you ready?"

Billy nodded.

"Say you kidnap my wife."

Billy gave a strangled yelp.

"No, just listen. Tomorrow night you do the very same thing. As if tonight was just practice. You come to the door. Neve answers. You show her the gun and you come into the house! You have some strong rope. A pair of scissors. At gunpoint you order me to tie up Neve. Once she's taken care of, you tie me up and say to me, in her hearing, that if I don't deliver fifty thousand dollars in cash to you tomorrow you will not let her go. Otherwise you'll kill her . . . you have to say that, I'm afraid. Then you bring her out to the car. Don't let her see the license plates."

"I don't think so," Billy said. "I think you're describing a federal crime."

"Well, yes," said Wildstrand. "But is it really a crime if nothing happens? I mean you'll be really, really nice to Neve. That's a given. You'll take her to a secure out-of-town location, like your house. Keep her blindfolded. Put her in the back bedroom where you keep the junk. Lay down a mattress there so she's comfortable. It'll just be for a day. I'll drop off the money. We'll time it. Then you'll let her out somewhere on the other side of town. She may have a long walk. Be sure she brings shoes and a coat. You'll drive back to wherever and turn in the car. I don't think we should tell Maggie."

"Maggie's gone, anyway."

Wildstrand's heart lurched, he'd somehow known it. "Where?" he managed to ask.

"Her friend Bonnie took her to Bismarck, just to clear out her head. They'll be back on Friday."

"Oh, then, this is perfect," said Wildstrand.

Billy looked at him with great, silent, dark eyes. His and Maggie's eyes were very similar, thought Wildstrand—that impenetrable

Indian darkness. They had some white blood and both were cream-skinned with heavy brown hair. Wildstrand felt extremely sorry for Billy. He was so frail, so young, and what would he do with Neve? She worked outside shoveling snow all winter and in summer she gardened, dug big holes, planted trees even. Billy kept shifting the gun from hand to hand, probably because his wrist was getting tired.

"By the way, where did that gun come from?" Wildstrand said.

"It belonged to my mother's father."

"Is it loaded?"

"Of course it is."

"You don't have ammunition for it, do you," said Wildstrand. "But that's good. We don't want any accidents."

## The Gingerbread Boy

WHEN BILLY PEACE knocked on the door the next evening, John Wildstrand pretended to have fallen asleep. His heart beat wildly and his throat closed as the quiet transaction occurred in the entryway. Then Neve walked into the room with her arms out and her square little honest face blanched in shock. She made a gesture to her husband, asking for help, but Wildstrand was looking at Billy and trying not to give everything away by laughing. Billy wore a child's knitted winter face mask of cinnamon brown with white piping around the mouth, nose, and eyes. His coat and his pants were a baked-looking brown. He looked like a scrawny gingerbread boy, except that he wore flowered gardening gloves, the sort that women used for heavy chores.

"Oh no, I'm going to throw up," Neve moaned when Billy ordered John Wildstrand to tie up his wife.

"No, you'll be okay," said Wildstrand, "you'll be okay." Tears dripped down his face and onto her hands as he tried firmly but gently to do his job. His wife's hands were so beautifully cared for, the nails lacquered with soft peach. Let nothing go wrong, he prayed.

"Look, he's crying," Neve said accusingly to Billy, before her husband tied a scarf between her teeth, knotting it hard behind her head. "Nnnnnn!"

"I'm sorry," said Wildstrand.

"Now it's your turn," said Billy.

The two of them suddenly realized that Billy would have to put down the gun and subdue Wildstrand, and their eyes got very wide. They stared at each other.

"Sit down in that chair," Billy said at last. "Take that rope and loop it around your legs, not around the chair legs," and then he gave instructions for Wildstrand to do most of the work himself, even had him test the knots, all of which Wildstrand thought quite ingenious of Billy.

Once Wildstrand had secured himself to the chair and Billy had gagged him, Billy told Neve to get on her feet. But she refused. Even as anxiety coursed through him, Wildstrand felt obscurely proud of his wife. She rolled around on the floor, kicking like a dolphin until Billy Peace finally pounced on her and pressed the barrel of the gun to her temple. Straddling her, Billy untied the cloth gag in her mouth and rummaged in his pocket. He drew out a couple of pills.

"You leave me no choice," he said, "I'm going to have to ask you to dry-swallow these."

"What are they?" asked Neve.

"Sleeping pills," said Billy. Then he spoke to Wildstrand. "Leave the money in a garbage bag next to the Flickertail Club highway sign. No marked bills. No police. Or I'll kill your wife. You're being watched."

Wildstrand was surprised that Neve took the pills, but then for some reason she always had been like that about taking pills, even asking the doctor to paint her throat when it was hardly pink—she'd always been a willing patient. Now she turned out to be a willing hostage, and Billy had no more trouble with her. He undid the rope on her legs and put a hobble on her ankle. She walked out dreamily, her coat draped over her shoulders, and John Wildstrand was left alone. It took him about half an hour of patient wiggling to release himself from the rope, which he left looped around the chair. Now what? He wanted desperately to call Maggie, to talk to her, hear the slow music of her voice. But for some hours, he sat on the couch with his head in his hands, replaying the whole scenario. Then he started thinking ahead. Tomorrow he would go in early. He would withdraw cash out of their joint accounts. Then he would take the cash and get in the car. He would drive out to the highway sign and make the drop. It would all be done before eleven A.M. and Billy Peace would free Neve west of town, where she could walk home or find a ride. There would be police. Investigation. Newspapers. But no insurance was involved. He'd have used all of their retirement money, but Neve still had the bank. It would all blow over.

## Helpless

A BLIZZARD CAME up and Neve got lost and might have frozen to death had not a farmer pulled her from a ditch. Because Billy had actually scooped up her snowboots as they left, and her coat was a big long woolen one that ended past her knees, she suffered no frostbite. She ran a fever for six days, but she did not develop pneumonia. Wildstrand nursed her with care, waited on her hand and foot, took a leave from the bank. He was shocked by how the kidnapping had affected her. Over the next weeks she lost a great deal of weight and spoke irrationally. To the police she described her abductor as quite large, muscular, with hard hands, a big nose, and a deep voice. Her kidnapper was stunningly handsome, she said, a god! It was all so bizarre that Wildstrand almost felt like correcting her. Though he was delighted, on the one hand, that she had the description so wrong, her embroidery disturbed him. And when he brought her home she was so restless. In the evenings, she wanted to talk instead of watch television or read the magazines she subscribed to. She had questions.

"Do you love me?"

"Of course I love you."

"Do you really, really love me, I mean, would you have died for me if the attacker had made you make a choice—it's her or you—say he said that. Would you have stepped forward?"

"I was tied to the chair," said John Wildstrand.

"Metaphorically."

"Of course, metaphorically. I would have."

"I wonder."

She began to look at him skeptically. Her eyes measured him. At night, now, she wanted lots of reassurance. She seduced him and scared him, saying things like, "Make me helpless."

"He made me helpless," she said one morning. "But he was kind. Very kind to me."

Wildstrand took her to the doctor, who said it was hysteria and prescribed cold baths and enemas, which seemed only to make her worse. "Hold me, tighter, squeeze the breath out of me." "Look at me. Don't close your eyes." "Don't say something meaningless. I want the truth." It was terrifying, how she'd opened up. What had Billy done?

Nothing, Billy insisted on the phone. Wildstrand was ashamed to be repelled by his wife's awkward need—it was no different from his own need. If she'd been this way earlier on, he recognized that maybe he would have responded. Maybe he wouldn't have turned to Maggie. Maybe he would have been amazed, grateful. But when Neve threw herself over him at night he felt despair, and she could sense his distance. She grew bony and let her hair go gray, long, out of control, beautiful. She was strange, she was sinking. She continually looked at him with the eyes of a drowning person.

## Murdo Harp

JOHN WILDSTRAND WENT to visit his father-in-law in the retirement home which his money had endowed. The Pluto Nursing Home. This place did not depress him, though he could see the reasons why it might. Murdo Harp was resting on his single bed, on top of a yellow chenille coverlet. He'd pulled an afghan over himself, one that Neve had knitted, intricate rainbow stripes. He was listening to the radio.

"It's me. It's John."

"Ah."

Wildstrand took his father-in-law's hand in his. The skin was dry and very soft, almost translucent. His face was thin, bloodless, almost saintly looking, even though Murdo Harp had been ruthless, a cut-throat banker, a survivor.

"I'm glad you're here. It's very peaceful and quiet, but I woke up at four A.M. before the rest of them this morning. I thought to myself, I hope someone will come. I want to go somewhere. And you came. It's good to see you, John. Where are we going?"

John ignored the question, and the old man nodded.

"How's my little girl?"

"She's just fine." No one had told Neve's father, of course, what had happened. "She has a cold," Wildstrand lied. "She's staying in bed to-day. She's probably curled up around her hot water bottle, sleeping."

"The poor kid."

Wildstrand resisted telling Neve's father, as he always did, "I'll take good care of her." How wrong, and how ironic, would that be? The hand relaxed and Wildstrand realized that his father-in-law had fallen asleep. Still, he continued to sit beside the bed holding the old man's slender and quite elegant hand. With someone this old a little wisdom might leak out into the room. There was, at least, a pleasant sensation of rest. To have given up. Nothing else was expected. The old man had done what he could do. Life was now the afghan and the radio. John Wildstrand sat there for a long time; it was a good place to consider things. The baby would be born in four months and Billy and Maggie were living in a sturdy little bungalow not far from Island Park. Billy was just about to start technical college classes. The last time Wildstrand had visited, Billy was just walking out the door. He shook hands but said nothing. He was wearing his old enfolding top-coat, a long, striped beatnik scarf, and soft, rumpled-looking boots.

As for Maggie, she was often alone. Wildstrand couldn't get away much because of Neve. Maggie understood. She was radiant. Her hair was long, a lustrous brown. They went into her bedroom in the mid-dle of the day and made love in the stark light. It was very solemn. He'd gone dizzy with the depth of it. When he lay against her, his perceptions had shifted and he saw the secret souls of the objects and plants in the room. Everything had consciousness and meaning. Mag-gie was measureless, but she was ordinary, too. He stepped out of time and into the nothingness of touch. Afterward, Wildstrand had driven back to Pluto and arrived just in time for dinner.

Leaving the old man, Wildstrand usually patted his arm or made some other vague gesture of apology. This time Wildstrand was still thinking of his time with Maggie, and he bent dreamily over Neve's father. He kissed the dry forehead, stroked back the old man's hair and thoughtlessly smiled. The old man jerked away suddenly and eyed Wildstrand like a mad hawk.

"You bastard!" he cried.

## The Gesture

ONE DAY NEVE was sitting in her bathrobe at lunch, tapping a knife against the side of a boiled egg. Suddenly she said, "I know who he was. I saw him in a play. Shakespeare. The play had two sets of twins who don't meet until the end."

John Wildstrand's guts went ice-cold and he phoned Billy as soon as he returned to the bank. Sure enough, Billy had been in the previous summer's production put on by the town drama club. He'd been one of the Dromios in *The Comedy of Errors*. Wildstrand put the phone down and stared at it. Neve was at the town library at that very moment looking through archived town newspapers. This was how it happened all of a sudden that instead of taking college courses, Billy bolted and joined the army, after all. Wildstrand hadn't thought that they would take him because he was underweight, but the army didn't care. Now he was terrified that Maggie's grief would affect the baby, for she was heartbroken and cried day and night when Billy was shipped off for basic training. She said that she couldn't feel things anymore, and turned away from Wildstrand when he visited and would not let him touch her. After six weeks, Billy sent a photograph of himself in military gear. He didn't look to have bulked up much. The helmet seemed to balance on his head, shadowing his unreadable eyes. His neck was still skinny and graceful. He looked about twelve years old.

One afternoon, Wildstrand drove home after having visited Maggie, and all the way down the highway the little face beneath the helmet was in his mind. When he entered his house he saw that Neve was working on another afghan. She raised her clear, blue eyes to his.

"I am leaving now," said Wildstrand. He put the car keys on the coffee table. "You keep everything. I have clothes. I have shoes. I'll make myself a sandwich and be going now."

John Wildstrand walked into the kitchen and made the sandwich and wrapped it in waxed paper. He walked out into the living room and stood in the center of the carpet. Neve just looked at him. Light blazed white across her face. She raised her hand, swept it to the side, then dropped it. The gesture seemed to hang in the air, as if her arm left a trail. Wildstrand turned and walked out the door, across town, and started hitchhiking back to Maggie along the highway. There was only a slight wind and the temperature was about sixty-five degrees. The fields were full of standing water and ducks and geese swam in the ditches. All through the afternoon, as he walked along, the horizon appeared and disappeared. He didn't take a ride until the sky darkened.

## The Lions

SHORTLY AFTER JOHN Wildstrand moved into the house with Maggie, the baby boy was born. In those dazzling moments after the birth, he had a vision. The baby looked like Billy. Stage Billy, tall Billy with no ass to speak of, Billy with big feet, who looked like he could hardly lift a water canteen. Billy's heart was pierced by thorns. Was there anyone more magnificent than Billy? John Wildstrand saw that Billy Peace was a kind of Christ figure, or a martyr like those in the New Testament. Only he was thrown to the lions in the cause of their happiness. Wildstrand had thought that, in his new life, Billy might grow in strength and valor and be exactly the person who Neve believed had abducted her. Now he saw that Billy already was that person and Neve had known. He also saw that Billy had told his sister about the kidnapping. All of this was depicted in the face of the tiny new infant. Wildstrand looked closer, and tried to see whether Billy would live or die. But before that picture came clear, the baby opened up its mouth and bawled. Wildstrand put the baby to Maggie's breast and when it latched on, he tried to touch the baby's hair. Maggie pushed away his hand with the same gesture that his wife had used to say good-bye, and he sank back into the hospital chair. He was dizzy with spent adrenaline. For a long time, he watched them from across the room.

## The Garage

ONLY TWICE DID John Wildstrand visit Pluto. The first time, he brought a trailer and loaded into it all that Neve had not disposed of—she'd thrown a lot of things away. But physical objects had ceased to matter to Wildstrand. He was sleeping out in Maggie's garage, by then, in a sleeping bag spread out on a little camp cot. He cuddled up next to the used car he'd bought. Maggie argued with him every day about going to the police, turning him in for the kidnapping.

"You'll lose everything"—Wildstrand waved his arm—"this house. And Billy will go to jail. Would you like that? You'll be out on the street. And what about little Corwin?"

Maggie had named the baby after her brother's best buddy in boot camp. He was now in Korea, stationed close to the DMZ. Billy was in danger and wrote weekly letters about his visions. Apparently, he was being contacted by powerful spirits who saved him time after time, and who promised to direct his life.

"He's never been religious," Maggie wept, "in his whole life. Now look at this! Look at what you did!"

Wildstrand despaired. There was no getting away from Billy; he would always control the situation, no matter where he was. Billy, with his bristle-headed army cut and unknown eyes, with his army boots and rifle. Now that he was a soldier and visited by angels, there was no hope. Even if nothing happened to him. In the months after his son's birth, Wildstrand had come to understand that he would never be forgiven for engineering the kidnap scheme, and he had lost Maggie's love. She was icy-angry—she implied that he was just like his Indian-hating grandfather and now spent all day caring for the baby and cleaning the house. Every so often, she would thrust a shopping list at Wildstrand, or make him help with heavy lifting. Beyond that, she didn't like him to get close to either her or the baby. He moved around the small house like a ghost, never knowing where to settle, never comfortable. He made a sorry den for himself in the basement, where he would go whenever it was too cold to sleep in the garage. Otherwise he stayed out there, listening to music, reading the newspaper. He'd found a job at the same insurance agency he'd always used, a low-level job assisting others in processing claims.

## The Entryway

ONE DAY, A homeowner's claim from his old address crossed his desk. Neve had filed a claim on everything that he had taken from the house, his own things, which she had pressured him to come and clear out. There were his expensive hand tools, each engraved with his name and an identification code, and records with their expensive record-playing equipment, even a brand-new television. Looking at the list, Wildstrand felt a glimmer of heat rise in his throat. His ears burned. He took his coat from the back of the office door, went back to the house that his and Neve's retirement money had bought, and packed up everything he'd kept in the garage. He drove back to Pluto with a full car and parked in the driveway of his former house.

After a while, Neve came to the window. She looked at him as he got out of the car, and he looked at her, through the window, which was like the glass of a dim aquarium. When she vanished, he was not sure whether she would come to the door or be absorbed into the gloom. But she did open the door at last, and beckoned him inside. They stood in the entry, quite close. Her hair had gone from gray to silver-white. A pulse beat in her slender throat. Her arms were stick thin, but she seemed to generate an unusual light. Wildstrand could feel it, this odd radiance. It seemed to emanate from her translucent skin. It occurred to him that he would sink down at the feet of this beautiful, wronged woman and kiss the hem of the wide-skirted dress that she was wearing.

"You filed a claim on all my stuff. I'm bringing it back," he said.

"No. I want the money. I need the money," she told him.

"Why?"

"We're sunk. They're not going to buy the bank out. They're opening a new one next to it."

"What about your father's accounts?"

"He'll live to be a hundred," said Neve. "John, he told me that you were seeing another woman all along."

"I don't know where he got that idea."

Neve waited.

"All right. Yes."

Her eyes filled with terrible tears and she began to shake. Before he knew it, Wildstrand was holding her. He shut the door. They made love in the entry, on the carpet where so many people paused, and then on the bench where visitors removed their boots and shoes. His remorse and shame was confusingly erotic. And her need for him was so powerful it seemed that they were going over a rushing waterfall together, falling in a barrel, and at the bottom Wildstrand cracked open and told her everything.

He had to, because of Billy Peace. On the entryway floor next to the boot rack, Wildstrand realized with utter instinctive certainty that Billy had helped himself to his wife's body when she was tied up and utterly helpless, kidnapped, on the mattress beside the junked pots and cast-off clothing. Wildstrand clung to Neve with the blackness washing over him, and talked and talked.

"I know he violated you," Wildstrand said, after he'd spilled everything else.

"Who? That boy? He was just a twerp," said Neve. "He never touched me. I said all of that stuff out of desperation, to try and make you jealous. Why, I do not know." She sat up and eyed him with calm assessment. "Possibly, I thought you loved me way deep down. I think I believed there was something in you."

"There is, there is," Wildstrand said to her, strangling on a surge of hope, touching her ankles as she got to her feet.

"When the snow was covering me, out in the ditch, I saw your face. Real as real. You bent over me and pulled me out. It wasn't the farmer, it was you."

"It was me," said Wildstrand, lifting his arms. "I must have always loved you."

She looked down at him for a long time, contemplating this amazing fact. Then she went upstairs and called the police.

## A Shiver of Possibility

IN THE YEARS after he was caught, tried, found guilty, and sentenced, Wildstrand was sometimes asked by friends he made behind bars, and other lawyers (of course, I asked him myself), what had caused him to admit what he had done. What caused him to tell Neve and, to boot, assume all responsibility? Sometimes he couldn't think of a good reason. Other times, he said that he guessed that it would never end; he saw that he'd be kicked from one woman to the other until the end of time. But after he gave his answer, he always came back to that moment he had opened his door to Billy Peace, and thought of how, when he saw the boy standing in the shining porch light, in the snow, with the dull gun and the sad face, he felt a shiver of possibility, and said, "Come in."

# Marn Wolde

# Satan: Hijacker of a Planet

### ❧

IT WAS A drought-dry summer when I met Billy Peace, and in the suspension of rain everything seemed to flex. The growthless spruce had dropped their bud-soft needles. Our popples stretched their full lengths, each heart-lobed leaf still and open. The great oak across the field reared out, its roots sucking water from the bottom of the world. On an afternoon when rain was promised, we sat on the deck and watched the sky pitch over reservation land. I could almost feel the timbers shake under my feet, as its great searching taproots trembled. Still, the rain held off. I left my mother sitting in her chair and went to the old field by the house, up a low rise. There, the storm seemed likelier. The wind came off the dense-grassed slough, smelling like wet hair, and the hot ditch grass reached for it, butter yellow, its life concentrated in its fiber mat, each stalk so dry it gave off a puff of smoke when snapped. Grasshoppers sprang from each step, tripped off my arms, legs, eyebrows. There was a small pile of stones halfway up the hill. Someone had cleared that hillside once to make an orchard that had fallen into ruin and was now only twisted silver branches and split trunks. I sat there and continued to watch the sky as, out of nowhere, great solid-looking clouds built hot stacks and cotton cones. I was sixteen years old.

I was watching the wash of ink, rain on the horizon, when his white car pulled into our yard. A tall man, thin and tense, but with a shy and open smile. His eyes were brown and melting, rich as sweet milk caramel. I would find out later that they could freeze black or turn any color under the sun. He was dressed very neatly, wearing a tie and a shirt that was not sweat through, still ironed crisp. I noticed this as I was walking back down to the yard. I was starting to notice these things about men, the way their hips moved when they hauled feed, checked fence lines, the way their forearms looked so tanned and hard when they rolled up their white sleeves. I was looking at men, not with intentions, because I didn't know what I would have done with one yet if I got him, but with a studious mind.

I was looking at them just to figure, for pure survival, the way a girl does. It is like a farmer, which my dad is, gets to know the lay of the land. He loves his land so he has got to figure how to cultivate it. What it needs in each season, how much abuse it will sustain, what in the end it will yield to him.

And I, too, in order to increase my yield and use myself right was taking my lessons. I never tried out my information, though, until Billy Peace arrived. He looked at me where I stood in the shade of my mother's butterfly bush. I'm not saying that I flirted right off. I still didn't know how to. I walked into the sunlight and stared him in the eye.

"What are you selling?" I smiled, and told him that my mother would probably buy it since she bought all sorts of things—a pruning saw you could use from the ground, a cherry pitter, a mechanical apple peeler that also removed the seeds and core, a sewing machine that remembered all the stitches it had sewed. He smiled back at me, walked with me to the steps of the house.

"You're a bright young lady," he said, though he was young himself. "Stand close. You'll see what I'm selling by looking into the middle of my eyes."

He pointed his finger between his eyebrows.

"I don't see a thing."

My mother came around the corner holding a glass of iced tea in her hand. While they were talking, I didn't look at Billy. I felt challenged, like I was supposed to make sense of what he did. At sixteen, I didn't have perspective on the things men did. I'd never gotten a whiff of that odor, the scent of it that shears off them like an acid. Later, it would require just a certain look, a tone of voice, a word, no more than a variation in the way he drew breath. A dog gets tuned that way, sensitized to a razor degree, but it wasn't that way in the beginning. I took orders from Billy like I was doing him a favor, the way, since I'd hit my growth, I took orders from my dad.

Except my dad only gave orders when he was tired. All other times, he did the things he wanted done by himself. My dad was not the man I should have studied, in the end, if I wanted to learn cold survival. He was too worn-out. All my life, my parents had been splitting up. I lived in a no-man's-land between them and the ground was pitted, scarred with ruts. And yet, no matter how hard they fought each other they had stuck together. He could not get away from my mother somehow, nor she from him. So I couldn't look to my father for information on what a man was. He was half her. And I couldn't look at the old man they took care of, his uncle whose dad originally bought the farm, my uncle Warren, who would stare and stare at you like he was watching your blood move and your food digest. Warren's face was a chopping block, his long arms hung heavy. He flew into disorderly rages and went missing, for days sometimes. We'd find him wandering the farm roads bewildered and spent of fury. I never saw Warren as the farmer that my dad was—you should have seen my father when he planted a tree.

"A ten-dollar hole for a two-bit seedling," he said. That was the way he dug, so as not to crowd the roots. He kept the little tree in water while he pried out any rocks that might be there, though our land was just as good as the best Red River soil, dirt that went ten feet down—rich, black clods you felt like holding in your fist and biting. My father put the bare-root tree in and sifted the soil around the roots, rubbing it to fine crumbs between his fingers. He packed the dirt in, he watered until the water pooled. Looking into my father's eyes you would see the knowledge, tender and offhand, of the ways roots took hold in the earth.

I believed, at first, that there was that sort of knowledge in Billy's eyes. I watched him from behind my mother. I discovered what he had to sell.

"It's Bibles, isn't it," I said.

"No fair." He put his hand across his heart, grinned at the two of us. He had seen my eyes flicker to the little gold cross in his lapel.

"Something even better."

"What?" My mother scoffed.

"Spirit."

My mother turned and walked away. She had no time for conversion attempts. I was only intermittently religious, but I suppose I felt that I had to make up for her rudeness, and so I stayed a moment longer. I was wearing very short cutoff jeans and a little brown T-shirt, tight, old clothes for dirty work. I was supposed to help my mom clean out her brooder house that afternoon, to set new straw in and wash down the galvanized feeders, to destroy the thick whorls of ground-spider cobwebs and shine the windows with vinegar and newspapers. All of this stuff was scattered behind me on the steps, rags and buckets. And as I said, I was never all that religious.

"There is a meeting tonight," he said. "I'm going to tell you where."

He always told in advance what he was going to say. That was the preaching habit in him, it made you wait and wonder in spite of yourself.

"Where?" I said finally.

He told me the directions, how to get where the tent was pitched. He spoke to me looking full on with sweetness of intensity. Eyes brown as burnt sugar. I realized I'd seen his picture before in my grandparents' bedroom. Billy's was the face of Jesus leaning his head forward just a little to listen for an answer as he knocked on a rustic door. I decided that I would go, without anyone else in my family, to the fairground field that evening. Just to study. Just to see.

❧

THE RAIN DROPPED off the edge of the world. We got no more than a slash of moisture in the air that dried before it fell. After the storm veered off, I decided to go to town. I drove a small sledge and tractor at the age of eleven, and a car back and forth into Pluto with my mother in the passenger's seat when I was fourteen years old. So it was not unusual that I went where I wanted to go.

As I walked over to the car, I passed Uncle Warren. He was sitting on a stump in the yard, looking at me, watching me, his gray hair tufted out, his chin white stubble, his eye on me, green and frozen.

Where are you going?

Town.

After that?

Back home.

Then?

I dunno.

Hell.

Maybe.

Hell, for sure.

Sometimes he would say that I was just like him, that I maybe was him, he could see it. He could see my whole structure. I couldn't hide. I told him shut up and leave me alone. He always said to me, you are alone. I always answered, not as alone as you.

In town, the streets were just on the edge of damp, but the air was still thin and dry. White moths fluttered in and out under the rolled flaps of the tent, but as the month of August was half spent there were no more mosquitoes. Too dry for them, too. Even though the tent was open-sided, the air seemed close, compressed, and faintly salty with evaporated sweat. The space was three-quarters full of singing people and I slipped into one of the hind rows. I sat in a gray metal folding chair, kept my eyes open, and my mouth shut.

He was not the first speaker, as it turned out. I didn't see him until the main preacher finished his work and said a prayer. He called Billy to the front with a little preface. Billy was newly saved, endowed with a message by the Lord, and could play several musical instruments. We were to listen to what the Lord would reveal to us through Billy's lips. He came on the stage. Now he wore a vest, a three-piece suit, a red silken shirt with a pointed collar. He started talking. I could tell you just about what he said, word for word, because after that night and long away into the next few years, sometimes four, five times in one day, I'd hear it over and over. You don't know preaching until you've heard Billy Peace. You don't know god loss, a barbed wire ripped from your grasp, until you've heard it from Billy Peace. You don't know subjection, the killing happiness of letting go. You don't know how light and comforted you feel, how cherished.

I was too young to stand against it.

>K

THE STARS ARE the eyes of God and they have been watching us from the beginning of the earth. Do you think there isn't an eye for each of us? Go on and count. Go on and look in the Book and total up all the nouns and verbs, like if you did somehow you'd grasp the meaning of what you held. You can't. The understanding is in you or it isn't. You can hide from the stars by daylight but at night, under all of them, so many, you are pierced by the sight and by the vision.

Get under the bed!

Get under the sheet!

I said to you, stand up, and if you fall, fall forward!

I'm going to go out blazing. I'm going to go out like a light. I'm going to burn in glory. I said to you, stand up!

And so there's one among them. You have heard Luce, Light, Lucifer, the Fallen Angel. You have seen it with your own eyes and you didn't know he came upon you. In the night, and in his own disguises like the hijacker of a planet, he fell out of the air, he fell out of the dark leaves, he fell out of the fragrance of a woman's body, he fell out of you and entered you as though he'd reached through the earth.

Reached his hand up and pulled you down.

Fell into you with a jerk.

Like a hangman's noose.

Like nobody.

Like the slave of night.

Like you were coming home and all the lights were blazing and the ambulance sat out front in the driveway and you said,

*Lord, which one?*

And the Lord said, *All of them.*

You too, follow, follow, I'm pointing you down. In the sight of the stars and in the sight of the Son of Man. The grace is on me. Stand up, I said. *Stand.* Yes and yes I'm gonna scream because I like it that way. Let yourself into the gate. Take it with you. In four years the earth will shake in its teeth.

Revelations. Face of the beast. In all fairness, in all fairness, let us quiet down and let us think.

Billy Peace looked intently, quietly, evenly, at each person in the crowd and quoted to them, proving things about the future that seemed complicated, like the way the Mideast had shaped up as such a trouble zone. How the Chinese armies were predicted in Tibet and that had come true and how they'll keep marching, moving, until they reached the Fertile Crescent. Billy Peace told about the number. He slammed his forehead with his open hand and left a red mark. *There,* he yelled, gut-shot, *there it will be scorched.* He was talking about the number of the beast and said that they would take it from your Social Security, your checkbooks, these things called credit cards—American Express, he cried, to Oblivion, they would take the numbers from your tax forms, your household insurance. That already, through these numbers, you are under the control of Last Things and you don't know it.

The Antichrist is among us.

He is the plastic in our wallets.

You want credit? Credit?

Then you'll burn for it and you will starve. You'll eat sticks, you'll eat black bits of paper, your bills, and all the while you'll be screaming from the dark place, *Why the hell didn't I just pay cash?*

Because the number of the beast is a fathomless number and banking numbers are the bones and the guts of the Antichrist, who is Lucifer, who is pure brain.

Pure brain gonna get us to the moon, get us past the moon.

The voice of lonely humanity in a space probe calling Anybody

Home? Anybody Home Out There? Antichrist will answer. Antichrist is here, all around us in the tunnels and webs of radiance, in the transistors, the great mind of the Antichrist is fusing in a pattern, in a destiny, waking up nerve by nerve.

Serves us right. Don't it serve us right not to be saved?

It won't come easy. Not by waving a magic wand. You've got to close your eyes and hold out those little plastic cards.

Look at this!

He held a scissors high, turned it to every side so the light gleamed off the blades.

The sword of Zero Interest! Now I'm coming. I'm coming down the aisle. I'm coming with the sword that sets you free.

Billy Peace started a hymn going and he walked down the rows of chairs, singing, and every person who held a credit card out he embraced, then he plucked that card out of their fingers. He cut once, crosswise. Dedicated to the Lord! He cut again. He kept the song flowing, walked up and down the rows, cutting, until the tough, trampled grass beneath the tent was littered with pieces of plastic. He came to me, last of all, and noticed me, and smiled.

"You're too young to have established a line of credit," he said, "but I'm glad to see you here."

Then he stared at me, his eyes hardened to the black of winter ice, cold in the warmth of his tan skin, so chilling I just melted.

"Stay," he said, "stay afterward and join us in the trailer. We're going to pray over Ed's mother."

⋊⋉

SO I DID stay. It doesn't sound like a courting invitation, but that was the way I thought of it at the time, and it turned out I was right. Ed was the advertised preacher, and his mother was a sick, sick woman. She lay flat and still on a couch at the front of this house trailer, where she just fit end to end. The air around her was dim, close with the smell of sweat-out medicine, and what the others had cooked and eaten, hamburger, burnt onions, coffee. The table was pushed to one side and the chairs were wedged around the couch. And Ed's mother, poor old dying woman, was covered with a white sheet that her breath hardly moved. Her face was caved in, sunken around the mouth and cheeks. She looked to me like a bird fallen out of its nest before it feathered, her shut eyelids bulging blue, wrinkled, beating with tiny nerves. Her head was covered with white wisps of hair. Her hands, just at her chest, curled like little bloodless claws. Her nose was a large and waxen bone.

I drew a chair up, the farthest to the back of the eight or so people who had gathered. One by one they opened their mouths and rolled their eyes or closed them tight and let the words fly out of them until they begin to garble and the sounds from their mouths resembled some ancient, dizzying speech. At first, I was so uncomfortable with all of the strangeness, and even a little faint from the airlessness and smells, that I breathed in with shallow gulps, and I shut the language out. But gradually, slowly, it worked its way in and I felt dizzy until I was seized.

The words are inside and outside of me, hanging in the air like small pottery triangles, broken and curved. But they are forming and crumbling so fast that I'm breathing dust, the sharp antibiotic bitterness, medicine, death, sweat. My eyes sting and I'm starting to choke. All the blood goes out of my head and down, along my arms, into the ends of my fingers. My hands feel swollen, twice as big as normal, like big puffed gloves. I get out of the chair and turn to leave, but he is there.

"Go on," he says. "Go on and touch her."

The others have their hands on Ed's mother. They are touching her with one hand and praying, the other palm held high, blind, feeling for the spirit like antennae. Billy pushes me, not by making any contact, just by inching up behind me so I feel the forcefulness and move. Two people make room and then I am standing over Ed's mother. She is absolutely motionless, still, as though she is a corpse, except that her pinched mouth has turned down at the edges so she frowns into her own dark.

I put my hands out, still huge, prickling. I am curious to see what will happen when I do touch her, if she'll respond. But when I place my hands down on her stomach, low and soft, she makes no motion at all. Nothing flows from me, no healing powers. Instead, I am filled with the rushing dark of what she suffers. It fills me suddenly as water from a faucet brims a jug, and spills over.

This is when it happens.

I'm not stupid, I have never been stupid. I have pictures. I can get a picture in my head at any moment, focus it so brilliant and detailed it seems real. That's what I do. That's what my uncle does when he's just staring. It's what I started when my mom and dad went for each other. When I heard them downstairs I always knew there'd be a moment. One of them would scream, tear through the stillness. It would rise up, that howl, and fill the house, and then one would come running. One would come and take hold of me. It would be my mother, smelling of smoked chicken, rice, and coffee grounds. It would be my father, sweat-soured, scorched with cigarette smoke from in the garage, bitter with the dust of his fields. Then I would be somewhere in no-man's-land, between them, and that was the unsafest place in the world. Except for the gaze grip of my uncle. So I would leave it. I would go limp and enter my pictures.

I have a picture. I go into it right off when I touch Ed's mother, veering off her thin pain. She grew up in Montana and now I see what she sees. Here's a grainy deep blue range of mountains hovering off the valley in the west; their foothills are blue, strips of dark blue flannel, and their tops are cloudy halls. The sun strikes through, once, twice, a pink radiance that dazzles patterns into their corridors so they gleam back, moon-pocked. Watch them, watch close, Ed's mother, and they start to walk. I keep talking until I know we are approaching these mountains together. She is dimming her lights, she is turning thin as tissue under my hands. She is dying as she goes into my picture with me, goes in strong, goes in willingly. And once she is in the picture she gains peace from it, gains the rock strength, the power, just like I always do.

# The Daniels

❧

WE WANDERED IN the desert three years, and I bore two children in the daze and rush of Billy's traveling visions. His cognitions came on us like Mack trucks, bowling us from tent to tent and town to town. He would howl with the signal, then writhe at tremendous sights he saw, shout for a pen and paper, growl and puke and wrestle with the knowledge until he lay calm on the bathroom floor, spent, saying to me, *Now, do you doubt?*

I never did. I had faith in Billy from that first night I heard him speak. I had faith and I cleaved to him, utterly. But as the months and then the years went by, I missed my mother and my father. I missed their ordinary routine, their low drama, even the familiarity of their quarrels. I missed that I could read their danger, and knew a safe place to be around them—in my pictures. I was having trouble with the pictures. I had to stay on this plane of existence with my babies, that was why. And because I could not disappear into my pictures I needed to go home.

❧

JUDAH IS FLUSHED and peaceful, lips red and soft as petals, his cheeks bright and marked with the seams of the fabric of my blouse. And Lilith, so small and hot, pressed into the folds of my skirt, sighs and falls into a glutted sleep.

"Let's go see Grandma and Grandpa," I say to my babies, thinking of my mother's face. She hasn't seen them yet.

Nothing can pry this idea loose, I am bent on it.

"Billy," I say when he walks in. "We're going home."

"No," he says without a beat of hesitation.

"We've got to," I tell him.

I've never crossed him before and my fierceness surprises, then shakes him.

"Your parents died when you were young," I tell him. "Your sister raised you until you went into the army, then she went to the dogs, I guess. So you don't really understand the idea of home, or folks, or a place you grew up in that you want to return to. But now it's time."

He sits down on the edge of the little bed in our motel room. I have made him a hot pot of coffee, which he drinks like he is listening.

"Tomorrow," I say.

I tell him that I have spoken to my parents on the telephone more often lately. As their grandchildren came along, they grew more resigned to Billy, and even will say hello to him on holidays and birthdays. I know if we go back home and bring the babies, things will be all right. My parents will come around. It seems to me that it is time for this to happen, for the break to be mended.

"I've never asked you for anything before," I say to Billy, and that is true. "I'm going home," I repeat.

"But I've just started my ministry here. I can't leave behind our membership."

We have signed on eight retired persons, who have liquidated all of their assets to join our congregation. We are based in motor homes, on land one of them has donated, in the Gallatin Valley near Bozeman. It's just two acres, and we're crowded together, always listening to the whine of someone else's radio.

"You've got reservation land," I said, "and we could get a bigger parcel of land out near my folks. We could buy up a building in town and open a God-based bookstore. But I want to live back where my family lives, close to the farm. I miss all that flat land, green crops, those clouds. We grew everything," I tell him. "The big crops, soybeans, flowers, flax. I miss the blue fields. The yellow mustard fields. Sun-flowers turning all day to catch the light. I miss the house garden. Mint for iced tea. Tomatoes big as your foot."

Billy thinks about it. Maybe, in the end, it is the mention of the farm's acreage, 888 acres, although he knows about my two brothers. It's not like I'm going to inherit the thing, or so it seems then. For one week, I can tell he's mulling it over and I say nothing, worried I'll tip the balance if I do speak, say the wrong thing or say too much.

Then one night, at meeting, he raises his arms and he makes the announcement. We are going to move. And I feel happy, so lucky, so proud as he is standing slim and handsome, fresh-faced and smiling, before his followers, that I don't think right then where they will live. The eight of them, the four of us, hold hands tight and pray in a circle. We sing for an hour, then split up. That night we all begin packing and several days later we set off in a caravan. It is not until we cross the county line that I realize with a jolt, though nothing is expressed, that the place Billy has in mind to park the trailers is my parents' farm. Where else?

When I ask him, he says, "I'll take care of their objections. I'll talk to them."

He grins. His silvery, curved sunglasses reflect me and reflect the land to either side, now absolutely flat. The sky is gray-gold with dust. The sun is huge and blurred, and seems to hang above us longer here and cast a richer and more diffused light. My parents have told me that there was a long, terrible heat wave this early May. It was a record spring, rainless and merciless. Although the temperatures have gone down somewhat, there has still been no rain, and the earth is suffering.

It is just like when I first met Billy. Another drought. But we'll end it.

"We'll bring rain," I say, excited, when we are just a few miles away from the farm. It is just something to say at the time, but Billy looks at me and starts to get reflective. We are waiting for the Armageddon that never came on Billy's date, which was just a preliminary date anyway, says Billy. This Armageddon we are waiting for is a different one than the usual, and the signs for it are multiplying, according to Billy's correlation between the Bible and the business pages. But while we are waiting for the universe to end, Billy gets the notion, as we turn down the road, that we should pray for rain to delay the inevitable. That is what he tells my folks, not fifteen minutes later. We have left the others parked at the turnoff.

I'm hugging and crying with my father and mother, and they're exclaiming over the babies. Uncle Warren is in the background, strained and vigilant. He's shaking with the volume of emotion set loose around him. And with his own thoughts. I am careful not to meet his raving eye. It is a prodigal's return. They are forgiving of me—it's each other they are hard on. They do not hold a grudge about my absence, even after all the trouble they've been through. They seem to accept Billy. Politely, in a grave voice, my mother beckons him up the stairs and into her domain. She is a glass collector—bowls, figurines, vases, tableaus. I hold Judah firmly in my grasp and give Lilith to my father. We walk into the living room and hear Billy exclaiming over the glass. He notices each and every artifact, runs his fingers along the curves of my mother's green unicorn, polishes a heavy blue egg with the side of his cuff. And after he has finished with the glass, he goes out to the sheds and the barns with my father. I don't know what they do out there, or what Billy says, but as they return Billy's hand is firm on my father's back and my father is frowning in concentration, ducking his head up and down. My father's face is long and tired. His eyes are the washed-out white-blue of an overworked German. His shock of white hair hangs thick between his eyes like the forelock of a horse.

"What did you speak to Dad about?" I ask Billy that night, as we're curled together on the three-quarter bed I slept in all my life. The children are down beside us in a trundle. I can hear their whimpering baby sighs.

"We talked about your brothers. One's hit the skids and the other would rather join the navy than go into farming. Plus they are having trouble taking care of your uncle. He wanders off. They found him half dead of exposure. Found him taking an ax to a cow."

"Ax to a cow?"

Billy shrugs and his voice gets intense now, the voice he uses at the ends of his sermons, the saving voice. "We could help them put your uncle in the state home, and you could have the farm if we just stayed here, you know that."

I do not answer for a long time. Outdoors, the night is still, just the sound of black crickets sawing in the cracks of the foundation, just the thin tangle of windbreaks and the dew forming and collecting on the powder-dry earth. I have been with Billy three years and I have spoken an unearthly language. I have spoken directly in the power, to spirit, but I'm still only nineteen, the age some girls start college. Some girls just finish high school then. I feel so old, so captured by life already. As we lay together in the dark, the yard lights off to save on the electric bills, as the moonless night covers us all, I feel something else, too. Half-awake and drifting, I feel the stark bird that nests in the tree of the Holy Ghost descend and hover.

I open my mouth to call Billy's name, but nothing. The wings flutter lower, scored white, and the down of its breast crackles faintly as the sparks jump between us. The bird flattens its wings across my breast, brushing my nipples. Then it presses itself into me, heated and full. Its wings are spread inside of me and I am filled with fluttering words I cannot yet pronounce or decipher. Some other voice is speaking now, a constant murmur in my head. Something foreign that I will hide from Billy until I understand its power. I'll hide it from everyone, I think, because it's rich and disturbing and something about it reminds me of my uncle and I wonder if his rage is catching.

The next morning, I put Lilith in her playpen outdoors, by the garden, and I set into weeding. The garden is in reach of the hose, so there's carrots feathering, and purple bush beans that will turn green when boiled. There's about ten rows of sweet corn, surrounded by a string fence hung with glittering can lids, to keep out raccoons. Later on in the summer, I'll walk the windbreaks looking for currants and juneberries, and still later chokecherries, wild plums to make a tart jam.

My mother comes out and stoops to the hoe, chopping the earth fine then carving in a little trench, putting in a late crop of Sugar Anns. She's leaner, and wrinkled with sudden age. Lines have webbed her cheeks and pulled down her eyelids, and even her full, pretty mouth is scored and creased. My first brother only calls for money, my other brother left three months ago and made his decision never to return. They didn't even mention that on the phone, but I do think I sensed the change occurring, the desolation. It is why I returned out of the blue, drawn by the sensation of my parents' loneliness, which I did not understand.

My father has been working the place practically alone, so he's let most of the fields go fallow and sold off all the stock but five milkers. Our return is already renewing his hopes, though. High on the tractor, my father goes to see what of the new hay is not yet burnt hollow, what may survive. Watching my mother's sharp elbows swing as she backs down the bean rows, hoeing, I think that maybe what Billy said isn't so terrible. Maybe it is not so awful to consider the reality of the situation. Maybe I should even get together with my parents and make some plans.

But there is no need. Billy says it all. Every night, back in Dad's office, Billy helps him straighten out the mess, helps file, and helps decide which bills to pay on and which to string along. Dad has agreed, with surprising disinterest, to let the retired people camp near an old burnt farmstead where a hand-pump well is still in operation. The end of our land bumps smack up to the reservation boundary. This was reservation, Billy says, and should be again. This was my family's land, Indian land. Will be again. He says it flat out with a lack of emotion that disturbs me. Something's there. Something's different underneath.

As one month and another month goes on, my husband, between attending to the needs of his people, guest-preaching for rain at revivals held all through the area, between learning how to run a tractor and use milking equipment and bale hay with my father, hardly sleeps. Billy seems to whirl from one thing to the next, his energy blooming, enormous, unflagging. The food he eats! Whole plates of spaghetti, pans of fresh rolls. There are nights he paces Dad's office, late, writing sermons and signing checks, for Dad has given him the power of signature. Sometimes at dawn I stumble downstairs for coffee and he is sitting there, grinning. Still up from the day before. Billy grows as the heat withers everything else. He drinks the well dry! That summer, we borrow from the bank and sink another well. Flushed and enormous, he splits the bottom of his pants.

"I never had parents." He chokes up, embracing my mother as she lets out and resews the seams of his pants. "I never knew what it was like to live in a family before."

She smiles at his drama, her face melting in the heat like wax. Uncle Warren watches from the corner, stiff as a stick doll, his jaw alone moving as he mutters an endless indecipherable low monologue. Sssssh, says my mother, keeping Uncle quiet.

My mother bakes a cake from scratch every day. Billy eats it. He earns money with his preaching, hires a lawyer to incorporate us all as a church, so we needn't worry over taxes. Soon, my parents' farmhouse becomes a focus. Each night, the rest of the congregation comes over and we all pray together, in the living room, crying and witnessing, begging forgiveness, and, when pure, sitting in a circle all together, channeling spirit. My mother is loud and extraordinary—who knew? My father more reserved, blinking at what she spills, the plenitude and triviality of her sins. As for Uncle Warren, his eyes grow pleading and he seems to cringe beneath the weight of all he hears. I begin, because Billy is so large and overpowering, to sit near my father on these nights. It is as if my dad needs protection. I think that he's grown more frail, although perhaps it's simply relative. He seems thinner because Billy has expanded to such a marvelous size, outweighing us all, and splendid in his new white suits.

Another month passes and Billy's chins double so he wears a thick flesh collar. We make love every night, but I am embarrassed. He is so loud, so ecstatic. I am tossed side to side on top of him, as if I am riding a bull whale. I make him wear a sleeveless undershirt so I can hold on to the shoulder straps like handles. The bed creaks like the timbers of a boat going down in a gale, and when he comes I feel heavy and swamped. I am afraid of getting pregnant again. I am afraid of what's happening. The house, once calm in its barbed, brown atmosphere, once lonely and predictable, crawls with people now. They are continually praying with my mother and cleaning savagely, with harsh chemicals. Everything smells of Pine Sol. The yard is gouged with the tire marks of cars. People break the branches off the butterfly bush to fan themselves when the spirit revs their temperature. And all this time, all this time, I don't speak in tongues or feel very much when I pray. I don't get my pictures back. All of that's gone.

I don't know who I married anymore. It's like he's supernatural. He is horribly tireless, exhausting everyone so much that we have to take shifts to keep up with him. I carry his shirts, socks, underwear, trousers, out to the clothesline to hang. They are so large now they do not require clothespins. I drape them like sheets and then I sit, worn-out, where I am hidden from his eye. He talks rain. He still talks Armageddon. The farm is made over to me now, and through me to Billy. He talks about the founding of the chosen. We are the ones, he says, who will walk through the fire. We are the Daniels. He holds our son up before the eyes of the congregation and the poor boy is small as a fish in his hands.

Finally, it is the picnic table and the iron bench that brings me to the end of this part of our life and the bigger, uncontrollable force that Billy becomes. The table is set out in the bare backyard, and it is made of sheet metal, steel pipes, and a welded cross bar, hammered into the ground. Dad made it for days it was too humid to eat indoors, and for general celebrations, of which we never had one. The whole area is laid out where the view is nice so that Mother, fond of her pretty yard and flowers, could gaze past a row of wild orange daylilies after she worked in the garden. She could pause, rest her eyes on a bit of loveliness. There is even an iron-lace bench for sitting on, maybe reading, though nobody ever opened a book there.

The August heat has let up briefly, then closed down again. Uncle Warren is chipping chicken shit off the perches, swearing in a low, grating tone at the hens that peck beside his feet. A few days ago, my mother crawled underneath a flowered sheet on the couch and now she will not rise. From her couch near the picture window, where she is quietly getting even thinner, my mother watches the picnic area, sees the sun rise and pass overhead. It is just a stubborn flu bug, she says, but there are times, watching as she simply lies still, her arms like straight boards placed to hold down the thin, puckery sheet, that I am afraid she'll die and I want to climb in next to her.

One humid afternoon I am sitting with my mother on the couch and we are watching Billy talk beneath the green ash tree with a few of the others. The babies are sleeping on the floor on folded quilts, with fans spilling air over them back and forth. Billy rarely drinks, and then, nothing stronger than wine. He is drinking wine now, a homemade variety from elderberries, made by a congregation member from a recipe passed down through her family. I suppose that the wine has got such a friendly history that Billy feels he can drink more than usual. And then, it is hot. The jars of wine are set in an icy cooler on the metal picnic table, and from time to time Billy lifts out a jar and drains it. As he talks, the sweat pours off his brow. His dark hair is wetted black, his body is huge, mounded over the iron bench. He lifts his thick arms to wrestle with a thought, drags it out of the air, thumps it on the top of his thigh. He is holding a rain prayer meeting, and as we sit in the heat of the afternoon, with the fans going, watching the others pray in the blazing sun, we notice that clouds are massing and building into fabulous castlelike and blazing shapes.

These clouds are remarkable, pink-gold and lit within. They are beautiful things. I point them out to my mother.

"Thunderclouds," she says, excited. "Push my couch closer to the window."

I should be out praying with the group, or cooking up a dinner for them all, or working on the garden to bring in tomatoes in case it does rain, in case those clouds bring hail. But I do nothing other than place a chair next to my mother's couch. Uncle Warren is sleeping with his eyes open, sitting straight in his chair. Lilith is limp and draped over a stuffed bear. I cover her with a crocheted afghan because a cool breeze has risen. My father enters the room. He has come to point out the clouds. Warren's eyes sharpen. Outside, Billy continues, wringing his hands into big golden fists, sobbing with the power, drinking the wine in swigs, shouting.

Now the wind rises, slapping the branches crazy. The clouds ride over the land, gathering and bunching, reflecting light. They are purple, a poisonous pink, a green as tender as the first buds of spring. The clouds cover the horizon and within the mass, as the thing opens over us, we see the heart of the storm, the dark side of the anvil shot through with an electric lacery of light.

A cold wind rises out of the ditches, driving before it the odor of sour mud water and then fresh. Droplets, soft and tentative, plop down and the thunder is a cart full of stones, rumbling closer.

Still they keep praying with their hands held up and their eyes tight shut. Beneath the whipping leaves, pelted and in danger, they huddle. Their voices are a windy murmur. His voice stands out among them, booming louder as the storm comes on.

A burst of radiance. The flowers fly into the air and scatter in the yard. Another crack so loud we're right inside of the sound. Billy Peace, sitting on the iron bench like an oracle, is the locus of blue bolts that spark between the iron poles and run along the lantern wires into the trees. Billy, the conductor with his arms raised, draws down the power. The sound of the next crack slams us back from the window, but we crawl forward again to see. A rope of golden fire snakes down and wraps Billy twice. He goes entirely black. A blue light pours from his chest. Then silence. A hushed suspension. Small pools of radiance hang in the air, wobble, and then disappear. A few drops fall, mixed with small, bouncing marbles of hail. Then whiteness tumbles through the air, ice balls smash down the mint and basil and lemon balm so the scents rise with the barbecue smell of burnt skin.

We say nothing. The babies sleep. And Billy Peace?

He is a mound, black and tattered, on all fours. A snuffling creature of darkness burnt blind. We watch as he rises, gathers himself up slowly, pushes down on his thighs with huge hands. Finally, he stands upright. I grab my mother's fingers, shocked limp. Billy is alive, bigger than before, swollen with unearthly power. We step away from the window. He bawls into the sky, shaking his head back and forth as the clouds open. Harsh silver curtains of water close across the scene. We turn away from the window.

"Mom," I say, "we've got to stop him."

"No one's ever going to stop him," she answers.

# The Kindred

ONE DAY, AS I am standing in a strip of shade, my uncle walks up and speaks to me, low, without looking at me.

It's on you, I can see it.

What's on me?

It's on you, I can see it.

What? What?

I can see it.

What?

You're gonna kill.

Shut up.

It's on you. You're gonna kill.

We put him in the state hospital and I stayed on the farm while my parents died. Billy left and toured his ideas until at last he developed a religion. Not a servant-to-God relationship, not a Praise Your Lord, not a Bagwam, not a Perfect Master, not a dervish or a mahara-ji. It was a religion based on what religion was before it was religion. Of course it had to be named and organized as soon as Billy Peace discovered it, but he tried not to use the trigger words. There was no God after Billings, no savior, for instance, by Minneapolis, where others told me Billy could have used it. By the time he and his followers backtracked across the border and then down, zigzagging home, there was only spirit. Most people did not understand this. Billy even let go of the concept of an Antichrist. The devil implied its opposite, and worshippers found the devil more attractive, Billy felt, than the woolly bearded father figure in their childhood dreams. It was like this, though it always changed. There was spirit, and that was vast, vast, vast, so vast we had to shut out the enormousness of it. We were like receivers, Billy said; our brains were biochemical machines, small receptors that narrowed down the hugeness of spiritual intelligence into something we could handle.

Our individual consciousnesses were sieves of the divine. We could only know what our minds could encompass safely. The task, as Billy saw it, was not to stretch the individual's barriers, as you might expect—not exactly that. Billy believed that a group of minds living together, thinking as one, had the potential to expand further than any individual. If we opened ourselves, all at once, in one place, we might possibly brush the outskirts, the edges of that vastness of spirit. A circle of linked rubber bands, touching fingertips, we sat some nights, all night, into morning, humming on the edge of that invert field, that sky. He took his time organizing his strategy and his purpose. He took care smoothing out the rough spots in the Manual of Discipline. And planning, raising money, finding people who met his standards. At first, he took the strong-willed, the purposeful, the cerebral, the experimental. Then he took the ones with rational explanations. Lately, he took the wounded, the ones with something missing, though they had to be organized at the same time. He looked for the ones who held down long-term jobs, especially. They had to have typed résumés. He took no one on faith. They had to sit with him, thinking, for hours. He had to test their quality of mind. They were not superstitious, they were not fundamentalists. They might believe the world was coming to an end and that the end would be an economic nightmare. They might believe in god if god was indivisible from light. They were never former Roman Catholics—it was like those were inoculated. Sometimes they were Jews a generation or two away from their own religious practice. Or Protestants, though few had ever been solid

Lutherans. No Baptists, no Hindus, no Confucians, no Mormons. No adherents of any other tribe's religion. No millenarians, no survivalists.

As for me, I didn't fit into any of those categories. On our travels south, I'd met a family who kept serpents and who believed they were directed to cast out devils by handling poisons. I'd stayed on in their church half a year, I'd sat with their grandmother Virginie, whose white hair reached to her waist. She said I never should cut mine. She'd grown eyes like a snake, a crack of darkness for a pupil, lips thin. One hand was curled black as a bone from the time she was bitten. The other lacked a ring finger. *You will get bit*, she told me, *but you will live through it in the power.* She gave me two of her serpents, one a six-foot diamondback, the other a northern copperhead with red skin and hourglass markings. *They have judgment in them*, she said. *And they have love.*

*So judge me*, I said when I held the snakes for the first time, *take me*, and they did. I found my belief. I knew from the first time that this was my way of getting close to spirit. Their cool dry bodies moved on me, skimmed over me, indifferent, curious, flickering, heavy, showing the mercy of spirit, loving me, sending a blood tide of power through me. I could set myself loose when I held the snakes. I became cold in my depth while my skin bloomed warm, calming them, and also I used pictures. I gave them the lovely heat, the flat rocks, the black rocks, the steady beating of the sun.

After I began to handle them in circle, the kindred stayed clear of me, and that was also a relief.

Still, I considered myself weak-willed, a follower, never speaking up if I could help it. I felt that I had no strong purpose or quality of mind. I was nice-looking but not anywhere near beautiful, I was young, I was younger than I had a right to be. I considered myself helpless, except when I held my serpents. Also, I had these pictures, and because I had them Billy would not let me go.

"Show me Milwaukee," Billy said one night.

That was where his family spent two years on relocation before his parents died. So I gave him Milwaukee as best I could. I lay there and got the heft of it, the green medians in June, the way you felt entering your favorite restaurant with dinner reservations, hungry, knowing that within fifteen minutes German food would start to fill you, German bread, German beer, German schnitzel. I got the neighborhood where Billy had lived, the powdery stucco, the old board-rotting infrastructure and the backyard, all shattered sun and shade, leaves, got Billy's mother lying on the ground full length in a red suit, asleep, got the back porch, full of suppressed heat and got the june bugs razzing indomitable against the night screens. Got the smell of Billy's river, got the first-day-of-school smell, the chalk and wax, the cleaned-and-stored-paper-towel scent of Milwaukee schools in the beginning of September. Got the milk cartons, got the straws. Got Billy's sister, thin and wiry arms holding Billy down. Got Billy a hot-dog stand, a nickel bag of peanuts, thirst.

"No," said Billy, "no more."

He could feel it coming though I avoided it. I steered away from the burning welts, the scissors, pinched nerves, the dead eye, the strap, the belt, the spike-heeled shoe, the razor, the boiling hot spilled tapioca, the shards of glass, the knives, the chinked armor, the sister, the sister, the basement, anything underground.

"Show me, show me." Billy was half asleep. He didn't know what he wanted to see, and of course I don't mean to imply that he would see the whole of my picture anyway. He would walk the edge of it, get the crumbs, the drops of water that flew off when a bird shook its feathers. That's how much I got across, but that was all it took. When you share like that, the rest of the earth shuts. You are locked in, twisted close, braided, born. And I could do it, just that much, and he needed it. Escape.

"Show me."

So I showed him, and I showed him. Another year passed and the discipline grew tighter and more intense as the spirit ripped into Billy and wouldn't spare us, either.

❧

ONE JANUARY NIGHT he came into the room and talked to the children and me all night, squeezing our faces in his thick, hot palms, slapping us to stay awake, urging us to stay aware.

"Listen up! Last things are on us!"

I wept and the children wept, but he would not let us sleep.

"There's something incongruent, something in you, something blocking the channel, something blacking out the peephole, narrowing the frequency."

"No, there isn't. These are your children."

"You are mine. Your lives are mine. I will do with you as spirit wills. Get down! Get down! Get down on the floor!"

He looked at us with a skeptical loathing, and the black hours passed. Finally, he nodded off. The children fell across my lap. By then I was all nerved up and wide awake, so I went to my glass boxes. I took out my serpents to pray with. They curled around me, in and out of my clothing, comforting. The serpents were listening, and I heard it, too. The chinook blew in. Just like that.

The temperature shifted radically. The warm wind could melt the deep snow packs in hours. I heard the rafters groan, the snow already dripping. I smelled dirt and rain. It was blowing through, and soon the winter grass, deep gray, blond, would poke through the drifts, The air was flowing, moving, warm currents of dark air heaving fresh out of the southwest across wet roads, slick roads. And then the wolf dogs came out, raising long muzzles to the air.

I started up in a moment of fear, and as I did, my copperhead struck me full on, in the shadow of my wing, too close to my heart not to kill me. *In the Lord,* I said, as I was taught, and I gathered up my red-back beauty. She wore time itself in those hourglasses and I felt the sand rush through them as I let her flow back into her case. Then I lay down. I let the poison bloom into me. Let the sickness boil up, and the questions, and the fruit of the tree of power. I let the knowing take hold of me. The understanding of serpents. My heart went black and rock hard. It stopped once, then started again. When the life flooded back in I knew that I was stronger. I knew that I'd absorbed the poison. As it worked in me, I knew that I *was* the poison and I was the power.

*Get away from him and take the children*, the serpent said to me from her glass box, as she curled back to sleep in her nest of grass.

><

LONG TRAIN RIDES, the slow repetitive suspense of travel. I had persuaded Billy to let me go all the way out to Seattle in order to raise money for the kindred. I took my snakes along, well fed in their pouches, curled to my body's warmth. If they became too active I'd set them back inside their leather cases on the cold floor by my feet. I'd made him let me go, although in some way I knew I would not return all the way, not after I was bit.

All the whole trip, I let it gather. On the way back, I let it come. Curled double among the sighs and groans of other passengers, I dozed and woke, cramped and sore, stiff in the bounds of my two-seater. In the dark Cascades I understood I was a darkness blacker than these mountains. The knowledge sank into my joints like something viral, and I sat from then on in quiet pain. That changed to fear somewhere in the Kootenai.

Outside the window, black and motionless, without limit, deep forest bowed in fresh snow. I considered what came next and hit a wall packed white. My children were behind it. My love for them was brute love. I would never let them go. Light broke just outside of Whitefish, Montana. Breakfast was announced. I made up my mind and secured myself within my decision. Once I had done this, my thoughts cleared. I sat down in the dining car and ordered eggs. They came with piles of browned cottage potatoes, buttered toast, grape jam in little cartons. I ate a few bites and drank milky coffee from a plastic cup. I watched the dark lodge pole, the yellow larch go by, more trees than some people see their whole lives. They turned like spokes, reached like arms, sifted snow like powder through their needles. Great spumes of whiteness puffed, crashing from their boughs.

Where a big derailment and grain spill had occurred two years before, a fat bear stood, a blackie stirred from hibernation, probably drawn by the lye-soaked and fermented wheat that the railroad workers had buried underground, behind an electric fence, out of reach. Everyone else in the car was deep in conversation or concentrating on burnt pancakes, mild tea. I was the only one who saw the bear and I said nothing. It swung its head, smelling diesel, harsh metal, maybe steam of boiling oatmeal. Perhaps it was used to the eastbound number 28 because it didn't lope off, didn't move away, just waited in its own shadow while we passed. My future seemed impenetrable, a cloud pack, fog socked in. And freedom seemed unreachable, like all that sweet grain bulldozed into the hill. My life was a trap that had closed on me with soft teeth, from under snow. Up here seems endless and free, so wide it hurts. It does hurt. For we are narrow, bound tight, hobbled, caught in sorrow out of mind.

Grass, water, summer fireweed and thistle, come save me now, I thought. I didn't call on god, though. He was on my husband's side.

When Frenchie picked me up at the station, I was gone already. Evidently, I looked and acted the same though, because Frenchie helped put my things into the back of the truck and got in front without comment. Billy didn't do things like pick passengers up at the depot, because that might have meant waiting around and he never sat still. Every moment of his time was now dedicated. Valuable.

"I'll buy you a meal," I said to Frenchie, "I raised a good ten thou." And I had.

Besides the waitressing job, which I used to pick up money when it was needed for some kind of equipment or spiritual campaign, I raised money for Billy by speaking at the big tent meetings and writing pamphlets and handling my snakes in the spirit-trance. All in all, I preferred waitressing. Just that the money at the stadium and tent revivals was so good. I knew that once I entered the compound it would be a long time before I saw much of the outside world again. That was why I got Frenchie to walk through the door of the 4-B's, home of the all-day breakfast, where I had worked a year and left with no hard feelings, even offers of a raise. It was as though I was a normal person there, any woman, and I needed to feel that now. Maybe I'd show a picture of my daughter, son, and nobody would comment on their gunnysack clothes, know their meaning, nobody would ask whether they had yet processed spirit.

Frenchie looked from side to side as he sat down, afraid. There was no rule exactly, about going to a restaurant to eat, but we both knew that we weren't supposed to, that we should be driving straight back to our home, to the kindred, that we should be saving money and not spending it on the second order of eggs that I wouldn't eat, or the weak black coffee that Frenchie would drink looking down into the brown pottery cup, refusing refills, feeling the hand of my husband on his shoulders, my husband's eyes heavy at the back of his neck, and Billy's voice, his voice always, radio-trained, pure and deep, full as thunder, round as hope. My husband's voice was perfect as he was perfect. Made in God. My husband's voice was redemption, a rope to hold in a whiteout. My husband's voice would change my mind as it had before, when I got back and entered into the mellow gold light surrounding him. I would sink in, go under, resistless in the dream that he dreamed with me in it. I would be a shadow, once more, a light thrown lovingly against a wall.

I drank my coffee slowly. I had to test myself by watching how I acted in front of one of us kindred. I was glad that it was Frenchie, who wasn't so observant. There was something scared and sidling about him, something not quite authentic. He had a handsome face if you really looked at it, nice bones, rich green eyes with thick brush eyelashes, firm mouth, straight nose. But he acted like a beaten animal—hunched, crept, spoke in an excusing lilt and never addressed you, just waited for you to speak. He took what he could get. That was his motto, I suppose. I didn't want to make him any trouble and so I didn't exchange more than a few polite words with another waitress I had known while employed at the 4-B's. I paid up with extra money I had been given in Seattle and not declared, and I said that we could go now, we could go home. But just before we left, I looked around the place, and even though it was a spare room, big and functional, with orange plastic booths and the usual salad island, even though in the realm of restaurants and cafés it was nothing special, light from outside the windows falling in rich bands of smoke was almost piercing to me in its promise.

When it was over, I would return here, I decided. I would sit down and unfold the silly napkin with the black and yellow bee, spread it out carefully onto my lap. I would order the all-day breakfast for my children. They would eat. And when I saw them eating, I would be able to eat too.

Until that time, no food would cross my lips but that I needed to gain strength, no movement would be wasted, no coin, no breath. From that moment on, I was a closed secret. I was everything the mountain knew. I was the unturned stone.

And the snake under it, that too.

&#10035;

SOME OF US lived in chicken coops, some of us lived in storage barrels, some of us lived outdoors beneath the solstice sun. Some of us lived deep inside the hills, some of us lived out on the range with cattle, or on tractors, or in an old Burlington boxcar. Some of us lived with husbands or wives, some with children, only children. Some of us were saved in heat, some of us were saved in winter's cold. Some of us were simply curious and had never been saved at all. Some of us lived right with Billy, back in the new log house, behind the fireplace, and all day our clothes smelled of pine pitch and smoke of midnight fires. I was his only true wife, with his name on me and my children, and that was my reward. His greater fidelity, that is—not the lesser, the procreation he quietly affirmed with others. He belonged to me in the greatest sense and held that fact to my face, a shining mirror.

By the time we got to the turn-off road, narrow and perfectly kept (not the rutted road the heavy equipment used), my hands were cold inside my knitted gloves. The ranch buildings came into distant view and, inside, I felt empty, hungry, ravenous but not for food. My skin was desperate to hold my children. We reached the guardhouse. Sweat trailed the inside of my arms. My face felt rigid with the effort of posing my features. I was cold all through, chilled to an ache, to the center. In the Manual of Discipline, to which all kindred must adhere, a guilty heart is a dead heart, burnt to a cindery knob, and it is to be rejected. Cast out. As we rode the curved drive, gravel crackling against the tires, I began to shake. My legs felt watery, unstable. My jaws hurt. I knew that Billy would look deep into me at first glance and see the black smoke, the steam, the blue radiance of betrayal. He would pray. He would look at me with triumph and take me back into our marriage, into the faith.

He called out to me, waving an arm in the air, pleased with me and pleased at the picture of the welcoming husband that he made. He was standing on the long porch of the two-story log house, the gray log house with the chinks cemented fast. He had not been waiting. He'd sent Deborah, the eternal penitent, his personal secretary. She had probably given him a blow job underneath his desk, then blotted her lips on a hankie and done the waiting. She had watched for us on the road and then summoned him from his office and the bank of phones and our all-night steno crew that never shut down. Deborah had come to get him and he had left his office, just in time to greet us, and he was impatient. I left the cab of the pickup like I was jumping off a high board into a pool of water, not knowing whether I could swim at all. Here was a new element, deep green, emotional, treacherous. I ran straight to him. Impetuous joy was what I wanted to convey. I ran to him and he held me against his tired, his soft, his body of the solid current. His was the only man's body I had known. I felt its frightful goodness, its secret extravagance of love for me. His heart beat hard underneath my cheek. I couldn't turn away.

Huge, soft, yet muscled with a hopeless power, Billy surrounded me. Not vast as he'd been when he'd absorbed the lightning, but big enough. I lost myself in the familiarity of flesh and voice. His voice was pink as the sky. His eagerness and pleasure at my return bloomed all around me as we went into the room where the children were playing, and where I was allowed to surprise them at their games.

I watched them for a moment, before they turned. I still had names for my children, though children's names were now forbidden. Mine were their old names, now secret names. I think that their father had forgotten what they were called.

Judah was sand-haired and tough. It always seemed that his wires were pulled tighter, sharper, that the connections were raw and quick, that he was not just more intelligent in mind but throughout his entire body. His eyes were large, sad, warm, his father's changing colors. Sometimes his deepened under strong emotion to a deep-set black. He had my features, people said, though I couldn't see it. I could tell Lilith's though; she looked like me. She looked like my grade school pictures, brows drawn together, frowning, always unprepared. She was shy and stubborn, both at once, and her sudden attacks of laziness were pure will, never helpless. I thought she was terribly intelligent, but there was no outside testing. I had no way of knowing exactly what she knew in relation to other children. Now she ran to me, gave herself to me with completeness, melting to me, smelling of salt and snow. I held them both close, put my face in the warm coarse hair. I breathed in their radiance, and we began to rise, light as cake. We hovered just an inch above the woven rug, turning, holding. From the door behind us, freezing air swirled around us and tightened.

⋇

DEEP IN THE night, every night, through the space across the great open center of the house, I woke to the comfort of the stuttering rings of telephones, the messages of the converted that came in after the monthly broadcasts that he taped here or in Grand Forks or Fargo or Winnipeg, then broadcast all over the world. Each ring brought cash. Women called to say they'd seen a light in the east, heard a voice rise from the laundry chute, felt power boil up between their knuckles, understood another exquisite language that hovered in the air all around them. Women called to say their loaves fell in the shape of Billy's face, their uncooked raw meat muttered his name. The little notes clipped around their checks told about their children, how when changing diapers they had known the call. Or how, when baking cakes, the straw came out of the batter with a continuous musical tone that signified salvation. They answered their home phone. Their own voice said Be Saved. Their washing machines refused to wash unless Billy's broadcast was playing. Their hands hurt with the knowledge and their sex lives were numbing them, hurting them. They were dying of dyspepsia, of cancer, of deadly warts, of an unusual virus, of hives, of internal parasites, of cerebral palsy, of cancer, of cancer.

Men wrote and called telling Billy their car radios exploded in the word, their power tools cried out, their names went dead, all of a sudden no one remembered who they were. They did not remember their own names either. Their fillings played his broadcasts in their heads. Their mothers had warned them and they hadn't listened. Men called trusting Billy with outrageous infidelities. Men wrote dying of enlarged hearts, enlarged prostates, of deep boils, of foul weather, of senile madness, of a wasting virus, of the kiss of tsetse flies, of food, of garden herbicides, of home-owner's accidents, of thrombosis, of clotted veins, of black depression, of cancer, of cancer. All night, through the whole night, the bank of telephones doodled and whined, and our people recorded these salvations. In the morning cheap onionskin littered the desks and floors and the testimonials were dragged across the carpet on the feet of tired typists to the bottom of the stairs.

⋈

"I CAN TELL it was a good trip," Billy said.

"Yes," I answered.

He put his hands on either side of my face, gazed into my eyes. He didn't really see me. He was looking at his own reflection. He was watching himself watch me and between him and his own regard of himself I was invisible.

"I like train rides," I said, so relieved I could taste blood in my mouth.

Then he said, "If you ever leave me, Marn, I will take the children. I will keep them. And you know what I will do with them."

He smoothed his hands across my hair, closed me against him, and then we shut the door to our room and he did as he sometimes did, one of the ways. He stood me next to the bed, took off my clothing piece by piece, then made me climax just by brushing me, slowly,

169

here, there, just by barely touching me until he forced apart my legs
and put his mouth on me hard. It took almost an hour, by the bedside
clock. It took a long time after that. He came into me without taking
off his clothes, the zipper of his pants cut and scratched. I cried out.
He pushed harder, then withdrew. He held my wrists behind my back
and forced me down onto the carpet. Then he bent over me and
gently, fast and slow, helplessly, without end or beginning, he went in
and out until I grew bored, until I wanted to sleep, until I moaned,
until I cried out again, until I wanted nothing else, until I wanted him
the way I had the very first time, that first dry summer.

The next morning, I took out the money in circle, counted it, and
offered it to Billy. He set it in a pile before him, blessed it, and handed
it over to Bliss, our treasurer. She was a heavy blond woman out of
Aberdeen, South Dakota, very competent and self-proud. She had a
bulldog's heavy face, drooping cheeks, a big ugly smile. And to think,
sometimes I had to laugh, I'd brought Bliss here. I had saved this
woman from venereal disaster. She had been a sexual dynamo, full
of blasted encounters, confessions, and still a kind of raw blood energy leached right from her through the boards of the floor. She was
diabetic and used long needle syringes for her injections, not the short
kind I'd seen others use. She gave the pain up, an offering, she said.
I thought she gave off a charred smell, myself. I thought she reeked,
but she professed to like me, and because she was also my children's
spirit mother I was forced to like her too, with all my heart. In fact,
she was a woman I was pledged to give my life to if she ever asked
me for it. Billy Peace had chosen Bliss, but she had, I thought, looking at her that new morning, the thick and punished hands of a
butcher.

She rose now, a larded green warrior in her sweat suit and army
jacket. She held out her thick hands and for a long moment we put
ours out, too, returning the energy. A song started and we had to let it
go around twice. Then she put her hands down and gave the financial
report. She shouted it out as though it were a kind of prayer, and since
it was all numbers and dizzy quotes of percentages and tax advan-

tages and ways that the money would go in here, come out there, look nice, still work for us, we all nodded at the right time, any time she asked for it, and smiled.

"All right," she said at last. "Bottom line. We need three to work a day job and give assistance with the profits."

"Let's all meditate on who," suggested Frenchie, lowering his head.

We did, all of us. Deborah's hand in mine was cold, cold as light. If I had anyone whom I counted as a friend it probably was Deborah, whose children were close in age to mine, and with whom I'd battled small temptations in the garden and the kitchen. She was a dark long-haired meek woman with exhausted eyes. My skin was pale, the palest it could be, Snow White pale, ghost pale, grass pale. Good skin, nice skin, not marred by a vein or freckle. Lilith had the same fine skin, the perfect covering, the wonderful elastic veneer that allowed for every interior change, compensated, stretched or shrank at will, smoothed or roughened with each change in weather. Sensitive skin that wrapped itself exquisitely over our bones. I sat there, holding hands, letting the energy pass through me and over me, absorbing the invisible rays of ardor and togetherness that we shoveled from ourselves into the middle of the circle. We basked in this communion, wallowed in it like animals on those mornings when we woke bereft.

I squeezed light from Deborah's palm, and she startled in surprise or pain.

"What's wrong?"

"Nothing, just the day before my cleansing," I whispered back.

She nodded and lowered her head again, into the steaming twilight of the morning's meditations. I looked up, a thing I'd never done before in circle. I unbolted my eyes and from under the edges of my scarf I looked straight into the eyes of Bliss, who was watching me with the money eyes. Empty eyes. I knew better than to meet those eyes. I had nearly tipped my hand. If she knew what I was thinking, what I wanted to do, it would be over before it started. If she even suspected. Bliss, the one I had to watch, the undoer, the stone turner. I smiled vaguely, as though I was confused, waking from and then submerging once again in my dream. I closed my eyes again and from inside my own dark consciousness I stared down, far down, into the shaft of an empty mine.

We were imaging gold. We were visualizing total and complete original support. We were seeing chunks, flakes, beads, veins, whole nuggets. We were seeing through the rock and gumbo, through igneous peat and shale, through the vestiges of lost black time, through the ivory teeth and petrified wood, through the bones and the tarry blood of dinosaurs. We were seeing gold, tasting it, biting gold coins, believing. We were going to start digging in the back field pretty soon.

⋈

I BEGAN TO keep a diary—not the usual written record, but a mental diary of important moments. Here is a list I memorized:

Billy walked into the bedroom one night and took a deep breath and sucked all of the air out of it.

Billy waited until I came out of the shower and stood outside the door and as I stood there naked and streaming water he dried me with the heated iron of his gaze.

Billy came toward me with his arms out, weeping, saying that no one could comfort him but me.

Billy made the children and me kneel until we fell over gasping.

We drank sour, clotted milk as he grabbed our necks, hissed in our ears.

He said he loved us to the very death, me, the children, that's why he would not take his eyes off us. He watched us sleep all night.

Billy put his head in my lap the next morning, and snored while I sat still for hours, thinking.

Billy caressed me until I fainted inside and then he stopped and fell asleep.

Billy said he wanted me and then he made himself come.

Billy brought me a little tray on which he'd placed a cup of steaming hot chocolate. With a boy's pride he watched me drink it.

Billy made me come with my eyes shut, with my mouth taped, with my ears sealed, with my legs and arms bound.

Billy said he was going to make me his forever. Wait right here.

Billy scratched the moving figure-eight sign of eternal life into the inside of my thigh with a needle. He sang to me to soothe me while I wept. He licked the blood away and pressed his mouth to my center to distract me while he touched the wound with alcohol. He rubbed raw ink, dark red ink, into the sign.

His was there, even darker.

The next night after he marked me, I brought my serpents into bed with me, naked. Get in, I said when my husband entered the room. Billy stretched his hand toward his pillow and the rattle shook.

Gentle, gentle, I said.

You get them out of there, said Billy. You get them out of here, Marn, please do it.

They loved to curl in my armpits where my heat was strongest. It brought out their scent, which was a powerful, raw odor pure as sex.

Look at them, Billy. They're my lambs of god, I said.

You get them out of here, Marn. They don't like me.

It's because your flesh is cold and you sweat cold, I said. They don't like the smell of sweat. And you're too full of light. Me, I'm dark inside. Hot.

There is something bad in you, said Billy. I wish that I could cast it out.

No you don't, I laughed. You wouldn't cast out what you needed worst. It's the bad in me you need so bad.

Put them away, put them away right now, he said.

But he loved to fuck me with the musk of the snakes on me. He was smelling his fear.

⋈

WORK BEGAN AFTER the meditation. I was on kitchen attention. This was work we all did, even Billy, though at rare intervals. Cooking was done with love of spirit, and because Deborah was my partner I had looked forward to the tasks, especially since, in the middle of the afternoon, we were allowed to bring our children from the binding compound.

We were careful and precious about the things we ate and what we fed to one another. We had to be. There wasn't much. We tried to grow hothouse and hydroponic produce and failed. Our chickens were picked off by hawks. Our turkeys looked up in the rain and drowned. The geese flew off. The goats ate the garden. Weasels got the baby pigs and coyotes got the calves. Nobody knew how to farm except me and I missed my dad. Every two months we bought a fattened hog or steer and butchered it in the big cement killing room—an ugly process. I'd bought a bolt gun so I could kill efficiently, and after the moment of slaughter I always left. I couldn't stand watching the others hack the animals apart. It was nothing but chaos and waste.

Whenever Deborah and I had our children for the afternoon, we cooked. At least there were two of us who knew how to cook. We connected the big pasta machine and mixed up our dough for that, as well as for our breads and cookies. We peeled and riced our carrots for a creamed soup with dill. Our other vegetable was store-bought broccoli and we worried over it until we realized that if we mashed it with bread crumbs we could bake it with cheese and milk and it would go around further. When, at two, we went to get our children, we were exhausted and happy with our work and I could almost have forgotten myself in the flower of the day except that I couldn't stop my eyes from catching on certain things—the lock on the gate of the play area, the intercom in diapering, the way the windows shut and locked from inside, the walls built heavy, reinforced, a bunker.

A year ago I would have said the bunker kept the children from harm, from the outside, from corrupting influences, from the clouds and confusion of all that lived and breathed and moved outside the kindred. Now, gathering Judah, now, holding Lilith, stroking her unbearable warmth, bearing the joy of her arms hard and fierce at my waist, her whisper, small and vehement, *Mother*, a word banned except in secret, between us, I thought different. I kept my eyes fixed empty and smiled with careful neutrality over her shoulder. Anguish, their caretaker, gleamed in dull bereavement, a woman who'd lost all of hers. Drunk, she'd dived out of the flaming trailer. Left, her children burnt. Not mine. She wouldn't get mine. I was gathering myself in order to escape with them.

Judah breathed, hot, against my neck. Something had happened, again. Maybe the thing with Anguish, her prying touch, which I had complained about to Billy. I could not afford to complain again and alert any suspicion in his heart, so when I questioned Judah I begged for it not to be Anguish.

"Did she?"

"No, uh-uh, it was just, I disappointed Father, just now, just a few minutes ago, he was here and I got so nervous, got so nervous I forgot the week's maxim from the manual and he derided me."

"Derided?"

"He gave me schedule."

I held Judah, grabbed him close. Schedule! It meant that instead of school, Judah would be on schedule. There was always one of us in the room where we held our circle. One of us had to stay there and suffer. Pain kept the room clear for spirit, Billy had been told. But Judah was too young!

When?

Tomorrow.

You're sick. I'll do it for you.

There was a rule that another of us could suffer for the scheduled if they were too ill or being cleansed. I took Lilith and Judah back to the kitchen and smiled and joked and held them, as did Deborah, her children, while I searched the cabinet.

"What are you looking for?"

It was Billy, behind me, his voice deep and musical. But I had already hidden the soy sauce—a bottle of it choked down and Judah would run a slight fever. Enough to keep him off schedule, while I went on.

✄

TO STAND STILL for an entire day, to lose yourself in immobility, to feel your blood pump painfully, pool—I feared schedule so much that adrenaline surged up in me at the certainty. To get ready for schedule I ran. I ran my long route, my rattlesnake route, my porcupine grass route. To run is to revel in a pretend freedom. I spring along slowly, matching my breathing to my stride, passing the usual fences and fence lines, and thinking. Running is like riding on a train after a while, a motion that allows thoughts to drop down clear from a place in your mind that surprises you.

I saw that I was running in a wide false circle, hopelessly awakened.

Awakened, things had changed in me. Schedule, I'd never questioned. And the harm and the casual pain. Part of processing spirit was a discipline of the afflictions, for we only meet our maker in the unmaking, Billy would say. We mainly chose for ourselves. Bliss had a calcified heart. She beat her chest, and instead of a tiny diabetic's needle she used a Novocain plunger, long and satisfyingly grim. Anguish mortified her fingernails. Frances slept on bare boards, no blanket. Ate flesh only, therefore stank. My friend Deborah practiced servile and incomplete sex and welcomed her migraines. Billy practiced—just being who he was. Pain enough.

I ran farther and faster, in the loop I was allowed, perfectly warm in my light clothes, in the strengthening sun. The prairie garter snakes were out that day, warming themselves on rocks tilted toward the sharpest rays. They were black with yellow stripes and innocent yellow bellies. If you touched them, held them, they smelled of rotted flowers. I knew some of them by size and temperament. They were not poisonous like my lambs in their aquarium, but I loved the harmless ones too. They coiled up in balls to ride the winters out. Now they were stretched out lank and warm. Sage jabbed the air where the snow had sunk away from the earth in hot patches. I jumped burnished old hanks of grass and ran cow pasture nipped down to the meek and sorry ground, and still the sage, the sage, that flammable green, and farther over the fence a formation of snow geese returning.

I stopped and flung my arms wide and I turned in six circles. Sky over me, sky under me, sky to my north and south. Sky to my west. One person underneath it all alive and wondering, soaked in the great surround. When I wheeled and bucked dust from my feet I was running for the pure joy of moving in the air, in this life, in this goodness soaking up through the dirt.

That, I brought back to my discipline.

The first two hours of schedule were the worst. The standing motionless seemed impossible. Every muscle that would ache hurt and every bone protested and the heart, bored with so much reverse direction and taut stillness, beat sullenly in my chest. I could hear it and the feeling of that bird moving in the cage of my ribs was a whir of sickness. The third hour, that was better, and the fourth was nothing. It passed like a hand on my forehead, for I was lost in what I was seeing. A warm curtain of pain billowed in, out with each breath, and then parted. Through the jammed sensation a door opened and my serpents slid out to speak with me. My prince of diamonds, my queen of red dust. They talked to me in low, protective whispers, and told me what to do.

I listened and questioned and made certain that I understood each step. Then I bowed to them for my freedom. I thanked them for my life. I saw how I'd hold my prince rattler's head to the cloth, and how I'd carefully milk the venom from his fangs into the small spice jar I'd cleaned and washed. I'd use three snakes more that way until I had enough venom to fill the syringe I'd taken out of Bliss's medical cabinet—she had a whole box in there. I'd let the snakes go. I'd break their aquarium to pieces and grind the glass up and pour it down the well. I'd stick the tip of the loaded syringe into an apple and I'd roll it in a piece of coloring paper. I'd carry it. Anguish would demand to see what kind of picture Lilith had drawn, but I would paste on a great glittering grin and tell her that I couldn't, that it was a surprise for her father, which was true.

※

IT'S ON YOU, I can see it.

What's on me? What?

It's on you, I can see it, you're gonna kill.

※

I WAS DOWN, I'd collapsed, and the only way I could possibly get out of my situation was to have professed a vision, which I did. I'd learned from Billy about telling what I was going to do in advance. I whispered in his ear. *I saw how I was going to fuck you.* The hatred was an animal so big I wanted to let it take Billy in its jaw. But I couldn't, not yet. There would be days and there would be days. There would be a time to run and a time to halt, a time to kill and a time to harvest. There would be a time to assemble and dissemble, a time to understand my vision and a time to carry it out. A time to hold myself away and hold myself away and a time very finally to give.

That time finally came.

I climbed my husband hotly and set my two thumbs at the pulse beneath his jawbone and I pressed and stroked until I had him cornered and weak and then like a cat I stole his breath. All that night I robbed him with my greed, making him hard with my mouth and drawing from him with all the rest of me, furious and careful, instructive when he waned, and punishing. Then good to him. Ironing. He lay still under me as under a warm iron. I drew myself over and over the sheet of his back and across and down his legs, molding to every part of him, soothing the evil twin away, unwrinkling that bad one who'd crumpled himself into Billy like an igniting wad and me the kerosene. I tied his hands to the sides of the bed and I measured his face with my own faceless hunger. Kissed him with my speechless lips. Set him task after task and then, when he'd finished, as the light increased, I decided that I hated him so much that I would not let him breathe until I'd soldered myself inside of him. Until I ruled him so that he could hurt no one. Until I entered his bowels like a stream of lead and hardened in his guts and drove him even crazier. No, I would not let him go until I sank through his bones like a wasting disease. Ate him from the inside, devouring his futility, filling him with a beautiful craving.

I took the needle filled with the venom of the snake and tipped with the apple of good and evil from beneath the child's drawing paper, and popped off the apple. Then I pushed the needle quickly, gently, like an expert, for I'd seen this many times in my pictures, right into the loud muscle of his heart.

*There*, I said, stroking his skin where I withdrew the needle, *there*, as his eyes opened, *there it will be scorched.*

And as he bucked and sank away I got the picture. I'd tie a loud necktie around his throat, winch him up into the rafters. Got Bliss cutting him down. Got the sight of him lying still in the eyes of others, got the power of it and the sorrow. I got my children's old gaze, got them holding me with quiet hands, and got them not weeping but staring out calmly over the hills. I got Bliss running mad, foaming, blowing her guts, laughing and then retrieving Billy's spirit from its path crawling slowly toward heaven, got the understanding she would organize the others and take over from Billy, but that before they could pin me down in the Manual of Discipline we'd have scooped up the money already and run.

Oh yes, I got us eating those eggs at the 4-B's, me and my children, and the land deed in my name.

# Evelina

# The 4-B's

❧

I WAS PULLING a double shift and it was that slow time in the afternoon between the lunch and early supper crowd. To keep busy, because you never knew when Earl the manager would poke his fat head out the door of his office, I was filling ketchup bottles. Earl called it consolidating. We had a hollow plastic ring with threads on both ends. You put the ring on a half-full ketchup bottle, then upended another bottle on top and let it drain into the first bottle. We had only two of these rings, so it took a while to fill all thirty-five ketchup bottles at the restaurant. Sometimes, if everything was very dull, like on that afternoon, I'd balance half the bottles on the others, mouth to mouth, without the rings. The arrangement was precarious. After filling each bottle I'd wipe it clean and set it on the booth, make sure the salt, pepper, and napkin dispensers were filled up too. Then I'd either study French in my Berlitz Self-Teacher or sneak-read the paperback I had in my pocket (a little black and purple copy of *The Fall* by Camus) or I'd stare out the window.

That afternoon, I was doing all three things. The ketchup bottles were balanced in the back booth. I had just put down Camus and was now muttering, *Je vais à Paris, je vais à Paris. Je n'ai jamais visité la belle capitale de la France.* I was also staring out the window. So I saw Marn Peace arrive with her two children—I guessed they were hers, though I'd never seen her with children before. I knew Marn from the summer before, when she'd worked at the 4-B's. I also knew she had married Corwin's uncle, Billy Peace. I was just about to graduate and was working at the 4-B's, saving money up for college.

Marn parked across the street, got out of the car, an old beat-up Chevy, and she and her children walked across the street to the 4-B's front door. There was a stiff, spring wind and they pushed into it, hair flying, as they crossed. Marn's hands were white and knotted and she was gripping her kids, hard, but the kids didn't look like they minded it. They weren't pulling away. They didn't look punished or grim or sad, like you might expect knowing where they came from. They looked amazed, that's what I thought. They looked like they were walking out of the funnel of a tornado. Like they couldn't believe the things they'd seen whirling around in there. After a few moments, I went to let them in, because they were standing in front of the old wood and glass double doors, stuck, as if the sidewalk had reached up and hardened around their ankles.

When I opened the door, Marn finally grabbed the heavy brass frame beside my hand, letting the kids go in under her arm. Marn's skin looked parched and stiff, her cheeks were knobs of bone. She was a small woman, hair the color of twine, ears sticking through the limp strands of a braid that reached nearly to her waist. She glanced at me, eyes wide—I could see the whites nearly all the way around the intense blue iris—and she made a gasping smile that showed all her long white teeth.

Later on, I thought maybe that was the way a person looks who has just murdered her husband, because there were all sorts of rumors that she had done in Billy Peace.

Marn and her children walked in and took the last booth open, farthest from the windows. I had the ketchups in the very last booth, behind them. Their table was set for four so I took one setting off. She waved away the menu and ordered three number eights, the breakfast special with steak. Well done for all of them. Coffee, orange juice, water with ice. It had been warm the day before, but turned cold and spring-raw today. They were dressed like winter and shed their coats.

"I'll take them," I offered, and she handed me her children's coats but kept hers beside her on the booth bench. "I've got stuff in the pockets."

I gave crayons to the kids—a boy and girl, mouse-haired and pallid but with those dark Peace eyes. They began to color the cartoon cow and chicken figures on their place mats. They set the crayons carefully aside when the food came, bowed their heads, and folded their hands in their laps. I put the plates down before them. They stayed poised like that, just waiting. Maybe they were waiting for ketchup. I grabbed a half-consolidated bottle and put it on their table. Marn picked up her fork.

"Lilith, Judah," she said, "pick up your forks. And just eat."

The girl picked hers up first, watching her mother closely. Then the boy did. Marn took a mouthful of hash browns. The children watched her. They forked up hash browns and placed the food between their lips, then began to chew. All of a sudden, Marn grabbed the ketchup bottle and dumped ketchup onto their plates, first the girl's, then the boy's, then her own. She reached over and cut up their meat with jerky, excited, little saws of her knife. She dropped the knife with a clatter and began to shovel food into her mouth. The kids started picking up speed, and soon they were hardly stopping to breathe. When the food was gone, the toast devoured down to the crumbs and last tubs of jelly, I refilled Marn's coffee and cleared their plates. I asked Marn if she wanted her check.

"No," she said, her thin cheeks flushed. The children sat back in the booth, stupefied and glowing. "We're gonna have dessert." The children's faces became very alert.

"Really," she said. She scanned the room and the street outside, then got up to go to the bathroom. While she was gone, I came and gave the kids menus again. They bent over the list, their mouths forming the words.

"Banana cream pie," said the boy finally.

"You got it," said Marn, sitting back down at the table.

"Could I have ice cream too?" the boy asked in a small voice, then looked down at his lap.

"Chocolate sundae," said the girl. She smiled. She had big, cute bunny teeth in front.

"With nuts?" I said.

She looked blankly at her mother and Marn nodded. I went back to the kitchen and made the desserts extra big with whipped cream on top of the ice cream and maraschino cherries stuck all over the mound.

"What the hell are you doing?" said Earl, coming up behind me.

"What's it look like?"

"Those are way too—"

Uncle Whitey said, "Get back in your office, fathead." Now that he was related to Earl by marriage, he enjoyed insulting him.

Earl did have a big, round, white head with pasty yellow hair that he glued to one side. He tried to run things in a military way even though he'd only lasted a week in the Marines. He hated that I brought books to work and when he saw my French book, he said, suddenly enraged, "The French are pussies."

"Take that word back," said Whitey, "or I'll fight you. Thou shalt not take that word in vain."

Earl opened his mouth, but Uncle Whitey kept talking. "Besides, my niece is going to Paris. She is in love with Paris. She's a saucy Francophile."

Whitey thought he was so clever.

"Okay, I take back the pussy part," said Earl. His face was red and his neck was getting thick. "But you scrape that damn cream off there," he said to me.

"I'll pay for the whipped cream out of my tips."

Often, once Earl left, we'd fry up a whole bag of popcorn shrimp and eat it. Plus I stole sugars, boxes of jelly, and especially the ketchup. I liked ketchup, hated running out. Earl couldn't fire Whitey because Whitey had married Earl's sister and she wouldn't let him.

"Jesus," said Whitey to Earl, "so what about the whipped cream? There's no other customers. I don't think those kids ever saw whipped cream before."

Earl peered out the slot of a kitchen window and saw Marn. I'd forgotten that he had a crush on Marn.

"Yeah," I said, "they're *her* kids."

"Oh," he said, disappointed, and I knew he hadn't realized that Marn had children, either. I put the desserts on a tray and backed through the swinging doors into the restaurant. Marn was smoking a cigarette and the children were watching her with fascination, as if they had never seen their mother smoke a cigarette before.

"Voilà," I said. The kids' eyes opened wide.

"Oh, nice," said Marn. She looked up at me and smiled, for real now, and she had the sweetest smile, with deep shadows at the corner of her mouth. She was almost beautiful when she smiled and looked into a person's eyes. There was something that drew you. I could see why Billy, I guess, and Earl, had crushes on her. She had a facile, tough, energetic little body.

Earl came to the booth and started offering Marn her old job back, trying to convince her, but she waved her hand and said, "You don't have to harangue me. I'll start whenever." Earl drew his head back into the hump of his shoulder, almost shy. Marn said that she'd come to town looking for Coutts, the lawyer. Earl looked over at me. I decided I'd better take down the ketchup bottles before he realized I had them all subtly balanced end to end.

"I need to get my land back," Marn said.

That's the first we heard of it.

"What are you going to do with it?" Earl asked.

"Start a snake ranch." Marn raised her eyebrows and tapped a cigarette smoothly from its package.

Just then the door opened, this time with a windy crack, and a heavyset blond woman in a quilted green jacket barged through, bawling, "There you are, there you are! Defilement!"

Marn threw down her cigarette, whirled, and jumped up, out of the booth. I heard her say to the children, "Bliss!" Then all of a sudden Marn was standing in the aisle of the restaurant with a steak knife in one fist. And a hammer in the other. What she'd had in her coat pocket. The children slipped underneath the table like they were practiced at evading this sort of danger. Bliss surged forward but halted when she saw the steak knife and hammer. Her skin was thick and pitted with old acne scars and her eyes and lips were swollen, red as if from weeping or a bad cold. Her coxcomb of rough, spiky hair shivered as she launched into a torrent of accusation. She lambasted Marn for murdering Billy

Peace and taking money from the group. As a result, Marn was going to be struck dead by something or someone who might be Bliss herself.

"Whoa," said Earl, planting himself, legs apart in a bravado stance, behind Marn and her tool-utensil weapons. "You're outta line," he told Bliss.

"Call the cops, then," Bliss bawled. "Call the cops and dump her in the slammer too!"

"She wasn't doing anything," said Earl.

"I was enjoying a peaceful meal with my children," said Marn, dancing a little on her toes. She was shedding electricity. This confrontation seemed to make her happy and it looked to me like she was ready to stick that knife right into the big woman. She was moving the point of it back and forth, as if trying to decide where it would go in easiest. Her other arm was cocked up with the hammer ready to come down. I was behind her and behind Earl, and Whitey was behind me. He'd come out to see what was going on.

"My goodness," said Whitey. He tapped me on the shoulder and leaned close to my ear. "Marn has a kamikaze grace, don't you think? Or would you call it catlike?"

"You have a crush on her too?"

"I'm content," said Whitey, "with very distant admiration. Let's stay behind Earl's abdominals."

Bliss paused and licked her lips. She shook her hands like she was wringing water off them. Her swollen red eyes went slitty and mean. She took a huge breath of air into her cheeks, gathering herself up, then crashed forward. She grabbed the arm with the hammer and twisted Marn's wrist. Then she slammed Marn into Earl, who staggered backwards slowly enough so I could step aside and let him plow his ass across the booth where I had been filling the ketchup bottles. The bottles went toppling away, cracking on the table, rolling across the floor, at first with the sound of cascading glass and then with smaller sounds of movement as they continued clinking and skittering. Whitey and I edged away, against the doors, ready to bolt through. Marn had dropped the hammer but the knife had entered Bliss's green coat under one arm and Marn was silently trying to rip it away. The serrated edges had been caught in the threads. Bliss began slamming her hands across Marn's face and shoulders; she was speechless at first, shocked with fear probably. Then, realizing that the knife hadn't penetrated and was hung up in the lining of her coat, she looked down, snarled, took two handfuls of Marn's hair, and started yanking. Marn yelled in pain, pushed forward again, and this time the knife went into Bliss. It only could've stuck in about an inch, nowhere near a vital organ, but when Marn stepped back Bliss fell away, clutching the handle, and began to weep with desolate fervor. There was ketchup all over the floor, but only a few of the bottles had broken. I don't think Bliss was bleeding much. You could still see the handle sticking out of the coat and most of the knife itself was even visible. As Bliss walked out the door, sobbing, we just watched her, saying nothing. She dragged herself over to a dull mustard-colored car I hadn't seen pull up, wrenched the door open, got in, and drove away.

"A mere flesh wound," Whitey said to me. He had shelves of crime and adventure paperbacks with sexy women on the covers wearing tight blue sweaters or low-cut red evening gowns. "But look, the aftershock of violence."

Marn was standing in the aisle with her arms hanging limp, shaking. The kids were still underneath the table. Earl was trying to ease himself off the top of the table without knocking any more bottles off. I took a few of the bottles out of the way, setting them down carefully on another table.

"You are fired," Earl told me shakily.

"I am not," I said.

"Yes, you are."

"What for?"

"I told you never to balance those ketchup bottles like that again. Plus, I am fed up with your attitude."

"Qu'est-ce que c'est," I said, "big whup."

"You can't fire her," said Whitey, "not only is she a woman of grace and intellect who will go far, but you don't have anybody else."

"Marn said she'd work."

"I won't, if Evey's fired," said Marn. She seemed pretty much recovered and crouched down to talk to her children, who crept out from under the table, into her arms.

"Careful now," said Marn. "Don't touch your heads to the table bottoms, people stick gum there."

Earl liked Marn partly because she not only cleaned off the tops of the tables, but scraped underneath at the gum and dried candy. Now she helped her children back onto the booth and settled them while I got rags and a bucket of water to wipe up the spilled ketchup. While we were doing this, a couple of people came in and I had to serve them, so I brought new coffee cups and dessert plates for Marn and Earl, because they'd sat down to make up a schedule.

One of the things I liked about the 4-B's was the motif of B's. There were four B's hooked together, an old livestock brand belonging to the first owner, but there were also honeybees. Bees here, bees there, bees printed on the napkins. The waitresses wore yellow shirts with black pants or skirts, our "uniform." I also liked that we didn't pool or share our tips, although that meant we bussed our own tables. At closing time, we had to mop down the floors, clean the booths, even wash the windows on slow days. We had to clean out the soda machines and maintain the bathrooms.

The restaurant had once been the National Bank of Pluto, and it was solid. The ceilings were high and the lights hung down on elegant brass fixtures fixed to decorative scalloped plaster bowls. There were brass rails along the counters and the floors were old terrazzo, the walls sheeted with marble, and in the corners there were a set of dignified marble half columns. The orange booths were set alongside the tall windows and light flooded from three sides under the old cornices.

Across from us there was a gas station and a reeking movie house that showed B movies. At times, a fake flower or decorative basket shop would spring up—some farm wife's hopeful crafts project outlet—or a secondhand clothing store that smelled of sweat and mice would suddenly appear in an old closed-down storefront.

Marn Wolde was brooding while her kids ate a second helping of pie when Mama dropped off Mooshum. He sat down in the booth with Earl, whom he liked to annoy. Earl left. Marn's children were so full their eyes drooped. She let them keel over in the booth. I brought their jackets for pillows, then poured out more fresh coffee. I brought Mooshum's sour cream and raisin pie. He would usually draw a line down the middle with his knife, and we'd each eat toward the mark. But that day we shared the pie three ways, with Marn.

"I think I look French, don't you?" I said to Marn.

"Well, you are French, aren't you?"

"La zhem feey katawashishiew," said Mooshum.

"Watch out," I said to Marn, "he's going to flirt with you."

"Aren't French girls pretty? You are."

"I'd rather be chic," I said. "Of course, I have to wear this uniform. But my brother Joseph is at the University of Minnesota. I've visited him twice. He's in science. I'm going to go into literature. I'm learning French, see?"

I showed her the Berlitz book I'd found on a stellar day in the mission rummage, brand-new, not a mark in it.

"Say something, say something!" Marn cried.

"La nord, le sud, l'ouest, et l'est sont les quatre points cardinaux!"

Mooshum looked disgusted. "That's not how it goes! She tries to speak Michif and she sounds like a damn chimookamaan."

"I sound *French*, Mooshum. Je parle français!"

"Ehhh, the French, Lee Kenayaen!" He swiped his hand at me and bit daintily, gingerly, into his pie. His new teeth had been hard to fit and loosened easily. I still missed his old teeth, how he used to shovel the food right past them. He seemed happier then, even when they hurt. And the toothaches had always been a good excuse for whiskey.

"You!" he said. "My girl, you're going to be famous in school. Like your brother." He nodded at Marn and winked. "No surprise coming from such forebears. She's outta the royal line, anyway, on both sides. The great chiefs and the blue blood Scots, she's related to Antoinette herself and through that the German—"

"The Mormons have come around the house again with their genealogy charts and they're trying to suck Mooshum into their religion by telling him that he's got kingly ancestors," I told Marn.

"I know it to be so," said Mooshum firmly, licking his fork. "And the Chippewa side, we're also hereditary chiefs. And we're quick. I escaped from Liver-Eating Johnson—he just got half my ear."

He tugged his damaged ear.

"What?"

"Listen," I said to Marn. Her children had gotten up and were coloring quietly in the next booth. "We'll split up the hours, you've got kids, so you take first pick."

"We'll adjust," she smiled, a little wan now. "And I think I'll cut my hair."

"What's this I hear," said Mooshum, "about a snake ranch?"

Marn opened her eyes wide at me and blinked.

"I need to see the judge, Evey."

"Come and live with us for a while," said Mooshum. "La michiinn li doctoer ka-ashtow ita la koulayr kawkeetuhkwawkayt."

"He says the doctor will treat your snakebites. He's the doctor, I'm sure. Just come over tomorrow and we'll visit Geraldine's. Judge Coutts will be there."

Marn laughed, but she looked spooked, too, and gathered up her children. After she left, I said to Mooshum, "You scared her away with that snake stuff."

He looked at me. "The old women talk about her. The old women know."

"So you've been with the old women again?"

"Not my precious lovey. Your mama won't bring me over there to visit. They have even hid the stamps on me! I cannot write to her!"

"I'll get you stamps," I said. "The worst Aunt Neve can do is not open the letter."

"You are a very good granddaughter," Mooshum beamed. "And for sure! You look more French than any girl around here."

*Judge Antone*
*Bazil Coutts*

# Shamengwa

FEW MEN KNOW how to become old. Shamengwa did. Even if Geraldine hadn't been his niece, I would have visited Shamengwa. I admired him and studied him. I thought I'd like to grow old the way he was doing it—with a certain style. Other than his arm, he was an extremely well-made old person. Anyone could see that he had been handsome, and he still cut a graceful figure, slim and medium tall. His fine head was covered with a startling white mane of thick hair, which he was proud of and every few weeks had carefully trimmed and styled—by Geraldine, who still traveled in from the family land just to do it.

He was fine-looking, yes, but there were other things about him. Shamengwa was a man of refinement who practiced clean habits. He prepared himself carefully to meet life every day. Ojibwe language in several dialects is spoken on our reservation, along with Cree, and Michif—a mixture of all three. Owehzhee is one of the words used for the way men get themselves up—neaten, scrub, pluck stray hairs, brush each tooth, make precise parts in our hair, and, these days, press a sharp crease down the front of our blue jeans—in order to show that although the government has tried in every way possible to destroy our manhood, we are undefeatable. Owehzhee. We still look good and know it. The old man was never seen in disarray, but yet there was more to it.

He played the fiddle. How he played the fiddle! Although his arm was so twisted and disfigured that his shirts had to be carefully altered and pinned on that side to accommodate the gnarled shape, yet he had agility in that arm, even strength. With the aid of a white silk scarf, which he chose to use rather than just any old rag, Shamengwa tied his elbow, ever since he was very young, into a position that allowed the elegant hand and fingers at the end of the damaged arm full play across the fiddle's strings. With his other hand and arm, he drew the bow.

Here I come to some trouble with words. The inside became the outside when Shamengwa played music. Yet inside to outside does not half sum it up. The music was more than music—at least what we are used to hearing. The music was feeling itself. The sound connected instantly with something deep and joyous. Those powerful moments of true knowledge that we have to paper over with daily life. The music tapped the back of our terrors, too. Things we'd lived through and didn't want to ever repeat. Shredded imaginings, unadmitted longings, fear and also surprising pleasures. No, we can't live at that pitch. But every so often something shatters like ice and we are in the river of our existence. We are aware. And this realization was in the music, somehow, or in the way Shamengwa played it.

Thus, Shamengwa wasn't wanted at every party. The wild joy his jigs and reels brought forth might just as soon send people crashing on the rocks of their roughest memories and they'd end up stunned and addled or crying in their beer. So it is. People's emotions often turn on them. Geraldine sometimes drove him to fiddling contests or places where he could perform in more of a concert setting. He was well-known. He even won awards, prizes of the cheap sort given at local or statewide musical contests—engraved plaques and small tin loving cups set on plastic pedestals. These he kept apart from the other objects in his house. He placed them on a triangular scrap of shelf high in one corner. The awards were never dusted. When his grandniece, Clemence's girl, was young, she asked him to take them down for her to play with. They came apart and had to be reglued or revealed patches of corrosion in the shiny gilt paint. He didn't care. He was, however, somewhat fanatical about his violin.

He treated this instrument with the reverence we accord our drums, which are considered living beings and require from us food, water, shelter, and love. They have their songs, which are given to their owners in sleep, and they must be dressed up according to their personalities, in beaded aprons and ribbons and careful paints. So with the violin that belonged to Shamengwa. He fussed over his instrument, stroked it clean with a soft cotton hankie, kept it in a cupboard from which he had removed two shelves, laid it carefully away every night in a case constructed to its shape, a leather case that he kept well polished as his shoes. The case was lined with velvet that was faded by time from heavy blood-red to a watery streaked violet. I don't know violins, but his was thought to be exceptionally beautiful; its sound was certainly human, and exquisite. It was generally understood that the violin was old and quite valuable. So when Geraldine came to trim her uncle's hair one morning and found Shamengwa still in bed with his feet tied to the posts, she glanced at the cupboard even as she unbound him and was not surprised to see the lock smashed and the violin gone.

Things will come to me through the grapevine of the court system or the tribal police. Gossip, rumors, scuttlebutt, b.s., or just flawed information. I always tune in and I even take notes on what I hear around. It's sometimes wrong, or exaggerated, but just as often there is contained a germ of useful truth. For instance, in this case, the name Corwin Peace was on people's lips, although there was no direct evidence he had committed the crime.

Corwin was one of those I see again and again. Of course, I knew more than I really should have about his origins. It would have been a miracle, I suppose, if he'd turned out well. He was a bad thing waiting for a worse thing to happen. A mistake, but one that we kept trying to salvage because he was so young. Some thought him of no redeeming value whatsoever. A sociopath. A borderline. A clever manipulator drugged dangerous ever since he'd dropped out of school. Others pitied him and blamed his behavior on his father's spectacular crime, or his mother's subsequent drinking. Still others thought they saw something in him that could be saved—perhaps the most dangerous idea of all. He was a petty dealer with a car he drove drunk and a string of girlfriends. He was, unfortunately, good-looking, with the features of an Edward Curtis subject, though the hard living was already beginning to make him puffy.

Drugs now travel the old fur trade routes, and where once Corwin would have sat high on a bale of buffalo robes or beaver skins and sung traveling songs to the screeching wheels of an oxcart, now he drove a banged-up Chevy Nova with hubcaps missing and back end dragging. He drove it hard and he drove it all cranked up, but he was rarely caught because he traveled such odd and erratic hours, making deals, whisking to Minneapolis, heading out the same night. He drove without a license—that had been taken from him. And he was always looking for money—scamming, betting, shooting pool, even now and then working a job that, horrifyingly, put him on the other side of a counter frying Chinese chicken strips. I kept careful track of Corwin because it seemed I was fated from the beginning to witness the full down-arcing shape of his life's trajectory. I wanted to make certain that if I had to put him away, I could do it and sleep well that same night. Now, although the violin was never seen in his possession and we had impounded the Nova, the police kept an eye on him because they were certain he would show his hand and try to sell the instrument.

As days passed, Corwin laid low and picked up his job at the deep-fryer. He probably knew that he was being watched because he made one of those rallying attempts that gave heart to so many of his would-be saviors. He straightened out, stayed sober, used his best manner, and when questioned was convincingly hopeful about his prospects and affable about his failures.

"I'm a jackass," he admitted, "but I never sank so low as to rip off the old man's fiddle."

Yet he had, of course. We just didn't know where he could be hiding it or whether he had the sense ultimately to bring it to an antiques dealer or an instrument shop somewhere in the Cities. While we waited for him to make his move, there was the old man, who quickly began to fail. I had not realized how much I'd loved to hear him play— sometimes out on his scrubby back lawn after dusk, sometimes, as I've mentioned, at those little concerts, and other times just for groups of people who would gather round at Clemence and Edward's house. It wasn't that I heard him more than once or twice a month, but I found, like many others, that I depended on his music. After weeks had passed a dull spot opened and I ached with a surprising poignancy for Shamengwa's loss, which I honestly shared, so that I had to seek him out and sit with him as if it would help to mourn the absence of his music together. One thing I wanted to know, too, was whether, if the violin did not turn up, we could get together and buy him a new, perhaps even a better instrument. I hesitated to ask him, as though my offer was a selfish thing. I didn't know. So I sat in Shamengwa's little front room one afternoon, and tried to find an opening.

"Of course," I said, "we think we know who took your fiddle. We've got our eye on him."

Shamengwa swept his hair back with the one graceful hand, and said, as he had many times, "I slept the whole damn time."

Yet in trying to free himself from the bed, he'd fallen half off the side. He'd scraped his cheek and the white of his eye on that side was an angry red. He moved with a stiff, pained slowness, the rigidity of a very old person. It took him a long time to straighten all the way when he tried to get up.

"You stay sitting. I'll boil the tea." Geraldine was gentle and practical. No one ever argued with her. Shamengwa lowered himself piece by piece back into a padded brown rocking chair. He gazed at me—or past me, really. I soon understood that, although he spoke quietly and answered questions, he was not fully engaged in the conversation. In fact, he was only half present, and somewhat disheveled, irritable as well, neither of which I'd ever seen in him. His shirt was buttoned wrong, the plaid askew, and he hadn't shaved the smattering of whiskers from his chin that morning. The white stubble stood out against his skin. His breath was sour and he didn't seem glad at all that I had come.

We sat together in a challenging silence until Geraldine brought two mugs of hot, strong, sugared tea and got another for herself. Shamengwa's hand shook as he lifted the cup, but he drank. His face cleared a bit as the tea went down, and I decided there would be no better time to put forth my idea.

"Uncle," I said, "we would like to buy a new fiddle for you."

Shamengwa took another drink of his tea, said nothing, but put down the cup and folded his hands in his lap. He looked past me and frowned in a thoughtful way. I did not think that was a good sign.

"Wouldn't he like a new violin?" I appealed to Geraldine. She shook her head as if she was both annoyed with me and exasperated with her uncle. We sat in silence. I didn't know where to go from there. Shamengwa had closed his eyes. He leaned far back in his chair, but he wasn't asleep. I thought he might be trying to get rid of me. But I was stubborn and did not want to go. I wanted to hear Shamengwa's music again.

"Oh, tell him about it, Uncle," said Geraldine at last.

Shamengwa leaned forward, and bent his head over his hands as though he were praying.

I relaxed now and understood that I was going to hear something. It was that breathless gathering moment I've known just before composure cracks, the witness breaks, the truth comes out, the unsaid is finally heard. I am familiar with it and although this was not exactly a confession, it was, as it turned out, something not generally known on the reservation. Shamengwa had owned his fiddle for such a long while that nobody knew, or remembered anyway, a time when he had been without it. But there had actually been two fiddles in his life. There was his father's fiddle, which he played while he was a boy, and then another, which came to find him through a dream.

## The First Fiddle

MY MOTHER LOST a baby boy to diphtheria when I was but four years old, said Shamengwa, and it was that loss which turned my mother strictly to the church. Before that, I remember my father playing chansons, reels, jigs, but after the baby's death my mother made

him put the fiddle down and take Holy Communion. We moved off
our allotment for a time and lived right here, but in those days trees
and bush still surrounded us. There were no houses to the west. We
were not considered to live in the settlement at all and we pastured
our horses where the Dairy Queen now stands. My mother out of
grief became rigid and tightly ordered with my father, my older
brother and sister, and me. Our oldest brother, or half brother, had
already left home. He went beyond her and became a priest. We understood why she held to strange laws, and we let her rule us, but we
all thought she would relent once the year of first mourning was up.
Where before we had a lively house that people liked to visit, now
there was quiet. No wine and no music. We kept our voices down because our noise hurt, she said, and there was no laughing or teasing by
my father, who had once been a dancing and hilarious man. I missed
the little one too. We had put him in the Catholic cemetery underneath a small, rounded, white headstone, where he lies to this day.

I don't believe my mother meant things to change so, but she and
my father had lost everything once already, and this sorrow she bore
was beyond her strength. As though her heart was buried underneath
that stone as well, she turned cold, turned away from the rest of us, lost
her feelings. Now that I am old and know the ways of grief I understand she felt too much, loved too hard, and was afraid to lose us as she
had lost my brother. But to a little boy these things are hidden. It only
seemed to me that along with that baby I had lost her love. Her strong
arms, her kisses, the clean-soap smell of her face, her voice calming
me, all of this was gone. She was like a statue in a church. Every so often we would find her in the kitchen, standing still, staring through
the wall. At first we touched her clothes, petted her hands. My father
kissed her, spoke gently into her ear, combed her short hair—she was a
full-blood and in the traditional way had cut off her hair in mourning. It
made a fat bush around her head. Later, after we had given up, we just
walked around her as you would a stump. Our oldest, my half brother,
came and visited. He took my brother away with him to serve at Holy
Mass. The house went quiet, my sister took up the cooking, my father
became a silent, empty ear, and gradually we accepted that the lively,

loving mother we had known wasn't going to return. If she wanted to sit in the dark all day, we let her. We didn't try and coax her out. More often, she spent her time at the church. She attended morning Mass and stayed on, her ivory and silver rosary draped in her right fist, her left hand wearing the beads smoother, smaller, until I thought for sure they would disappear between her fingers.

Just after the great visitation of doves, we heard that Seraph had run away. While the rest of the family went to church to pray for his return, one day, I became restless. I wished that I could run away too. I'd been left home with a cold and my sister had instructed me to keep the stove hot—I wasn't really all that sick but had produced a dreadful, gravelly cough to fool my sister into letting me skip church. I began to poke around, and soon enough I came across the fiddle that my mother had forced my father to stop playing. So there it was. I was alone with it. I was now five or six years old, but I could balance a fiddle and before all of this I had seen my father use the bow. That day, I got sound out of it all right, but nothing satisfactory. Still, the noise made my bones shiver. I put the fiddle back carefully, well before they came home, and climbed underneath the blankets when they walked into the yard. I pretended to sleep, not because I wanted so badly to keep up the appearance of being sick, but because I could not bear to return to the way things were. Something had happened. Something had changed. Something had disrupted the nature of all that I knew. You might think it had to do with my brother running away. But no. This deep thing had to do with the fiddle.

Freedom, I found, is not only in the running but in the heart, the mind, the hands. After that day, I contrived, as often as I could, to stay alone in the house. As soon as everyone was gone I took the fiddle from its hidden place beneath the blankets in the blanket chest, and I tuned it to my own liking. I learned how to play it one note at a time, not that I had a name for each distinct sound. I started to fit these sounds together. The string of notes that I made itched my brain. It became a torment for me to have to put away the fiddle when my parents or my sister came home. Sometimes, if the wind was right, I sneaked the fiddle from the house even if they were home and I played out in the woods. I was always careful that the wind should carry my music away to the west, the emptiness, where there was no one to hear it. But one day the wind might have shifted. Or perhaps my mother's ears were more sensitive than either my sister's or my father's. Because when I had come back into the house, I found her staring out the window, to the west. She was excited, breathing fast. *Did you hear it?* She cried out. *Did you hear it?* Terrified to be discovered, I said no. She was very agitated and my father had a hard time to calm her. After he finally had her asleep, he sat an hour at the table with his head in his hands. I tiptoed around the house, did the chores. I felt terrible not to tell him that my music was the source of what she heard. Even then, though I would not have understood all that my father despaired of, sitting there in the lamplight with his head in his hands, I did know that it had to do with my mother and my secret music and that my father thought she heard something she had not. I did know it would have helped him had I admitted the truth. But now, as I look back, I consider my silence the first decision I made as a true musician. An artist. That I must play was more important to me than my father's pain. I said nothing, but was all the more sly and twice as secretive.

It was a question of survival, after all. If I had not found the music, I would have died of the silence. The rule of quiet in the house became more rigorous and soon my sister fled to the government boarding school. But I was still a child, and if my mother and father sat for hours uttering no word, and required me to do the same, where else was my mind to take itself but music? I saved myself by inventing songs and playing them inside my mind where my parents could not hear them. I made up notes that were not music, exactly, but the pure emotions of my childish heart. As of yet, nobody had thought of school. The stillness in my mother had infected my father. There are ways of being abandoned even when your parents are right there.

We had two cows and I did the milking in the morning and evening. Lucky, because if my parents forgot to cook at least I had the milk. Sometimes I made my supper on a half a warm, foamy bucket. Maybe a little bannock to soften in the milk and chew. I can't say I really ever suffered from a stomach kind of hunger, but another kind of human hunger bit me. I was lonely. It was about that time I received a terrible kick from the cow, an accident, as she was usually mild. A wasp sting, perhaps, caused her to lash out in surprise. She caught my arm, and although I had no way to know it, shattered the bone. Painful? Oh, for certain it was, I remember, but my parents did not think to take me to a doctor. They did not notice, I suppose. I did tell my father about it, but he only nodded, pretending that he had heard, and went back to whatever he was doing.

The pain in my arm kept me awake, and I know that at night, when I couldn't distract myself, I moaned in my blankets by the stove. But worse was the uselessness of the arm in playing the fiddle. I tried to prop it up, but it fell like a rag-doll arm. I finally hit upon the solution, a strip of cloth, that I have used ever since. I started tying up my broken arm at that early age, just as I do now. I had of course no idea that it would heal that way and that as a result I would be considered a permanent cripple. I only knew that with the arm securely tied up I could play, and that I could play saved my life. So I was, like most artists, deformed by my art. I was shaped.

There was bound to come a time when I slipped up, but it didn't come for a while, and by the time it did I was already twelve years old. My father, my mother, and I had gotten used to our strangeness by then. I went to school because the truancy agent finally came and got me. School is where I got the name I carry now. The full-blood children gave it to me as a kind of blessing, I think. Shamengwa, the black and orange butterfly. It was an acceptance of my "wing arm." Yet, even though a nun told me that a picture of a butterfly in a painting of our lady was meant to represent the Holy Spirit, I didn't like the name at first. But I was too quiet to do anything about it. My bashfulness about the shape of my arm caused me to avoid people even once I was older, and I made no friends. Human friends. My true friend was hidden in the blanket chest, anyway, the only friend I really needed. And then I lost that friend.

My parents had gone to church, but there was on that winter's day some problem with the stove there. Smoke had filled the nave at the start of Mass and everyone was sent straight home. So my mother and father arrived when I was deep into my playing. They listened, stand-ing at the door rooted by the surprise of what they heard, for how long I do not know. I had not heard the door open and with my eyes shut not seen the light thereby admitted. I finally noticed the cold breeze that swirled around them, turned, and we stared at one another with a shocked gravity that my father broke at last by asking, "How long?"

I did not answer, though I wanted to. *Seven years. Seven years!*

He led my mother in. They shut the door behind them. Then he said, in a voice of troubled softness, "Keep on."

So I did play, and when I quit he said nothing.

Discovered, I thought the worst was over. I put the fiddle away that night. But next morning, waking to a silence where I usually heard my father's noises, hearing a vacancy of presence before I even knew it for sure, I knew the worst was yet to come. My playing woke something in him. That's what I think. That was the reason he left. But I don't know why he had to take the violin. When I opened the blanket box and saw that it was missing, all breath left me, all thought, all feeling. For months after that I was the same as my mother. In our loss, we were cut off from all the true, bright, normal routines of liv-ing. I might have stayed that way, gone even deeper into the silence, joined my mother on the dark bench from which she could not re-turn. I would have lived on in that diminished form except that I had a dream.

The dream was simple. A voice. *Go to the lake and sit by the southern rock. Wait there. I will come.*

I decided to follow these direct orders. I took my bedroll and a scrap of jerky, a loaf of bannock, and sat myself down on the scabby gray lichen of the southern rock. That plate of stone jutted out into the water, which dropped off deeply from its edges into a green-black depth. From that rock, I could see all that happened on the water. I put tobacco down for the spirits. All day, I sat there waiting. Flies bit me. The wind boomed in my ears. Nothing happened. I curled up when the light left and I slept. Stayed on the next morning. As a mat-ter of fact, the next day too. It was the first time I had ever slept out on the shores, and I began to understand why people said of the lake there is no end to it, when of course, as I always thought, it was bounded by rocks. But there were rivers flowing in and flowing out, secret currents, six kinds of weather working on its surface and a hidden terrain underneath. Each wave washed in from somewhere unseen and washed right out again to go somewhere unknown. I saw birds, strange-feathered and unfamiliar, passing through on their way to somewhere else. Listening to the water, another music, I was for the first time comforted by sounds other than my fiddle playing. I let go. I nibbled the bannock, drank the lake water, rolled in my blanket. I saw three dawns and for three nights I watched the stars take their positions in the crackling black heavens. I thought I might just stay there forever, staring at the blue thread of the horizon. Nothing mattered. When a small bit of the horizon's thread detached, darkened, proceeded forward slowly, I observed it with only mild interest. The speck seemed both to advance and retreat. It wavered back and forth. I lost sight of it for long stretches, then it popped closer, over a wave.

It was a canoe. But either the paddler was asleep in the bottom, or the canoe was drifting. As it came nearer, I decided for sure it must be adrift. It rode so light in the waves, nosing this way, then the other. Always, no matter how hesitant or contradictory, it ended up advancing straight toward the southern rock and straight toward me. I watched until I could clearly see there was nobody in it before I recalled why I had come to that place. Then the words of my dream returned. *I will come to you.* I dove in eagerly, swam for the canoe—this arm does not prevent that. I have learned, as boys do, to compensate and although my stroke was peculiar I was strong. I thought perhaps the canoe had been badly tied and slipped its mooring, but no rope trailed. The canoe had lost its paddler somehow, gotten away from its master. Perhaps high waves had coaxed it off a beach where its owner had dragged it up, thinking it safe. I somehow pushed the canoe ashore, then pulled it up behind me, wedged it in a cleft between two rocks. Only then did I look inside, at the gear it held. There, lashed to a crosspiece in the bow, was a black case of womanly shape that fastened on the side with two brass locks.

That is how my fiddle came to me, said Shamengwa, raising his head to look steadily at me. He smiled, shook his fine head and spoke softly. And that is why no other fiddle will I play.

## Silent Passage

CORWIN SHUT THE door to the room in the basement where his mother's boyfriend was letting him stay, temporarily. Standing on a door propped on sawhorses, he pushed his outspread fingers against the foam panel of the false ceiling. He placed the panel to one side and groped up behind it among wires and underneath a pad of yellow fiberglass insulation, until he located the handle of the carrying case. Corwin dragged it toward him, overhead, bit by bit until he could tip the case and instrument through the hole into his arms. He bore it down, off the unstable, hollow-core door, to the piece of foam rubber that served as his mattress and through which, every night, he felt the hard cold of the concrete floor seep into his legs. He had taken the old man's fiddle because he needed money, but he hadn't thought much about where he would sell it. Who would buy it. Then he had an inspiration. He'd hitch down to Fargo with the fiddle. He'd get out at West Acres Mall and he'd bring the violin there in its case and sell it to a music lover.

Corwin got out of the car and carried the violin into the mall. In his own mind, he liked to quote himself. There are two kinds of people—the givers and the takers. I'm a taker. Render unto Corwin what is due him. His favorite movie of recent times was about a cop with a twisted way of looking at the world so you couldn't tell if he was evil or good you only knew that he could seize your mind up with language. Corwin had a thing for language. He inhaled it from movies and rock lyrics, television. It rubbed around inside him, word against word. He thought he was writing poems sometimes in his thoughts, but the poems would not come out of his hands. The words stuck in odd configurations and made patterns that raced across the screen of his shut eyes and off the edge, down his temples into the darkness of his neck. So when he walked through the air-lock doors into the warm cathedral space of the central food court, his brain was a mumble of intentions.

He was very proud of his leather jacket which had most of what he owned inside of it, in the inner pockets. And as always he was hyperaware of his own good looks. People treated him like a good-looking person. Others, who knew him well or whom he had burned, avoided him. But this problem was nothing he could fix now. The only way, he imagined, to redeem himself was through impressing people on a level he had not yet reached. He fantasized. As a rock star, the subject of a *Rolling Stone* interview. Who was the real Corwin Peace? Now, taking a seat in the central court, peering at the distracted-looking customers, he understood that none of them was going to outright buy the fiddle. He got up and walked into a music store and tried to show the instrument to the manager, who only said, "Nah, we don't take used." Corwin walked out again. He tried a few people. They shied away or turned him down flat.

Gotta regroup, Corwin told himself, and went back to sit on the central length of bench he had decided to call his own. That was where he got the idea that became a gold mine. It was from a TV show, a clip of a woman passing a musician in a city street and he was playing a saxophone or something of that sort, and at his feet there was an open instrument case. She stopped, and smiled, and threw a dollar in the case. Corwin took the violin out of the case, laid the open case at his feet. He took the violin in one hand and the bow in the other. Then he drew the bow across the string and made a terrible, strange sound.

The screech echoed in the food court and several people raised their lips from the waxed-paper food wrappers, then lowered the wrapped food when they saw Corwin. He looked back at them, poised and frozen. It was a moment of drama—he had them. An audience. He had to act instantly or lose them. He made a flowery, low bow. His move was elegant, the bow in one hand and the instrument in the other. It just came out of him. As though he was accepting an ovation. There were a few murmurs of amusement. Someone even applauded. These sounds acted on Corwin Peace at once, more powerfully than any drug he had yet tried. A surge of zeal filled him and he took up the instrument again, threw back his hair, and began to play a silent, swift passage of music.

His mimicry was impeccable. Where had he learned it? He didn't know. He didn't touch the bow to the strings, but he played music all the same. Music ricocheted around between his ears. He could hardly keep up with what he heard. His body spilled over with drama. He threw every move he'd ever seen and then some. When the music in his head stopped, he dipped low, did the splits, which he'd practiced not knowing why. He held the violin and bow overhead. Applause broke over him. A skein of dazzling sound.

## The Fire

THEY PICKED UP Corwin Peace pretending to play the fiddle in a Fargo mall and brought him to me. I have a great deal of latitude in sentencing. In spite of my conviction that he was probably incorrigible, I was intrigued by Corwin's unusual treatment of the instrument. I could not help thinking of his ancestors, the Peace brothers, Henri and Lafayette. Perhaps there was a dormant talent. And perhaps as they had saved my grandfather, I was meant to rescue their descendant. These sorts of complications are simply part of tribal justice. I decided to take advantage of my prerogative to use tribally based traditions in sentencing and to set precedent. First, I cleared my decision with Shamengwa. Then I sentenced Corwin to apprentice himself with the old master. Six days a week, three hours in the morning. Three hours of practice after work in the early evening. He would either learn to play the violin, or he would do time. In truth, I didn't know who was being punished, the boy or the old man. But now at least, from the house we began to hear the violin.

><

IT WAS THE middle of September on the reservation, the mornings chill, the afternoons warm, the leaves still thick and poignant in their final sweetness. All the hay was mown. The wild rice was beaten flat. The radiators in the tribal offices went on at night but by noon we still had to open the windows to cool off. The woodsmoke of parching fires and the spent breeze of diesel entered, then, and sometimes the squawl of Corwin's music from just down the hill. The first weeks were not promising, and I was reminded of the fact that in order to play any instrument well, a person usually must begin as a child. Perhaps, I thought, it was just too late. Then the days turned uniformly cold, we kept the windows shut, and until spring the only news of Corwin's progress came through Geraldine and from reports made by Corwin's probation officer. I didn't expect much. But Corwin showed up at Shamengwa's every day at eight A.M. It was not until the first hot afternoon in early May that I opened my window and actually heard Corwin playing.

"Not half bad," I said that night when I visited Shamengwa. "I listened to your student."

"He's clumsy as hell, but he's got the fire," said Shamengwa, touching his chest. He had improved, physically, along with Corwin's musicianship. I could tell that he was proud of Corwin, and I allowed myself to consider the possibility that history is sometimes on our side, and an act as idealistic as putting an old man and a hard-core juvenile delinquent together had worked, or had had some effect, or hadn't ended up, anyway, a disaster.

The lessons and the relationship outlasted, in fact, the sentence and through the summer we heard further slow improvement. Fall came and we closed the windows again. In spring we opened them, and one or two times heard Corwin playing. The summer went, and we heard assurance in the music, so much so that we were reminded, sometimes, of the master. Then Shamengwa died.

His was an ideal and peaceful death, the sort of death we used to pray to Saint Joseph to give us all. Asleep, his violin next to the bed, covers pulled to his chin. Found in the morning by Geraldine. There was a large funeral with the usual viewing, at which people filed up to his body and tucked flowers and pipe tobacco and small tokens into his coffin to accompany Shamengwa into the earth. Everybody said, as they do, *Oh, he looks at peace, the old man*. Geraldine placed a monarch butterfly upon her uncle's shoulder. She said she had found it that morning on the grille of her car. Clemence and Whitey held each other outside the church. Then I saw Clemence was holding Whitey up—he was drunk. Edward came and supported Whitey from the other side and went in and got into one pew. Shamengwa's brother, Seraph, was settled in between Evelina and Joseph. They were patting his shoulders and arms. He was speechless for once. He looked broken, or brokenhearted. He didn't even look up when Father Cassidy walked to the pulpit and solemnly, with much grinding of the gears, clearing of the throat, and springing up and down on his toes, began the eulogy.

*I come now before you in the holy spirit of forgiveness to bless the soul of Seraph Milk*

"What?" hissed Geraldine, "he's got the wrong brother!" She tried to signal the priest with a wave of her hand. But Father Cassidy was on his own track now, and Seraph had perked up a little.

*Seraph Milk who died unhoused, refusing Extreme Unction or the anointment of holy oils. Though his soul may be in hell we have no way of knowing for sure as he was always good at getting out of sticky situations, his family tells me, and moreover, sometimes the saints intercede for sinners on a whim. The Virgin Mary could be looking after him, although in my very presence Seraph Milk expressed doubt upon two specific foundations of our Catholic faith—the Immaculate Conception and the Virgin Birth. His own words were and I quote: I think she pulled a fast one!*

The old reprobate improved remarkably. His lip drooped open in a smile. He motioned those around us ready to stand up and protest that he was happy to listen. And anyway, the priest was gathering power, his voice boomed and nobody could have stopped him.

*Seraph Milk is now discovering whether or not his other hero, Louis Riel, was right when he proposed the belief that hell was neither infinite nor very hot. We have argued this many times! The Metis believed in a merciful God, you see, but it is my sorry duty to report that God is also just and although His Almighty Compassion may war with his sense of righteousness, he must consider whether we on earth would take him seriously were he not to punish sinners, heretics, liars, fornicators, drunkards, and those who celebrate the Feast of the Ass, as Seraph Milk informed me he did regularly with his brother, who may be greeting him one day in the future, playing a fiddle that spouts the devil's flames and wringing holy torment from its bow. But all of this is not to say that Seraph Milk necessarily deserves the hell he does not anticipate.*

A few people got up from their pews and made furious motions but were pulled back down by others.

*Nay!* Father Cassidy raised his fingers. *There was much good in this man, too, much virtue. Seraph Milk was a true patriarch and was said to love and indulge his children. Though heavily addicted to drink in his youth, he gave it up to some degree, perhaps too late in life to really matter to his wife, but all the same he cut back. From time to time he'd even taper off. Fortunately his young grandchildren, Joseph and Evelina, were not unduly influenced and have turned out as well as can be expected. Their mother is of course a regular communicant in this church, and the Church in its mercy decided to bury her father. No, it is really not for me to say that Seraph Milk belongs in hell, as I am but a servant of God the Father, the Son, and Holy Ghost. Seraph spoke of doves, so I ask that upon his soul there may rest the most generous spirit of blessing by the Holy Spirit, which is represented by the person of a pure white dove. I ask this blessing in spite of Seraph Milk's expressed wish that I "keep my trap shut about the pagans." In spite of his secret tippling and his open disregard for the laws and dispensation of our mother the Holy Catholic Church I ask that in His mercy God the Father excuse the sins and degradations of Seraph Milk and allow him to join his long suffering wife, Junesse, who has surely earned her way through her own gentle guidance of Seraph.*

It was Clemence who couldn't take it anymore. She shook Whitey and Mooshum's hands off her and strode to the front. She actually opened the coffin and plucked the violin from where it had been tucked up close to Shamengwa. Father Cassidy fell silent as she brandished the instrument at him. He then saw Seraph/Mooshum waving from the second pew, and his jaw fell slack. Clemence looked like she might take a swing at the priest, but instead she gave the violin to Geraldine, who rose and stood before the parish, motioning to the paralyzed Father Cassidy that it was now her turn to speak.

"A few months ago, Uncle told me that when he died, I was to give this violin to Corwin Peace," Geraldine told everyone, "and so I'm offering it to him now. And I've already asked will he play us one of Shamengwa's favorites today?"

Mooshum was still waving and smiling at Father Cassidy, who'd staggered backwards and sat down against the nave wall, wiping his head.

Corwin had been sitting in the rear of the church and now he walked up to the front, his shoulders hunched, hands shoved in his pockets. He was extremely sad. The sorrow in his face surprised me. It made me uneasy to see such a direct show of emotion from one who had been so volatile. But Corwin's feelings seemed directed once he took up the fiddle and began to play a chanson everyone knew, a song typical of our people because it began tender and slow, then broke into a wild strangeness that pricked our pulses and strained our breath. Corwin played with passion, if imprecision, and there was enough of the old man's energy in his music and stance so that by the time he finished everybody was in tears.

Then came the shock. Amid the rustling of Kleenex, the dabbing of eyes and discreet nose blowing, Corwin stood, gazing into the coffin at his teacher, the violin dangling from one hand down at his side. Beside the coffin there was an ornate communion rail. Corwin raised the violin high and smashed it on the rail, once, twice, three times to do the job right. Father Cassidy squeezed his eyes shut. His lips moved in prayer. I was in the front pew and suddenly I found myself standing next to Corwin. I'd jumped from my seat as though I'd been prepared for this type of thing. I grasped Corwin's arm as he laid the violin carefully back into the coffin beside Shamengwa, but then I let him go, for I recognized that his gesture was spent. He walked to his place at the back. My focus changed from Corwin to the violin itself because I saw, sticking from its smashed wood, a small roll of paper. I drew the paper out. The stuff was old and covered with an antique, stiff flow of writing. Wholly shaken, Father Cassidy began the service all over again. People sat still, dazzled by the entertainment of it all. I fit the roll of paper into my jacket pocket and returned to my seat. I didn't exactly forget to read the paper—there was just so much happening directly after the funeral, what with the windy burial and then the six-kinds-of-frybread supper in the Knights of Columbus hall, that I didn't get the chance to sit still and concentrate. It was evening and I was at home, finally sitting in my chair with a bright lamp turned on behind me, so the radiance fell across my shoulder, before I finally read what had been hidden in the violin all these years.

## Letter

I, HENRI BAPTISTE Parentheau, also known as Henri Peace, leave to my brother, Lafayette, this message, being a history of the violin which on this day of Our Lord August 20, 1888, I send out onto the waters to find him.

A recapitulation to begin with: Having read of LaFountaine's mission to the Iroquois, during which that priest avoided having his liver plucked out before his eyes by nimbly playing the flute, our own Father Jasprine thought it wise to learn to play a musical instrument before he ventured forth into the wastelands past Lac du Bois. Therefore, he set off with music his protection. He studied and brought along his violin, a noble instrument, which he played less than adequately. If the truth were told, he'd have done better not to impose his slight talents on the Ojibwe. Yet, as he died young and left the violin to his altar boy, my father, I should say nothing against good Jasprine. I should, instead, be grateful for the joys his violin afforded my family. I should be happy in the happy hours that my father spent tuning and then playing our beauty, our darling, and in the devotion that my brother and I eagerly gave to her. Yet, as things ended so hard between my brother and myself because of the instrument, I find myself wishing we never knew the violin, that she never had been brought before us, that I'd never played its music or understood her voice. For when my father died, he left the fiddle to both my brother Lafayette and me, with the stipulation that were we unable to decide which should have it, then we were to race for it as true sons of the great waters, by paddling our canoes.

When my brother and I heard this declaration read, we said nothing. There was nothing to say, for as much as it was true we loved each other, we both wanted that violin. Each of us had given years of practice, each of us had whispered into her hollow our despairs and taken hold of her joys. That violin had soothed our wild hours, courted our wives. But now we were done with the passing of it back and forth. And if she had to belong to one of us two brothers, I determined it would be myself.

Two nights before we took our canoes out, I conceived of a sure plan. When the moon slipped behind clouds and the world was dark, I went out to the shore with a pannikin of heated pitch. I decided to interfere with Lafayette's balance. Our canoes were so carefully constructed that each side matched ounce for ounce. By thickening the seams on only one side with a heavy application of pitch, I'd throw off my brother's paddle stroke—enough, I was sure, to give me a telling advantage.

Ours is a wide lake and full of islands. It is haunted by birds who utter sarcastic or sorrowing human cries. One loses sight of others easily and sound travels, skewed, bouncing off the rock cliffs. There are caves containing the spirits of little children, flying skeletons, floating bogs, and black moods of weather. We love it well, and we know its secrets, in some part at least. Not all. And not the secret that I put in motion.

We were to set off on the far northern end of the lake and arrive at the south, where our uncles had lighted fires and brought the violin, wrapped in red cloth, set in its fancy case. We started out together, joking. Lafayette, you remember how we paddled through the first two narrows, laughing as we exaggerated our efforts and how I said, as what I'd done with the soft pitch weighed on me, "Maybe we should share the damn thing after all."

You laughed and said that our uncles would be disappointed, waiting there, and that when you won the contest things would be as they were before, except all would know that Lafayette was the faster paddler. I promised you the same. Then you swerved behind a skim of rock and took what you perceived to be your secret shortcut. As I paddled, I had to stop occasionally and bail. At first I thought that I had sprung a slow leak, but in time I understood. While I was painting on extra pitch you were piercing the bottom of my canoe. I was not, in fact, in any danger, and when the wind shifted all of a sudden and it began to storm, no thunder or lightning, just a buffet of cold rain, I laughed and thanked you. For the water I took on actually helped steady me. I rode lower, and stayed on course. But you foundered—it was worse to be set off balance. You must have overturned.

*The bonfires die to coals on the south shore. I curl in blankets but I do not sleep. I am keeping watch. At first when you are waiting for someone, every shadow is an arrival. Then the shadows become the very substance of dread. We hunt for you, call your name until our voices are worn to whispers. No answer. In one old man's dream everything goes around the other way, the not-sun-way, counterclockwise, which means that the dream is of the spirit world. And then he sees you there in his dream, going the wrong way too.*

*The uncles have returned to their cabins, hunting, rice beds, children, wives. I am alone on the shore. As the night goes black I sing for you. As the sun comes up I call across the water. White gulls answer. As the time goes on, I begin to accept what I have done. I begin to know the truth of things.*

*They have left the violin here with me. Each night I play for you, Brother, and when I can play no more, I'll lash our fiddle into the canoe and send it out to you, to find you wherever you are. I won't have to pierce the bottom so it will travel the bed of the lake. Your holes will do the trick, Brother, as my trick did for you.*

✠

HERE WAS AT least a partial answer to my grandfather's question of what had happened to the two Peace brothers, Henri and Lafayette, who had once promised to bury him, but who instead had found him meat and hung a crucifix around his neck. More than that, the canoe did not sink to the bottom of the lake, that was one thing. Nor did it stray. That was another. Sure enough, the canoe and its violin had eventually found a Peace through the person and the agency of Shamengwa. That fiddle had searched long for Corwin. I had no doubt. For what stuck in my mind, what woke me in the middle of the night, after the fact of reading it, was the date on the letter. 1888 was the year. But the violin spoke to Shamengwa and called him out onto the lake in a dream almost twenty years later.

"How about that?" I said to Geraldine. "Can you explain such a thing?"

She looked at me steadily.

"We know nothing" is what she said.

I was to marry her. We took in Corwin. The violin lies deep buried, while the boy it also saved plays for money in a traveling band now, and prospers here on the surface of the earth. I do my work. I do my best to make the small decisions well, and I try not to hunger for the great things, for the deeper explanations. For I am sentenced to keep watch over this small patch of earth, to judge its miseries and tell its stories. That's who I am. Mii'sago iw.

# Evelina

# The Reptile Garden

❧

IN THE FALL of 1972, my parents drove me to college. Everything I needed was packed in a brand-new royal blue aluminum trunk—a crazy-quilt afghan my mother had crocheted for my bed, a hundred 4-B's dollars' worth of brand-new clothes, my Berlitz Self-Teacher, the *Meditations* by Marcus Aurelius (a paperback copy from Judge Coutts), a framed photograph, a beaded leather tobacco pouch that Mooshum had owned since I could remember, and which he casually handed to me, the way old men give presents, and from my father a stack of self-addressed envelopes each containing a new dollar bill. He had special stamps on each envelope that he wanted postmarked—some on particular days.

The other freshmen were moving into their dormitory rooms with their parents helping haul. I saw boxes of paperbacks, stereo equipment. Dylan albums and acoustic guitars of golden varnished wood. Home-knitted afghans, none as brilliant as mine. Janis posters. Bowie posters. Brightly splashed print sheets, hacky-sacks, stuffed bears. But as we carried my trunk up two flights of stairs, dread invaded me. In spite of my determination to go to Paris, I had actually dreaded leaving home even to go as far as Grand Forks, and in the end my parents did not want me to, either. But I had to go, and here I was. We walked back down the stairs. I was too miserable to cry and I do not remember our final embraces, but I watched my mother and father as they stood beside the car. They waved to me, and that moment is a clear, still picture. I can call it up as if it was a photograph.

My father, so thin and athletic, looked almost frail with shock, while my mother, whose beauty was still remarkable and who was known on the reservation for her silence and reserve, had left off her characteristic gravity. Her face, and my father's face, were naked with love. It wasn't something that we talked about—love—and I was terrified of its expression from the lips of my parents. But they allowed me this one clear look at it. Their love blazed from them. And then they left. I think now that everything that was concentrated in that one look—their care in raising me, their patient lessons in every subject they knew to teach, their wincing efforts to give me freedoms, their example of fortitude in work—allowed me to survive myself.

The trunk was quickly emptied, my room was barely filled. I had framed a picture of Mooshum dressed up in his traditional clothes. He had a war club in one hand, but he was smiling in a friendly way, his dentures a startling snow-white. His headdress, a roach with two eagle feathers, bobbed on ballpoint-pen springs attached to fishing swivels. His head was cocked at a jaunty angle. A heart-shaped mirror in the middle of his forehead was supposed to snare the hearts of ladies in the crowd. I had a picture of my great-uncle, too, a modest black-and-white photo in which he held his violin. Books to my chest, I curled up beneath the afghan and looked first at Mooshum, then at Shamengwa, and then out the window. I think I realized right then that this place was where I'd spend most of my first semester.

The white girls I knew listened to Joni Mitchell, grew their hair long, smoked impatiently, frowned into their poetry notebooks. The other girls—Dakota, Chippewa, and mixed-blood like me—were less obvious on campus. The Indian women I knew were shy and very studious, although a couple of them swaggered around furious in ribbon shirts with AIM-looking boyfriends. I didn't really fit in with anybody. We were middle-class BIA Indians, and I wanted to go to Paris. I missed my parents and my uncles and was afraid that Mooshum would die while I was gone.

My roommate was a stocky blond girl from Wishek who was so dead set on becoming a nurse that she practiced bringing me things—a cup of water or, when I had a headache, aspirin. I let her take my blood pressure and temperature, but would not let her practice on me with a shot needle. I spent most of my time in the library. I hid out there and read in the poetry section. My favorites were all darkly inspired, from Rimbaud to Plath. It was the era of romantic self-destruction. I was especially interested in those who died young, went crazy, disappeared, *and* went to Paris. Only one survivor of edgeless experience interested me, and she became my muse, my model, my everything. Anaïs Nin.

I was lost in soul-to-soul contact. I checked her out of the library, over and over, but when summer came I needed her, worse than ever. I had to bring her back with me to keep at my side while I worked at the 4-B's, while I hung out the family laundry, while I rode Geraldine's old pinto with Joseph. Anaïs. I bought all of her diaries—the boxed set. A huge investment. Hard to explain—she was so artistically driven, demure and yet so bold, and those swimming eyes! I made it through the summer. By the time I came back in the fall to live off-campus in a beautiful old half-wrecked farmhouse, I was soaked in the oils of my own manufactured delirium.

Like Anaïs, I reviewed every thought, all visual trivia became momentous, my faintest desire a raving hunger. I kept Anaïs with me at all times, though the difference in our lives had become a strain. Anaïs had had servants to feed her and clean up after her. Even her debauched lovers picked her clothing off the floor; her dinner parties were full of social dangers and alarms, but afterward, she didn't have to do the dishes. All the same, I, too, kept careful and replete diaries. Each notebook had a title taken from a diary entry by Anaïs. That fall's diary was called "Sprouting in the Void."

As Anaïs would have done, I wrote long letters to Joseph. He wrote short ones back. Corwin drove me to school and I read aloud from her diary all the way. He only liked it when she had sex—otherwise he said she was "way up in her head." Corwin visited from time to time. Our grade school romance was a joke between us, and his theft of my uncle's violin forgiven after the funeral. He was a dealer, and supplied my friends.

I'd moved in with a household of local poets, hippies, and everyone was dirty. I tried to be, too, but my standards of cleanliness kept me from truly entering into the spirit of the times. I had learned from my mother to keep my surroundings in order, my dishes washed, my towels laundered. The sagging clapboard house where we lived had one bathroom. Periodically, as nobody else ever did, I broke down and cleaned. It made me hate my friends to do this, and resent them as I watched the filth build up afterward, but I couldn't help it. My fastidiousness always overwhelmed my fury.

Late that fall, past midnight, I had one of my bathroom-cleaning fits. I got a bucket, a scrub brush, and a box of something harsh-smelling called Soilax. I ripped an old towel in four. I wet the bathtub down, the toilet and the sink, and then shook the Soilax evenly across every surface. I looked around for a moment and remembered the putty knife I'd stashed in the basement closet. I fetched it, and a plastic bag, and then I began to scrape away the waxlike brown patches of grease, hair, soap, scum, the petrified ropes of toothpaste, the shit, the common dirt.

The cleaning took a couple of hours and the light over me seemed harsh once I quit, because I'd emptied the fixture of dead flies. But when the light poured down out of its clean globe, a few lines of poetry occurred to me.

> My brain is like a fixture deep in dead flies.
> How I long for my thoughts to shine clear!
> Disperse your crumpled wings, college students and professors of UND,
> Let your bodies blow like dust across the prairies!

I jotted those lines in the notebook, which I always carried in the hip pocket of my jeans. "Sprouting in the Void" was almost filled. I wanted to take a hot bath to remove the disinfectant stink, but what I'd done in patches just made the tub look dirtier, and wrong, like I'd disturbed an ecosystem. So I showered very quickly, then went downstairs, where there was as usual an ongoing party. This one was a welcome-home party for a fellow poet who'd walked back across the Canadian border that day and was going underground, as he kept saying, loudly. He was also going to shower in my clean bathroom. I deserved to drink wine. I remember that it was cheap and very pink and that halfway through a glass of it Corwin took a piece of paper from a plain white envelope and tore off a few small squares, which I put in my mouth.

She tried everything, Anaïs; *she* would have tried this! *Spanish dancer*, I cried to Corwin—he was my third or fourth cousin. She was in love with her cousin. *Eduardo!* I said to Corwin, and kissed him. This all came back to me much later. For because of the wine, I was not aware that I had taken blotter acid, even after all of its effects were upon me— the hideous malformations of my friends' faces, the walls and corridors of sound, the whispered instructions from objects, a panicked fear in which I became speechless and could not communicate at all. I locked myself into my room, which I soon realized was a garden for local herpetofauna and some exotics like the deadly hooded cobra, all of which passed underneath the mop board and occasionally slid out of the light fixtures. I was in my room for two days, sleepless, watching red-sided garter snakes, chorus frogs, an occasional Great Plains toad. I passed in and out of terror, unaware of who I was, unremembering of how I'd come to be in the state I was in. My reclusiveness was so habitual and the household so chaotic that no one really noticed my absence.

On the third day, only one eastern tiger salamander appeared, *Abystoma tigrinum*. It was comforting, an old friend. I began to sense a reliable connection between one moment and the next, and to feel with some security that I inhabited one body and one consciousness. The terror lessened to a milder dread. I ate and drank. On the fourth day, I slept. I wept steadily the fifth day and sixth. And so gradually I became again the person I had known as myself. But I was not the same. I had found out what a slim rail I walked. I had lost my unifier of sensations, lost mind, lost confidence in my own control over my sanity. I'd frightened myself and it was all the more a comfort to return to the diaries. Anaïs was so deeply aware of her inner states. She was descriptive of the effects of the world upon her—the time of day, the sky, the weather, all affected her moods. I began to shake as I read some of her entries, so filled with detail. I needed someone to pay close attention to the world I had nearly left behind.

"Everything. The house bewitches me. The lamps are lighted. The fantastic shadows cast by the colored lights on the lacquered walls . . ."

That was her bedroom in September 1929.

No reptiles for Anaïs. My own dread kept returning. It was as though in those awful days I'd switched inner connections and now the fear seemed wired into me. Panic states. Temporary shocks—if I were even slightly startled, I could not stop shaking. Frightful but momentary breaks with reality. Daydreams so vivid they made me sick. I managed to function. Because I was so quiet anyway, I hid these dislocations of mind. Only, I had determined that I did not somehow belong with the careless well of the world anymore. I belonged with . . . Anaïs. On campus, I watched the well-fed, sane, secure, shining-haired and leather-belted ribbons of students pass me by. I would never be one of them! Instead, as I could not dance—what was Spanish dancing anyway?—and as I could not yet go to Paris, I decided that I must live and work in a mental hospital.

I got my Psych 1 professor (the course was nicknamed Nuts and Sluts) to help me find a position just for one term. I was hired as a psychiatric aide. That winter, I packed a suitcase and took an empty overheated Greyhound bus to the state mental hospital, where I trudged through blinding drifts of cold and was shown to a small room in a staff dormitory.

## Warren

MY ROOM WAS small, the walls a deep pink. In my diary I wrote: *I shall cover them with scarves.* I had a single bed with an oriental print spread. The lush landscape had pagodas, small winding streams, bent willows. This, I liked. There was a mirror, a shiny red-brown bureau, a tiny refrigerator on a wooden table, a straight-backed blue chair. Blue! My secondary muse—the color blue. I took the refrigerator off the table, and made myself a desk. I put everything away, my long skirts and the hand-knitted turquoise sweater I wore constantly. I'd met none of the other aides yet. There was someone in the next room. The walls were thin and I could hear the other person moving about quietly, rustling the clothes in her closet. There were rules against noise, against music, because the people on the night shift slept all day. My shift would begin at six A.M. So I showered down the hall and dried my hair. I laid my uniform out on the chair, the heavy white rayon dress with deep pockets, the panty hose, the thick-soled nurse's shoes I bought at JC Penney.

As always, I woke in time to shut off the alarm just before it rang. I boiled water in my little green hot pot and made a cup of instant coffee. The sky was a pre-dawn indigo. I put on a long, black coat I'd bought at the Goodwill, a coat with curly fur of some sort, like dog fur, on the collar and cuffs. It was lined with satin, and maybe wool blanketing, too, for it was heavy as a shield. The air prickled in my nose, my skin tightened, and an intense subzero pain stabbed my forehead.

I walked across the frozen lawn to the ward and sat down in the lighted office. The nurse coming on duty introduced herself as Mrs. L. because, she said, her actual name was long, Polish, and unpronounceable. She was tall, broad, and already looked tired. She wore a baggy tan cardigan along with her uniform, and a nurse's cap was pinned into her fluffy pink-blond hair. She was drinking coffee and eating a glazed doughnut from a waxed-paper bag.

"Want some?" Her voice was dull. She turned to one of the other aides coming on and said that she'd had a rough night. Her little boy was sick. They all knew one another, and the talk swirled back and forth for a few minutes.

"What am I supposed to do? Can you give me something to do?" I asked in a too bright, nervous voice.

"Listen to this," Mrs. L. laughed. "Don't worry, there's plenty. None of the patients are up yet."

"Except Warren," said the nurse who was going off duty. "Warren's always up."

I walked out of the office into the hall, which opened onto a huge square room floored with pink and black linoleum squares. The walls were a strange lavender-gray, perhaps meant to be soothing.

The curtainless windows were rectangles of electric blue sky that turned to normal daylight as the patients rose and slowly, in their striped cotton robes, began wandering down another corridor that led into the big room from the left. Everyone looked the same at first, men and women, young and old. Mrs. L. handed out medications in small paper cups and said to me, pointing, "Go with Warren there, and make sure he takes it."

So I went with Warren, the night owl, an elderly—no, really *old*— man with long arms and the rope-muscled and leathery body of a farmer who has worked so hard he will now live forever—or certainly past the reach of his mind. His tan was now permanent, burnt into the lower half of his face and hands. There was a V of leather at his neck from a lifetime of open shirt collars. His legs and stomach and chest and upper arms would be deadly pale. He was already dressed neatly—he always dressed and shaved himself. He was wearing clean brown pants and a frayed but ironed plaid shirt and he was starting to walk. He popped the pills down and didn't miss a step. He walked and walked. He was from Pluto and probably related to Marn Wolde, but she'd never mentioned him. I watched Warren a lot that first day because I couldn't believe he'd keep it up, but he didn't stop for more than a breath, filling up on food quickly at the designated times, then strolling up and down the corridors, crisscrossing the common room, in and out of every bedroom. To everyone he met, he nodded and said, "I'll slaughter them all." The patients answered, "Shut up." The staff didn't seem to hear.

The first day's schedule became routine. I woke early to record my dreams and sensations, then I dressed, putting a pen and small notebook in my pocket, plus a tiny book I'd sent away for—a miniature French dictionary made of blue plastic. I'd not given up. I noted everything, jotted quickly in a stall on bathroom breaks. At breakfast time I walked down through the steam tunnels to the dining room. My job as an escort was to see that no one hid in the tunnels or got lost. I ate with the patients, put my tray in line and waited to see what landed on it. Farina, cold toast, a pat of butter, a carton of milk, juice if I was early enough, and coffee. There was always coffee, endless, black acid in sterilized and stained Melmac cups. I ate what they gave me, no matter what, ravenous and forgetful. I did the same at lunch. Mashed turnips. Macaroni and meat sauce. Extra bread, extra butter. I began to think of food all day. Food occupied my thoughts. The food began to take up too much of my diary. There was nothing new to say about it in English, so I began to describe the food in French. Soon, there was nothing new to say about it in either language.

I was assigned to an open ward. The patients could sign out if they wanted to walk the ice-blasted grounds. As long as they were not gone past curfew they could go anywhere. There was also a lot of sitting. It was supposed to be part of my job to listen to people, draw them out, provide a conversational backdrop of reality, tell them when they were having fantasies.

Warren talked of the war sometimes, but one of the nurses told me that he wasn't a veteran. "I was reviewing the troops. They marched by and turned their eyes upon me as they passed. I turned to General Eisenhower and I said, 'Mentally, you're not a very good president.' His aide turned and looked at me. He was in civilian clothes . . ." And so on. His monologues always ended with "I'll slaughter them all." Always the same. I wanted to edit his mental loop, instead I walked with him. He would try to give me money—dollar bills folded fine in a peculiar way. We took a few turns around the halls, always at the same time. I knew everyone's routine. I knew each person's delusion, the places their records had scratched, where the sounds repeated.

Lucille, in the patients' coffee room where snacks were fixed, ate cornstarch from a box by the spoonful.

"We must put that away," I told her. My voice was changing, growing singsong, indulgent and coaxing, like the other staff. I couldn't stand the sound of myself.

"I ate this when I was pregnant," said Lucille. "Did you know I was artificially inseminated nine times?"

"Please, Lucille, give me the spoon."

"I put all nine of the kids up for adoption, one after the other, but they didn't like it. Know what they did?"

"They didn't blow spiders under your door. You just imagined that. So don't say it, and give me the spoon."

"They blew spiders under my door."

"Hey!"

I snatched the spoon and box away. One quick grab and they were both mine.

"Nobody blew spiders under your door."

"My children did," Lucille said stubbornly. "My children hated me."

Warren came in. He had been looking more disorganized, unshaved, his shirt buttoned wrong, his pants unzipped. His hair stuck to all sides in clumps. But for about five minutes, we held a perfectly normal conversation. Then he mentioned General Eisenhower and was off. I left, carrying the box of cornstarch.

## Nonette

MRS. L. WAS admitting a new patient, a young woman sitting with her back to me. I paused in the door of the office. There was something about the woman—I felt it immediately. A heat. She was wearing a black dress. Her eyes were angry blue and her lips very red. Her skin was pasty and shiny, as though she had a fever. Her blond hair, maybe dyed hair, was greasy and dull. She swiveled in the chair and smiled. She was about my age. Each of her teeth was separated from the next by a thin space, which gave her a predatory look. I handed the cornstarch box to Mrs. L., who put it absently on the windowsill.

"This is Nonette," she said.

"Is that French?" I asked. That was it. She looked French.

The new patient didn't answer but looked at me steadily, her smile becoming a false leer.

Mrs. L. pursed her lips and filled in blank spots on the forms. "Nonette can sleep in twenty. Here's the linen key. Why don't you help her settle in?"

"Fetch my things along," Nonette ordered.

"Evelina's not a bellhop," said Mrs. L.

"That's all right." I lugged one of Nonette's suitcases down the corridor. She smiled in an underhanded way and dropped the other suitcase once we were out of Mrs. L.'s sight. She waited while I carried it to her room, and watched as I took her sheets, a pillowcase, a heavy blanket, and a thin spread of cotton waffle-weave from the linen closet. Her room was one of the nicer ones, with only two roommates. It had built-in wooden furniture, not flimsy tin dressers, and the bed was solid. It even had all four casters on the legs.

"Fuck this dump," said Nonette.

"It's not bad."

"You're a bitch."

"You're a bidet."

In a Salvation Army store I had acquired a 1924 edition of a French dictionary called *Nouveau Petit Larousse Illustré*. I'd gotten to the B's. The page with the word *bidet* also had beautiful tiny engraved pictures of a biberon, a biche, a bicyclette, and a bidon.

Nonette's mouth twisted open in scorn. I left. The next day Nonette was extremely friendly to me. When I walked onto the ward, she immediately grabbed my hand as though we'd interrupted some wonderful conversation the day before, and she tugged me toward the glassed-in porch, which was freezing cold but where patients went to talk privately. I sat down beside Nonette in an aluminum lawn chair. I was wearing a sweater. She had on a thin cotton shirt, button-down style, a man's shirt with a necktie and men's chino pants. Her shoes were feminine kitten heels. Her hair was slicked back with water or Vitalis. She was an odd mixture of elements—she looked depressed but, it could not be denied, also chic. Today she wore black eyeliner and her face was prettier, more harmonious in the subdued light.

She didn't smoke. "It's a stinking habit," she said when I lit up. I was smoking the ones with low tar and nicotine because I was smoking too much there, constantly, like everyone else, and my chest ached.

"I should quit." I stubbed out my cigarette. "What do you want to talk about?"

"I wanted to talk to someone my age, not those jerks, shrinks, whatever. You're not bad-looking either. That helps. I wanted to talk about what's bothering me. I came to get well, didn't I? So I want to talk about how really, truly, sick I am. I've talked about it, I know I have, but I haven't really *told* it. Or if I have, then nothing happened anyway. So that's why I want to talk about it."

She paused for a moment and leaned toward me. When she did her whole face sharpened, her eyebrows flowed back into her temples, her mouth deepened.

"If I could just be born over," she said, "I'd be born neutral. Woman or man, that's not what I mean. I wouldn't have a sex drive. I wouldn't care about it, need it or anything. It's just a problem, things that you do, which you hate yourself for afterward. Like take when I was nine years old, when I had it first. He was a relative, a cousin, something like that, living with us for a summer."

"Where?" I asked.

"Not in stupid France," she answered. "Anyway, he comes in without knocking and kneels by my bed. He uncovers me and he starts giving it to me with his mouth. And I'm like, at first I don't know what, ashamed of it. I could buy a hook for my door, though; I could tell on him. I don't, though, because I get so I want it. He strips himself naked. He teaches me how to jerk him off. And then he does it to me again.

"I'm a little girl, right, I don't even wash very well. Next time he brings along a washcloth and cleans me first. We have a ritual. Where's my mother and father? They sleep at the other end of the hall, down the stairs, with the fan going in their room. And my cousin is a fucking Boy Scout! Was he going for a fucking merit badge? Anyway, he goes home. Things happen. I think I already feel different, I am different. There is a smell on me, sex, that no one else in my schoolroom has. I look at the older boys. I know what's coming. I go searching for it.

"Look at you . . ." She laughed suddenly, drawing away. "You're, like, fascinated . . ."

She stared out the windows onto the snowy grounds. "I'm not French," she said gently. "I'm messed up. I'm in a state hospital. I think I want a sex-change operation. I want to be a man so I won't have to put up with this shit."

"I'm not giving you shit."

Her mouth gaped mockingly. "Oh, look at you, trying to be tough. You're not tough. You're like, a little college girl, right? Who the hell cares. I'm from the university, too, I have a Ph.D. Pretty Hot Dick. I am a man, posing as a woman. You want proof?" Then her face closed in, bored. "I'm just kidding. Get the fuck away from me."

"I'm sorry," I said to her. "You're really beautiful."

She wouldn't say anything, wouldn't look at me now.

"You're an Indian or something, aren't you," she mumbled. "That's pretty cool."

I went back into the common room and played gin rummy with Warren, who couldn't concentrate. I didn't think he was taking all of his medication, but if he had discovered a way to hide it he was pretty slick. We watched him every morning. He seemed to swallow. His mouth was empty.

A policeman was standing in the office the next morning, drinking a cup of coffee with Mrs. L. He'd just brought Warren back. After we finished playing cards, Warren had marched outside, through fields, down a narrow road that ran west, and twenty miles later was turned in as he crawled into a farmyard. Warren had fallen and bloodied the side of his head. He was sleeping now, sedated, and it was not until late afternoon that he rose, came out to sit in the lounge, one side of his head swollen dark and bandaged. I sat down next to him.

"I hear you had a bad day." These words popped from my mouth. Yet I was curious. Perhaps it was cruel to be so curious. I asked about the voices he heard—if they were hard on him.

He straightened, shrugged a little. He was wearing a different, almost-new yellow shirt. He ran a hand up his face gently, exploring with his fingers. Then he reached into his pocket and pulled out one of his little folded-up dollar bills. He tried to give it to me.

"No," I said, curling his dry fingers around the money.

"Please." His old eyes begged, moist and red. "I did it because they told me . . . ," but he choked on what he might say and his voice was a crow's croak. He rubbed his face and closed his eyes. And then I

saw, just around the edges of his face, in the balled musculature and
the set of his eyes and jaw, that he was inside a waking dream. He
raised his arms. He recoiled. He sat down in a chair and began taking
apart some invisible thing in his lap. Then he went statue-still and
lifted his head. Gazed off to the side in a fugue of stillness, listening.

## The Kiss

NONETTE AND I were sitting on the frigid sunporch, and this time
she was also smoking.

"I'm only doing this disgusting thing so that I won't be disgusted
by the fact that you're doing it," she said.

I shrugged and dragged hard. She was belligerent in a low-key way
that nobody took too seriously. And she had told that story about being raped by her cousin, the Eagle Scout, to every nurse, aide, doctor,
and other patient available. It was just a conversation opener. Here, of
course, it was not supposed to matter whether or not the story was
true because the important thing was her need to tell it. I was now
trained to think that. Nonette wore a man's black suit, a gravedigger's
suit, a Charlie Chaplin bowler. All too big and comically masculine.
She took my cigarette from my hands and crushed it out. Then she
suddenly reached out and held my face in the cup of her palm. She
leaned toward me and kissed me. There was nothing upsetting about
it, at first, it was no different than the other times I'd kissed someone
for the first time. There was the same tentative heat, the same curiosity. Only she was supposed to be crazy, I was supposed to be not
crazy, and we were women. Or maybe Nonette was just troubled, I
was less troubled, and she claimed she was a man. She pretended she
was a man. Or she pretended that she was pretending.

She drew back into her chair, settled, crooked one leg up, and
hugged her knee. She stared at me, assessing my reaction. I was suddenly and completely charged with an electrifying embarrassment. I
burned and burned, losing control. I forced myself to rise, and even so
I stumbled, awkward and big, to the door of the sunporch and the
entrance to the ward. She was still watching, now smiling.

The truth is, the fact is, I didn't know at the time women could kiss women in that way anywhere but in Paris. I didn't think it could happen, or had never heard of it happening, in North Dakota. I was staggered with tender surprise.

Later on, I was sent to check on Nonette. She had gone to her bed, pulled the covers down, and slid underneath with all of her clothing on. I could see her heavy shoes sticking out the bottom. The sight of her boot soles filled me with pity and joy.

>|<

THERE WAS NOTHING in the many stories of reversal and romance among my aunts and uncles to guide me here. A kiss from another girl set me outside the narrative. None of the family stories could touch me. I was in Anaïs's story now. A dangerous love that could destroy. At the same time, I was so scared of what the kiss might actually lead to that I couldn't think of anything to do but eat. I stocked my little room with food and did not stop eating long enough to think. Boxes of crackers lined the wall. Fruit yogurt in the cold space between the window and the storm glass. Cans of soda. Fruit pies and peanuts, bags of apples. I talked on the phone in the hallway for hours, smoking, tracking down my housemates, friends, even Corwin, who was distant with me. I didn't really care. I kept him on the phone as long as possible because, after hanging up, there was nowhere to go but back into my room, where the food waited. As long as I was eating I could concentrate on what I was writing or reading. My eye traveled over the pages, my hand from bag to mouth. For the hours until the hour I could fall asleep, this worked. I didn't have to figure out what I was doing, what Nonette was doing, why I couldn't think of her and why I couldn't stop thinking of her.

>|<

AFTER ESCORTING A patient to the beauty parlor one late morning, I am returning alone through the steam tunnels underground when she is there. She is walking toward me with no escort.

"I have a pass." Nonette grins, stopping when we're face-to-face.

We're standing close and there's no one else in the tunnel, lit by low bulbs, whitewashed and warm, branching off into small closets and locked chambers full of brooms and mops and cleaning solvents. Her face is clear and bright, her hair a rumpled gold in the odd light; her eyes are calm and full with no makeup. She is beautiful as some-one in a foreign movie, in a book, a catalogue of strange, expensive clothes. There is green in her eyes today, her eyes are sea glass. I can almost taste her mouth, it's that close again, pink, fresh with tooth-paste. She is wearing jeans, a white sweatshirt, sneakers, and gym socks. I am wearing my cheap white uniform of scratching false mate-rial with tucks and a front zipper. She puts her fingers on the tongue of the zipper at my throat. She laughs.

"Got a slip on?"

I take her hand around the wrist, my thumb at her pulse.

"Stop, stop," she pretends, but her voice is soft. I follow her around a corner, then a sharp turn, through a door, and we are right in the middle of the pipes, some wrapped with powdery bandages of asbes-tos, some smooth, boiling copper conduits. My cap snags. I let it fall. We walk into the nest of pipes and duck low, underneath the biggest, walk down the cast stone steps to the other side, a kind of landing, completely closed in. Behind us there is a wall of rough brick and flag-stone that smells of dirt, of fields in summer with the sun beating down just after a heavy rain. The heat brings out the smell.

"Let's sit down," she says. "I'd like to get you stoned but I don't have anything."

I'm still holding her wrist. There is barely room to stand. The pipes, running parallel, of different lengths, graze the tops of our heads.

We sit down together. I'm shaking but she's very calm. Anyway, it isn't the way I thought it would be. After the first few moments, there is nothing frightening at all about kissing her or touching her. It is familiar, entirely familiar, much more so than if I were touching a boy I'd never touched before. The only thing is I keep shaking, trembling, because our bodies are the same, and when I touch her I know what she is feeling just as she knows when touching me, so it seems both normal and unbearable. We don't take our clothes off, do anything, just touch each other lightly on our arms, our throats, our hands, and kiss. Her whole face is burning, and soft, like flower petals.

She says, "That's enough." I should go back now and she will follow. Any longer, and they'll miss us. As I walk back down the corridors of whitewashed stone, through the five doors, back onto the ward, I begin to imagine how things really are. I invent her story. My thoughts take off. Nonette came here in obvious need, and I was here for her. She was here for me. I came here not knowing that I would meet the one I'd always needed. A week, maybe three, and she will be all right. I'll leave with her.

"Nonette said you asked for a patient visit." Mrs. L. sits behind her desk, a stack of forms beneath her spread hands.

"Yes," I say, though I didn't ask. But I'm smiling, slowly blooming at the idea. Nonette's idea.

"We like to encourage our aides to work with the patients during off-duty hours, and I don't see anything wrong with it, as long as you know that she presented here with some real problems."

"I know that. I've talked to her about them."

"Good."

Mrs. L. waits, watching me a little too carefully. I am not supposed to know a whole lot about each patient's personal history, not more than the patient wants me to know.

"Look," I say, "she told me about her cousin forcing himself on her. I know she came here out of control, and I still don't know exactly what precipitated it. I don't know what she's dealing with at home, at school, or if she's going back there. The thing is, I really like Nonette. I'm not doing this because I feel sorry for her."

Mrs. L. bites her lip. "Your motives are good, I know that. But you've got to know, to understand, she's on lithium and we're adjusting her dosage. She's depressive, and then she has her manic spells."

"We're just going to make a batch of cookies."

Mrs. L. smiles at me approvingly, and signs the pass.

•

There is a small kitchen in the basement of the staff dormitory, just one room with a stove and some cupboards, a fridge, an old wooden table painted white, and six vinyl chairs. We make our favorite cookies. Both of us like molasses cookies, not baked hard in the middle. We make three batches and bring them upstairs, to my room. The cookies are still warm as we eat them, crumb by crumb, sitting on my bed with the cookies in our fingers. We drink cold milk. Later, we take our clothes off. It isn't strange at all, the covers pulled back, the willows on my bedspread bending over the streams and the curved Chinese bridges. She has small breasts, pointed, the nipples round and rough, slightly chapped because she doesn't wear a bra beneath her shirts.

I hold her hips and she sits over me. She is older than me by two years and knows so much more. How to come sitting up. She spreads her legs and shows me, with a clinical cool, then bends over me while she is coming and begins to laugh. We begin to laugh at everything I've never done, and then we do it. She shows me how to start off light and slow, barely brushing each other, so when we come it will happen again, and again, and it will be endless between us. Just before nine o'clock I walk Nonette back to the ward, a bag of cookies in one hand.

"Do you think about, you know . . ." I finally ask her, at the door.

"Do I think about what?"

Nonette looks at me, her face bland and empty, smiling. She looks more and more like a girl in a ski commercial. Healthy. When she came that afternoon, she made me look into her eyes, deep with pleasured shock. Now her eyes are scary cheerleader eyes.

"Do I think about what?" she says again.

I look down at my feet in boots. *About what is going to happen to us?* I am dressed in jeans, a coat and sweater, like a normal person, like her. I don't answer. It is a night so cold and dark the snow makes squeaking noises as it settles in drifts along the big, square yard. All night, the trees crack. You can hear them, the tall, black pines. I stand there as Nonette walks into the hospital, as the glass and steel doors shut behind her with the movie-ending sound of metal catching, holding fast. The locks are automatic, but, still, I try them once she disappears into the bright corridor.

"I'm going home next week," she says one morning. "My parents said okay."

Her parents? Why haven't I ever seen them? A sudden burst of energy pulses from the center of my chest, grabbing all along my nerves. I clap my hands, fast, making sounds to divert the awful feeling, and then I wring them in the air, shedding the pain like drops of water.

Nonette looks at me and shakes her head, smiling. "Are you all right?"

I catch my breath, let it out slowly. "Have they been down to visit?"

"Sure. You work days. They drive down for dinner, then we visit in the early evening."

"Next week, next week."

My face stretches in a stupid smile and she twinkles back, into my eyes. Super cute! Popular! She's not okay, I think. She's crazier than I am if she can deny this. She must be. I tear my gaze away and feel my chest blaze. My ribs glow, hot, the bars of a grill, sending warm streaks washing to my feet. My thoughts spin a series of wild if questions. *If she wasn't crazy, if I was, if this was not out of the ordinary, if it couldn't be helped, if I were wrong, if people could see, if this thing with her was a new thing, the first of many, if she left here, if it meant nothing, if she didn't care at all about me.* I step away from her. She has a lovely face, so gentle, a kind and pretty face. An American face. She is wearing a blue sweater, a plaid skirt, knee-high stockings, ultra-normal Midwest catalogue clothes.

"Come and see me?" My voice is miserable.

"Sure! I will!"

My throat half shuts and I gulp at air. I struggle to get a good, deep breath. The air hurts, flowing deep. I'm smoking way too much. She doesn't mean it, of course she doesn't, not now, not ever. I am part of what she thinks is her illness, a symptom of which she thinks she has been cured. She, on the other hand, is what I was looking for. I can hardly breathe for wanting her so terribly. I walk away with my hands shaking in the scratchy white cloth of my pockets. I keep going and without punching out I walk back down the corridors of the hospital, out the doors, across the snowy central lawn and straight to my room.

## Nonette's Bed

I CALL IN sick the next morning, and the next morning after that. Two days go by. I can't make it to the telephone. I can barely force myself to get up and walk to the bathroom. At some point, I tack a note to my door. I forget what I've written. Once I'm in bed again a kind of black-hole gravity holds me there, or maybe it is fear. All I know is that the air is painful. Acid flows back into my brain. My thoughts are all flashbacks. I see moving creatures in the Chinese landscape of the bedspread and I throw it in the corner of the room. And there's pain, gray curtains I can't push aside. I breathe pain in, out, and the stuff sticks inside of me like tar and nicotine from cigarettes, making each breath just a little more difficult. A week goes by and then Mrs. L. comes to the door and calls, "Can I come in? Can you answer?" I try. I open my mouth. Nothing comes out. It is such a peculiar feeling that I start to laugh. But there is no sound to my laugh. I go to sleep again, sleep and sleep. And the next time I awaken Mrs. L. is in the room, sitting at the side of my bed, and she is using the voice she uses with the others.

"We're going to move you," she says. "We've called your mother." Which is how I end up in Nonette's bed after all.

I am sitting on the cracked green plastic sofa in the patients' lounge, wearing my nurse's shoes, only now with no uniform, just baggy jeans and a droopy brown sweater. I have talked to my mother on the phone and tried to persuade her not to worry about me, that I only need a rest, that I am all right and will be back in school when the next quarter starts. I have signed myself in, I'm nineteen, and I can do this. I have told my mother that I'll use this voluntary commitment as a rest period—but the fact is, I am afraid. I fear losing my observer, the self that tells me what to do. My consciousness is fragile ground, shaky as forming ice. Every morning, when I open my eyes and experience my first thought, I am flooded with relief. The *I* is still here. If it goes, there will be only gravity. There were body magnets underneath the bed in my little pink nurse's aide room. There are magnets beneath the bed here, too, but they have a comforting power since it was Nonette's bed and something of the lost happy calm of her skin, her hair, the length of her pressed against me, resides in the bed along with the drag and pain.

Warren enters the patients' lounge. He sees me sitting on the sofa and he walks over, in his careful and dignified way, and he stands before me. He is wearing a rust-colored jacket and gray woolen slacks. He has dressed in his best clothes today. Maybe it is Sunday. He is wearing a striped tie of rich, burgundy, figured silk, and a shirt with turned-back French cuffs. Instead of cuff links, I see that he has used two safety pins.

"You should have cuff links," I mutter.

"I'll slaughter them all," he says.

"Shut up," I answer.

✄

I LIE THERE days, and more days and days. I do not get out of bed. I do not read Anaïs Nin—she cannot possibly help me now. I am past all that and, anyway, she helped get me into trouble by providing the treacherous paradigm of a life I was always too backwards, or provincial, or Catholic, or reservation- or family-bound to absorb and pull off. I no longer want adventure. The thought of Paris is a burden. I'll never see the back of Notre-Dame or visit the bird market or eat a croissant. The coffee I drink will always be transparent. Which is all right, as I am sick of endless coffee here. No, I'd better figure out where I am in this life. So I lie there trying to work it out in my mind.

I try to start with the beginning—my family. When Joseph comes to visit me I decide that we should be more honest with each other, resume the depth of our relationship, and so I start by telling him about my drug experience and the days of watching reptiles.

"What species?" he asks. He is studying to be a biologist.

"Well, the usual. But I also saw cobras."

"That surprises me."

"They were so real, too."

"I wonder what part of the brain harbors such acute hallucinatory details, I mean, of something you've never seen in real life?"

"The reptile brain, asshole."

"I didn't mean to be insensitive," he says after a pause. "I took drugs too."

"What?"

"Marihootiberry. It didn't do much."

"Probably because it was oregano."

"I got A's in botany," he reminds me.

"You got A's in everything. You're not helping my depression. Look around you, it sucks, contrary to what the fans of suicidal poets think. Why don't you go discover some kind of cure?"

Joseph looks at me thoughtfully, then turns his attention to the people around us in the lounge. There is Lucille, glaring at linoleum tile, disheveled, and Warren, pacing, and others so dull and gray, slumped in torpor. Seeing the ward through his eyes, I am all of a sudden very disturbed. I've grown used to being part of this.

"You're not one of the crazies," he says then, half-choking, a little desperate. I can tell now that it is dawning on him something might really be wrong. His sympathy wrecks me. Joseph quietly takes my hand, which is even worse. For your brother to hold your hand. This is like some deathbed experience. I shake his hand away but pat his wrist. He sits with me for a long time and we don't talk and that is peaceful. After a while he gets choked up again and says that he will go into drug research. I whack him on the arm as hard as I can, and he smiles at me in relief.

⋈

MY MOTHER AND father come down every weekend to see me. All I do when they visit is cry in sympathy for their worry over me, or fall asleep, and after they go home I miss them—my father who left the bank knowing that he didn't have the stomach to turn down loans or foreclose like old Murdo. My father who like his uncle Octave collected only stamps. He went away to the war—came back for love—left money for love—my father the schoolteacher hero.

And there is my mother, who loves Mooshum and keeps him going by taking away the bottle and walking him around the yard or down the road every day. I realize that I can only think of her in relation to other persons, and I am pained all over again at what seeing me in this hospital must do to her. I try to think of one thing that is all about Clemence, like my father with his stamps, Joseph's salamanders, Mooshum telling stories, but I can't think of anything.

I do think of how I have grown up in the certainty of my parents' love, and how that is a rare thing and how, given that they love me, my breakdown is my own fault and shameful. I think of how history works itself out in the living. The Buckendorfs, the other Wildstrands, the Peace family, all of these people whose backgrounds tangled in the hanging.

I think of all the men who hanged Corwin's great-uncle Cuthbert, Asiginak, and Holy Track. I see Wildstrand's strained whipsaw body, and Gostlin walk off slapping his hat on his thigh. Now that some of us have mixed in the spring of our existence both guilt and victim, there is no unraveling the rope.

I think of Billy Peace, whose meek and shattered-looking members included at least one Buckendorf, a Mantle also. One or another of the kindred would materialize sometimes beside a person in the grocery store and seemed lost in wonder at the aisles of plentiful food. Some adherents blended back in with the other town and reservation people as they took modest little jobs. Billy's radio hour was taken by another voice. The little tracts we used to find in the Pluto or Hoopdance phone booths, or tucked in wayside rests, were more and more rare, then tattered, just souvenirs of the existence of Billy Peace, perhaps on another plane, those gone too.

Light falls through the wire-glass windows in a gentle swell. Mooshum told me how the old buffalo hunters looked beneath the robe of destruction that blanketed the earth. In the extremity of their hunger they saw the frail crust of white commerce lifting, saw the green grass underneath the burnt wheat, saw the buffalo thick as lice again, saw the great herds moving, flattening that rich grass beneath their hooves. Looking up, they saw the sky darkening with birds that covered it so that you could not see from one end to another. They flew low, a thunder. Sometimes doves seem to hover in this room. At night, when I can't sleep, I hear the flutter of their wings.

I'm just a nothing, half-crazy, half-drugged, half-Chippewa. I think of Mooshum and Shamengwa sitting long into the afternoon. In the bed where Nonette curled—so warm, so golden—I see the beauty of women holding out their Latin missals and walking through the wheat in white dresses, praying away the doves in an ancient, foreign, magisterial tongue. And Sister Mary Anita Buckendorf, for whom my passion should have clued me, and Corwin Peace, who also had a hand in this, I think of them.

I might go back and visit Sister Mary Anita. It might be a good thing to do. To speak to that monstrous, gentle face, to tell her that I've fallen from the church but that I still have visions, sometimes, of the mad swirl of her habit as she made adroit backhand catches and threw out a black-shod foot for balance. How the black wool snapped out in the air and then eddied back down around her ankles as she took a skipping hop and blazed the ball back to the catcher.

## The Concert

ONE DAY, CORWIN Peace comes to visit me.

I am surprised, but not embarrassed. He's learned where I am from my aunt, and is feeling bad about my desperate phone calls. He remembers the acid he fed me, and how I locked myself into my room for days after I took it. He says he decided that he should look me up. So one day as I am slowly crushing one cigarette after another into a sand-filled coffee can—there are six or seven cans in the patients' lounge, always full of butts—in walks Corwin. He is dressed in a long, black sheriff's riding duster, but he wears a strange orange woolen hunting cap with a low brim over his eyes. He has on high-top tennis shoes, bellbottom jeans, a ripped T-shirt. Under the dramatic duster, he is carrying his new violin.

"Sit down." I gesture with a newly lighted cigarette. I try to look bored, but actually I am excited. Corwin sits down in a plastic arm-chair and rests the violin case on his lap. His face is long and beautiful, his Peace eyes black and haunted. He has a short scraggle of unmowed beard. His ponytail flows down under his cap and snakes down his back. Corwin has always had lush brown lashes and those straight-across dramatic eyebrows. He can look at you steadily from under those minky brows, like his mother. He has some of what his uncle must have had to attract so many followers—that odd magnetism. When he smiles, his crooked teeth look very white. He doesn't smoke.

"So," he says.

"So," I say.

We nod for a while like two sages on a hill. Then he opens the case and picks up his fiddle. As he tunes it, making such unfamiliar noise, the patients come out of their rooms or are attracted from down the corridor. The nurses venture from their station and stand, arms folded, chewing gum. Their mouths stop moving when he starts play-ing, and some of the patients sit down, right where they are, a couple of them on the floor, as if the music has cut through the big room like a scythe. After that first run of notes, the music gathers. Corwin plays a slow and pretty tune that makes people's eyes unfocus. Lucille's mouth forms a big O and she huddles into herself. Warren stands rooted, stiff and tall. Others sway, they look like they might weep, but that changes quickly as Corwin picks up tempo and plucks out a lively jig that has a sense of humor in the phrasing. At this point, Warren leaves his wall and begins to walk around and around the room, faster and faster. The music ticks along in a jerky way, a Red River jig. Then something monstrous happens. All sounds merge for a moment in the belly of the violin and fill the room with distress. My throat fills. I jump up. Alarm strikes through us. Warren stops walking and backs up flat against the wall. But Corwin draws some note out of the chaos in his hands, and then draws it further up and up, further, until it is unbearable, and at that very point where it might become a shriek, the note changes key a fraction and breaks into the most lucid sweetness.

Warren slides down the wall, his hand over his heart like he is taking the pledge. His head slumps down onto his chest. The rest of us sit back down, too. Calm rains upon us and a strange peace fills our stomachs and slows our hearts. The playing goes on in the most penetrating, lovely, endless way. I don't know how long it lasts. I don't know when or if it ever really ends. Warren has fallen over. A nurse plods over to check his pulse. The playing of the violin is the only thing in the world and in that music there is dark assurance. The music understands, and it will be there whether we stay in pain or gain our sanity, which is also painful. I am small. I am whole. Nothing matters. Things are startling and immense. When the music is just reverberations, I stand up. The nurse is checking her watch and frowning at it first, then down at Warren, then at her watch again. I stand next to Corwin as he carefully replaces his violin in its case and snaps the latches down. I look at my cousin and he looks at me—under those eyebrows, he gives his wicked, shy grin and points his lips in a kiss, toward the door.

"I can't leave here," I say.

And I walk out of that place.

><

WHEN I LEFT the hospital with Corwin, I took my purse and my diary and nothing else. I left Anaïs—the entire boxed set—annotated. In the margins where she described tall buildings—*phallic?* And where she noted the cast of light on a Paris afternoon—*impressionistic?* Where she loved a woman, question marks, exclamation points, checks, and stars. I didn't know if I could actually bear leaving the safety of the hospital, but I just kept going until we reached Corwin's car. I'd lost a lot of weight and hardly exercised, so I was dizzy and had to ask Corwin to stop the car once so I could puke.

Corwin was living with my aunt and Judge Coutts, and he said that the two of them had changed his life and given him self-confidence. When he first moved in, he hadn't entirely stopped using or supplying (of course the two of them didn't know this), but after I went to the mental hospital he meditated on this form of commerce and ended up laying it down for good. He was straight now, he said, which gave me an opening.

"Well, I'm not. I'm a lesbian," I told him.

He said I couldn't be. I didn't dress like one.

"Like you'd know," I said.

He says he did know. He'd been around. "They dress like me, aaaay."

We drove along quietly for a while.

"I'm really sorry I gave you that acid, man," he said. "Did it, you know, change your head around?"

"You mean did it make me a lesbian?"

He nodded.

"I don't think so."

We drove some more. We'd known each other stoned, sick, drunk. We'd beaten each other up in Catholic school, so silence between us was comfortable, even a relief. I looked out the cracked car window—the world was beautiful all along the road. Some of the fields were great mirrors of melted water. Golden light blazed on the slick surface. I started feeling better. Sitting in a car with the boy whose name I had written a million times on my body, and besides that, in blood, and telling him about Nonette and having him take it pretty much in stride took some of the dark glamour from my feelings.

"Do you actually know any lesbians?" I asked.

"Not to talk to," he said. Then, a moment later, "Or any I could set you up with, if that's what you want."

A heated flush rose along my collarbone.

"Hey," Corwin said after a while, "you don't have to go anywhere with this thing just yet. Take it easy."

I didn't answer, but I felt better thinking I did not have to rush out and do anything about being a lesbian. I could just exist with it and get used to it for as long as I wanted. Nobody could tell from looking at me. I looked basically the same, though frail. And I looked sad. I knew because my mother said my sadness made her cry. But sitting in the car knowing I looked sad made me feel self-consciously sad, which isn't really sadness at all.

As we passed onto the reservation, I saw that the ditches were burning. Fires had been set to clear spring stubble, and the thin smoke hung over the road in a steady cloud. After Corwin dropped me off at our house, I sat with Mooshum outside, drinking cool water from tall galvanized water cans. After a while, I thought I'd be all right. Something about those cans—maybe the galvanizing—always made the water taste good.

As the sun went down, light shot through the smoke and turned the air around us and off to the west orange gold. A strange, unsettling radiance crept up the sides of the trees and houses. Mooshum and I watched until the light began to recede. The air turned fresh and blue. It was very cold, but still we sat until the darkness had a brown edge to it, and Mama came to the door.

"Come in here, you two," she said, her voice gentle.

## *Walking on Air*

A FEW DAYS later, I rang the bell at St. Joseph's convent. About two feet up a dog had scratched to get in many times, scoring it white. I waited, rang again, and heard a faint tink-tonk sound deep inside. There was a firm step, and then Mary Anita herself pulled the door open. She no longer wore the strict black habit, but regular clothes. Nunnish clothes, a baggy cream sweater set and a long blue A-line skirt. Soft tie shoes instead of elegant black nun boots. Her hair surprised me, a foresty brown with gray streaks and swirls, vigorous and beautiful, though she had cut it short. She peered steadily at me. Her eyes had weakened, perhaps, and she blinked behind round glasses, then took them off as she opened the door.

"Evelina Harp!"

Her huge face lighted, but her eyes were still. She gestured me inside and so I entered, wiping my feet carefully on the rough mat. The walls were a calming tan color and the place smelled clean, like there were no old or extra things in it. I followed her into a small receiving room, which contained a couch, an easy chair, a box of Kleenex balanced on the chair's arm. On the wall, there was an arrangement of dried flowers in a red willow basket. A crucifix hung over the dark television. She told me that she was happy to see me and asked me to sit down. She was much smaller now—the weight of her jaw had pulled her face down and changed the angle of her neck so she hunched and peered up from underneath her delicate brows, giving her look a penetrating gravity.

We fell into an awkward silence, and then she asked me how I was.

"Not so good," I said.

There was another silence, longer now, and I wished that I hadn't come.

"What is wrong?" Her gaze was tender and lingered on me. She was very happy that I'd visited, I could see, and now she was worried about me, one of her endless flock. I couldn't bear to tell her the truth, so I said something else.

"I've been thinking about becoming a nun!"

"Oh!" She clapped her milk-white hands. Her skin was pure and clear, translucent almost. A frightening joy shone out of her, then faded.

"It would be extraordinary if you had a vocation." Her voice was hesitant.

"I'm really thinking about it."

"Truly?" She folded her hands like the wings of birds. We both looked at her hands and I thought of the Holy Spirit, the dove settling to sleep, silent and immaculate.

"I think not," she said suddenly, raising her eyes to mine. "It's just that I don't see you in the convent," she continued, gently. "Have you had some sort of special experience you'd like to share with me?"

I smiled in dumb surprise and had really no idea what was going to pop out of my mouth. "I was in a mental hospital."

She looked at me sharply when I said that, but when I smiled, she laughed, that tinkly musical laugh that surprised people. "Yes, yes. . . . - Were you cured?"

"I guess so." I paused, less awkward now. "Maybe you're right about the convent. The problem is, I don't believe in God anymore."

Her eyes narrowed under the silky brows. Her gaze, though quiet and neutral, unsettled me.

"Sometimes I don't either," she said. "It's hardest when you don't believe."

"I imagined that you, I mean of all people . . ."

"No," she said, "not a firm faith."

"So the reason you became a nun"—my voice was low, I felt I might be pressing her too far now, but I wanted to know—"was it because you're a Buckendorf? Because a Buckendorf hung Corwin's great-uncle?"

She concealed her reaction behind a lifted hand, and took some time to answer.

"To live my life atoning for another person's sin?" She said at last, her voice scratchy and faint. "I wouldn't have had the strength. But then again, the hanging undoubtedly had something to do with my decision, growing up and finding out. Knowing one could be capable."

"One could be?"

"Anyone, perhaps. My father said that his grandfather was very kind, the kindest one of all. And yet he always knew he'd been one of the lynching party. My father was never able to put him there, in his thoughts. A couple of times he said he spoke of it. He spoke of your grandfather."

"Mooshum?"

I leaned forward and waited, but she hesitated.

"I'm not sure . . . but you asked. You want to know." Her lucid eyes combed me over. "All right, dear, I'll tell you. I believe your grandfather used to drink in those days. Your Mooshum told Eugene Wildstrand that he and the others were at the farmhouse. Mooshum told how they had found that poor family."

I couldn't look at her suddenly. I could only see Mooshum. A ragged flush rose from deep inside of me, a flood of pure distress. "He must have been stinking drunk to tell that," I said.

Nowhere in Mooshum's telling of the events did he make himself responsible. He never said that he had been the one who betrayed the others, yet instantly I knew it was true. Here was why the others would not speak to him in the wagon. Here was the reason he was cut down before he died.

Although I knew Mary Anita spoke the truth, I could not help arguing, and my voice rose. "They put a rope around his neck! He almost died. They tried to hang him, too."

Sister Mary Anita's hands twisted in agitation. "Yes, my dear. Wildstrand cut him down at the last moment, yes. From what I heard, though, they never meant to hang him all the way. They wanted to terrify him, to intimidate him. A false hanging will do that."

Sister Mary Anita touched the bottom of her face lightly with her knuckles, then gazed over my head, at the crucifix I thought. She was looking at the basket of dried flowers—black-eyed Susans, the little brown thumbs of prairie coneflowers, rusty Indian paint, cattails—all recently gathered from the ditches and pastures.

"The boy made that basket," said Mary Anita.

I rose, stepped across the room, and examined the basket—the wands, brittle and ancient, were more widely spaced than the best baskets, and a bit loose, the weaving not tight but irregular; it was a basket that a boy might make. Sister Mary Anita scraped out of the room, her feet uncertain on the floor now, and while she was gone I sat down, bent over, and held my head in my hands. *Mooshum.* When she came back, she had a brown paper bag, folded over on top. She didn't sit down and when I stood up to take the bag in my arms, I saw that she was tired and wanted me to leave. She remembered at the door.

"I'll pray for your vocation," she said. "And your sanity, too." She brightened and made a small joke. "They are not mutually exclusive."

I walked back down the hill and entered our house. Joseph and I still had our tiny alcove bedrooms—though his was full of all of his things now, plus Mama's sewing. Mooshum still slept in the little pantry off the kitchen. I went to my room, sat down on the bed, opened the paper bag, and peered inside. There was a pair of laceless boots, tongues dragging, leather dark and cracked with age. I took the boots out of the bag and held them in my arms. If I lifted one out and turned it over to look at the bottom, I knew I would see the nailed-on cross.

When I'd walked into the house, I had awakened Mooshum and now I heard him making his unsteady old man's way down the hall to my room. Nobody else was home.

"Want to play cards?" he said at my door.

I turned around and held the boots out, one gripped in each hand. Mooshum looked at me strangely, arrested by my attitude. He pushed his fingers through his scraggly hair, touched his sparse unshaven bristles, white against his skin, but of course he didn't recognize Holy Track's boots.

"Evey?"

I shook the boots at him. He cocked his head to the side, opened his long fingers, and took the boots when I shoved them toward him.

"Turn them over," I said.

He did and as he stared at the soles he bent slightly forward, as if they had gotten heavy. He turned away from me in silence and made his way back down the hall to his couch, which he fell into with the boots still in his hands. I thought that I'd maybe killed him. But he was frowning at the wall. I sat down next to him on the lumpy cushions. He put the boots carefully between us.

After a while, he spoke.

"I passed out cold, so I never knew when they cut me down. I lay there I don't know how long. When I came to, I looked up and there was these damn boots with the damn crosses on, walking, the boy was still walking, on air."

"They let him dangle there, choking to death, and watched him."

Mooshum shrugged and put his hands to his eyes.

A dizziness boiled up in me. I jumped to my feet.

"You're the only one left," I said.

"Tawpway," said Mooshum, complainingly, "and now you killed me some, too. I am sick to look on these old boots and think of Holy Track."

"You're the one who told!"

He rifled his pockets, took out his grubby, balled-up handkerchief, and tried to give it to me. I pushed it back.

"I did sober up for a long time, though, after that, some."

We looked down at the splayed boots.

After a while Mooshum picked up the boots and said he wanted me to drive him someplace. So I got the keys and helped him out of the house and into the car.

"Where am I going?"

"To the tree."

I knew where the tree was. Everybody knew where the tree was. The tree still grew on Marn's land, where Billy Peace's kindred used to stay. People had stopped going there for a while, but come back now that the kindred had disappeared. The tree took up the very northwest corner of the land, and it was always full of birds. Mooshum and I drove silently over the miles, then parked the car on a tractor turnout. When we slammed the car doors, a thousand birds startled up at the same instant. The sound reverberated like a shot bow. They flew like arrows and disappeared, sucked into the air.

We walked over dusty winter-flattened grass into the shadow of the tree. Alone in the field, catching light from each direction, the tree had grown its branches out like the graceful arms of a candelabra. New prayer flags hung down—red, green, blue, white. The sun was flaring low, gold on the branches, and the finest of new leaves was showing.

Mooshum knotted the laces, handed the boots to me. I threw them up. It took three times to catch them on a branch.

"This is sentiment instead of justice," I said to Mooshum.

The truth is, all the way there I'd thought about saying just this thing.

Mooshum nodded, peering into the film of green on the black twigs, blinking, "Awee, my girl. The doves are still up there."

I stared up and didn't have anything to say about the doves, but I hated the gentle swaying of those boots.

# All Souls' Day

❦

SO AFTER ALL, Mooshum saw in the skies of North Dakota an endless number of doves cluttering the air and filling heaven with an eternity of low cries. He imagined that the blanket of doves had merely lifted into the stratosphere and not been snuffed out here on earth. By this flurry of feathers, he was connected to the great French writer whose paperback I picked up again after abandoning Anaïs Nin. I read it so often that I sometimes thought of Judge Coutts as the judge-penitent, who bore my mother's name, and waited at a bar in Amsterdam for someone like me. I didn't know what I was going to do now. Albert Camus had once worked in a weather bureau, which made me trust his observations of the sky.

It was a warm Halloween night, and I had come home from school to help celebrate Mooshum's favorite holiday. To get ready for the trick-or-treaters, I drizzled warm corn syrup onto popcorn, larded my hands, and packed popcorn into balls until we had about a hundred or more stacked in a big steel bowl. We had backup—two vast bags of sticky peanut butter kisses. Our house was first on the road and everyone from out in the bush came into town on Halloween nights. Mooshum glared sadly at the treats. He didn't like peanut butter and the popcorn balls would be a problem, as he had never adjusted to his dentures.

"I could not bite the liver out of anyone with these dull choppers," Mooshum said.

I pulled out a bag of pink peppermint pillows. He plucked one out, set it on his tongue, and closed his eyes. The little wisps of his hair fluttered in the breeze from the door.

"I miss my brother," said Mooshum, fingering his mangled ear. "I even miss how he shot me."

"What?"

"Oh yai," he said, "this ear, didn't you know? It was him."

Mooshum told me that the fall after he and Junesse returned to the reservation he followed his younger brother out hunting. Somewhere in the woods Mooshum had hidden the bear's skin that ordinarily draped the family couch. Pulling the skin over himself, Mooshum managed a convincing ambush, rising suddenly from a patch of wild raspberry pickers and flinging himself forward in a mighty charge. Shamengwa fled as Mooshum pursued, fled with a loaded gun, but turned and shot with an awful cry as he tripped and fell.

"That bullet took my ear," Mooshum said, chopping the side of his hand at his head. "Clipped me good."

My mother sat down with us, and stirred sugar into a cup of tea.

"My brother pissed himself all the way down his legs that time. Did you ever know that?" Mooshum said.

"No!"

They started snuffling behind their hands. "Shame on you, Daddy," said Mama. "You're the one who peed himself." They suddenly fell silent. Mooshum rocked back on his chair's rear legs. He'd shrunk so that his soft, old green clothes were like bags, and his body inside was just lashed-together sticks.

Mama finished her tea, got up, and threw a couple of big hunks of dough on the cutting board. She started kneading, thumping them hard and shoving the heels of her hands in, a practiced movement I'd seen a thousand times. She was setting the dough to rise before going out with my father. They were attending some church-sponsored event that was supposed to be an alternative to the devil's inspiration, trick-or-treating. Father Cassidy still worked on the family, though more by habit than with any real hope.

Mooshum chewed and spat; his new coffee can was a red Folger's.

"They still won't give me a stamp!" He hissed behind Mama's back.

"Give me the letter," I said. "I'll mail it."

Mama was leaving, a spiderwebby lace scarf at the collar of her neat navy blue coat. My father wore a starched green shirt and a plaid jacket. His face was tired and resigned.

"He'd rather of stuck here with us," Mooshum said as they went out the door.

"He needs some relief," I said.

My father's class that year was dominated by two big unstable Vallient boys, who were uncontrollable. Most of my father's days were filled with conflict. He said that he couldn't take teaching anymore and had decided to sell his stamp collections and retire. Of course, we thought it was just talk, but he was conducting an auction by mail. Letters with the crests of stamp dealers appeared in the post office box.

After they left, Mooshum and I sat beside the door. Mama had wrapped each popcorn ball in waxed paper and twisted the ends shut. I opened one and began to eat it. There was an excited knock and the first wave of trick-or-treaters hit. We got the usual assortment of bums and pirates, some sorry-looking astronauts, a few vampires out of *Dark Shadows*, ghosts in old sheets, nondescript monsters, and bedraggled princesses with cardboard crowns. A lot of the older kids were motley werewolves or rugaroo with real fur stuck on their faces and wrists.

"This ain't no fun yet," said Mooshum.

For the next ones who came, I hid around the back of the door while Mooshum sat in darkness with the bowl of popcorn balls in his lap and a flashlight held under his chin. The kids had to approach and pluck the treat from the bowl, but only the toddlers were anywhere scared enough for Mooshum. A couple of older kids even laughed. He tried moaning some, rolling his eyes to the whites.

"They are hardened!" he said when they left.

"It's not easy to scare kids these days with all they see." I attempted to comfort him, but he was downcast. We tried the same thing with the next bunch, but not until he bit into a popcorn ball as one little boy approached, and his dentures stuck, and he took the ball out and held it toward the kid with the teeth in it, did we get a real satisfying shriek.

After that, when a child approached, I turned the flashlight on Mooshum and he bit into the popcorn ball, leaving his teeth in the gluey syrup. The kids had to reach underneath the hand and the popcorn ball with the teeth in it. We kept it up until one mom, who was carrying her two-year-old in a piece of white sheet, said, "You're unsanitary, old man!" That hurt Mooshum's feelings. He put his dentures back in sulkily and gave out peanut butter kisses with a stingy fist to the next three groups. There was a short hiatus, and I ate a kiss, which tasted faintly of peanut butter, more of glue. Mooshum's dentures were so loose now that he clacked and spat.

I finished handing out the treats, shut the door, and turned back with the bowl of candy. Mooshum was gone.

"Don't look yet!" he cried from the kitchen.

I walked straight back to see what he was up to, and nearly dropped over. He was wearing nothing but a pair of boxer shorts made of tissue-thin cotton, and he was stretching a big wet hunk of Mama's fresh, soft, new-risen bread dough over his head. He'd plopped it there and now it oozed horribly down his face, his neck, over his shoulders. His ears stuck out of the dripping mask. Strings of dough hung around his arms and he'd taken more bread dough and slapped it on his chest and stomach and thighs. His eyes peered out of the white goo, red and avid as a woodpecker's. He'd filled his mouth with ketchup. When he grinned, it leaked from his toothless mouth and down his chin. He saw my face, whirled, and ran out the back door. There was a clamor of voices yelling trick or treat. I dropped the bowl and chased him out the back door, but he'd already disappeared. I was creeping around the front when I saw him rise from the yew bush, the flashlight trained on himself from underneath. He shrieked—a barely human, shocking squeal. He tottered toward the kids and I knew when he grinned the ketchup grin, because the five boys yelled in fright and broke ranks. Three bolted and sprang off quick as jackrabbits. One dashed a little way before he tripped. The last one picked up a rock and winged it.

The rock hit Mooshum square in the center of his forehead. He fell full length, the flashlight skidding out of his fist, just as my parents drove up and jumped out of the car. I picked up the flashlight and trained it on Mooshum as Dad turned him over. Mama fell to her knees. Mooshum's eyes were wide-open, staring, and his forehead was bleeding all down his nose and cheeks. Mama put her arms around Mooshum's shoulders and shook him, trying to make his eyes focus. I knelt beside him and tried to take his pulse, but I can hardly find my own pulse so I couldn't tell if he was dead or not. I put my ear to his chest.

"Let's get him to the hospital," said Dad.

Mooshum woke and trained his eyes with great affection on my mother. "A good one, that."

Then he closed his eyes and went to sleep. He snored once. Mom said, "What's he covered with?" I answered, "Bread dough." We waited for the next snore. There wasn't one. Dad bent over Mooshum, pinched his nose shut, tipped his head back and opened his jaw with his thumb. He blew a long breath into Mooshum. Ketchup bubbled and leaked down Mooshum's neck.

"Did his chest move?" Dad wiped the ketchup off his mouth. He didn't even ask about the ketchup.

"Yeah."

He bent over and blew four more times into Mooshum. Then Mooshum stirred and coughed himself back to consciousness.

We decided to load him into the car, and in the relief of the moment we seemed to carry Mooshum effortlessly. I sat in the backseat with his head in my arms, and as we sped toward the hospital I felt his breath go out, and not come in, but then start up, like a sputtering outboard.

In the emergency room, he caused a stir. The nurses called every-one else over to look at him in his bread dough until Dad got mad, said, "Quit gawking. You're supposed to be professionals!" and shut the curtain around us. The doctor on call made it to the emergency room in five minutes. He was a young doctor, doing his government payback with the IHS, and he stepped around the curtain still shrug-ging on his white coat. The nurses must not have told him about the ketchup and the bread dough, but the doctor did pretty well. His mouth shook but he withheld laughter. Mooshum frowned in the bread dough mask, the ketchup drooling out the corners of his mouth, down his neck. Mama touched his hands tenderly and lightly as she folded them onto his chest. As we stood there looking at Mooshum, it seemed that his face slowly changed, relaxing into contemplation; contentment at the corners of his mouth. Dad gasped and wiped his face. The nurses were out there again, listening to us. We stood there for an endless amount of time, in a buzzing suspension.

"He looks happy," said Mama. "He looks like he's coming back."

Mooshum started breathing steadily.

"I'm going to die now," he sighed.

"No you're not, Daddy."

"Yes, I am. I want my lovergirl to visit me. Here in the hospital. Call Neve! It is my final request!"

"They're not even going to keep you here, Daddy. They're letting us take you home."

"No, baby girl, I am gone." He appeared to pass out, and Mama shook him, but just then Father Cassidy bounded lightly between the curtains. He had a spark in his eye and the good book in his hands. Mama would not step aside, so the priest had to crane to look into Mooshum's face.

"Am I still in time?" he asked loudly. "One of the nurses sent word."

Mooshum frowned and opened his eyes.

"There is time! How fortunate!" Father Cassidy muttered a fervent prayer. He had the Holy Oils along in a little kit. He began to fussily arrange them on the stainless steel bedside table. Mooshum gave a groan of irritation and sat up.

"If you won't let me die in peace, then I'll live, though I do not want to. You won't get me this time, Hop Along, I'll extend my life!"

Mooshum swung his legs over the side of the table and stood shakily. Dad and Mama held him from either side. He drooled a last bit of ketchup. "I have been told in the Indian heaven we live with the buffalo. I am content with that. Anyway, you have already spoken for me in the church. I couldn't have wished for a better send-off."

"I've apologized for that dozens of times," said Father Cassidy. He began with hurt dignity to pack away his vials of oil and to primly refold the starched white napkins that came in his kit.

Mama helped Mooshum into Dad's topcoat. He seemed stronger by the minute. He was still shedding dough, in dried flakes now. Father Cassidy noticed and asked what happened.

"He put dough on himself," I said.

Father Cassidy shook his head and snapped the top of his handy leather case. He was still talking cozily to the nurses when we left. A year later, he quit the priesthood, went home, grew a beard, and became an entrepreneur. He sold Montana beef, shipped it to Japan and all over the world. We'd see him on billboards and in his TV commercials. His distinctive skipping bound, his calflike and happy energy, became a trademark for the beef industry and made him very rich.

⚹

BEFORE I WENT back to school that weekend, Corwin came to my house and picked me up. We got into his car and drove out to a deserted place far off in the middle of a flat field where we could see lights coming from a distance. We climbed into the backseat with the windows half open—it was an unusually warm November night— and we kissed. Strange, intimate, brotherly. Then hurting each other, greedy with heat. We pulled our clothes away but suddenly stopped, confused, overwhelmed by a shy aversion. We sat there holding hands until we dozed off. The light lifted and the edges of the earth showed streaks of fire. The sun would rise soon. I studied Corwin in the soft gray light. His face looked swollen and bruised—we were all cramped and stiff from sleeping bent together. Maybe he'd been crying, secretly. He stroked my face, tucked my hair behind my ears, then put his other hand between my legs.

"Hey, Evey?" Corwin's teeth flashed. "You and me are supposed to marry. We're supposed to love unto death, until death do us part." His face was serious and exciting with the light creeping in a blaze up his throat and mouth. His eyes were masked in a slash of shadow.

"We'll go to Paris," he said. "We'll visit Joseph at the U and take a plane from there. Paris, just like you always wanted. We'll fuck in the street, fuck in the cathedral, fuck in the fucking coffee shops, you know?"

"Which cathedral?" I asked.

"The most beautiful one," said Corwin, "the one with the best statues."

"All right," I said. "Which coffee shop?"

"An all-night one with very tall booths. It could happen."

"How about the street? Which street?"

"All streets. We'll take a map."

I had studied the map on the endpapers of my book—an astonishing maze.

"We'd better get there soon," said Corwin. "They're probably building new streets in Paris right this minute."

"What if I don't want to, being a lesbian?"

Corwin fell silent; after a while he spoke.

"So you think it might be permanent?"


Driving slowly home, we passed an old man shambling along, coat flapping, hair streaming. It was Mooshum. We stopped the car just ahead, then turned around on the empty highway and cruised up beside him. He continued to stumble eagerly forward, so I jumped out and pulled him over to the car.

"Hey, get in!"

He looked at me, distracted.

"Oh, it's Evey."

"Get in the car, Mooshum, where are you going?"

"Visiting around."

He let me put him in the car and, once he was in, he said in a grand voice, "Take me to lovey!"

"Okay." I looked at Corwin wearily. He was staring straight ahead. "It's my aunt, Neve. He wants to go and see her."

"Why not?" said Corwin, shifting gears with a gesture of resignation.

As we were driving to Pluto, I realized that by now my mother was probably talking to the tribal police. She would be frantic over Mooshum. So as soon as Aunt Neve answered the door—wearing a bathrobe, no makeup, hair matted flat—I told her that I needed to use her telephone. Mooshum and Corwin sat down on Aunt Neve's springy golden couch and waited while she left the room to brew some coffee. Mooshum flapped his hands at Corwin and hissed at him to leave. I turned away from them with the phone and put my hand over one ear.

"Mama? I've got Mooshum and we're at Aunt Neve's."

Mama said a few explosive things, but was mostly relieved. She said something to Dad, then said, "Here, your dad needs to talk to you."

"Evey? Are you at—"

"Aunt Harp's."

"Oh!"

His voice was strained, tense, more excited than I'd ever heard. "Look," he said, "is there any way you can take a look at her mail?"

"What?"

My father told me that Mooshum raided his stamp collection when Mama refused to send one of his letters, and he glued several valuable, *extremely valuable* (my father's voice shook a little), stamps on an envelope he sneaked into the mail two days before. I opened my mouth to say that I'd mailed the letter for Mooshum, but thought better of it.

"I got a little upset last night," said Dad. "This morning he decided to take off . . ."

Just then the doorbell rang.

"Will you get that, dear?" Aunt Neve called from the bedroom, her voice a melodious trill. I was pretty sure that when she came out she would look perfectly groomed.

I set the phone down and answered the door. It was the postman with a postage-due letter among the other mail. I paid the postage with coins from my pocket and tucked the letter into my bra. I closed the door, set the rest of the mail on the neat little side table, and picked up the telephone.

"Well, I've got it. The letter has a one-cent stamp on it, blue, Benjamin Franklin."

I could hear my father struggling with some emotion on the other end.

"It's called the Z Grill. Honey, if you get that stamp back here safely, I promise I'll send you to Paris."

I put the phone down. My father never called me, or anyone, honey. And this was the second time that morning I had been promised a trip to Paris. I stared at Mooshum. His hair was a clean silver, swept into a neat tail. His teeth were back in, a white slash in his rumpled face. He was perfectly shaved. His clothes were spotless, shoes polished. He had his handkerchief out to touch the drip off the end of his nose.

Mooshum gave me a significant look that I understood to mean *get out of here*, so I grabbed Corwin's hand. We sneaked quickly out, back to the car, and immediately peeled out back onto the road. Once we were driving, we tried again to talk, but nothing came out right. I put my hand on Corwin's leg, but he just let it sit there and we both fell silent. It was awkward and my arm began to ache with the strain.

"We better start saving for our tickets," he said before I got out of the car. We were parked in the road outside of my house.

I kissed him, and left. When I looked out the window of the house about ten minutes later, the car was still there. The next time I looked, it was gone.

Aunt Neve kept Mooshum at her house that night. Just as I was about to head back to school the next morning, she pulled up in her yellow Buick. I watched from the doorway as Mooshum extricated himself from the passenger's side and walked around the front of the car, quick like a young man, brushing his hand across the hood and staring hawklike through the windshield at Aunt Neve. As Aunt Neve drove away, he stood waving slowly. The Buick disappeared, but he didn't move. He kept his hand in the air until he shrank and became old again. When he finally turned and shuffled toward the house, I walked down the steps and took his arm.

"Awee!" His face was full of emotion as we climbed the steps. "At last, my girl. If only Father Hop Along was here. I almost wish it. At last, I have something to confess."

✖

I WAS NAMED for Louis Riel's first love, a girl he met soon after his release from Beauport Asylum, near Quebec in 1878. He had been locked up there for treatment after suffering an attack of uncontrollable laughter during Holy Mass. Riel's Evelina was blond, tall, humble, and a lover of sweet flowers. It was Mooshum who actually suggested to Mama that she name me for this lost love of Riel's, and he was always proud that she had taken his suggestion.

✖

FOR MONTHS, ALL winter, in fact, my father held a grudge toward Mooshum for nearly sabotaging his retirement by stealing not only the Z Grill, but a three-cent Swedish stamp issued in 1855 and colored orange instead of blue. That one was returned for insufficient postage. At least Mooshum had used a return address, I observed, looking at the envelope over Christmas break.

"Don't joke. This is our family's future," said my father.

Mooshum had used a harmless paste of flour mixed with spit to stick it onto the envelope. The stamp did not even bear a killer or cancellation, because the postman in Pluto hadn't known quite how to handle the mistake, except to ask at the door for postage. Dad had gently soaked both stamps off the envelopes and put them back on their album pages. He showed me all of his favorite stamps. Until he agreed to a price by mail, he planned to put the whole collection in a safe-deposit box that was not in his sister's bank.

In late March, driving to Fargo with the collection, my father hit a patch of black ice and spun off the road, rolling the family car to the edge of a beet field. It was a sudden and deceptive freeze. He was alone, and unconscious, so the stamp albums were left behind. Since the windows were shattered entirely from the frames, much of what was in the car flew out as the car rolled, popping open the doors. The albums were left somewhere in a cold drenching rain that began soon after he came to consciousness at St. John's Hospital. He asked for his stamps at once, but of course the last thing the doctors were interested in was a stamp collection.

After we got to the hospital and made certain that Dad was all right, Joseph and I went looking for the stamps. We found the albums about a hundred feet from where the car had come to rest. The leather-bound books were splayed open, warped, and ruined. We picked stamps off cattails and peeled stamps from wet clods of mud. When we brought what we'd found to his hospital bed, Dad looked sick. He pretended to fall asleep. Our mother said, "He is in despair." We hadn't known the stamps could really be that valuable.

It was weeks before Dad was strong enough to go home. Most of the stamps we found were so fragile that once dried, when he tried to handle them, they disintegrated into a minute confetti. I saw him try to reconstruct the Benjamin Franklin Z Grill stamp myself. I'd found that stamp in the beet field attached to a rotting root. Perhaps the chemicals in the fertilized soil had attacked the paper. It was no use. When he lifted the stamp with a tweezers, it fell into a little heap of incredibly precious dust, which he caught as it sifted down.

My father took a deep breath, then looked at me.

A moment passed. He asked me to come with him to the back door and watch half a million dollars vanish.

*Ready?* he said.

And we stood together in the sun as he blew across the palm of his hand.

# *Road in the Sky*

**❧**

ON THE DAY that Aunt Geraldine finally married Judge Coutts, with all of us in attendance, there was a herringbone trail of clouds running east to west that resembled a dusty road. I noticed it before anybody else spoke of it, I think, and pointed it out to the judge. *I'll walk that road with Geraldine,* he said at once. Tears came into his eyes.

They were not married in the Catholic church (a disappointment to Geraldine and my mother). Besides his lingering outrage at Shamengwa's botched eulogy, my mother said that Judge Coutts was unwilling to confess and be absolved of his sins. He told Hop Along that he could not regret having sex out of wedlock and refused to be sorry, although he said the priest could feel free to absolve him anyway. Father Cassidy said he would not solemnize their vows under such conditions. So they were married by the tribal judge who preceded Judge Coutts, on a gentle swell of earth overlooking a field of half-grown hay in which the sage and alfalfa and buffalo grass stood heavy— Mooshum's old allotment land.

They said their vows and were pronounced husband and wife. Judge Coutts kissed Geraldine and people hugged all around. We could see from the judge's face that he felt immediate relief, as if he were a man coming out of surgery, still half-anesthetized, but understanding that survival was now assured.

Our respective families had become accustomed to having within the ranks an unwed couple living in sin. Aunt Geraldine seemed surprisingly willing to accept her role as the family scandal, and Judge Coutts had always been afraid that she liked the part, in fact, too well to relinquish it. Now he kept looking at the sky, clutching Geraldine's hand and pointing upward.

*Now I don't have to walk that old dusty road alone*, I heard him say, in what I guess was a slightly dizzy, maudlin fit. She touched his face with her handkerchief and said, *Buck up, Judge.* Tears were streaming from his eyes and he didn't know it. His mother was still alive enough to be there—a tiny, gnarled lump of a lady in a silver wheelchair.

"Listen," she said, beckoning him close. "Stop crying. You can't have people thinking you're soft."

But she was smiling, everyone was smiling, there was a giddy air of resolution. Approval arched over them like a rainbow of balloons. Corwin played for us of course—he was the only entertainment. When we are young, the words are scattered all around us. As they are assembled by experience, so also are we, sentence by sentence, until the story takes shape. I didn't want to go. I didn't know what would happen to me, bad or good, or whether I could bear it either way. But Corwin's playing of a wordless tune my uncle had taught him brightened the air. As I walked away I kept on hearing that music.

*Judge Antone*
*Bazil Coutts*

# The Veil

❧

AFTER THE WEDDING we got into the car bannered Just Married. White balloons, cans, and plastic fringe dragged from the bumpers. I took Geraldine's hand and held it on the seat between us as we rattled all the way to the Knights of Columbus hall. We'd been allowed to rent it even without a church wedding and now, I knew, from the KC kitchen ovens great roasters of meat soup, baked beans, frybread, potatoes, and roasted chicken were being lugged to the serving table. We'd pass by and fill our plates, eat in an exciting good-natured garble of cheer. Our wedding cake was four white-on-white layers embellished with glittering sugar roses. When it came time to cut the cake, I put my hand over Geraldine's fist as she gripped the knife. We smiled for pictures as the knife melted through the base of the cake.

Clemence removed the top for us to take home—a cakelet. The plastic groom was painted into a judge's robes and the bride wore a white suit. Her shoulder-length hair was black and waved like Geraldine's. Evelina had made the souvenir. "I'd like to keep this on my desk," I said, plucking the tiny couple off the cake and stashing it in my pocket.

So Geraldine and I began married life, at last.

❧

WE HAD DECIDED to save our money for a real honeymoon and go somewhere exotic later on—it was enough that we'd just be allowed to reassume our domestic life. We had the weekend before us. Someone, probably Evelina, had taped a sign on the front door. No Visitors. We left the sign up and entered our house, closed the door, stood in the little hallway. I removed Geraldine's white boxy hat with its pretty mesh veil. Then I put her hat back on, suddenly, and drew her veil down over her face and kissed her through the veil. The stiff little holes printed on her mouth then caught between our lips and tongues. In that moment, we coveted each other so intensely that we walked straight into the bedroom and did not emerge until late in the evening, dizzy and at peace. She remembered the little cake and fetched it. We froze the cake top to eat on our first anniversary. We made toast and tea and brought our plates and cups back into the bedroom, which wasn't in its usual order. Geraldine's suit was crumpled across a chair, the coat splayed open to reveal the glossy satin lining. Her small wedding hat had whirled into the corner and the veil seemed to have dissolved like sugar icing. Geraldine took a bite of toast and a light sift of crumbs scattered across the yoke of her robe and her naked collarbone. I leaned over and brushed the crumbs off; my hand lingered and then slipped inside, to her dark nipple.

*I don't think*, said Geraldine, *I really don't*, but then she gave me that smile, close up, and slid over me, opening the robe.

❈

I WONDERED IF we'd ever leave that bed. I didn't want to. Old love, middle love, the kind of love that knows itself and knows that nothing lasts, is a desperate shared wildness. I lay beside her in the dark. She was a silent sleeper, grave and frowning through her weighty dreams. As I do sometimes to fall asleep, I imagined myself hovering above ourselves, then rising, dissolving through the roof and taking a dark ride over the reservation and the neighboring towns. It did not work this time, but had the opposite effect. My brain became too alert. The adrenaline and unaccustomed naps had revved me. My thoughts spun. Life crowded in, the trivial and the vast. I thought of everyone who'd come to our wedding. I was moved all over again by how the Milk family had embraced our marriage. Their happiness had been genuine and there was nothing held back, nothing of the faint disapprobation I had feared, not even from Clemence. My long involvement with a married woman off the reservation, in Pluto, was surely known to them. I had no illusions that I'd kept my doomed first love private from anyone but C.'s husband. Yet they seemed to have shrugged away my past. Geraldine, after all, had made me prove myself.

As for Geraldine, if she knew about what I had done, and whom I'd loved, she never spoke, and I was always grateful to her for that. But although I have never told her the truth of my *before*, what occurred in Pluto, I'm sure that she knew why I stayed single for so long, and lived so quietly with my mother all those years before I met her. I never told her that it started when I was a boy not out of high school. I never told her about my first love or explained the difficult hold it had on me—I never told her about C.

I wish that I could say on the night following our wedding I thought of only Geraldine. But the crumbs in our bed and the honey in our tea reminded me of other times, and a different bed. I do not think it was disloyal of me to lie next to Geraldine and recall that history, so sad in many ways. For at the same time I was quickened with wonder, and gratitude. After I was stung, I never thought that love would come my way again. I never thought I would love anyone but C.

# Demolition

THE FIRST WOMAN I loved was slightly bigger than me. In bed, C. moved with the agility of a high school wrestler; she was incredibly quick. First she'd be on top and then in a split second underneath me with no break in the fluidity of our motion. It was like we were going somewhere every time we got in bed, cross-country or on a train trip, and we'd have trouble with hunger while making love. In certain favorite positions I'd get famished and weak. She'd make a sandwich or two and bring the food to bed. Sometimes there would be a glass of milk on the wooden table beside the headboard, and there was always a little squeeze bear full of honey, which she drank from like a bottle. She was a great believer in the restorative powers of milk and honey. On occasion, to rejuvenate me, she'd squirt the honey into my mouth, then dip a cloth into the cool glass of milk, and wipe me down. In summer, I soured in the heat, and one day my mother noticed when I walked in the door. My love affair with C. was clandestine, and I told my mother on the spur of the moment that I'd gotten work at the creamery.

She misheard me.

"What? The cemetery?"

"Yes," I said.

Which is how I really did end up working in the Pluto cemetery. So that my lie would not be found out, I walked over there the next day hoping to get a job. I was hired by a man named Gottschalk, who had been there most of his life. His little office was plastered with news clippings and obituaries. He had mapped out the graveyard and knew everything about each person buried there: when they'd come to the town and what they had done, how the family had come to choose that particular stone or monument, cause or moment of death, what property they'd left behind. My grandfather Coutts was buried there already, his grave marked by a tall limestone obelisk with these words at the base: *Qui finem vitae extremum inter munera ponat naturae.* It is as natural to die as to be born. There was a space next to him for his wife. She'd remarried and never taken it. There was my father, too, with a nice dark stone wide enough for two. He also was given to quotes, though not in Latin. He liked Thoreau (perhaps why he stayed in North Dakota), and he detested all trivialities. *Blessed are they who never read a Newspaper, for they shall see Nature, and, through her, God.* My mother had already had her name incised next to his, along with her birth date. There was a blank for her death date, which I didn't like, but she was comforted.

Gottschalk pointed out some additional space and observed that my grandfather had bought a large family plot. There was room for me and my wife, even a couple of kids. It seemed far off and laughable then, but as time has passed I have become increasingly grateful that those places next to my ancestors lie empty and waiting. I have also looked at Geraldine and wondered if she would consent to be buried next to me, but have not yet had the courage to ask.

I was seventeen when I began digging graves for the Pluto dead. I measured with string and used four tent pegs to anchor the string in a rectangle. Later, we bought a chalk roller of the same sort they used to mark the high school football field. I took the grass off in sections, peeling it like a scalp, and laid the squares on a piece of wet burlap. I used a toylike backhoe and finished the graves by hand with a straight spade. After the burials, I'd cover up the coffins and make a mound so that the ground wouldn't dent once the dirt had settled. I cut the grass, too, with a finicky gas mower, and learned how to trim the trees so that they would grow in a graceful, natural shape. I learned how to keep the death records in order, and after a while I knew the cemetery map as well as Gottschalk did. I could easily guide people when they needed assistance finding a relative, or wanted to see the war memorial, the ornate Russian ironwork crosses, or the humble, common fieldstones that marked the graves of a family murdered here long ago.

The thing is, this was just supposed to be a summer job before I went to college. But once I started having sex with C., I couldn't leave sex, or leave her, or leave the town. Besides, once I started spending my days among the dead, I grew used to the peace and quiet, as Gottschalk had told me I would. I even started adding to his clippings of interesting people, places, or events. One controversy at the time was the proliferation in our town of bars that featured striptease dancers. There was a community battle as to exactly how naked they should be allowed to get. We clipped and posted all of the editorials.

"If people could see things as we do," said Gottschalk. "No matter how small the G-string or how big the pasty, we all end up in the ground."

Six months after that remark, I dug his grave. I prepared his last resting place with unusual care, as befitted one who had so precisely cared for the journey of his fellow citizens. There was really no one else to take Gottschalk's place, and so at the age of twenty I became the manager of the Town of Pluto Cemetery, which helped a great deal in keeping my love secret—nobody wanted to date me.

I don't mean that women were put off by my line of work. On the contrary, it often seemed to fascinate them. But there was a certain lack of future in it, which girls could see. Once it was discovered that I was contented with my work, I wasn't bothered, even though I went to bars and such. I got on the radical pro side of going entirely topless because I liked watching Candy, who took suckers from her regulation G-string and tossed them to us. They were hygienically wrapped safety pops. At one time a patron of the bar had inhaled a straight stem sucker, perhaps in delight at one of Candy's novel moves. I hadn't had to bury him, but it was close. So she gave out the same kind of suckers as grocery stores give kids. In fact, that's where she got them—free. I got to know Candy, wanted her to stay in business, and was delighted to make C. jealous enough to fight with me.

While I was seeing Candy, or actually, just flirting with her, C. renovated her old house in order to be near me.

At one time the cemetery was set on the western edge of town, but the neighborhood has grown and now it is bounded by blocks of houses, all with their backs turned, politely or in dread, away from the gravestones and monuments. After the fight about my friend the stripper, C. moved her office to her house, which had a yard abutting the cemetery. She remodeled the living rooms and built-in the porch as a reception area. She left the back leafy and private. I could leave Gottschalk's old office, which had become mine, or walk from our equipment shed, which was set just outside a windbreak of pines, and enter C.'s back door without being seen. The thing is, we never could part, though C. did lose weight, shrink down considerably, and after a while she was no longer bigger than me.

⋊⋉

MY LIFE WENT calmly along for five years after Gottschalk died. One day in early June, just after the lilacs and the mock orange had folded, I started, as always, working among the roses, the iris, and then the peonies. This succession of color and scent has always taken me out of myself, sent me spinning. As soon as I got up each morning, I started working in the gardens around the house. The bees were out, their numbers unusual in our yard, and I was surrounded by their small vibrating bodies. They followed me as I worked, but I like bees. They seem to know that I respect their nature, admire their industry, and understand that they are essential to all that grows. I brushed them off gently, as I always do. In fact, I have been stung only twice in my whole life. After I finished weeding and watering, I went quietly into Mother's room, where she slept upright with a canister of oxygen. The rigors of her condition made her sharp and bitter for a time, but even when she was feeling awful, we still enjoyed each other's company. She was a sharp-boned little Chippewa woman. She liked to joke, had been very dedicated to my father, and was to me.

"Where are you going?" Her voice was a rasp by then. Of course she knew where I was going, but wanted to get her line in.

"To work."

"You'll be digging a grave for me soon!"

"No, I won't."

"Yes, you will!"

She cried this out with baleful joy in her voice. I wheeled her to the bathroom door and she rose, supported herself on the railing I'd installed.

"Shoo!"

I closed the door. We were both dreading the day when even this last piece of privacy would be taken from between us. We were both thinking about the Pluto Nursing Home, but to get her in there we would have to sell the house, which was a beautiful and comforting old place on a double lot, where I'd gardened and planted all my life. Mother wanted to leave the house to me. To that end, she was cheerfully trying to die. Mother weakened herself by not eating and hoped to suffocate herself in her sleep by not using her oxygen. Her natural toughness was not fooled by these tricks.

"All right, I'm done," she called out. In the kitchen, she ate a bit of toast and sipped a cup of coffee. I tried to get her to drink some water, but she was trying to dehydrate herself, too. As she did every day, she asked me what I'd be doing in the evening. It worried her that I hardly went out anymore.

"I'm going to play poker with you, Mom, then I'm watching the news and turning out the lights."

"You really need a wife, you know."

"Yes, I do."

"You're not going to find one by sitting home with your mother."

"I know the one I want."

"Give up on that old, tough hen!" she said, swiping at me. She had found about C. quite some time ago. "Get yourself a spring chicken and give me a grandchild, Bazil. She cured your cancer, but she's no good for you otherwise."

As a boy, I'd had a strange series of lumps on my head. They came and went until C. had affected a miracle cure—which was painless, as I remember, and left no mark. My mother has always been convinced that I had brain cancer, though it couldn't have been much more than cysts or warts. Still, I don't correct my mother as she thinks I owe my life to C., and that confuses the issue about our being lovers. I even say, sometimes, "Well, I'd be dead without her," when my mother begins to pester me.

⚛

I WAS ALWAYS eager to get to the graveyard in early summer. So few people died then. Mostly, there were just visitors. When I was working there, we had the most picturesque cemetery in the state. We were in brochures. Where the full sun hit, the peonies were just bursting from their compact balls into spicy, shredded, pink confetti-petaled flowers. I brought a Mason jar to fill for C. I usually went over to her place just after five o'clock, when her receptionist left. I was careful to pass quickly through her backyard, along the fence.

I remember that day specifically, because it was the day that she told me that she was getting married to the man who had remodeled her office.

"It's the only way I can break this off," she said.

I was bewildered. "I'm old enough now. Why don't you marry me?"

"You know the answer. I'm so much older."

I was twenty-five.

"I thought it was going to stop mattering, some day."

"I used to think so, too."

"You think I care what people think? I don't care what people think!"

"I know that."

She had her profession, her standing, the trust of her patients to think about. I'd heard all of that again and again.

"Can't it be over now?" she asked, her voice weary.

"No," I told her, my voice as hard as hers was tired.

And it wasn't over, although she married Ted Bursap, a general contractor. Ted was only five years younger than C. He believed that there was a future in Pluto, and his wife had just conveniently died. I'd buried her myself—in plain pine. I'd taken that as a sign of Ted's cheapness, though it's possible that's what she'd wanted. C.'s marriage so grieved me that I started correspondence courses in my father and grandfather's profession, and found I liked the law. Of course, there was a terrific law library in the house, two generations of law and philosophy books. Not to mention fiction and poetry, but I'd already gone through those. I disappeared in the evenings. That is when I discovered my grandfather's papers, and when because of him I began reading Lucretius, Marcus Aurelius, Epictetus, and Plotinus. For a while, everything written since A.D. 300 seemed useless, except case law, which fascinated me and told me that nothing had changed since those men had written.

Now that I was getting myself ahead, my mother approved of my not going out in the evenings. For a year after C.'s wedding, she and I were finished. I tried not to even look in the direction of her house. But we could not stay apart. One dusty summer evening, I watched from the cemetery as the sun turned white hot and then red. Through the pine trees, I followed this enormous ball of fire as it sank in the west. I looked in the direction that I had resisted looking, and saw Ted pull out of the driveway in his pickup. I walked between the graves and through the backyard the way I used to do, and there she was, waiting for me on the back kitchen steps. She had waited there every afternoon at five o'clock, all that year. She couldn't help herself, she said, but she'd promised herself she never would let me know, that she'd let me get on with my life.

Ted, it turned out, had gone to Hoopdance to work out a bid on some small construction job, and he would be an hour there and an hour back, at least. Those two hours were different from any we had ever spent before. The whole time we made love, in deepening light, we watched each other's faces as the expressions came and went. We saw the pleasure and the tenderness. We saw the helplessness deepen. We saw the need that was a beautiful sickness between us.

The only problem with those old philosophers, I thought as I was walking back through the graves, was that they didn't give enough due to the unbearable weight of human sexual love. It was something they correctly saw, though, as hindering deliberation, at war with reason, and apt to stain a man's honor, which of course I accepted.

Ted never found out, but I told myself that he might not even have cared. From what I had seen, love and sentiment had never interested him much.

Ted had built many of those newer houses in Pluto, those with only a backyard cemetery view, and he was also responsible for many of the least attractive buildings in town. I'd hated Ted even before he married the woman I loved, but afterward, of course, I thought often of how happy I would be to bury him, how fast I'd dig his grave. And then after I began seeing C. again, coming home, knowing that Ted got to sleep with her all night, I'd imagine how satisfying it would be to cover Ted up and put a stone on his head. Just a cheap flawed rock. No quote. Next to his poor pine-boxed wife. I had also hated Ted Bursap because of the way he ruined this town—Ted bought up older properties—graceful houses beginning to decay and churches that had consolidated their congregations or lost them to time. He stripped them of their oak trim or carved doors or stained-glass windows, and sold all that salvage to people in the cities. He tore down the shells and put up apartment buildings that were really so hideous, aluminum-sided or fake-bricked, with mansard shingled roofs or flimsy inset balconies, it was a wonder the town council couldn't see it. But they wouldn't. Pluto has no sense of character. New is always best no matter how ugly or cheap. Ted Bursap tore down the old railroad depot, put up a Quonset hut. He was always smiling, cheerful. He did not love his wife the way I did; she had not saved his life, either—she had only fixed his hernia. They never had passion, she told me, although Ted was a patient man and treated her well.

Once we got back together, I had Ted to avoid, as well as C.'s receptionist and all of her patients—the whole town, in fact. But C. was the shout and I was the echo. I loved her even more. There were times we were so happy. One afternoon, she let me into the darkened entryway between the garage and kitchen. Inside, she had the blinds pulled, too.

"You want some eggs?" she asked. "Some coffee?"

"I'll take some coffee."

"A sandwich?"

"That sounds good. What kind?"

"Oh . . ." She opened the refrigerator and leaned into its humming glow. "Sardines and macaroni."

"Just the sardines."

She laughed. "A sardine sandwich."

She made the sandwich for me carefully, placing the sardines just so on the bread, the lettuce on top, scraping the mustard onto both slices with a steak knife. She put the plate before me. This part of my day—five to six o'clock—was always spent in her kitchen with the window blinds shut and the lights on, no matter if it was sunny or dark. And although Ted could walk in almost any time and find nothing objectionable in our conversation or behavior with each other, we had continued as lovers. Just not often, like before. We were the main connection, the one who saw and understood. I told C. everything that was happening to me, from dreams to books I'd read to my mother's health, and C. did the same with me. We never talked about the future anymore—she refused to, and I had to accept that. The present was enough, though my work in the cemetery told me every day what happens when you let an unsatisfactory present go on long enough: it becomes your entire history.

I'd already picked my quote: *The universe is transformation.*

I watched C.'s hair change from a sun-stroked blond, darkening as she delivered one baby after another in Pluto. I saw her wear it clipped short, and then she let it grow into a wavy mass that vibrated against her neck as she cooked, as she turned her head, as she walked, as she lay beside me or swayed on top of me or held me from beneath. Gray strands and shoots arched from her side part back into a loose top-knot. Her hair turned back to sunny blond, as she began to touch it up. She grew it longer. By that time, its silken luster had dulled. I saw her eyes go from a direct blue, the shade of willowware china, dark and earnest, to a sadder washed-out color. Her eyes faded from all they saw as she healed and failed, and failed and healed. I even watched her clothes change, the newly bought shirts with the sizing in them go limp over time, losing status; from dress-up blouses that she wore to church, they became the paint-spattered clothes she threw on to water the lawn. I saw her skin freckle, her throat loosen, her teeth chip, her lips crease. Only her bones did not change; their admirable structure stayed sharp and resonant. Her bones fitted marvelously beneath her nervous skin.

That day, since Ted was in Fargo on business, we decided it was one of our rare days and we went down to the basement. There was a back door and side door to the basement. There was a way out of the room that we used, and a kind of alarm, which was her dog, Pogo, who would bark at anyone who entered the house, even Ted. We were very careful. We did not upset the balance of things. We were never discovered. Only, because our times were so far between and our caution was so great, the intensity built.

Where before it was like we were taking a trip, now making love became a homecoming. We realized that we were lost in the everyday world. So lost that we didn't even know it. And when we made love, it was as though we had come a long distance. As though all the days and weeks apart we were traveling, staving off weariness, and at last we had arrived. When we were at home, in each other's arms, lying in the cool of the basement afterward, it seemed that the world had spun into place around us. It seemed our harmony should be reflected in the order of the house, yard, and town. But when I left, I saw that only the cemetery was in perfect order, as I'd always kept it. Only the dead were at equilibrium.

As I walked home, I thought about C.'s skin, the tiny freckles, and the scent of dish soap on her hands, the sardine oil, the white bread, the animal closeness when she opened her legs. I was used to the smothered emptiness, the sick longing I went through every time we parted. It would smooth out, it would even out, over the weeks. *The universe is transformation*. But for us, nothing changed.

>k<

THE MOMENT I walked in the door, I knew that something was different. Something had happened—to Mother. The silence was peculiar. The suspension. As if we were playing some game where she was waiting to be found. I walked through each room, calling for her. As I've said, the house was wonderfully built, and large. At last I saw that she was crumpled at the foot of the basement stairs. The lights were off. She'd stumbled, or, more likely, thrown herself down on purpose. She moaned a bit and I grabbed the phone and called the ambulance. Then I crouched next to her, squeezing and straightening out each limb, checking for breaks.

No, she didn't have a broken limb. But she was as brittle as dried sticks, and the fall had jolted her mentally. She went in and out of what was real. Because she was in good health, she might live years, I was told, or only hours, as she was anxious and ready to die. No one could tell me much over the days she was in the hospital, so I finally made the call. I decided it was time to sell the house and put her in a safe place where she could talk to other old people and live easier, where she could perhaps improve.

"It's all right," I said. Her eyes were empty and her pupils had dilated until it seemed I was staring into the blackness of her mind.

I called the real estate agent from the hospital, and made arrangements for Mother to enter the Pluto Nursing Home. There was a double room available, and we got on the waiting list for a single. The van from the home came to the hospital, and I rode along with a brown leather suitcase of her things. That suitcase had belonged to my father, and I remembered her packing it for his trips to Bismarck. All the way to the retirement home, she would not speak. As we were settling her into her room, she suddenly barked, "This is not what I had in mind!"

She was terribly frail. If I'd brought her home, I was sure she would succeed in killing herself and maybe, even at the home, she would starve herself anyway. She looked at the tray of pudding with contempt. Sipped a little coffee and said, again, "I tell you, this is not what I had in mind."

It was surprising how quickly she got used to the place. Over the next couple of months, she made a friend of her roommate and began to join the others playing cards and sharing shows she always liked to watch on television. She even gained a few pounds, and got her hair done and a manicure from the stylist who donated her time every week. I had to say that Mother looked good, that the decision was right. I had forgotten how social she was before her decline. Only, the house was not selling and I had already dropped the price.

"Nobody with the income level that we need is moving here," said the agent. "And the doctors, lawyers, and so on, they all build new at the edge of town."

"Maybe we could sell it to the town. It could be a museum. See how carefully I've kept it?"

"You've done a beautiful job. I wish I could afford it, myself. We do have one interested party, but I've hesitated to mention him because he's right up front talking about demolition."

"Ted." I knew. That he would want the house had, of course, occurred to me. I'd never sell it to him.

"Ted Bursap," the realtor said, nodding. "He'll give you your asking price."

"The tear-down king. I don't think so."

"Well." The real estate agent shrugged. "At least we've got him in our back pocket."

"Yeah, sit on him! William Jennings Bryan stayed in this house when he came through on a stump speech. The windows were made out east and shipped here in huge sawdust crates. The interior moldings and woodwork are mahogany, the library panels—"

"You're real attached, I know."

I was too attached to give up the house—it was true. I figured and finagled, but all we had ever had was the house. My salary from the cemetery endowment was just enough through the years to maintain us, pay medical bills and my tuition, and keep the house in good shape, even though I did most of the repairs myself and had let the back wall go to the bees. I knew they were in there. In summer the wall vibrated with their sensuous life. All winter it was quiet as they slept. I had finished my law degree as I was waiting for the house to sell, and I decided to take the state bar exam. Perhaps I'd try to get a loan, I would take out a homeowner's loan and pay it off once I'd hung out my shingle. In the evenings, I sat on the back porch studying like mad, listening to the bees gather the last sweetness before going to sleep. Their hum made the whole house awaken and I could not abandon it or them. After dusk, I sat in the paneled library, appreciating the stillness and the clean odor of the swept and dusted rooms. I thought how nice it would be to live there with C. I imagined it; I got lost in imagining it. I dreamed it when I fell asleep in my chair. All of a sudden I woke in blackness, alive to desolate knowledge.

In that moment, I knew what those who kill themselves over love know; I saw what passed before the eyes of dying men who fought idiotic duels. I'd wasted my life on a woman. All I had was this house. I called the agent.

"Okay," I told him. "Sell the place to Ted."

※

THE VERY NEXT day, I put all that my parents and I had ever owned into storage, and I moved out of the house into a motel. I soon heard that Ted had begun. I knew how he worked. His crew would dismantle the inside, prying off even the old bead board in the pantry, yanking out light fixtures, chipping the shadowy gold tiles from around the fireplace, disassembling the elegant staircase, packing up the stained glass. Once the inside was gutted, Ted would rent a giant new machine with a great toothed bucket that he operated to claw the shell of lath and plaster to splinters.

I sat in my room at the Bluebird, trying to read. I was scheduled to take the bar that week, but I couldn't concentrate. It was as though the house was calling out to me, telling me that it loved me, that its destruction was a cruel and unnecessary adjunct to my decision to break things off with C. I couldn't see what was happening to the house, but I could feel what Ted was doing as though it was happening to me. The poor motel room, so shabby with its faded wallpaper of fluttering swallows, the sagging mattress on its rickety bed, the sink of chipped gray porcelain, and worst of all—an attempt at cheer—a paper bluebird in a glassless frame, only filled me with low dread. I could feel myself chopped into, gutted, chipped out, destroyed. Finally, on the third day, reduced to bones or beams, I decided to act.

I left the Bluebird and walked in the warm summer air to C.'s. For the first time, I went in through the front door, the office door, without knocking. Her receptionist told me that she was busy with a patient, and squawked when I walked right past her into the examining room, which was empty. I shut that door and went out into the back, into her kitchen, where I surprised her as she was loading a brand-new dishwasher. She had shed her white coat and was wearing a light cotton sweater the color of cantaloupe. Her pants were honeydew green. Her glass earrings and her necklace combined both colors.

We stared at each other, and the sun went behind a cloud. The light in the kitchen changed from amber to gray. Her clothes deepened in color to rusted iron and bitter sage.

"Did Ted tell you that I sold him my house?"

From the look of shock on her face, I knew that he hadn't, and I also knew, because I'd told her repeatedly of the situation with my mother, that she understood immediately what had happened.

"Is he . . ."

"Of course."

"I'll stop him!"

"Just let him."

"Just let him?"

"Pack your stuff," I said. "We'll go now. Our age won't be an issue in the city, and you can start a new practice. Leave Ted the house. Let's go."

Behind her, the dishwasher swished on, the water purred in and heated up. She turned away from me and faced the counter.

"I forgot to add the cups," she said.

A cloud of steam shot out as she opened the door to put in two coffee mugs, but when she closed it and looked at me, I loved her again and I could not give her up..

"Buy my house from Ted. I'll pay you back, and we can live there."

"Is he working over there now?"

"Yes."

She wiped her hands carefully, the way doctors do.

What had she decided? She walked out the front door and I followed her. The walk to my house was about a mile, and this was the first time that we had ever been seen in public together, which, for a moment, made me happy. And then, when we were almost at the house, I understood that the fact that she'd allowed herself to be seen in public with me meant our love was over for good.

><

WHEN WE ARRIVED, I saw that one crew was pulling out the front-porch columns, and another had started work on the rear wall of the house. Ted was in the back, in the gardens, and I tried not to gasp at the way he had allowed the workers to trample the blooms of portulaca and the still-green clumps of sedum into the mulched ground. The bees were everywhere, more than usual, and I felt a terrible guilt at having betrayed them. I apologized in a whisper as I looked around the back, as I saw Ted on the machine that he would use to tear into the back wall of the house.

C. shouted for him to quit. He turned off the engine and she walked over and began to talk to him, her back to me. But he was at an angle and I could see that although he was listening to what she was saying, he was actually looking at me. He looked at me as if I'd taken something from him. A hard look, an easy flicker. Although I was unaccustomed to seeing Ted with her, I did understand that he knew. On some level, not a conscious level but deep down, he knew, as a man knows. He turned from C. and restarted the machine—he rammed it forward. Its claw made a rip in the wall and he backed it up to make another, but before he could move forward again, there was a roar louder than the motor. A darkness poured from my house. A ripsaw whined. A sweetness exploded from the back wall, and Ted and C. were swarmed by the bees.

I was stung only twice, I think by young bees that did not know me.

I retrieved C. and carried her straight to the garage. When I went back for Ted, I saw that he had fallen under a moving cloud that had stung him into silence. Honey dripped from the gash he made in the clapboards; honey dripped from the backhoe. I walked over to him and stood there and watched the bees moving across his back. They seemed finished with their fury; some flew off to repair the hive. As I waited for him to move, I reached out and tasted the honey from the claw of his machine. It was dark in the comb, and rich with the care I'd put into the flowers. I took a bigger piece of comb, brushed off a bee or two, and stuffed the dripping wax into my mouth. C., who had come to the door of the garage, saw me do this. She said it was the most cold-blooded act she'd ever witnessed—me eating honey while I watched Ted lie unconscious underneath the moving bees.

I've always known that in her life she witnessed far worse; still, it was my simple tasting of the honey that caused her to allow Ted to continue with his teardown once he recovered and went back to work. The strange thing is, although he survived a massive number of bee stings then, one single bee sting did him in about a year later. His throat closed, and he was gone before he could even shout for help.

I passed the bar exam and decided to practice Indian law. I got some land back for one tribe, went to Washington, helped with a case regarding tribal religion, one thing and another, until I jumped at the chance to come back. Only not to Pluto, but to the reservation where I would marry Geraldine and where, all along, the truth was waiting.

Although we asked Mother to live with us, she refused, and insisted on remaining in Pluto. When I visited her, I would walk the town and invariably pass the empty lot where our house had stood.

Ted had died before deciding what flimsy box to erect, and the lot had gone to weeds.

One day as I was standing there, a car drove past and then stopped. An aged woman in a baggy summer dress got out and began to walk back toward me. Her dress, a lurid pink floral pattern, threw me off. As she drew near, I recognized C. She'd never worn a flower print before, only solid colors, and she had let her hair go white. Also, she had developed the hunch of an elderly, soft-boned woman. She looked pleased when she saw the look on my face.

"Didn't I tell you I would get old?"

"I didn't believe you," I said.

C. didn't seem concerned in the least at my awkwardness. Rather, it confirmed her belief, I suppose, and she said in a taunting voice, "Did you think I'd stay beautiful? Age gracefully?"

Staring into her face, I saw expressions—shame, defiance, maybe satisfaction—but no tenderness that I could recognize.

"You did what you did," I said, at last.

"I had to so you'd leave."

I took a step toward her, but she turned from me and stomped back to her car. I watched her drive off. After a moment, I walked up the limestone steps and through the phantom oak-and-glass front doors of the house where I grew up. I paced the hall, entered the long rectangle of dining room, rested a hand on the carved cherrywood mantel, then passed into the kitchen. The house was so real around me that I could smell the musty linen in the cedar closet, the gas from the leaky burner on the stove, the sharp tang of geraniums that I had planted in clay pots. I lay down on the exact place where the living room couch had been pushed tight under the leaded-glass windows. I closed my eyes and it was all around me again. The stuffed bookshelves, the paneling, the soft slap of my mother's cards on the table.

I could see from the house of my dark mind the alley, from the alley the street leading to the end of town, its farthest boundary the lucid silence of the dead. Between the graves my path, and along that path her back door, her face, her timeless bed, and the lost architecture of her bones. I turned over and made myself comfortable in the crush of wild burdock. A bee or two hummed in the drowsy air. The swarm had left the rubble and built their houses beneath the earth. They were busy in the graveyard right now, filling the skulls with white combs and the coffins with sweet black honey.

>K

ABOUT A MONTH after our wedding, I was sitting with Geraldine. Between segments of the national news, we were chatting about some illness she'd once had, or I'd once had. C.'s name came up and Geraldine said, "Oh, that doctor who won't treat Indians."

"What?"

In all the time that I knew C., in all time that I'd made love to her, I never knew such a thing. And there I was, a member of our tribe—which proved how off-reservation my mind-set was, growing up. But it was also strange I hadn't heard this in my capacity as a judge, or from my mother. Then I remembered my head bumps.

"Are you sure?"

"Oh, she won't."

"How so?"

Geraldine switched off the television, then returned to sit down beside me. By talking of C. we had already violated our tacit rule in which she was not mentioned. And it had gone further. Geraldine did not believe me.

"You must have known."

It was the first time that my involvement with C. was acknowledged between us. Part of me wanted to drop the subject forever, but another part insisted I defend my innocence.

"I didn't know."

My words sounded false even in my own ears. There was a sudden cleft of space between us. Stricken, I said something I've always wished I could take back.

"But she treated me."

Geraldine raised her eyes to mine, then looked away. I had seen disappointment.

"They always need an exception," she said.

Geraldine then told me of several cases, over the years, where the doctor had turned people down—even in a crisis—and how she had let it be known, generally, that she would not treat our people. They all knew why. It was more than your garden-variety bigotry. There was history involved, said Geraldine. I understood, then, that I'd known everything and nothing about the doctor. Only later did I realize: if I had been the same age as C., it would not have mattered. Even though she'd cured my head bumps, become my lover, I'd always be her one exception. Or worse, her absolution. Every time I touched her, she was forgiven. I thought the whole thing out—as Geraldine says, I took in the history. I had to swallow it before I accepted why Cordelia loved me and why she could not abide that she loved me. Why she would not be seen with me. Why tearing down my house was her only option. Why to this day she lives alone.

# Doctor Cordelia Lochren

# Disaster Stamps of Pluto

※

THE DEAD OF Pluto now outnumber the living, and the cemetery stretches up the low hill I can see from my kitchen, in a jagged display of white stone. There is no bar, no theater, no hardware store, no car repair, just a gas pump. Even the priest comes only once a week to the church. The grass is barely mowed in time for his visit, and of course there are no flowers planted, so by summer the weeds are thick in the old beds. But when the priest does come, there is at least one more person for the town café to feed.

That there is a town café is something of a surprise, and it is no run-down questionable edifice. When the bank pulled out, the family whose drive-in was destroyed by heavy winds bought the building with their insurance money and named it the 4-B's. The granite façade, arched windows, and twenty-foot ceilings make our café seem solid and even luxurious. There is a blackboard for specials and a cigar box by the cash register for the extra change people might donate to the hospital care and surgeries of a local boy whose hand was amputated in a farming accident. I spend a good part of my day, as do most of the people left here, in a booth at the café. For now that there is no point in keeping up our municipal buildings, the café serves as office space for town council and hobby club members, meeting place for church society and card-playing groups. It is an informal staging area for shopping trips to the nearest mall—sixty-eight miles south—and a place for the few young mothers in town to meet and talk, pushing their car-seat convertible strollers back and forth with one foot while hooting and swearing as intensely as their husbands, down at the other end of the row of booths. Those left childless or, like me, spouseless, due to war or distance or attrition, eat here. Also divorced or single persons who, for one reason or another, ended up with a house in Pluto, North Dakota, as their only major possession.

We are still here because to sell our houses for a fraction of their original value would leave us renters for life in the world outside. Yet however tenaciously we cling to yards and living rooms and garages, the grip of one or two of us is broken every year. We are growing less. Our town is dying. I am in charge of more than I bargained for when, in the year of my retirement, I was elected president of Pluto's historical society.

At the time, it looked as though we might survive, if not flourish, well into the next millennium. But then our fertilizer plant went bust and the farm-implement dealership moved to the other side of the reservation. We were left with agriculture, but cheap transport via the interstate had pretty much knocked us out of the game already. Our highway had never been improved, so we began to steadily diminish, and as we did, I became the repository of many untold stories such as people will finally tell when they know there is no use in keeping secrets, or when they see that all that's left of a place will one day reside in documents, and they want those to reflect the truth.

My friend Neve Harp is one of the last of the original founding families. She is the granddaughter of the speculator Frank Harp, who came after the first town-site party failed in its survey. Frank arrived with members of the Dakota and Great Northern Town Site Company, who were establishing a chain of towns along the Great Northern tracks. They hoped to profit. These town sites were meticulously drawn up into maps for risk takers who would purchase lots for their · businesses or homes. Farmers to every direction would buy their supplies in town and patronize the entertainment spots when they came to ship their harvests via rail.

Now, of course, the trains are gone and we are still here, stranded.

The platting crew moved by wagon and camped where they all agreed some natural feature of the landscape or general distance from other towns made a new town desirable. When the men reached the site of what is now our town, they'd already been platting and mapping for several years and had used up in naming their sites presidents and foreign capitals, important minerals, great statesmen, North American mammals, and the names of their own children. To the east lay the neatly marked out town sites of Zeus, Neptune, Apollo, and Athena. They rejected Venus as conducive, perhaps, to future debauchery. Frank Harp suggested Pluto and it was accepted before anyone realized they'd named a town for the god of the underworld. It was always called Pluto, but the official naming of the town did not occur until the boom year of 1906, twenty-four years before Pluto was discovered. It is not without irony, now, that Pluto is the coldest, loneliest, and perhaps the least hospitable body in our solar system, but that was never intended to reflect upon our little municipality.

Dramas of great note have occurred in Pluto. In 1911, five members of a family—parents, a teenage girl, and an eight- and a four-year-old boy—were murdered. In the heat of things, a group of men ran down a party of Indians and what occurred was a shameful piece of what was called at the time "rough justice." The town avoids all mention. My thoughts veer off, too. As it turned out, it was soon found that a neighbor boy apparently deranged with love over the daughter had vanished, and so for many years he remained the only suspect. Of that family, but one survived—a seven-month-old baby who slept through the violence in a crib pushed unobtrusively behind a bed.

In 1928, the owner of the National Bank of Pluto fled the country with most of the town's money. He tried to travel to Brazil. His brother followed, persuaded him to return, and most of the money was restored. By visiting each customer personally, the brother persuaded everyone that their accounts were now safe and the bank survived. The owner killed himself. The brother took over as president. At the very apex of the town cemetery hill, there is a war memorial. In 1949, seventeen names were carved into a chunk of granite that was dedicated to the heroes of both world wars. One of the names, Tobek Hess, is that of the boy believed to have murdered the family. He went to Canada and enlisted early in the First World War. Notice of his death reached his older sister, Electa, who was married to a town council member and had not wanted to move away like the mother and father of the suspect did. Electa insisted that his name be added to the list of the honorable dead. But unknown community members chipped it out of the stone so that now a roughed spot is all that marks his name, and each Veterans Day only sixteen flags are set into the ground around that rock.

There were droughts and freak accidents and other crimes of passion, and there were good things that happened, too. The seven-month-old baby who survived the murders was adopted by the same Oric and Electa Hoag, who raised the baby in pampered love and, once she grew up, at great expense sent her away to an Eastern college, never expecting that she would return. When she did in nine years, she was a doctor. The first female doctor in the region. She set up her practice and restored the house she had inherited, where the murders had taken place—a small, charming, clapboard farmhouse that borders the cemetery on the western edge of town. Six hundred and eighty acres of farmland stretch from the house and barn. With the lease money from those acres, she was able to maintain a clinic and a nurse, and to keep her practice going, even when her patients could not always pay for her services.

One thing shamed her, only, one specific paralysis. She was known to turn Indians away as patients; it was thought that she was a bigoted person. In truth, she experienced an unsteady weakness in their presence. It seemed beyond her control, as was the other thing. She loved someone far too young for herself, inappropriate in that other way, too, but in his presence her feelings gripped her with the force of unquestionable fate. Or a mad lapse, she now believes.

At the same time those feelings were often the only part of her life that made sense. To try and break that bond, she married, but was widowed. She formed a final relationship with a university swimming coach whose job did not permit him to leave the campus for long. They had always intended that he would move to Pluto once he retired. But instead, he married a student and moved to Southern California, so he could have a year-round pool.

><

THE BROTHER OF the suicide banker was Murdo Harp. He was the son of the town's surveyor and the father of my friend. Neve is now in her seventies like me; she and I take daily walks to keep our joints oiled. Neve Harp was married three times and kidnapped once—she survived all four events. She has returned to her maiden name and the house she inherited from her father. She is a tall woman, somewhat stooped for lack of calcium in her diet, although on my advice she now ingests plenty. She is one of those interested in restoring authenticity to town history. Both Neve and I have always had the habit of activity, and every day, no matter what the weather (up to blizzard conditions) our two- or three-mile walk takes us around the perimeter of Pluto.

"We orbit like an ancient couple of moons," she said to me one day.

"If there were people in Pluto, they could set their clocks by us," I answered, "or worship us."

We laughed to think of ourselves as moon goddesses.

Most of the yards and lots were empty. There hasn't been money in the town coffers for street repairs and the majority have been unimproved or left to gravel. Only the main street is paved with asphalt now, but the rough surfaces are fine with us. They give more purchase. We don't want to slip. Breaking a hip is our gravest dread. Once you are immobile at our age, that is the end.

"I've been meaning to tell you why Murdo's brother, Octave, you know, tried to run away to Brazil," she told me one day, as though the scandal had just occurred. "I want you to write the whole thing up for the town historical newsletter. I would like the truth to become part of our official record now!"

I asked Neve to wait until we finished our walk and sat down at the café, so that I could take notes, but she was too excited by the story beating its wings inside of her, alive and insistent that morning for some reason, and she had to talk as we made our way along.

"As you remember," said Neve, "Octave drowned himself when the river was at its lowest, in only two feet of water. He basically had to throw himself upon a puddle and breathe it in. It was thought that only a woman could have caused a man to inflict such a gruesome death upon himself, but it was not love. He did not die for love." Neve paused and walked meditatively for about a hundred yards. Then she began again. "Do you remember stamp collections? How important those were? The rage?"

I said that I did remember. People still collect stamps, I told her.

"Yes, yes, they dabble like my brother Edward," she said. "But for Octave the stamps were everything. He kept his stamp collection in the bank's main vault. One of this town's best kept secrets is exactly how much money that collection was worth. Even I was not aware of it until very recently. When, as you know, our bank was robbed in 'thirty-two, the robbers forced their way into the vault. They grabbed what cash there was and completely ignored the fifty-nine albums and twenty-two specially constructed felt boxes framed in ebony. That stamp collection was worth many times what the robbers got. It was worth almost as much money as was in the entire bank, in fact."

"What happened to it?" I was very much intrigued, as I'd heard only confusing rumors.

Neve gave me a sly, sideways look.

"My brother took bits and pieces of that collection, but he had no idea what was really there. I kept most of the stamps when the bank changed hands. I like looking at them, you see. They're better than television. The collection is in my front room. Stacked on a table. You've seen the albums but you've never commented. You've never looked inside of them. If you had, you would have been enchanted, like me, with the delicacy, the detail, and the endless variety, at first. Later you would have wanted to know more about the stamps them-selves and the need to know and understand their histories would have taken hold of you, as it did my uncle, my brother, and as it recently has me, though thankfully to a much lesser degree. Of course, you have your own interests."

"Yes," I said, "thank God for those."

As we passed by the church, we saw the priest was there on his visit. The poor man waved at us when we called out a greeting to him. No one had remembered, so he was cutting the grass. He looked sad and overworked.

"They treat the good ones like simple beasts," said Neve. Then she shrugged and we pressed on. "In reading my uncle's old letters, going through his files, I've made a discovery. His specialty, for all stamp collectors begin at some point to lean in a certain direction, was what you might call the dark side of stamp collecting."

I looked at Neve, thinking that I'd seen dark tendencies in her myself, but still surprised about the stamps.

"After he had acquired the Holy Grails of Philately—British Guiana's one-cent magenta, Sweden's 1855 three-cent issue which is orange instead of blue-green, as well as many stamps of the Thurn and Taxis postal system and superb specimens of the highly prized Mulready cover—my uncle's melancholia drew him specifically to what are called errors. I think Sweden's three-cent began it all."

"Of course," I said, "even I know of the upside-down airplane stamp."

"The twenty-four-cent carmine rose and blue Invert. Yes!" She seemed delighted. "I've been reading through his notes and combing through the collection for that one. He says that he began to collect errors in color, like the Swedish stamp, very tricky, then overprints, imperforate errors, value missings, omitted vignettes, and freaks. He speaks of one entire album page devoted to a seventeen-year-old boy, Frank Baptist, who ran stamps off an old handpress for the Confederate government. I've yet to determine which it was, but am sure I'll find it."

Neve charged across a gravelly patch of road, much elated to share the story, and I hastened to stay within earshot. Stopping to catch her breath, she leaned on a tree and told me that about six years before he absconded with the bank's money, Octave Harp had gone into disasters—that is, stamps and covers (envelopes or similar materials) that had survived the dreadful occurrences that test and destroy us. These pieces of mail, marked by experience, took their value from the gravity of their condition. They were water stained, tattered, even bloodied, said Neve. Such damage was part of their allure.

By then, we had come to the former bank/café, and I was glad to sit down where I could take a few notes on Neve's revelations. I borrowed some sheets of paper and a pen from the owner, and we ordered our coffee and sandwiches. I always have a Denver sandwich and Neve orders a BLT without the bacon. She is a strict vegetarian, the only one in Pluto. We sipped our coffee.

"I have just read a book I ordered," said Neve, "on philately, in which it says that stamp collecting offers refuge to the confused and gives new vigor to fallen spirits. I think Octave was hoping he would obtain something of the sort. But the more he dwelt on the disasters, the worse he felt, according to my father. He would brighten whenever he obtained something valuable for his collection, though. He corresponded with people all over the globe; it was quite remarkable. I've got files and files of his correspondence with stamp dealers. He would take years tracking down a surviving stamp or cover that had been through a particular disaster. Wars, of course, from the American Revolution, the Crimean War, the First World War. Soldiers would frequently carry letters on their persons, of course. One doesn't like to think how those letters ended up in the hands of collectors. But he preferred natural disasters and, to a lesser extent, man-made accidents." Neve tapped the side of her cup. "He would have been fascinated by the *Hindenburg* and certainly there would have been a stamp or two involved, somewhere. And our modern disasters, too, of course."

I knew what she was thinking of, suddenly—those letters mailed on the day we lost our thirty-fifth president, or the mail, I pictured White House thank-you notes, that had been waiting, perhaps, in Jackie's purse. I went a little cold with dismay to think that many of these bits of paper were perhaps now in the hands of dealers and for sale all over the world to people like Octave. Neve and I think very much alike, and I saw that she was going to sugar her coffee—a sign of distress, since she has a bit of a blood sugar problem.

"Don't," I said. "You'll be awake all night."

"I know." She sugared her coffee anyway and put the glass canister back. "Isn't it strange, though, how time mutes the horror of events, how they cease to affect us in the same way? But I began to tell you all of this in order to explain why Octave left for Brazil."

"With so much money. Now I'm starting to imagine he was on the trail of a stamp."

"You're exactly right," said Neve. "I was talking to my brother yesterday, and oddly enough, he remembered that our father told us what Octave was looking for. This object had entered the possession of a very wealthy Brazilian woman. In his collection notes he mentions a letter that survived the explosion of Krakatoa in 1883, a Dutch stamp placed upon a letter written just before and carried off on a steamer. He had a letter from the sack of mail frozen onto the back of a New Hampshire mail carrier who died in the east-coast blizzard of 1888. An authenticated letter from the *Titanic*, too, but then there must have been quite a bit of mail recovered for some reason, as he refers to other pieces. But he was not as interested in sea disasters. No, the prize he was after was a letter from the year A.D. 79."

I hadn't known there was mail service then, but Neve assured me that mail was extremely old, and that it was Herodotus who'd coined the motto "Neither snow nor rain nor dead of night etc." over five hundred years before the date she'd just referred to, the year Mount Vesuvius blew up and buried Pompeii in volcanic ash. "As you may know," she went on, "the site was looted and picked through by curiosity seekers for a century and a half after it was discovered, before anything was done about preservation. By then, quite a number of recovered objects had found their way into the hands of collectors. A letter that may have been meant for Pliny the Younger, from the Elder, apparently surfaced for a tantalizing moment in London, but by the time Octave could contact the dealer the parchment had been stolen. The dealer tracked it, however, through a shadowy resale into the hands of a Portuguese rubber baron's wife, a woman with obsessions similar to Octave's—though she was not a stamp collector. She was interested in all things Pompeii, had her walls painted in exact replicas of Pompeii frescoes—women whipping each other, and so on."

"Imagine that. In Brazil."

"No stranger than a small-town North Dakota banker amassing a world-class collection of stamps."

I agreed with her, and tried to remember what I could of Neve's uncle.

"Octave was, of course, a bachelor."

"And he lived very modestly, too. Still, he hadn't money enough to come near purchasing the Pliny letter. He tried to leave the country with the bank's money and his stamp collection, but the stamps held him back. I think the customs officials became involved in questions regarding the collection—whether it should be allowed to leave the country, and so on. The Frank Baptist stamps were an interesting side note to American history, for instance. Murdo caught up with him in New York City. Octave had had a breakdown and was paralyzed in some hotel room. He was terrified that his collection would be confiscated. When he returned to Pluto, he began drinking heavily, and from then on he was never the same."

"And the Pompeii letter, what became of it?"

"There was a letter from the Brazilian lady, who had still hoped to sell the piece to Octave, a wild letter full of cross-outs and stained with tears."

"A disaster letter?"

"Yes, I suppose you could say so. Her three-year-old son had somehow got hold of the Pompeii missive and in his play reduced it to dust. So in a way it was a letter from a woman that broke his heart."

There was nothing more to say and we were both in thoughtful moods by then. Our sandwiches were before us and we ate them.

Neve and I spend our evenings quietly, indoors, reading or watching television, listening to music, eating our meager suppers alone. If a volcano should rise out of the ancient lake-bed earth and blow, covering us suddenly with killing ash, ours would be calm forms, preserved sitting gravely as the fates, staring transfixed at a picture or a word. I have seen other plaster forms in books. I know the ones from Pompeii were first noted as mysterious absences in the solid ash. When the spaces were filled with plaster, and the volcanic debris chipped away, the piteous nature of those final human moments were revealed. Sometimes, I think I am more akin to that absence, before the substance. I am less the final gesture than the void preceding it. I have already disappeared, as one does when long accustomed to one's own company.

Yet, I find my time from dusk to midnight wonderful. I am not lonely. I know I haven't long to enjoy the luxuries of privacy and silence and I cherish my familiar surroundings. Neve, however, misses her two stepchildren and stepgrandchildren from the last marriage. She spends many evenings on the telephone, although they only live in Fargo and she sees them often. Both Neve and I find it strange that we are old, and we are both amazed at how quickly our lives went— Neve with her abduction and her multiple marriages and I with my own painful ecstasies. We are often surprised when we catch sight of ourselves.

As I often remind myself, I am fortunate in my age to have a good companion like Neve, though she does luxuriate in dark thoughts sometimes.

That night, she does have an episode of black moodiness brought on by the sugar in her coffee, though I do not say so, when I answer her first phone call. She speaks as she sometimes does of the strange beauty of her kidnapper, and what she taught him, or he taught her, on the mattress in the back room of his house. He became a decorated veteran and, when he returned from Korea, grew in charismatic perversity—he became the leader of a religion marked by unfathomable laws. A few leftovers have migrated, worn out and twisted, into the local churches over the years. But I've heard about Billy's insatiable penis way too many times. I divert her, and she finally hangs up. But later on, she makes an odd discovery.

Flanked by two bright reading lamps, I am quietly absorbing a rather too sweet novel sent by a book club that I subscribe to, when the telephone rings again. Speaking breathlessly, Neve tells me that she has been looking through albums all evening with a magnifying glass. She has understood something that she should have realized long ago.

"My brother has the real collection," she says, her voice squeaking in huge distress. "I took the money and let him paw through the stamps. At the time, I didn't know. I hadn't any idea that he knew what he was looking for. The upshot is: mine are worthless. His are worth . . ." She cannot speak. Her voice catches and she mews softly. Her lips are pressed against the receiver. "A million. Maybe. He cheated me."

I restrain my laughter and do not say, "Everybody knows you cheated him!"

As she has continued to sift through Octave's papers and letters, she has found something else that distresses her. In a file that she had never before opened, a set of eight or nine letters, all addressed to the same person, with canceled stamps, the paper distorted as though it had been wet, the writing smudged, each varying from the other by some slight degree—a minor flaw in the cancellation mark, a slight rip. She had examined them in some puzzlement and noticed that one bears a fifty-cent violet Benjamin Franklin issued two years after the cancellation, which was dated just before the sinking of the *Titanic*.

"I am finding it very hard to admit the obvious," she said, "because I had formed such a sympathetic opinion of my uncle. But I believe he was experimenting with forged disaster mail, and that what I found was no less than evidence." She sounds furious, as though he had tried to sell her the item himself. (Perhaps, I think, she has.) "He was offering his fake authenticated letter to a dealer in London. There were attempts at, and rejections of, certification letters, too."

I try to talk Neve down, but when she gets into a mood like this all of her rages and sorrows come back to her and it seems she must berate the world or mourn each one. True, she has some tenuous family outside the area and will not be trapped here like me. But I do not want her to say it. As soon as possible, I put the phone down, and my insipid novel as well. Neve's moods are catching. I try to shake off a sudden miasma of turbulent dread, but before I know it I have walked into my bedroom and am opening the chest at the foot of my bed and I am looking through my family's clothes—all else was destroyed or taken away, but the undertaker washed and kept these (kindly, I think) and he gave them to me when I moved into this house. I find the somber envelope marked Jorgenson's Funeral Parlor, and slip from it the valentine, within its own envelope, that must have been hidden in a pocket. It is a hideous thing, all schmaltz and paper lace. I note for the first time the envelope bears a commemorative stamp of the Huguenot monument in Florida. What a bloody piece of history to place on a valentine, I think, and yet, inadvertantly appropriate.

Sometimes I wonder if the sounds of fear and anguish, the thunder of the shotgun, is hidden from me somewhere in my brain, the most obscure corner. I might have died of dehydration as I wasn't found for three days, but I don't remember that, either—not at all—and have never been abnormally afraid of thirst or obsessed with food or water. Apparently, so I've been told, I was fed by one of the Indians later hanged. No, my childhood was very happy and I had everything—a swing, a puppy, doting parents. Nothing but good things happened to me. I loved getting high marks and having friends. I was chosen queen of the prom. I never underwent a shock at the sudden revelation of my origins, for I was told the story early on and came to accept who I was. The only thing is, I was allowed to believe that the lynched Indians had been the ones responsible. I believed that until Neve Harp set me straight—in fact, showed me all the clippings. Told me all the points of view. And now I think that my adopted mother even suspected that somewhere in our area there still might reside the actual killer, not Tobek but another—invisible, remorseful. For we'd find small, carefully folded bills of cash hidden outdoors in places Electa or I would be certain to find them—beneath a flowerpot, in my tree house, in the hollow handles of my bicycle—and we'd always hold the wadded square up and say, "Santa Claus has been here again." But truly, I am hard-pressed to name more than the predictable sadnesses that pass through one's life. It is as though the freak of my survival charged my disposition with gratitude. Or as if my family absorbed all of the misfortune that might have come my way. I have loved intensely. I have lived an ordinary and a satisfying life, and I have been privileged to be of service to people. Most people. There is no one I mourn to the point of madness and nothing I would really do over again.

So why when I stroke my sister's valentine against the side of my face, and why when I touch the folded linen of her vest, and when I reach for my brothers' overalls and the apron my mother died in on that day, and bundle these things with my father's ancient, laundered, hay-smelling clothes to my stomach, and press, and why, when I gather my family into my arms, do I catch my breath at the wild upsurge, as if a wind had lifted me, a black wing of air? And why, when that happens, do I fly toward some blurred and ineradicable set of features that seems to rush away from me as stars do? At blinding speeds, never stopping?

When Pluto's empty at last and this house is reclaimed by earth, when the war memorial is toppled and the bank/café stripped for its brass and granite, when all that remains of Pluto is our collected historical newsletters bound in volumes donated to the local collections at the University of North Dakota, what then? What shall I have said? How shall I have depicted the truth?

The valentine has always told me that the boy's name should not have been scratched from the war memorial. Not only were innocent people hanged, unbearably murdered for nobody's justice, but even that boy was not the killer after all. For my dead sister loved him in return, or she would not have carried his message upon her person. And if he had her love, he probably fled out of grief and despair. Perhaps he'd been there. Perhaps he'd seen her dead. Poor Tobek. But if not the boy, who was it? My father? But no, he was felled from behind. There is no one to accuse. Somewhere in this town or out in the world, then, the being has existed who stalked after my brothers and destroyed them as they fled toward the barn, who saw the beauty of my sister and mother and shot them dead. And to what profit? For nothing was taken. Nothing gained. To what end the mysterious waste?

An extremely touchy case came my way about twenty years ago. The patient was an old farmer who'd lived his life on acreage that abutted the farthest edges of our land. Warren Wolde was a taciturn crank, who nevertheless had a way with animals. He had a number of peculiar beliefs, I am told, regarding the United States government. Certain things were never mentioned around him—Congress being one, and all of the amendments to the Constitution. It got so his opinion was avoided, for fear he would fly into a sick, obliterating rage. Even if one stuck to safe topics with him, he looked at people in a penetrating way they found disquieting. But Warren Wolde was in no condition to disquiet me when I came onto the farm to treat him. Two weeks before, the farm's expensive blooded bull had hooked then trampled him, concentrating most of the damage on one thigh and leg. He'd absolutely refused to see a doctor and now a feverish infection had set in and the wound was necrotic. He was very strong, and fought being moved to a hospital so violently that his family had decided to call me instead and see whether I could save his leg.

I could, and did, though the means was painful and awful and it meant twice-daily visits, which I could ill afford in my schedule. At each change of the dressing and debridement, I tried to dose Wolde with morphine, but he resisted. He did not trust me yet and feared that if he lost consciousness he'd wake without his leg. Gradually, I managed to heal the wound and also to quiet him. When I first came to treat him, he'd reacted to the sight of me with a horror unprecedented in my medical experience. It was a fear mixed with panic that had only gradually dulled to a silent wariness. As his leg healed, he opened to my visits, and by the time he was hobbling on crutches, he seemed to anticipate my presence with an eager pleasure so tender and pathetic that it startled everyone around him. But he'd shuck off his forbidding and strange persona just for me, they said, and sink back into an immobilizing fury once I'd left. He never quite healed enough to take on all of his old tasks, but lasted pretty well for another

few years before he went entirely senile and was sent down to the
state hospital. At an advanced age he died naturally, in his sleep, of a
thrown blood clot. To my surprise, I was contacted several weeks
later by a lawyer.

The man said that his client, Warren Wolde, had left a package for
me, which I asked him to send in the mail. When the package arrived,
addressed in an awkward script that certainly could have been
Wolde's, I opened the box immediately. Inside were hundreds upon
hundreds of wadded bills of assorted (mainly small) denominations,
and of course I recognized their folded pattern as identical to the bills
that had turned up for me all through my childhood. I called the lawyer, who connected me with the nurse who'd found Wolde dead, and
I asked if she could shed any light on his state of mind.

It was the music that killed him, she said.

I asked what music and she told me that Wolde had collapsed when
a visitor named Peace had played a little violin concert in the common
room. He'd died that night. I thanked her. The name Peace upset me.
I could perhaps believe that the money gifts and the legacy were only
marks of Wolde's sympathy for the tragic star of my past, and, later,
gratitude for what I'd done. I might be inclined to think so, were it not
for so many small, strange truths. The name, the violin that belonged
to the name, the music that spoke the name. And the first few times I
had come to treat Wolde, I remember, he reared from me in a horror
that seemed too personal, and pitiable. There had been something of
a recalled nightmare in his face—I'd thought so even then—and I'd
not been touched later on by the remarkable change in his character.
On the contrary, it had given me a chill.

⋊⋉

THOSE OF YOU who have faithfully subscribed to this newsletter know
that our dwindling subscription list has made it necessary to reduce
the length of our articles. So I must end here. But it appears, anyway,
that since only the society's treasurer, Neve Harp, and I, have con-
vened to make any decisions at all regarding the preservation and
upkeep of our little collection, and as only the two of us are left to

contribute more material to this record, our membership is now closed. We declare our society defunct. We shall, however, keep walking the perimeter of Pluto until our footsteps wear our orbit into the earth. My last act as the president of Pluto's historical society is this: I would like to declare a town holiday to commemorate the year I saved the life of my family's murderer.

The wind will blow. The devils rise. All who celebrate shall be ghosts. And there will be nothing but eternal dancing, dust on dust, everywhere you look.

Oh my, too apocalyptic, I think as I leave my house to walk over to Neve's to help her cope with her sleepless night. Dust on dust! There are very few towns where old women can go out at night and enjoy the breeze, so there is that about Pluto. I take my cane to feel the way, for the air is so black I think already we are invisible.

THANK YOU: Terry Karten, this book's editor; Trent Duffy, this book's copy editor; Deborah Treisman; Jane Beirn; and Andrew Wylie. Thanks also to Sandeep Patel, M.D.

The author gratefully acknowledges the editors of the magazines and anthologies in which parts of this novel have appeared in different form: "The Plague of Doves," *The New Yorker* and *The O. Henry Prize Stories 2006*; "Sister Godzilla," *The Atlantic Monthly*; "Shamengwa," *The New Yorker* and *The Best American Short Stories 2003*; "Town Fever," *North Dakota Quarterly*; "Come In" (as "Gleason"), *The New Yorker* and *The Best American Mystery Stories 2007*; "Satan: Hijacker of a Planet," *The Atlantic Monthly* and *Prize Stories 1998: The O. Henry Awards*; "The Reptile Garden" and "Demolition," *The New Yorker;* and "Disaster Stamps of Pluto," *The New Yorker* and *The Best American Mystery Stories of 2005*.

As in all of Louise Erdrich's books, the reservation, towns, and people depicted are imagined places and characters, with these exceptions: Louis Riel, and also the name Holy Track. In 1897, at the age of thirteen, Paul Holy Track was hanged by a mob in Emmons County, North Dakota. The section "Town Fever" draws upon a Red River town-site speculation in 1857 by Daniel S. B. Johnston.

Any mistakes in the Ojibwe or Michif language are the author's and do not reflect upon her patient teachers.

Part of the proceeds of this and all of Louise Erdrich's books help fund Birchbark Books, an independent bookstore, and Birchbark Press, an Ojibwe-language publishing venture, located in Minneapolis, Minnesota (www.birchbarkbooks.com). This book is printed on recycled paper.

## About the author

## About the book

## Read on

Insights,
Interviews
& More . . .

# A Conversation with Louise Erdrich

*Where were you born, Louise?*

I was born in Little Falls, Minnesota, and grew up in Wahpeton, North Dakota. I am an enrolled member of the Turtle Mountain Chippewa, Pembina Band.

*You have a rich ethnic heritage— Ojibwe and French on your mother's side, German on your father's side. How would you describe this mix?*

Fry bread and sauerkraut.

*In an earlier P.S. you owned up to throwing "terrible tantrums" as a small child. How would you characterize your childhood between tantrums?*

Between tantrums I was a model child and made my parents very happy.

*What is your earliest memory of reading and being influenced by a book?*

I was astounded at a young age by Orwell's *Animal Farm*—the greatest pig story ever written!

*Is it true that you wore cowboy boots at Dartmouth?*

Red ones, with very pointy toes. I had also just dyed my long hair red and gotten a permanent. I was a startling

*" Is it true that you wore cowboy boots at Dartmouth?*

*Red ones. "*

2

addition to Dartmouth's Native American program. I was very lucky to go to Dartmouth. It was 1972, the first year of co-education and one of the earliest years of Dartmouth's re-commitment to native education.

***Do you have any unusual or otherwise compelling anecdotes about your collegiate experience?***

Working in the stacks at Baker Library was a source of great joy, as was Orozco's devastating mural in the basement. One panel shows a huge skeleton in a black academic cap and gown giving birth to baby academics contained in bell jars.

***Is it true that you once worked as a flagwaver for a road crew? If so, what are your memories of the job?***

Tears of boredom and hot feet.

***Speaking of jobs, you opened a bookstore in Minneapolis (Birchbark Books and Native Arts) in June of 2000. Do you spend a fair amount of time there?***

I get to work the floor a little and suggest books, but I am not allowed near the computer cash register. I check in every day. Otherwise I am busy writing.

***What has been your biggest surprise in operating a bookstore?***

That this quixotic, enjoyable effort by obsessive book lovers works at all. That we have remained open. ▶

## Meet Louise Erdrich

Persia Erdrich

LOUISE ERDRICH is the author of twelve novels, as well as volumes of poetry, children's books, and a memoir of early motherhood. Her novel *Love Medicine* won the National Book Critics Circle Award. *The Last Report on the Miracles at Little No Horse* was a finalist for the National Book Award. In 2009, she published *The Red Convertible: Selected and New Stories, 1978–2008*, the first and only collection of her award-winning short fiction. She lives in Minnesota with her daughters and is the owner of Birchbark Books, a small independent bookstore. ᦓ

**A Conversation with Louise Erdrich**
(*continued*)

*You have said that both sides of your family were given to oral storytelling. Prior to writing each novel, do you find yourself sharing its basic story aloud with, say, your daughters?*

Often, yes. My daughters are great readers and very direct in their reactions.

*Do you have any writerly quirks? When and where do you write? PC or pen?*

I write by hand in large notebooks, then transfer the draft to computer. As for writerly quirks, I'm afraid my family knows them better than I do. I am a very ordinary person. I do keep a number of interesting things near my computer, though—a shrine to the BVM made of seashells, exquisite Huichol masks, and a bust of H. P. Lovecraft by Gahan Wilson, which I received in 1997.

*What do you rely upon for stimulation when you are writing? Do you observe any particular beverage ritual?*

Earl Grey tea with cream and lump sugar. About one gallon per day. Also, from late summer through midwinter, five or six of the apples that my father grows in his Wahpeton orchard. Northwest Greenings are my favorite.

*Do you have any pet hates?*

Loud, persistent buzzing noises of mechanical origin. For instance, leaf

66 I do keep a number of interesting things near my computer, though—a shrine to the BVM made of seashells, exquisite Huichol masks, and a bust of H. P. Lovecraft by Gahan Wilson, which I received in 1997. 99

blowers. Besides that, unkindness small and vast.

**What single thing would improve your quality of life?**

Perhaps a doppelgänger would be nice—someone to do publicity, give coherent lectures, read to schoolchildren, put up Christmas lights, and so on, leaving me in my chair to write books.

**What is the most important lesson life has taught you?**

Never rationalize anything that feels wrong.

**What engages your time outside of family, the bookstore, and writing?**

That seems to take up most of it, but I do study the Ojibwe language.

**What are your goals and dreams?**

To rear happy children; to write the best books I can; to be accidentally "raptured"—although, come to think of it, the most interesting people will surely be left down here on earth. ∾

# From Mustache Maude to 9/11
## The Story Behind the Book

**The Title**

"The title actually came from a very old newspaper clipping. The incident that begins the book was true. There was a plague of doves, and the congregation of a Catholic church was gathered in order to try and walk through the fields praying to drive away the doves and prevent them from eating the crops. This was in North Dakota.

"It haunted me as some of the other historical pieces in this book did. It took a long time to put them together but this particular story also includes one of my favorite characters from North Dakota history. Her name is Mustache Maude. She was a real woman; she was a rustler; she was also a rancher. And she did pick up a pig from time to time" (from an interview with Liane Hansen, National Public Radio's *Weekend Edition*).

**Inspiration**

"The book revolves or spins off of a lynching of Native Americans—Native American men, young men. One boy was only thirteen years old. This particular incident, which occurred in 1897, would not leave my thoughts. I wrote around it for many years and put together differing stories. . . .

"My mother is Chippewa, or Ojibwe, Turtle Mountain Ojibwe. My father is non-Indian. This book talks about what it's like for a community to come to terms with an unresolved act of cruel injustice. This act of vengeance reverberates throughout the whole community for generations. But by the end, people are so intertwined and intermixed that one of the descendants of both the lynchers and the victim says, 'There's no unraveling the rope. We're all in this together' " (from an interview with Amy Goodman, *Democracy Now!*).

**The Writing**

"The novel was started in pieces, some of it started way back in the 1990s. . . . I had pieces of it put together for a long time, and they just really took on a shape only a few years ago.

"I realized I should work with these people and figure out what was going on. It turned out I was writing a mystery. And I was very happy because I had never written a mystery before. So then I went back and constructed it that way" (from an interview with Geeta Sharma-Jensen, *Milwaukee Journal Sentinel*).

**Voice**

"A voice that is going to take over a story is someone you will have prepared for quite some time without knowing it. . . . I've been reading what the judge in this book read, Marcus Aurelius, *The Roman Stoic*, for it informs the judge's voice" (from an interview with John Freeman, *St. Petersburg Times*). ▶

❝ 'And I was very happy because I had never written a mystery before. So then I went back and constructed it that way.' ❞

**From Mustache Maude to 9/11** *(continued)*

## Structure

"I'm trying to tell a story that goes back and forth through time, showing the influence of history on the passions and decisions of people who live in the present" (from an interview with Liane Hansen, National Public Radio's *Weekend Edition*).

## Vengeance

"Erdrich . . . sees parallels between the hunger for vengeance that followed the murders of six members of a North Dakota farm family in Emmons County more than a century ago and the aftermath of 9/11.

" 'I think vengeance, rather than sitting back and allowing justice to be done over time, is really so much a part of our history. And unfortunately, it's part of our present, as well. . . .

" 'This is common after any sort of horrific event. There's a terrible thirst for someone to blame, for someone to be caught and punished right away, and immediately. We saw that after 9/11. I felt the same thing in my own heart. . . . And it became twisted around until we're in Iraq" (from an interview with Jeff Baenen, Associated Press). ∾

# Have You Read?
## More by Louise Erdrich

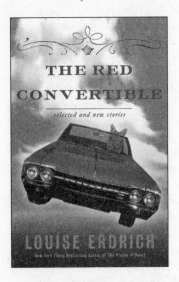

### THE RED CONVERTIBLE

This unique volume brings together, for the first time, three decades of stories by one of the most innovative and exciting writers of our day.

Erdrich is a fearless and inventive writer. In her fictional world, the mystical can emerge from the everyday, the comic turn suddenly tragic, and violence and beauty inhabit a single emotional landscape. Each character in these stories is full of surprises, and the twists and leaps of Erdrich's imagination are made all the more meaningful by the deeper truth of human feeling that underlies them.

In "Saint Marie," the ardent longing that propels a fourteen-year-old Indian girl up the hill to the Sacred Heart Convent and

**Have You Read?** *(continued)*

into a life-and-death struggle with the
diabolical Sister Leopolda fuels a story
of breathtaking power and originality.
"Knives" features a homely butcher's
assistant, a devoted reader of love stories,
who falls for a good-looking predator,
a traveling salesman, with devastating
consequences for each of them. "Le Mooz"
evokes the stinging flames of passion in
old age—"Margaret had exhausted three
husbands, and Nanapush had outlived his
six wives"—with unexpected humor that
turns suddenly bittersweet at the story's
close. A passion for music in "Naked
Woman Playing Chopin" proves more
powerful than any experience of carnal or
spiritual love; indeed, when Agnes DeWitt
removes her clothing to enter the music
of a particular composer, she sweeps all
before her and transcends mortality and
time itself.

In *The Red Convertible*, readers can
follow the evolution of narrative styles,
the shifts and metamorphoses in
Erdrich's fiction, over the past thirty
years. These stories, spellbinding in
their boldness and beauty, are a
stunning literary achievement.

"A wondrous short story writer . . .
creating a keepsake of the American
experience. . . . A master tuner of the
taut emotions that keen between parent
and child, man and woman, brother and
sister, and man and beast."

—Liesl Schillinger,
*New York Times Book Review*

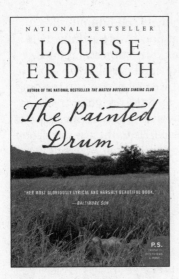

## THE PAINTED DRUM

While appraising the estate of a New Hampshire family descended from a North Dakota Indian agent, Faye Travers is startled to discover a rare moose skin and cedar drum fashioned long ago by an Ojibwe artisan. And so begins an illuminating journey both backward and forward in time, following the strange passage of a powerful yet delicate instrument, and revealing the extraordinary lives it has touched and defined.

Louise Erdrich's *Painted Drum* explores the often fraught relationship between mothers and daughters, the strength of family, and the intricate rhythms of grief with all the grace, wit, and startling beauty that characterizes this acclaimed author's finest work.

"With fearlessness and humility, in a narrative that flows more artfully than ever between destruction and rebirth, Erdrich has opened herself to possibilities beyond what we merely see—to the dead alive and busy, to the breath of trees and the souls of wolves—and inspires readers to open their hearts to these mysteries as well." —*Washington Post Book World*

**FOUR SOULS**

Fleur Pillager takes her mother's name, Four Souls, for strength and walks from her Ojibwe reservation to the cities of Minneapolis and Saint Paul. There she seeks restitution from and revenge on the lumber baron who has stripped her reservation. But revenge is never simple; her intentions are complicated by her dangerous compassion for the man who wronged her.

"Full of satisfying yet unexpected twists. . . . *Four Souls* begins with clean, spare prose but finishes in gorgeous incantations and poetry."
—*New York Times Book Review*

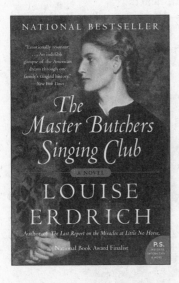

## THE MASTER BUTCHERS SINGING CLUB

Fidelis Waldvogel leaves behind his small German village in the quiet aftermath of World War I; he sets out for America with his new wife, Eva—the widow of his best friend, killed in action. Finally settling in North Dakota, Fidelis works hard to build a business, a home for his family, and a singing club consisting of the best voices in town. But his

**Have You Read?** *(continued)*

adventures in the New World truly begin when he encounters Delphine Watzka, a local woman whose origins are a mystery, even to herself. Delphine meets Eva and is enchanted; she meets Fidelis and the ground trembles. . . .

"An enrapturing plunge into the depths of the human heart."
—*Washington Post Book World*

"[A] masterpiece. . . . Erdrich never hits a false note." —*Pittsburgh Post-Gazette*

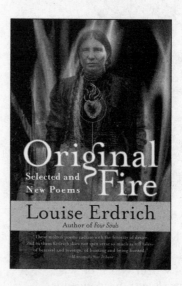

**ORIGINAL FIRE:**
**SELECTED AND NEW POEMS**

In this important new collection, her first in fourteen years, Louise Erdrich has selected poems from her two previous books of poetry (*Jacklight*

and *Baptism of Desire*) and added
new poems to create *Original Fire*.

This profound and accessible
collection anticipates and enlarges
upon many of the themes, and even
the characters, of Erdrich's prose.
A sequence of story poems called
"The Potchikoo Stories" recounts
the life and afterlife of the questing
trickster Potchikoo; here, Erdrich
echoes the wit and humanity of the
inimitable Nanapush, who appears
in several of her novels. Similarly, the
group of poems called "The Butcher's
Wife" contains the germ of Erdrich's
novel *The Master Butchers Singing Club*.

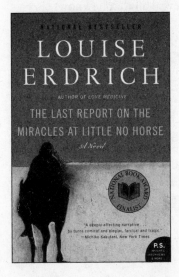

**THE LAST REPORT ON THE MIRACLES
AT LITTLE NO HORSE**

A finalist for the National Book Award,
*The Last Report on the Miracles at Little*

*No Horse* tells the story of Father Damien Modeste, who for more than half a century has served his beloved people, the Ojibwe, on the remote reservation of Little No Horse. Now, nearing the end of his life, he dreads the discovery of his physical identity, for he is a woman who has lived as a man. To complicate his fears, Father Damien's quiet life changes when a troubled colleague comes to the reservation to investigate the life of a perplexing, difficult, possibly false saint, Sister Leopolda. Father Damien alone knows the strange truth of Sister Leopolda's piety and is faced with the most difficult decision of his life: Should he reveal all that he knows and risk everything? Or should he manufacture a protective history though he believes Leopolda's wonder-working is motivated by evil?

"A deeply affecting narrative. . . . Ms. Erdrich uses her remarkable storytelling gifts to endow it with both emotional immediacy and the timeless power of fable. . . . By turns comical and tragic, the stories span the history of this Ojibwe tribe and its members' wrestlings with time and change and loss."
　　　　—Michiko Kakutani, *New York Times*

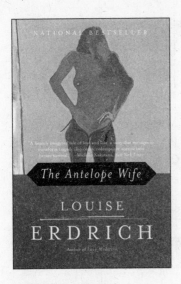

## THE ANTELOPE WIFE

When a powwow trader kidnaps a strange and silent young woman from a Native American camp and brings her back to live with him as his wife, connections to the past rear up to confront an urban community. Soon the patterns of people's ancestors begin to repeat themselves with consequences both tragic and ridiculous.

"Spiritual yet pragmatic, Erdrich's deft lyricism affirms while it defies the usual lines separating the mythical from the daily. Erdrich leads every event in her book to its outer limits, so no detail is mundane. And each scene contains bits of hilarity, extravagance, and horror."
—*Boston Globe Sunday Magazine*

**Have You Read?** *(continued)*

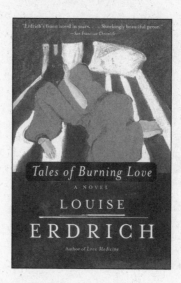

### TALES OF BURNING LOVE

Jack Mauser has women problems; he's been married five times and none of his wives really know him. This becomes strikingly apparent when all his wives, marooned in the same snowbound car, start to tell stories about their onetime husband. He's a man with a talent for reinvention and a less than circumspect regard for the truth. But as the women talk, their stories begin to revive them; they start thinking about Jack in a whole new light.

"Erdrich's finest novel in years. . . . Shockingly beautiful prose."
—*San Francisco Chronicle*

**THE BLUE JAY'S DANCE: A BIRTH YEAR**
**(nonfiction)**

*The Blue Jay's Dance* is a poetic meditation on what it means to be a mother. Describing her pregnancy and the birth of her child, Erdrich charts the weather outside her window and the moods inside her heart. It is, she says, "a book of conflict, a book of babyhood, a book about luck, cats, a writing life, wild places in the world, and my husband's cooking. It is a book about the vitality between mothers and infants, that passionate and artful bond into which we pour the direct expression of our being."

"The language in this book is stunning, elastic, often full of silence. . . . Erdrich is forthright and tough-minded in her intentions, generous in her speculations, and courageous in her vulnerability before her readers. *The Blue Jay's Dance* is a book that breaks ground."

—*Boston Globe*

### THE BINGO PALACE

Seeking direction and enlightenment, charismatic young drifter Lipsha Morrissey answers his grandmother's summons to return to his birthplace. As he tries to settle into a challenging new job on the reservation, Lipsha falls passionately in love for the first time. But the object of his affection, the beautiful Shawnee Ray, is in the midst of deciding whether to marry Lipsha's boss, Lyman Lamartine. Matters are further complicated when Lipsha discovers that Lyman, in league with an influential group of aggressive businessmen, has chosen to open a gambling complex on reservation land—a development that threatens to destroy the community's fundamental links with the past.

"Beautiful. . . . *The Bingo Palace* shows us a place where love, fate, and chance are woven together like a braid, a world where daily life is enriched by a powerful spiritual presence."

—*New York Times*

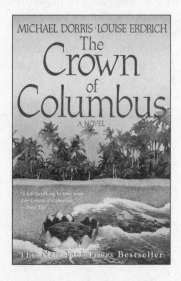

**THE CROWN OF COLUMBUS**
(cowritten with Michael Dorris)

A gripping novel of history, suspense, recovery, and new beginnings, *The Crown of Columbus* chronicles the adventures of a pair of mismatched lovers—Vivian Twostar, a divorced,

pregnant anthropologist, and Roger
Williams, a consummate academic,
epic poet, and bewildered father of
Vivian's baby—on their quest for the
truth about Christopher Columbus
and themselves. When Vivian uncovers
what is presumed to be the lost diary of
Christopher Columbus, she and Roger
are drawn into a journey from icy New
Hampshire to the idyllic Caribbean
in search of "the greatest treasure of
Europe." Lured by the wild promise of
redeeming the past, they are plunged into
a harrowing race against time and death
that threatens—and finally changes—
their lives. A rollicking tale of adventure,
*The Crown of Columbus* is also a
contemporary love story and a
tender examination of parenthood
and passion.

"The rare novel that is both literature
and good fun."　　　—*Barbara Kingsolver*

**TRACKS**

"We started dying before the snow, and like the snow, we continued to fall." So begins Nanapush as he recalls the winter of 1912, when consumption wiped out whole families of Ojibwe. But the magnificent Fleur Pillager refuses to be done away with; she drowns twice in Lake Matchimanito but returns to life to bedevil her enemies using the strength of the black underwaters. This is a book about love, loss, endurance, and survival.

"Erdrich captures the passions, fears, myths, and doom of a living people, and she does so with ease that leaves the reader breathless."     —*The New Yorker*

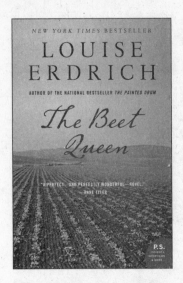

### THE BEET QUEEN

Two children, Karl and Mary Adare, leap from a boxcar one chilly spring morning in 1932. Karl and Mary have been orphaned in a most peculiar way. The children have come to Argus, in the heart of rural North Dakota, to seek refuge with their aunt, who runs a butcher shop. So begins this enthralling tale, spanning some forty years and brimming with unforgettable characters: ordinary Mary, who causes a miracle; seductive, restless Karl, who lacks his sister's gift for survival; Sita, their lovely, ambitious, disturbed cousin; Celestine James, Mary's lifelong friend; and Celestine's fearless, wild daughter Dot—the Beet Queen.

"[Erdrich] is a luminous writer and has produced a novel rich in movement, beauty, event. Her prose spins and sparkles." —*Los Angeles Times*

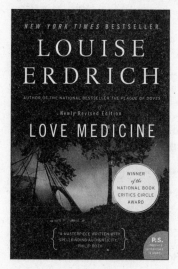

**LOVE MEDICINE**

Winner of a 1984 National Book Critics Circle Award, Louise Erdrich's beloved first novel is now newly revised by the author—the Definitive Edition of the book that introduced one of contemporary literature's most innovative voices. Set on and around a North Dakota reservation over fifty years, *Love Medicine* tells of the intertwined fates of two families, the Lamartines and the Kashpaws. Their world is harsh and hazardous, full of old grievances and bad decisions, but it is illuminated by the kind of love that can leave a person crazily empty or full to overflowing with its spellbinding magic.

**Have You Read?** *(continued)*

"The beauty of *Love Medicine* saves us from being completely devastated by its power."　　　　　—Toni Morrison

"A dazzling series of family portraits. . . . This novel is simply about the power of love."　　　　　*—Chicago Tribune*

## The Birchbark House Books (for children)

### THE BIRCHBARK HOUSE

Her name is Omakayas, or Little Frog, because her first step was a hop and she lives on an island in Lake Superior. Louise Erdrich's first book for children, a National Book Award Finalist, introduces readers to this wise and passionate seven-year-old and her family: Tallow, the woman who adopted Omakayas when she was just a baby, the only survivor of a smallpox epidemic, and siblings Pinch, Neewo, and Angeline. As the family harvests the year's food, weathers the harsh winter, and tell stories handed down for generations, Erdrich vividly captures the language and culture of the Ojibwe in the nineteenth century. But the satisfying rhythms of their life are shattered when a visitor comes to their lodge one winter night, bringing with him an invisible enemy that will change things forever—but that will eventually lead Omakayas to discover her calling.

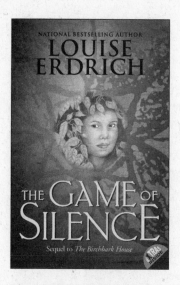

**THE GAME OF SILENCE**

*On that rich early summer day, anything seemed possible.*

It is 1850 and the lives of the Ojibwe have returned to a familiar rhythm: they build their birchbark houses in the summer, go to the ricing camps in the fall to harvest and feast, and move to their cozy cedar log cabins near the town of LaPointe before the first snows.

The satisfying routines of Omakayas's days are interrupted by a surprise visit from a group of desperate and mysterious people. From them, she learns that the *chimookomanag,* or white people, want Omakayas and her people to leave their island and move farther west. That day, Omakayas realizes that something so valuable, so important that she never knew she had it in the first place, could be in danger. Her home. Her way of life.

Winner of the Scott O'Dell Award for Historical Fiction, *The Game of Silence* continues Louise Erdrich's celebrated series, which began with *The Birchbark House*, a National Book Award nominee.

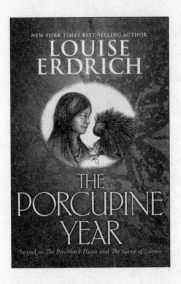

**THE PORCUPINE YEAR**

*Here follows the story of a most extraordinary year in the life of an Ojibwe family and of a girl named "Omakayas," or Little Frog, who lived a year of flight and adventure, pain and joy, in 1852.*

When Omakayas is twelve winters old, she and her family set off on a harrowing journey. In search of a new home, they travel westward from the shores of Lake Superior by canoe, along the rivers of northern Minnesota. While the family has prepared well, unexpected danger, enemies, and hardships will push them to the brink of survival. Omakayas continues to learn from the land and the spirits around her, and she discovers that no matter where she is, or how she is living, there is only one thing she needs to carry her through.

Richly imagined, full of laughter and sorrow, *The Porcupine Year*, an ALA Notable Book, continues Louise Erdrich's celebrated series, which began with *The Birchbark House*, a National Book Award Nominee, and continued with *The Game of Silence*, winner of the Scott O'Dell Award for Historical Fiction.

*Praise for Louise Erdrich's Birchbark House Books*

"Erdrich is a talented storyteller. She has created a world, fictional but real: absorbing, funny, serious, and convincingly human."
　　　　　—*New York Times Book Review*

"Readers will welcome the return of richly drawn characters."
　　　　　—*Booklist* (starred review)

"Readers who loved Omakayas and her family in *The Birchbark House* have ample reason to rejoice in this beautifully constructed sequel. . . . Hard not to hope

**Have You Read?** *(continued)*

for what comes next for this radiant nine-year-old."
                    —*Kirkus Reviews* (starred review)

"This meticulously researched novel offers an even balance of joyful and sorrowful moments while conveying a perspective of America's past that is rarely found in history books."
                    —*Publishers Weekly*

Don't miss the next book by your favorite author. Sign up now for AuthorTracker by visiting www.AuthorTracker.com.